TOM HOLT

In Your Dreams

orbit

An *Orbit* Book

First published in Great Britain by Orbit 2004
This edition published by Orbit 2005

Copyright © Kim Holt 2004

The moral right of the author has been asserted.

*All characters and events in this publication are fictitious
and any resemblance to real persons, living or dead,
is purely coincidental.*

A CIP catalogue record for this book
is available from the British Library.

ISBN 1 84149 219 1

Printed and bound in Great Britain
by Mackays of Chatham plc

Orbit
An imprint of
Time Warner Books UK
Brettenham House
Lancaster Place
London WC2E 7EN

In memory of

JAMES HALE
(1946-2003)

Sweet charioteer

Chapter One

Twenty-five past five on a cold autumn Friday. Outside, Central London growled and shoved its way homewards in a blaze of white, green, red and amber light. In the cashier's office on the top floor of 70 St Mary Axe, Benny Shumway glanced up at the clock on the wall opposite his desk. Time to cash up, then home.

He leaned forward, grabbed a handful of pink cash chits out of his in-tray and leafed through them quickly, his mind adding up the numbers faster than silicon could ever manage: a quick note in the Big Ledger, another in the Small Ledger and the One True Ledger and the Other Ledger, a precise thumb-click on the end of his silver Parker ballpoint. Five feet two inches tall, bearded and windscreened by bottle-end spectacles as thick as tank armour, Benny Shumway worked with the speed, precision and assurance of a Japanese swordsman.

Last chore: the banking. He flipped open the lid of the cash box, took out a thick wad of fifty-pound notes and riffled through them like a New Orleans gambler shuffling cards. £12,850. It being Friday night (no cash to be left on the premises over the weekend), he pulled the paying-in book out of the top drawer of his desk, uncapped a Bic one-handed, jotted down the amount, date, account details; flicked out the slip, put the book away, laid the slip on top of the neatly faced-up banknotes, recapped the Bic.

The paying-in slip bore the words *BANK OF THE DEAD* in twelve-point Garamond capital italics.

Whistling a long-forgotten tune, Benny Shumway dipped in his pocket, produced a genuine all-brass Zippo and thumbed the wheel. As the flame caught and blossomed, he picked up the stack of currency, plus the paying-in slip, and held the flame against the short end. The notes caught; he turned his wrist, expertly nursing the infant fire, while with his other hand he reached for what looked like a wide, flat-bottomed tourist-ware brass Benares ashtray. Just as the flames were about to lick his fingertips, he dropped the blazing money into the tray and watched as it curled into white ash.

That done, Benny Shumway wriggled into his overcoat, flipped off the lights and trotted down the stairs. He was two minutes behind schedule, but luckily the goblins hadn't locked up yet.

At twenty to six, Paul Carpenter was standing beside the road, hating his car.

It hadn't been his idea in the first place; but he'd been too shocked to refuse at the time, and by then it was too late. Promotion from junior clerk to clerk meant that he was entitled to a company car. Since the company in question was J. W. Wells & Co., the car wasn't your run-of-the-mill Volkswagen Polo. In fact, until a few months ago, it had been a third-level sorcerer's apprentice employed by Gebruder Faust Gmbh of Frankfurt, one of J. W. Wells's oldest and most intransigent business rivals. It (or she) had accepted the sideways promotion with stoical good grace (after all, as Ricky Wurmtoter, the pest-control partner, had said at the time, it could have been worse; could've been a

Ford, or even – cruelly and unusually – a Rover Metro), and up till now, Paul and Monika had got on reasonably well together.

Up till now.

He'd tried magic, of course. Where engine trouble was concerned, magic was his first resort, and also his last. Since he'd joined JWW six months ago, he'd learned quite a lot of rudimentary magic, as was essential if he was to pull his weight as an employee of the oldest and most respected firm of sorcerers and thaumaturgical consultants in the UK. He'd learned that magic is just a fancy term for the process of turning things from how they are to how they ought to be. And a Volkswagen Polo ought to go *vroom* when you press the accelerator pedal.

'Please?' he asked nicely; but that failed too. He swore under his breath. The car radio clicked into life.

'*Ich kann dich horen,*' it said reproachfully. '*Das is nicht höflich.*'

Paul scowled. It had been a long day; six o'clock start, driving from London to a pub car park in some godforsaken place in outer Gloucestershire to hand over a brown A4 manila envelope to (he shuddered just thinking about it) a red-eyed, rat-headed goblin wearing a Marks & Sparks suit three sizes too big for it. 'Talk English, for crying out loud. I know you can.'

The car radio tutted at him. 'You should make effort,' it said. 'Is bad enough for me being car.'

'I'm sorry,' Paul muttered. Monika had a lovely voice, but she did tend to be bossy. 'Can you tell me what's wrong with you?'

'*Ja, ja,* is obvious. *Die Zylinderkopfdichtung* is *undicht.* Anybody should know this.'

Paul sighed. 'The what is what?'

'*Zylinderkopfdichtung*.' Monika clicked her virtual tongue. 'I do not know what it is in English. But it is very bad. I am very sick. You must call for assistance.'

'Yes, right,' Paul snapped. 'And I expect you know how I'm supposed to go about finding a garage in the middle of nowhere at six o'clock on a Friday—'

'*Natürlich*,' Monika interrupted. 'In my glove box is 1996 edition of AA Members' handbook. On page 386 is list of local garages. Third from top is Gorse Hill Motors, telephone number . . .' Paul pressed keys on his mobile. Nobody answered for a very long time. Just as he was about to ring off, a voice said, 'What?'

Paul took a deep breath. 'Hello,' he said. 'I wonder if you could help me. My car's broken down and, um, I was hoping, can you come out and sort of fix it?'

A long silence; then the voice said: 'Hang on, I'll get someone.'

'Thanks,' Paul said. It was either a woman's voice or a child's; if he'd been on oath, he'd have had to say it was probably the latter. *Well*, he thought, *family-run business in rural Gloucestershire, nothing unusual about that.*

'Well?' said another voice.

'Hello,' Paul said. 'I was wondering if—'

'Skip all that,' said the new voice; and this time, absolutely no doubt about it, this time it was definitely a kid; a girl, somewhere between seven and nine. 'What's the problem?'

'Um,' Paul said. 'Well, it was making this horrible sort of clonking noise, and then it started blowing out great clouds of blue smoke, and now it won't go at all.'

The unseen seven-year-old clicked her tongue. 'Cylinder-head gasket,' she said. 'All right, we'll come and pick it up. Where are you?'

'Um, I'm not sure.' Monika would know, of course; she had some kind of satellite navigation system that told her where she was to the nearest centimetre. Unfortunately he couldn't make head nor tail of it, and he couldn't very well say, *Hold on, you'd better ask my car.* He leaned in through the driver's door and stared at the little screen where the ashtray should have been. 'Well, if this road's the B5632—'

'It isn't.'

'Oh.' He wasn't sure how the kid knew that, but he wasn't going to argue. 'In that case, I don't know.'

''S all right,' said the kid wearily. 'We've got you. Hang on, we'll be there in twenty minutes.'

The kid had rung off. Paul shrugged and sat in the driver's seat. It was too cold to stand about in the open.

'You are calling the garage?' Monika asked.

Paul nodded. He knew she could see him, though he had no idea what with. 'They're sending someone,' he replied. 'Twenty minutes.'

'*Sehr gut.*' She groaned softly. 'It hurts, but I am brave. We play Hangman?'

Paul sighed wearily. 'Oh, all right,' he said.

For some reason, Monika loved playing Hangman, though her limited English vocabulary didn't help; also, she got very tense when she lost. In the event, it only took eighteen minutes for the pick-up truck to arrive, but it seemed much longer.

'Here is garage,' Monika announced suddenly. A moment later, a pair of bright white eyes flared in the rear-view mirror. Paul got out.

'You the breakdown?' said a voice from the darkness, as the truck drew up beside him.

'Yes, that's . . .' Paul broke off. Another one who sounded like a child. Wasn't there some gas or something that made your voice go all high and squeaky? The truck doors opened. Two small figures climbed out and walked towards him.

The one on the left was male, very short blond hair, shirt-tails hanging out under a green pullover, age probably ten. On the right, a nine-year-old girl with a ponytail, wearing lilac jeans and matching trainers. The girl was carrying, apparently without effort, a toolbox that looked like it weighed more than she did.

'What's the problem?' asked the girl briskly.

It took Paul a moment to answer. 'Um, it was making this terrible clunky noise, and there was a lot of blue smoke, and now it won't go at all.'

The girl looked up at him. She had clear blue eyes and freckles. 'Keys?'

Paul blinked. 'Sorry?'

'Keys,' she repeated irritably.

'Oh, right. In the ignition.'

She nodded. 'All right,' she said. 'Stand back.' Paul did so, and apparently ceased to exist. The boy jumped into the driver's seat, leant over and flipped the bonnet lock; where-upon the conversation between him and the girl became technical, and Paul tuned out.

He'd seen weirder things, true, ever since he joined JWW. He'd seen goblins, real ones with round red eyes and tusks, and found out that they owned the freehold of 70 St Mary Axe. He'd seen a human being turned into a photocopier before his very eyes, and learned that the long stapler used for tacking sheets of A3 together was in fact the firm's senior partner, transfigured into a stapler a century ago during a particularly savage bout of office politics; in fact, he'd been the one who rescued Mr Wells senior from the curse, though quite how he'd managed that he wasn't quite sure. He'd seen all manner of disconcerting things lately and had reached the point where he could think round them or over them, like a knight in chess. But one of the parameters that helped him cling on to the shirt-tails of his sanity was that all the weirdness happened inside the office, or else on work-related forays where he could at least prepare himself beforehand. If weirdness was going to jump out at him on all sides like this, he felt that he probably wasn't going to be able to cope for much longer.

'I was right,' the girl said, with an expensive-sounding sigh. 'Cylinder-head gasket's blown.' She took a step back, and surveyed the car as though it was something very sad which should have been avoided. 'You're looking at a strip down, cylinder-head refacing, new gasket, fan belt, refit, add your recovery cost and VAT on top, it's going to be something around four hundred quid however you look at it. More than this old heap of junk's worth, if you ask me.'

The car radio started talking very fast in German. The girl leaned in and switched it off, something that Paul had never been able to do, though he'd tried very hard.

'Actually,' he said, 'it's not my car. Belongs to the company.'

'Oh, right.' The girl shrugged. 'Well, it's up to you. We'll fix it for you if you want us to, but ...'

Naturally, Paul couldn't explain why the car had to be fixed. 'That'd be great,' he said. 'Will it, um, take long?'

The way she didn't answer suggested that yes, it would.

'Hop in the back,' the girl said, pointing towards the pick-up. 'We'll give you a lift as far as the garage.'

Luckily it wasn't far, though such things are relative when you're sharing the back of an open truck with chains, coils of rope and a soggy tarpaulin. All the way, Paul tried to assure himself that once they reached the garage it'd be all right, there'd be grown-ups there who'd do the actual engineering, and possibly even offer a rational explanation. He tried not to think about the fact that his car was apparently sentient, and that the girl hadn't mentioned anything about using anaesthetics while she was performing surgery. He'd never heard a Volkswagen scream, and he was in no hurry to find out what it sounded like.

The garage looked ordinary enough, until the wide galvanised-iron doors opened and revealed three more under-twelves, all dressed in oily overalls. There was a grubby-looking teddy bear on the office desk, and a Barbie calendar on the wall instead of the usual Pirelli. Apart from that, it could've been any small country garage anywhere.

A carrot-topped six-year-old with her hair in bunches unhitched Monika from the truck and pushed her into the workshop. Treading warily round the fact that it was way past her bedtime, Paul asked her if there was any chance of doing the repairs tonight, since he had an important meeting first thing in the morning.

She looked at him; and Paul noticed with alarm a look in her eyes that reminded him of goblins, or rather of one particular goblin, who happened to be the mother of one of the firm's partners and who also, for reasons best known to herself, fancied him rotten. 'Maybe,' the child said, and grinned, making Paul wish he hadn't asked. 'I s'pose we could do you the express service,' she went on, and winked broadly. 'But you'll have to promise not to tell.'

'Fine,' Paul heard himself say. 'I'd really appreciate it, because—'

The kid leered at him. 'Right,' she said. 'Push off. You can wait outside, I'll call you when we're done.'

Clearly, they didn't want him to see, which was fine by him. Ever since he'd had the use of a car who talked back when he spoke to it, he'd tended to come over faint at the sight of oil. It was cold out on the forecourt, but the rain was only a light drizzle. He found a relatively sheltered spot behind a pile of dead tyres, and huddled. In the distance somewhere, an owl hooted.

'Hey, you.' The doors slid back, and yellow light engulfed him. He looked up, startled. He didn't know how long he'd been standing there, but he was sure they couldn't have finished already. 'All done,' the ginger-haired girl said, grinning at him round the edge of the door. 'You can come in now.'

A kid he hadn't seen before (small, fair-haired, glasses) turned the key and started the engine. Monika purred; no rattle, no smoke. 'That's great,' Paul said awkwardly. From the expressions on the children's faces he had the idea that some kind of miracle had been achieved while he'd been standing outside. He wished he knew enough about cars to appreciate it properly. 'Um, how much do I owe you?'

Carrot-top gave him a rather grubby invoice. At least they had handwriting like proper children, and they spelt cylinder with two 1's. Whatever the express service entailed, it came expensive, and Paul didn't relish the thought of what Mr Shumway was going to say about it in the morning.

'Cash,' Carrot-top added.

'Oh.' Paul looked down at her, worried. 'I'm very sorry,' he said, 'I haven't got that sort of money on me.' He took out his wallet, just in case the Folding Money Fairy had left him a four-figure surprise. She hadn't. 'I can do plastic,' he said. 'Or,' he remembered, 'a company cheque.' Mr Shumway had let him loose with the firm's chequebook, on the strict understanding that any misuse thereof would be punished by unspeakable atrocities. 'Otherwise, I don't—'

'Cash,' the child repeated; and then she caught sight of the JWW chequebook, lying inside Paul's open wallet. *BANK OF THE DEAD*, unmissable on the cover. She looked like she had the knack of reading upside down. 'Or a cheque'll do fine,' she said pleasantly.

'Um,' Paul replied. It had just occurred to him that, according to Mr Shumway, the term 'misuse' specifically included giving JWW cheques to anybody outside The Business. Given who JWW banked with, he could see Mr Shumway's point. 'Actually,' he said, 'maybe that wouldn't be such a good idea. If someone could give me a lift to the nearest cashpoint—'

'A cheque,' the girl repeated firmly, 'will do just fine. We've got a stamp,' she added, making it sound like a threat.

So Paul wrote her a cheque. The girl waved away the card, then took the cheque in her left hand, produced a cigarette lighter and—

'And then,' Paul said, 'you'll never guess what she did.'

Sophie yawned. 'Set light to it,' she said, pouring water from the kettle into her hot water bottle.

Paul looked at her. 'Yes,' he said. 'How did you—?'

Sophie had joined JWW on the same day as Paul; they'd

found out the great secret together, at roughly the same time that they'd discovered that they were, somewhat improbably, in love. But whereas there were still mornings when Paul woke up and assumed his recent memories were the shrapnel from a particularly bizarre dream, Sophie seemed to have adapted remarkably well to the ambient weirdness. She tightened the hottie-bottle stopper and yawned again. 'Bank of The Dead,' she said. 'You don't know, right?'

Paul nodded.

'It's a Chinese thing originally,' she said. 'They believe it's your duty to provide for your ancestors in the next world by sending them money; you buy Bank of The Dead banknotes with real money, and then you burn them, which credits their account.'

Paul frowned. 'Yes, but surely that's just a—'

'Tax fiddle, yes,' Sophie said, her hand in front of her mouth. 'Other companies bank offshore, but JWW has to go one better.' She opened the kitchen door. 'You think that's strange, you wait till you see what happens when you use a Bank of The Dead cashpoint card in an ordinary machine. Well, I'm going to bed. G'night.'

''Night, then,' Paul said. He felt faintly disappointed; not that it was the most grippingly fascinating story ever or anything like that, but . . . Still; on balance, he approved of the way that Sophie could shrug off the bizarre and the disturbing, the way he still couldn't. A sense of perspective, he supposed you'd call it, a vitally important part of being grown-up and all that stuff he'd never quite been able to master. But so long as she had one, he didn't have to. That's partnership for you, the Jack Sprat equilibrium. She had her own special strengths, and he—

Paul still couldn't see what the hell Sophie saw in him.

He caught sight of his reflection in the kitchen window, and found no answers there; tall, thin, unfinished-looking young Englishmen aren't hard to find, the supply tends to exceed demand, whereas beautiful, intelligent, courageous, resourceful, small thin girls with enormous eyes are a scarce commodity, always highly sought after, even if they do have an unfortunate manner which you can get used to very quickly . . .

Yes, he thought, ordering the kettle to boil, *but*. In the time they'd been together, she'd started to change. It was as though Life was an exam the term after next, and she'd already started revising, and he hadn't. Where he still drifted from day to day, trying to keep out of the way of the more alarming variants of weirdness and counting himself lucky every time he got home in the same shape he'd left in, she— She was getting *serious* about things, in an admirable but not entirely comfortable way. At work, she tried hard; at home, she cared about stuff like spin-dryers and radiators and putting money aside for the electricity bill; and yes, someone had to do all that kind of thing and for sure he wasn't capable of it, but even so. It couldn't be too long, could it, before she got sick to death of the sight of him, and—

Frowning, Paul ordered the boiling water into his teacup, then remembered that he'd forgotten the tea bag. He had, of course, assumed that once he'd won the girl of his dreams, that would be that; the story would be over, and somehow complete. Exam thinking again; once he'd passed, he'd get his little bit of paper with the curly writing and his name and grade, and then he'd have his Maths GCSE for ever and ever. Nobody could take it away from him, and he wouldn't ever have to do it again. But there was rather more to being in love. You had to stick at it, or you could lose everything, just like that. *Not fair*, growled Paul's inner child. Not fair at all.

Somehow, tea seemed to have lost its relevance; he tipped the hot water down the sink, dried the cup and put it away. (He now lived in an environment where cups didn't live on the draining board any more; when had that happened, and how?) The kitchen clock told him it was time to go to bed, since he had to be up bright and early in the morning for the Important Meeting. Oh well.

Perched on the edge of his side of the bed (asleep, Sophie displayed territorial ambitions unparalleled since the collapse of the Mongol empire) Paul fell into troubled sleep, the sort in which the dreams are all the more alarming because you're pretty sure you're still awake. He dreamed that he was in something like a hospital ward, except that there were no nurses or drips or legs in plaster; a dormitory of some kind, except that all the people lying asleep in the beds – hundreds of them, maybe even thousands – were grown-ups. Sophie was there, lying on her side, dead to the world. He knew that something was wrong, but there was nobody to ask; and then countess Judy di Castel'Bianco, the Entertainment Sector partner at JWW, was standing next to him, with a clipboard in one hand, smiling.

'It's all right,' she told him kindly. (In real life, he hadn't spoken to her since his interview.) 'They can't feel anything, it doesn't hurt. And it's necessary,' she added, with possibly a hint of remorse. 'And be realistic; it wouldn't have lasted anyway, you're far too immature. This way, you're spared the pain. It's for the best, you'll see that in the end.'

That made sense, apparently; so did the fact that the ward (it was definitely a hospital now) was suddenly full of children, like the ones at the garage, and, wearing white coats, they were walking up and down between the beds. Some of them wheeled trolleys laden with food and drink: cheese omelettes, strong-smelling coffee. Others were inspecting the sleepers – thumbing back eyelids, forcing lips apart with little wooden spatulas, checking pulses and drawing samples of blood. From time to time they found one who wasn't working any more; they took them away on trolleys and brought replacements.

When they came for Sophie ('Over here,' Judy di Castel'Bianco called out. 'Hurry, she's been dead for hours'), he woke up.

The notice hanging from Ricky Wurmtoter's doorhandle was, as usual, both alarming and profoundly unhelpful. It read *BEWARE OF THE PREDATORS*.

Paul had regarded Ricky Wurmtoter, the partner specialising in pest control, with suspicious caution ever since he'd taken Paul out to lunch on the day he'd joined the firm. Probably Mr Wurmtoter was just being nice; he was the youngest and most affable of the partners, looked and dressed like a movie star trying to be inconspicuous, spoke with a faint German accent and owned (among other things) a flying white horse that could get from London to north of Manchester in the time it took to boil an egg. His work mostly consisted of slaying dragons (who, being attracted to stored accumulations of wealth, tended to be a serious nuisance to museums, art galleries and banks), vampires, werewolves, manticores and other monstrous creatures that Paul had, until recently, fondly believed didn't exist; accordingly he was out of the office a lot of the time, and Paul hadn't had much to do with him since that initial lunch.

Paul hadn't been inside Mr Wurmtoter's office before, and he was pleasantly surprised at how normal it was, at least by JWW standards. Apart from a couple of stuffed and mounted heads on the wall that would lead to a mass pulping and rewriting of textbooks if they ever fell into the hands of the scientific community, and a huge walk-in safe in one corner, there were just a plain desk, three chairs and an almost empty bookshelf.

'Paul,' Mr Wurmtoter said, turning round and smiling pleasantly. 'Thanks for joining us. You know Benny Shumway, I'm sure.'

Paul knew Benny Shumway, no doubt about it. Instead of snarling at him, however, the cashier raised his left hand and waggled his fingers. Paul sat down next to him and tried to look keen and eager.

'As I'm sure you know,' Mr Wurmtoter said, 'it's JWW policy for trainees like yourself to spend a month or so in each department, so we can see where your strengths lie and you can make up your mind which area you'd like to specialise in. Now, as I understand it, you've done your time with Dennis Tanner scrying for mineral deposits – he's really pleased with your work for him, by the way, though I expect you're sick to the teeth of staring at photos of bits of desert all day – and you made a start on sorcery and magic with Humph Wells, before—' Mr Wurmtoter hesitated. It was Paul and Sophie who'd uncovered Humphrey Wells's treachery towards his uncle, the firm's senior partner; Humphrey Wells now served the firm in the capacity of Xerox machine, on the grounds that the copier is the most hated item of equipment in every office in the world. 'And since then,' he went on, 'you've been doing odd jobs for all of us while we've been restructuring in the light of – well, you know.' He paused, fiddled with the large claw he wore on a chain round his neck, and went on: 'So really, it's time you both got back on track with your vocational training, and I'd like it if you'd consider coming and working in my department for a while.'

He paused again, clearly waiting for a response. Paul, who had a feeling that he didn't really have a choice in the matter, mumbled, 'Yes, lovely, thanks,' or words to that effect.

'Great,' said Mr Wurmtoter. 'The thing of it is, though, I'm going to be away on a job with Jack — Mr Wells Senior — and it's likely to take quite some time. While I'm away, Benny here'll be looking after things for me, and so you'll be working with him. Is that going to be OK?'

Like he could say no, with Mr Shumway sitting next to him. 'Sure,' he muttered.

Mr Wurmtoter smiled. 'That's fantastic,' he said. 'The fact is, Benny knows the pest business inside out, don't you, Ben?'

Mr Shumway nodded; exceptional economy of movement.

'Actually,' Mr Wurmtoter continued, 'if there was any justice, he'd be the PC partner here instead of me. But—'

'But I retired,' Mr Shumway interrupted. 'While I still had something to retire with.' He shifted slightly in his chair until he was staring into Paul's eyes through his extremely thick-lensed glasses. 'What Rick hasn't told you is that pest control is dangerous, as in death or horrible injuries. Also, you've got to kill things. Strikes me you might not want to do that.'

'Well,' Paul said, once he'd got his voice back, 'no, not really. I don't think I've ever killed anything on purpose,' he added, 'not even spiders or things like that. Usually I try and catch them and—' He tailed off. Although, obviously, he didn't want to be seconded to the dragon-slaying department for six months, he didn't want to give the impression that he was totally pathetic and feeble, even if it was true. 'I don't know,' he confessed. 'What do you think?'

Mr Wurmtoter was smiling again. 'Well,' he said, 'here's where Benny and I agree to differ. Benny reckons that pest controllers are born, not trained, and you need to have the old killer instinct if you're going to make the grade. I can see his point, but I've always felt that anybody who wants to do this job is probably too crazy to be allowed to do it, if you see what I mean. After all, it's not like treating woodworm or putting down mousetraps. The sort of pests you'll be up against are highly intelligent sentient life forms; if dragons and harpies and frost-giants were allowed to go to university, you wouldn't be able to stick your head out the door in Oxford or Cambridge without getting it bitten off. Which is why,' he went on, 'a gung-ho attitude – no offence, Ben – isn't a survival trait in this area. A healthy instinct for staying alive and an ability to sense and assess danger is what you need, together with the ability to get on and do the job when the claws are out and the flames are licking round your toes, even though you're so scared you can hardly breathe – because, take it from me, doesn't matter how brave you are, when you're on the warm end of twelve tons of angry dragon, that's how scared you'll be. Better to have someone who knows he'll be scared right from the start, rather than a guy to whom absolute terror comes as a nasty shock. Do you see what I mean?'

Paul's mouth had suddenly gone dry. 'Um,' he said.

'And I think,' Mr Wurmtoter said, glancing at Mr

Shumway and then looking back, 'I think that after the way you handled Humph Wells and a really bad situation, I think you've probably got what it takes. Of course,' he added casually, 'if you really feel you aren't cut out for the job, that's perfectly fine. I'll have a word with Judy di Castel'Bianco, and you can go and do your stint with her, and Sophie can come in with Benny and me.'

Shit, Paul thought; and it occurred to him at that moment that Ricky Wurmtoter probably was very good at his job. At least he had the knack of laying a good trap. 'No, that's fine,' he heard himself croak. 'When do I start?'

Benny Shumway walked with Paul back to the office that Paul shared with Sophie. Benny didn't say anything for a while; then he stopped dead, just outside the closed file store. 'You probably got the impression I don't want you working for me,' he said abruptly. 'Right?'

'Well . . .'

'Right.' Benny Shumway grinned. 'But no hard feelings,' he said. 'Ricky was an arsehole, springing that or-else bit on you. He knows that you two can't just tell JWW where to stick their rotten jobs, for fear of what Dennis Tanner'll do to the both of you for breach of contract; he needs someone to help mind the store while he's off gallivanting for three months, he doesn't want your girlfriend because he's got a really unreconstructed view of what women should and shouldn't do in the workplace, so you're it, by default. All that I-think-you-got-what-it-takes stuff was just flannel.' He sighed. 'That's Ricky for you. Of all selfish bastards, a selfish bastard who likes to be liked is probably the worst. Never mind, though,' he added, reaching up and slapping Paul on the back with spine-jarring force.

'You'll be all right, I guess. At least,' he added, with a slight edge to his voice, 'you will by the time I'm through with you.'

'Um, thanks,' Paul said nervously. 'How do you mean?'

'You'll see,' replied Benny Shumway, grinning. 'Right, about you, let's see. Do you work out at all?'

It took Paul a moment to figure out what he was talking about. 'Well, no,' he admitted.

'I see. Done any martial arts? Judo, karate, tae kwon do?'

'No.'

'Basic weapons skills? Fencing, ken-jutsu, marksmanship training? How are you with high explosives?'

'Um.'

Benny's grin was threatening to unzip his face. 'Poisons?' he asked. 'Wilderness survival techniques?'

'Not really,' Paul said.

'That's all right, then.' Benny Shumway beamed up at him. 'One thing I can't stand is a bloody know-it-all. How about doing exactly what you're told? You any great shakes at that?'

'Oh yes,' Paul said confidently. 'I've been doing that all my life.'

'Perfect,' Benny said. 'In that case, there's a fair chance that you might get through this without me having to send you home to your family in a matchbox. Finish up what you're doing, we'll make a start on training you first thing tomorrow.' Suddenly, without warning, he stuck out his hand for Paul to shake. 'Welcome to heroism.'

Paul looked at him. 'Excuse me?'

'That's the other name for pest control, fighting monsters, what we do. We're your actual heroes.'

Paul studied him for a moment, then thought of the

reflection that he'd seen in the window the previous evening. 'Are we?' he said. 'Oh, jolly good.'

'He's a dwarf,' Sophie explained, as they worked through the last of the Mortensen printouts (apparently meaningless computer spreadsheets that had to be sorted by date order).

'Well, yes,' Paul said. 'At least, he's a bit on the short side, but I wouldn't go as far as—'

'No,' she interrupted, 'a *dwarf*. You know; the ones who live in caves under mountains. Fearless warriors, skilled craftspeople, really into gold and wealth and stuff. Don't you ever read books?'

'But—' Paul started to say; and then he thought, *Fearless warrior, well, yes; don't know about skilled craftsperson, but he's the cashier, so I guess that figures.* 'Oh,' he said. 'Oh, right. How did you—?'

Sophie scowled impatiently at him. 'Well,' she said, 'it's obvious, surely. I mean, you *have* read the office procedures manual, haven't you?'

Oh, Paul thought, *that*. 'Yes,' he lied. He'd been meaning to, of course, ever since they'd come to work one morning and found two copies of it on their shared desk: two enormous calf-bound, breeze-block-thick volumes, four thousand pages crammed with tiny, intimidating print. Two days afterwards, Paul had surreptitiously weighed his copy on the post-room scales: four and a half kilos, whatever that was in real money. He was planning to get around to reading it any day now.

'Well, then,' Sophie said. 'Anyway.' She looked past him, at the far wall. 'Is that what you want to do?' she asked. 'Hunt monsters, kill dragons, that sort of thing?'

Paul thought for a whole fifty-thousandth of a second before answering, 'No, of course not. It sounds horrible and dangerous. But I don't think I've got a choice.'

Sophie nodded. 'You could always refuse,' she said. 'I mean, stand up for yourself, just tell them straight, you won't do it.'

'You think they'll listen?'

'No.'

'Nor me.'

'But it's so——' She glared at him, as though being the victim was his fault. 'I mean, why can't they find someone else to do their silly work for them? Why's it got to be you?'

But it doesn't have to be me, Paul didn't say; *they could make you do it instead. Which is why*— Instead, he said: 'It won't be so bad. I got the impression that most of it's just boring and tedious, anyhow – not actually dangerous. I mean, they don't charge around waving swords and dressed in armour any more.'

'Don't they? How would you know?'

'I don't,' Paul admitted. 'But it stands to reason, doesn't it? I mean, technology's moved on, hasn't it? Benny Shumway was talking about explosives and poisons——'

'And other really safe things to be around,' Sophie said. 'And besides, it's *wrong*. These are *endangered species* that you're talking about exterminating. You've just got to look at that Ricky Wurmtoter creep to see what sort of a man he is. Probably got a dragon's-foot umbrella stand in his office. I mean, what harm did a dragon ever do you?'

'None,' Paul said. *Yet*, he thought. 'Look, there's no point giving me a hard time about it, it's the last thing I want to do. Or rather,' he added, scowling, 'the last thing but one. The *last* thing I want to do is give Mr Tanner an excuse to do horrible things to me for breach of contract. Or had you forgotten—?'

'No, of course not,' Sophie said quickly. 'But even if he did, it wouldn't *kill* you. And you wouldn't be killing harmless dragons, either. I really think you've got to be firm this time. Take a stand.'

'Sophie—'

There were all sorts of things he could say; all sorts of things, just crying out to be said – how it was all very well for her, she wasn't the one who'd been volunteered to fight bloody dragons, she was going to spend the next three months learning about the Entertainments Sector, probably going to film premières and swanning about at drinks parties round swimming pools meeting the stars. Also, what exactly would she do, if she'd been the one to draw the short straw? Also, why the hell did she think he was giving in so tamely, if not because if he refused she'd be forced to do it, and then she'd be the one who'd get blown up or eaten by dragons? It showed how much he'd learned in the last six months, even without reading the office-procedures manual, that he didn't say any of these things, or anything at all.

'What?' she demanded.

'Nothing.'

Sophie gave him a scowl that would've stripped barnacles off the underside of an oil rig, and went back to sorting through Mortensen printouts. Paul did the same, vaguely aware that World War Three had been postponed at the last moment. *Our first fight*, he thought, but it didn't make him feel any happier about it.

Usually they went out for lunch, to the small Italian sandwich bar round the corner where she'd once bought him an epoch-making ham roll. But today she had a meeting with Judy di Castel'Bianco, to learn more about what she'd be doing; it would probably last all afternoon, and she'd see him back at the flat. Fine, he thought; with Sophie in that kind of mood, it'd probably be just as well. He spent the lunch hour and the rest of the day shuffling spreadsheets, and was about to call it a day (twenty-five past five; everybody was required to be off the premises by five-thirty, because of the goblins) when Ricky Wurmtoter came in.

He came in without knocking, which was unusual in itself. Also he looked ruffled, almost worried. He had a suitcase, and Paul noticed that he wasn't wearing his claw pendant.

'Paul,' he said, 'sorry to bother you. I've got a favour to ask.'

'Sure,' Paul answered nervously.

'Would it be all right—' Ricky Wurmtoter, mumbling? Never in a million years. 'Look,' he said, and if it'd been anybody else, Paul would have thought *furtive* or even *guilty about something.* 'I don't like to ask, but could I borrow that door thing of yours? You know, that thing you used to get into the place where Humph Wells marooned those two clerks?'

What surprised Paul most of all was that Ricky Wurmtoter was *asking.* Ever since Paul had chanced upon the Acme Portable Door, a thin plastic sheet that, when pressed against a wall, turned into a door that opened onto anywhere or anywhen you wanted it to, he'd been expecting at any moment to be yelled at for misappropriating it and ordered to give it back immediately. He'd found it, after all, in a desk drawer; by no stretch of the imagination could it be described as *his*, and since it was clearly a rare and valuable piece of equipment, he was amazed that nobody had noticed it was missing. He'd finally reached the conclusion that no one (apart from himself, Sophie, Mr Tanner's mother and the firm's senior partner) knew that it was him who'd got it. But apparently Mr Wurmtoter knew too, and here he was asking nicely.

'Um,' Paul said.

'I'll let you have it back just as soon as I've finished with it,' Mr Wurmtoter went on — totally weird, he was practically pleading. 'Only, it just might make all the difference for this job I've got to do; and, well, the sooner I get the job done and get back here, the sooner you'll be taken off pest-control duty and put in with Caz Suslowicz or Theo van Spee or somebody. How about it?'

'Sure,' Paul repeated. He reached into his inside pocket and produced the cardboard tube in which the Portable Door lived. What with one thing and another, he hadn't used it for months, hadn't even given it a thought. Even so, he felt curiously reluctant to let go of it, and when Ricky Wurmtoter practically snatched it from him, he felt a tiny flicker of anger, a minuscule urge to fight—

'Thanks,' said Ricky Wurmtoter, visibly sagging with relief. 'That's really kind, you're a pal.' While Paul was still speechless, he added, 'Well, won't hold you up any longer, you'd better be getting a move on if you don't want to run into any of Dennis's loathsome relatives. Thanks again, Paul, I won't forget this, you're a real life-saver. And you will get it back, promise.' Mr Wurmtoter grinned awkwardly, sneezed ferociously, and more or less ran out of the room.

Oh, Paul thought. *A pal. Me.* Also a life-saver — a *real* one, too, not just some kind of cheap imitation. On the other hand, he reflected, he was now minus one extremely useful enchanted object, which could well have come in handy when (for example) faced with an angry fire-breathing dragon. Presumably that was why Mr Wurmtoter – *his pal* Ricky Wurmtoter – wanted it so badly. Oh well.

Won't mention this to Sophie, he thought, though he wasn't quite sure why. He put on his coat and headed for the front office.

No goblins as such; but Mr Tanner's mum was on reception. That is, behind the reception desk was a stunningly lovely chestnut-haired beauty he'd never seen before in his life, who winked at him as he went past. Mr Tanner's mum was a goblin; like the rest of her kind she could assume human shape at will, and she made no bones about the fact that she fancied him rotten, something he tried very hard not to think about. Pretending that he hadn't noticed, he hurried past and didn't slow down till he reached the bus stop.

It's not true that it's easier to get from Bokhara to Tashkent on a three-legged camel than to travel from the City to Kentish Town by bus. It just seems that way, particularly when you're in a hurry. Paul had found out long before that magic doesn't work on traffic jams (implying, rather disturbingly, that traffic in Central London is *meant* to be permanently gridlocked), so he spent the journey fretting and looking at his watch, which if anything appeared to be running backwards. His idea had been to get home before Sophie did, tidy the flat, do the washing-up, cook dinner and generally impress her with his caring, responsible side. After dinner, he'd smear a solemn look onto his face and suggest that it was time they had a Serious Talk about Us, which would please her no end; Us was probably her favourite topic of conversation, and although generally speaking he tended to lose the thread after the first few minutes, it never seemed to matter, so long as he agreed with everything she said and maintained eye contact. That was the plan; a sort of pre-emptive apology for whatever it was he'd done, or was about to do, wrong. Unfortunately, infuriatingly, it looked like sixty thousand cars had sworn to stop him or die trying.

When Paul eventually set toe to pavement, it was thirty-five minutes after his ETA. As he scuttled homewards from the bus stop, he quickly reshuffled his plans. If he still managed to get home first, the main priority was the washing-up, followed by a quick skirmish with the dirty laundry on the bedroom floor. Most important of all would be that he suggested the Serious Talk. Basically, once he'd tabled the motion, that'd be his duty done for the day. He could rely on her to do all the serious talking.

When he unlatched the door and flopped through it, his first reaction was relief. She wasn't there, so obviously she hadn't got home yet. Then he saw the envelope.

It was on the kitchen table, and it said *Paul* in her hand-writing; and that was very bad, because when she left him little notes to say she'd just nipped down to the shop or the video library, she wrote them on yellow stickies and stuck them on the fridge door. An envelope on the table, with *Paul* on it, couldn't possibly be anything good. Feeling as though some malevolent joker had opened him up and stuffed him with newspaper, he sat down and opened it.

Paul—

We're finished. When I got home tonight I realised that there's no point going on. I care about you and I know you care about me but I also care about us and I know you don't.

It's not your fault, it's just that you're you and I'm me and I can't see any way round that, and if we tried we'd end up with neither of us being who we are. I'm sure you can see that, can't you?

They want me to go and do three months at the Hollywood office – I didn't know they had one but presumably they do – and when I get back I'll come and get the rest of my things. I've sent the landlord a cheque for my half of the rent, so you don't need to worry about that. If you need to get in touch with me I suppose you can call me at the office out there, but I'd rather you didn't. There isn't anything left to say, really.

I'm sorry, Paul. I didn't mean it to end up like this, but I think we both knew it was coming, sooner or later, and it's best to get it over and done with rather than dragging on. I think we've both been kidding ourselves all along. It's not because you're a bad person or anything that you've done. I should have been honest with myself earlier, and then it'd never have got this far. Don't forget that the rubbish has to go out on Thursday evening. I think the seal's gone on the vacuum cleaner.

I hope everything works out for you.
Sophie

Chapter Two

A *nd then I woke up*, he told himself, *and it had all been a dream.*

People are sometimes easily overlooked. The holes they leave behind when they aren't there any more are far harder to miss. It made Paul think of science lessons at school. He'd never been able to get his head around concepts like negative numbers and antimatter, but now it made complete sense. Everywhere he looked, and even when he closed his eyes, all he could see was the absence of Sophie, the gap where she used to be, should have been, no longer was. It was so large, it dominated the landscape so much that he was pretty sure it must be visible from orbit, like the Great Wall of China or the lights of the San Francisco freeways. *Maybe* (he speculated, not that he gave a shit) *that's what ghosts are*; the huge empty spaces left behind when someone dies, kept wedged wilfully open by the self-destructive human mind. Above all, for some crazy reason, Sophie's tangible absence put him in mind of the ridiculous Portable Door, except that it was a gap in Nature that opened only into the past, and through which it would be extremely perilous to go. Paul made himself a strong cup of tea, but it didn't really help much. He considered going to the pub on the corner and drinking himself into a spongy mess, but he had to go to work tomorrow and learn how to fight stupid dragons. Just on the off chance he tried magic, but he gave himself a headache concentrating very hard, and when he opened his eyes Sophie still wasn't there. That figured: magic only repairs that which has got screwed up. In this case, apparently, the mistake had already been rectified.

There wasn't anything on the telly apart from game shows and snooker, and he wasn't in the mood. He tried going to bed, but the hole next to him was so wide and deep that he was afraid he'd roll into it and never climb out; so he sat in the armchair. He'd have read a book, only all the books on the shelf were hers.

At three o'clock in the morning, Paul came to the conclusion that he didn't like himself very much; which was a pity, since he was stuck with him, forsaking all others.

At seven o'clock he got dressed, shaved, combed his hair. There wasn't any bread, and the milk wasn't entirely liquid. Magic would've set it right, but he couldn't be bothered. He went to work.

The receptionist smiled at Paul as he went past the front desk, which showed how much she knew about anything. He really didn't want to go to his office, because there'd be a hole on the other side of the desk he didn't particularly want to meet. *Fuck Ricky Wurmtoter*, he thought; *just when I could use a Portable Door, he's got it.* But he went and sat opposite the hole for a few minutes, until suddenly he remembered that he was supposed to report to Benny Shumway first thing to begin his Heroism lessons.

'Sorry I'm—' he started to say as he opened Mr Shumway's door, but the office was empty. He stood on the threshold, frowning. He'd been at JWW long enough to know that the cashier's absence (*Dammit*, he thought, *is* nobody *here any more? Pretty soon, I'll have the whole place to myself*) could mean many things. It could be an intelligence test, the first step in his training; or maybe, twenty years ago, Mr Shumway had sold his soul to the Evil One and the bailiffs had just been round to collect him; or maybe he'd just nipped across the landing for a quick pee. For once, though, not knowing what was going on didn't bother him particularly. One of the advantages of nothing mattering any more is that nothing matters. Paul sat down and stared out of the window. Some trick of the light meant that he saw his own reflection, rather than the buildings opposite. He didn't like looking at that. Depressing.

'Great,' said a voice behind him. 'You're here, finally. I've been all over the place looking for you.' Mr Shumway didn't sound happy, but that was hardly unusual. Paul noticed that in addition to his customary shabby charcoal-grey suit, he had a pair of safety goggles pushed up onto his forehead, and a pair of scorched leather gloves. He took these off and stashed them in a desk drawer. 'Right,' he went on, 'since we're late starting, and since we've already met, we won't bother with the getting-to-know-you crap. *Beowulf.*'

Paul wondered if that was dwarvish for 'atishoo'. 'Sorry?'

'*Beowulf,*' Mr Shumway repeated. 'Fine, you've never heard of it.' He opened another drawer, picked out a dog-eared paperback, and tossed it at Paul. Much to Paul's surprise, he caught it. 'Read it carefully, it's got a lot of useful stuff. For your information, it's an Anglo-Saxon epic poem about a guy who fights monsters. I'm assuming you've already read sections five, nine and forty-six of the office procedures manual—'

Normally, Paul would have lied; but nothing mattered

any more, so why not tell the truth? 'Sorry, no,' he said.
'I—'

'Bloody hell.' Mr Shumway clicked his tongue. 'Look,'
he said, 'I know this is all an unwarranted intrusion on your
free time and you don't want to be here, but I've got work
to do. I'm a realist, so I don't expect you to help; but I *do*
expect you to try as hard as you can not to be a bloody
nuisance. Do as you're told, do your homework, and don't
waste my time. Understood?'

'Sorry,' Paul replied, as guilt welled up inside him like
the contents of a backed-up toilet. 'It's just that—'

Suddenly, alarmingly, Mr Shumway grinned. 'I know,' he
said. 'Makes you feel a bit like you've just been kicked in
the nuts. I remember one time I got told to get lost by the
love of my life, I went straight out, got completely blasted,
woke up in hospital. Got discharged a week later, married
the nurse. Fifth wife. Nice kid, had a nose like a parsnip.
Don't worry about it,' he added cheerfully, 'you're probably
better off. Great thing about getting dumped is, it means
you're now at liberty to go back to the sweetshop and try
a few new flavours. It's only boring people and doves that
mate for life, and have you ever seen a cheerful dove? Anyway,'
he said, moving a pencil so that it lay exactly parallel with
the edge of the desk, 'that's enough about that. No point
you hanging about here if you haven't done the background
reading. I suggest you piss off somewhere quiet and read
those chapters in the manual, and when you've done that,
come back and we can get started.' He hesitated, sneezed
like a cannon shot, and wiped his nose on a huge red-and-
white handkerchief. 'Right?'

'Right,' Paul replied, slightly dazed.

'Fine. That means you can leave the room. Goodbye.'

Paul was through the door and halfway to the stairs when he heard Mr Shumway's voice behind him, calling out, 'Remember, *Beowulf*. Get it read.' When he looked round, he saw Mr Shumway's door closing.

So, Paul thought as he trailed back down the stairs, *everybody in the office seems to know; probably knew before I did. Not a problem, saves me having to do the embarrassing explanations.* Probably better off, Shumway had said. Was there a current Mrs Shumway? Paul hadn't heard about her if there was, but that didn't mean a great deal. No framed picture on the desk, for what that was worth. He went back to his office and took the procedures manual down off the shelf, feeling his tendons creak as they took up the strain. As he did so, it occurred to him that Mr Shumway hadn't said go back to your office and read the chapters, he'd just said somewhere quiet. Possibly just a sloppy choice of words, but perhaps it was compassion; maybe Mr Shumway had shared confined spaces with people who weren't there, and understood. Well, it was an interpretation, and Paul could read a fat, dull book just as easily somewhere else as here.

He couldn't quite bring himself to leave the building; but, during the course of his wanderings, he'd noticed a small room on the fifth floor that nobody seemed to use for anything; it had been empty except for a plain, old-fashioned wooden desk and a chair, just right for hiding in. Assuming, of course, that it was still there.

It was, although the desk and chair had now been joined by a ratty old green steel filing cabinet and four ancient-looking VDUs. He sat down, pulled out a drawer of the filing cabinet to rest his feet on, and opened the office procedures manual.

There are some books you just can't manage to read, no

matter how hard you try. Your eye skids off the page like a file off hardened steel, and twenty minutes later you find you've read the same paragraph half a dozen times and still can't make head nor tail of it. Paul sighed, dumped the manual on the table, which shook like a jelly under its bulk, and fished Mr Shumway's paperback out of his side pocket.

Beowulf was slightly easier going, though there wasn't a great deal in it. Still, the pages were smaller, and there were fewer words on each one, and at least there wasn't a love interest. Paul couldn't help feeling a little concerned at the fact that he'd been given it to read as coursework; the actual monster-fighting stuff was a bit vague and seemed to assume previous knowledge of swordsmanship and the like; also, the hero who fought the dragon ended up dead, which didn't inspire confidence. Maybe that was the point, and he'd been given it to read so that he'd know how *not* to set about fighting dragons. No point trying to second-guess the syllabus. He ploughed on until he reached the end, by which time it was five to one: lunch. For some reason, it seemed extremely important that he should leave the building for a while. He put the book back in his pocket, left the manual where it was, and headed for the front office.

The receptionist smiled at Paul again as he walked past; odd, he reflected as he walked out onto the street, because he was fairly sure that she wasn't Mr Tanner's mum (who leered rather than smiled; he could recognise her through any of her disguises at twenty-five yards). Another odd thing was that she hadn't been all that pretty. Invariably, the girls behind the reception desk (a different one each day) were always stunningly gorgeous, for the simple reason that they were either Mr Tanner's mum or one of his aunts, both of whom wore human shape the way film stars wear clothes – nothing but the best, and never the same outfit twice. The girl who'd smiled at him, however, had been pleasant-looking but nothing more, and there hadn't been that all-the-better-to-eat-you-with shine on her teeth that Paul had come to recognise as the hallmark of goblinesses in mufti. A genuine human being on reception? What was the old firm coming to?

As to where he was going to spend his precious fifty-five minutes of liberty, he had no idea. The Italian sandwich bar was out, obviously; also the pub on the corner, which would be crammed to the doors with gaps where Sophie wasn't. That just left the Starbucks at the end of the road; a grim, joyless place that reminded him of an airport late at night, but it was better than walking the streets. He bought a cup of coffee and a Danish pastry, and sat down at the only empty table.

'Mind if I join you?'

He looked up, and for the third time that day found himself looking down the barrel of the same unprovoked smile. 'Please,' he muttered, 'help yourself.'

She sat down next to him, carefully settling her own cup of coffee and Danish pastry on the wobbly table top. 'You don't remember me, do you?' she said.

Well yes, Paul thought, *of course I do; you're the new receptionist, I saw you about three minutes ago.* 'Um,' he said.

'I'm Melze,' she said. 'Demelza Horrocks. Laburnum Grove Primary School.' Her grin was entirely human; not a pointed tooth in sight. 'You promised to marry me when we were both grown up, but I guess it must've slipped your mind.'

'Oh.' Paul must've looked as startled as he felt, because she laughed. He couldn't understand; why would anybody lie about a thing like this? Clearly she wasn't Melze, because she'd had freckles and four missing front teeth and a nose like a small doorknob, and she'd only been about four feet tall— But, Paul suddenly realised, she wasn't lying after all. She was still there, in the triangle between eyebrows and chin; like the listed building surrounded by modern developments. In this case, gentrification. 'You've changed,' he heard himself say.

'Thank you,' she replied. 'So've you. What're you doing in a dump like that?'

'It was the only job I could get,' he replied sheepishly.

'Same here.'

Bloody hell, he was thinking. Demelza *Horrocks*. 'That can't be right,' he said. 'At school you were the clever one, you got into Wiffins and everything. I thought everybody who went there ended up as doctors or accountants.'

She smiled. 'Not quite,' she said. 'I was headed in that direction, sure, but I never actually arrived. Dropped out of Uni in my second year – boy trouble – did bar work for a couple of years until I suddenly realised you can't be nineteen for ever and ever, and by then, apparently, I was too incredibly ancient to be any use to anybody. So I learned typing and stuff, and here I am.' She shrugged. 'Wasted opportunities, all that. I could've been a chimney sweep if only I'd got the right A levels.'

Paul didn't understand that, so he assumed it must be a quotation or something. 'That's a pity,' he said. 'I guess,' he added, 'unless you're amazingly happy and well adjusted and so on.'

She grinned. 'No,' she said.

'Oh.' Something occurred to him. 'Um, Melze,' he said awkwardly, 'you do *know* about JWW, don't you? Only—'

She laughed. 'About what they do? Yes, of course I know.

First thing they told me at the interview. Pretty weird, but like they said, that aspect of things won't affect me, really. All I'll be doing is answering the phone and normal, boring stuff like that.'

Paul frowned. They hadn't told him anything of the sort at *his* interview; it had taken him several weeks and an armed confrontation with a dozen red-eyed goblins before he found out. 'It's not so bad,' he said, on the principle that she probably wanted to hear something upbeat. 'So long as you're out of the door by half-five, that is. That's when—'

'I know,' she said. 'They told me. Also, don't leave personal property in the desk drawers unless you want it shredded by four-inch claws. You should see the second-floor ladies' loo, by the way. I guess the partners never think to go in there when they're making good the damage on a Monday morning.'

That reminded Paul of something else. 'Did they happen to mention,' he said as casually as he could manage (about as casual as the Buckingham Palace sentry, unfortunately), 'why they needed a receptionist? Only, up till now a couple of the goblins—'

'Mr Tanner's mother, yes. Haven't you heard? She's pregnant, apparently, and goblins are rather old-fashioned about maternity leave and stuff.'

'Bloody hell.' One good thing – no, two, or make that three. First, the joyful thought of how Mr Tanner was going to react when presented with a baby brother or sister. Second, if Mr Tanner's mum was going to be out of circulation for a while, he'd be able to get out of the habit of scanning every attractive female he passed in the street for signs of twinkling eyes and feral grins. Third; third, fourth and fifth, Melze was going to be there, every day from now on, and he'd always liked Melze. A lot—

Oh shit, he thought. *Not again.*

She was eating her Danish pastry. She'd been a messy eater when she was nine, and she hadn't changed; bits of pastry shrapnel were spattered around her nose, chin and mouth. He caught himself noticing her mouth, and quickly looked away. That was *very* bad; because (up till now) Melze was the only female of approximately his own age with whom he'd ever felt comfortable. When they'd been kids together, they'd got into trouble splashing about in her dad's stagnant, leaf-clogged goldfish pond, hunting mosquito larvae with a butterfly net; they'd mangled balsa-wood aircraft and tangled kite strings in shrubs together, fought over alleged rule infringements in marathon Monopoly tournaments, broken each other's toys. They'd been *friends*, even though she was technically a girl. It'd been like *E.T.* and all those other movies where a human and an alien forge bonds of friendship across the species divide. And now – now she'd betrayed all that, he couldn't help feeling, because she'd metamorphosed into a beautiful, or at least pleasant-looking, or at least not hideously deformed, young woman, one of those dangerous creature who break your heart and leave you notes and go away, filling the world with black holes . . .

'Quite.' Melze was still chattering happily away, apparently oblivious of her own foul treachery. 'You must know, is it true that goblins can make themselves look just like people? That could be – well, awkward, I suppose.'

'Very,' Paul heard himself say. 'Especially since you can't trust them any further than you could sneeze them out of a blocked nostril. Have you come across them yet?'

'Hardly.' She smiled again, but this time he was ready for her, and looked away. 'It's only my first day, remember? I've met all the partners, though. That Ricky Wurmtoter – he's a specimen, isn't he?'

Paul wasn't quite sure what she meant by that, but caught himself feeling suddenly and furiously jealous, just in case it signified lust. 'He's gone off on some job,' he said quickly. 'Won't be back for ages. In fact, I'm, um, filling in for him till he gets back.'

'Really?' Melze was looking at him with her oncoming-lorry-headlight eyes. 'But he does all the dragon slaying and vampire hunting and stuff, doesn't he?'

'That's right.'

'Cool.' He was still looking away, but he could feel the smile. He could probably have toasted muffins over it. 'And that's what you do, is it?'

'Yes,' Paul squeaked. 'Well, some of the time. I help out with a lot of different stuff, actually. While I'm making up my mind which field I want to specialise in, you know.'

'Amazing.'

(But this is *wrong*, yelled a little voice inside his head. This time yesterday, you were in love with Sophie for ever and ever. In fact – how do the time zones work, is California eight hours behind or eight hours in front? – quite possibly, where Sophie was right now it was probably still yesterday; and already, here he was: Paul Carpenter, love's lemming, adding to his already impressive collection of Frequent Faller points. The rebound is one thing, but the human heart shouldn't be a pinball machine. *Wrong*—)

'Well,' his voice said, ignoring all that, 'it's just a job, really, better than digging peat or stacking shelves. I'd have jacked it in long ago, only—' Yet another nasty thought struck him. 'Melze,' he said, 'have they made you sign a contract or anything? Only, there's this clause—'

She shook her head. 'They told me about that,' she said. 'That's just for the professional staff. General help like me, we can come and go as we please. I suppose they reckon we can't give away trade secrets to rival firms because we don't know any, and if we tried to blow the whistle on them, for being wizards and all, or sell the story to the tabloids, nobody'd believe us because we're just silly girls.' She shrugged. 'Which is fine,' she said. 'Actually, I think I'll stick around for a while. I mean, it's weird, yes, but it's a bloody sight better than the dump I was at before. One ten-minute coffee-break, and the staff room had cockroaches.'

'That's—' Paul bit off the rest of the sentence. He'd been about to say, *That's wonderful, I'm so glad you're going to be working here.* But why not? After all, she was his oldest friend. 'That's disgusting,' he said. 'What's the coffee room like, by the way? I've never dared go in there.'

'Haven't you? Why not? Is there a manticore in the cupboard under the sink or something?'

Worse than that, it's always full of girls. All a manticore can do is eat you. 'I don't think so,' he said. 'But you never know around here. I mean, one of the staplers in the front office turned out to be the senior partner.'

Melze giggled. 'I heard about that,' she said; and then (slight change of tone of voice): 'Wasn't it you who rescued him?'

'Yes, me and—' Pause. 'Me and one of the other clerks. She's not here any more, though. Got posted to the Hollywood office.'

Paul had done his best to gloss over the obtrusive pronoun, but Melze was on to it like a ferret on a lame rat. She didn't say anything, but the focus of her eyes changed a little. 'And how about you, then?' she said. 'Anyone special?'

And that, Paul couldn't help thinking, was a bloody good question. 'No,' he said. 'Not right now.' He hoped she'd grown out of the knack of knowing when he was lying. 'You?'

She shook her head; and he made a point of not noticing the way her hair floated round her shoulders. 'Not since the creep at Uni, really. Before him, lots. All messy and horrid. Truth is,' she went on, 'I'm not particularly good at—' He could hear her open the inverted commas – 'relationships. Someone once said I fall in love like a young subaltern going over the top in 1914. A bit harsh, but basically true. I'm surprised you're still on the loose, though.'

Eek, Paul thought. That was a topic that ought to be sealed off by angels with flaming swords and Rottweilers. Time for a change of subject. 'So, how's your family?' he asked.

'Fine,' Melze replied, with a trace of a sigh, 'just as normal and boring as ever. Dad's been made sales manager for the whole of the South-East, which is nice. Mum's still making soft toys for the Red Cross. What about your lot?'

Paul grinned feebly. 'My parents emigrated to Florida last year,' he said. 'Sold the house, all the furniture and stuff. I get a phone call once or twice a month – three in the morning usually, because of the time difference – and Mum tells me all about how she doesn't like the people next door, because their dog digs up the flower beds. Haven't told them about JWW. No point, they'd just think I was trying to be funny.'

Melze clicked her tongue sympathetically. 'They always were a bit – well, self-centred.'

'As a gyroscope,' Paul replied. 'I always liked your parents better than mine. At least, yours always seemed pleased to see me.'

Melze shrugged. 'And what about your uncle, the one who was always away travelling in exotic places?'

Paul had to think for a moment. 'Uncle Ernie? Haven't heard from him in years. I assume he's still alive, or someone'd have told me, but we lost touch ages ago.'

'It's a pity when that happens,' Melze said. 'I mean, there's times when it's a bit claustrophobic, having a close family like ours, but at least we stay in touch.'

They chatted about families for a while, until he'd quite forgotten who he was talking to; and then, quite unexpectedly, it was five to two, and there was only just enough time left to get back to the office.

He left her at the front desk and wandered back to his room, thinking, *All this and dragons, too.* Dragons, on the other hand, were probably something you could learn how to cope with, given time and patient tuition.

After all that, it was hardly surprising that Paul found it extremely difficult to get his head around the office procedures manual that afternoon. At the best of times, he'd have had problems coming to terms with stuff like—

For a fully grown urban dragon (draco vulgaris Robinsonii) *in a built-up area, the Pest Control (Residential & Commercial Districts) Regulations 1964 Schedule 2, paragraph 2(i)(b) mandates the use of a tungsten or depleted-uranium projectile of at least 0.577" diameter not exceeding 800 grains avoirdupois in weight with a muzzle energy of not less than 3,000 ft/lbs. Exploding projectiles are forbidden under the 1964 Regulations except where their use has been*

expressly authorised in advance by the proper officer of the
appropriate area directorate; authorisation will only be granted
where at least two of the following criteria obtain—

—and with all the other stuff on his mind, the book might as well have been written in Sanskrit for all the sense he could make of it. At least the boredom was reassuring; it was hard to be freaked out by anything so excruciatingly dull. A few things stuck in his mind: for instance, under the Wildlife & Countryside Act 1979 as modified by the Supplementary Regulations Order 1981, it was illegal to kill a vampire by driving a wooden stake through its heart between February 1st and November 22nd unless you held a valid extermination licence issued by the Ministry of Agriculture, and a qualified veterinary surgeon had to be present to ensure that all procedures were carried out humanely and without causing undue suffering to the vampire. On the other hand, the owner or tenant of farmland was entitled to snare unicorns by means of virgins or other approved devices, providing that he could prove that they'd caused damage to growing crops or standing timber.

Half-past five was running late that day. When the clock on the opposite wall eventually condescended to get there, Paul slammed the book shut – he'd have to finish it off at home, but there was a copy (*Sophie's; remember her?*) at the flat – and practically sprinted for the front office; not that he had any reason to get there before anybody in particular went home or anything, but— He heard someone call his name, and stopped. He recognised the voice, even though he hadn't exchanged more than a few words with Judy di Castel'Bianco since his interview. She spoke with what sounded to him like an American accent overlying something else he couldn't quite place. Back when Mr Tanner had told him what the various partners in the firm actually did, he'd said that she looked after the Entertainment Sector. The letters after her name on the company letterhead apparently stood for Queen of the Fey, whatever the hell that meant.

'Mr Carpenter,' she repeated, materialising out of her office like a Starfleet away team. 'I was wondering, could you spare me a moment?'

Oh well, Paul thought; and then, *Never mind, there'll be other days.* 'Sure,' he said, trying to sound polite.

She was looking at him. Her eyes, he noticed, were large and a very light blue, almost silver.

'You're not in a hurry, or anything?' she said.

'Um, no. Not at all.'

Judy di Castel'Bianco was silent for a moment, studying him intensely, like a cat watching a mouse. 'If you're concerned about getting out of the building after the door is locked, I do of course have a key.'

'Great,' Paul said helplessly. 'Fine.'

Another second and a half of intense scrutiny; then: 'If you'd care to follow me,' she said, and disappeared. For a moment, Paul was rooted to the spot. Then it occurred to him that she must've just walked round the corner and he hadn't been paying attention. He followed, and there she was, opening the door of the small conference room.

Today the room was L-shaped, its long side at right angles to the street. Judy di Castel'Bianco sat down at the head of the long, polished walnut table and nodded towards a chair on her left. As Paul sat down, it struck him that something was odd, but he wasn't sure what it was.

'I'll get straight to the point,' she said, steepling her

unusually long fingers on the table top. 'First, I should mention that it's not this firm's policy to interfere in any way in the personal lives of members of staff; nor is it my place as a partner to pass judgement or anything of that sort. However, I'm aware that my decision to assign Ms Pettingell temporarily to our Los Angeles office may be having repercussions on your—' She frowned slightly. 'Your relationship,' she said, and she spoke the word as if it were an unfamiliar loanword from a foreign language and she wasn't quite sure how it should be pronounced.

'Actually—' Paul started to say, but apparently she couldn't hear him. She was looking past him; only just, a matter of fifteen degrees or so. It was as if she couldn't actually see him, but had a fairly good idea of where he was likely to be.

'Obviously,' she went on, 'if Ms Pettingell's assignment is causing any difficulties in your respective personal lives, I and we as a firm naturally regret that most sincerely. However—' She hesitated, apparently unsure about something. 'If I may speak frankly,' she went on, 'and please note that I'm making these observations in a purely unofficial capacity; I can't help but feel that this situation may actually be all for the best, in that the relationship' (the same slight stumble over the word) 'in question was perhaps not entirely advisable, considering the interests of both parties. I don't claim any special insight in these matters, but you might care to consider the position in that light.'

Judy di Castel'Bianco stopped speaking and looked at him, as though they were in a play and she'd just given him his cue. Paul looked back at her, and wondered what the hell he was supposed to say. He hadn't noticed before how extremely high and sharp her cheekbones were. Who were the Fey, anyhow?

'It's all right, actually,' he mumbled, 'we'd just sort of, well, split up. I mean, it was her idea rather than mine, but I think we both knew we weren't, you know, going anywhere. I mean, I'd sort of got the idea that maybe—'

Mercifully, she interrupted before Paul could embarrass himself into a coma. 'Fortuitous,' she said. 'It would appear, then, that the situation has worked out quite well. Presumably it will be easier for you to adjust, if you aren't faced with the prospect of working closely with Ms Pettingell while coming to terms with the cessation of the relationship.'

It took Paul a moment or so to translate that. 'Absolutely,' he said. 'I guess we both need a bit of space,' he added. (That was what Sophie would have said.) 'So, like you were saying, you've done us both a bit of a favour, really. So,' he went on, though he knew that trying to make awkward silences better by filling them with the first words that come into your head is like dowsing a fire with petrol, 'no hard feelings, is about it, really. It's all just, um, perfectly fine.'

'Indeed.' Now she was looking off to his other side, just a tad. 'It's very fortunate that you feel that way. I trust I haven't offended you by raising the subject.'

'Oh, no, no,' Paul said quickly. 'Best to get it all out in the open, and, um, very nice of you to care, I mean be concerned.' How old was she? The line of her mouth was so hard you could've engraved glass with her lips, but her skin was as smooth as a sixteen-year-old's. 'Um, was that it? Or—'

'That's all,' Judy di Castel'Bianco replied. 'Thank you for

your time. If you'd care to follow me, I'll see that you leave the building without any problems.'

That made him wince, reminding him of the only time he'd been in the place after the front door was locked. That was, of course, the time he'd tried to rescue Sophie from the armed goblins who'd kidnapped her. 'Thanks,' he mumbled, but she'd already left the room.

As he'd feared, the goblins were already coming out to play. He'd seen them once or twice since that first traumatic encounter, but the sight of them still made him want to find the nearest sofa and hide behind it. It wasn't any one thing in particular – the red eyes, the pig, ape, dog faces, the coarse brown and grey fur, the claws – more the overall effect of everything put together.

But if goblins spooked Paul, it was nothing compared to the effect that Countess Judy seemed to have on goblins. They didn't seem to like her at all. As she rounded a corner with Paul in tow and walked into a small knot of them, busily playing toss-the-fire-extinguisher, they spun round, shrieked and scampered away in all directions. A small, rat-faced specimen they bumped into on the second-floor landing backed into a corner with its paws over its eyes, whimpering. Another jumped down a whole flight of stairs to get out of her way, landing painfully on one knee and crawling off like a wounded crab. Either the Countess didn't notice or she was so used to that sort of thing that it didn't occur to her to make any comment; but Paul couldn't help noticing that every time she came within fifteen yards of a goblin, her skin actually seemed to glow with a very faint blue light, which clashed horribly with her lipstick.

All in all, he was relieved when the front door closed

behind him; in fact, he told himself, he could probably use a drink.

For once, the pub on the corner wasn't too crowded, and he was able to sit down at a table in the corner. Plenty to think about; in fact, the trick would be *not* thinking about most of it. For example: what made the Countess think that she was under some kind of obligation to explain, or even to apologise? That didn't strike Paul as being JWW's style at all; nobody had apologised or made excuses when he found out that he wasn't actually allowed to resign, on pain of being made to do horrible things to himself and others. Of course, it wouldn't have mattered anyway if he still had the Portable Door – he could be in Hollywood, California in the time it took to fish the Door out of its cardboard tube and spread it on the wall. But Ricky Wurmtoter had the Door now, so that wasn't an option; besides, there wouldn't be any point going, would there? It occurred to him to wonder whether Mr Wurmtoter had relieved him of the thing just in case he was tempted to go over there and make a nuisance of himself, hanging around in the front office while she hid out back. *Unlikely*, he decided. He felt sure that JWW had more efficient ways of stopping him from being a pest—

Pest. Pest control. *Yuck.*

In the morning, he'd be reporting to Mr Shumway, assuming he managed to get through the rest of the stuff he had to read without falling asleep. A few days ago, he'd have thought it was impossible to imagine a situation where he'd actually be pining for the Mortensen printouts, or the long afternoons he'd spent staring at photographs of bleak Australian desert, scrying them for hidden bauxite deposits. Now, apparently, he was set on a course that would probably, at some stage, involve him in actual physical danger. After all, it stood to reason that if sorting out dragons and monsters and whatever called for the services of your Ricky Wurmtoters and Benny Shumways, warlike men whose time came expensive, then inevitably those buggers must be *dangerous* – teeth and claws and all manner of unpleasantness posing a severe risk to one's health. Paul wasn't sure he liked the idea of that, not one little bit. Up till then, telling JWW where to stick their job and risking the full force of Mr Tanner's warped imagination had been out of the question. But.

But there was a substantial difference between being magically compelled to wander up and down Oxford Street wearing nothing but a coat of blue emulsion, announcing to all the world that you're a little flower fairy, and actual definitive death. Although Paul was probably more afraid of Mr Tanner than of anyone else he'd ever met in his entire life, he was fairly sure that Tanner wouldn't go so far as to kill him dead if he refused to carry on working for the old firm. A dragon, on the other hand, or a werewolf or a gorgon or a manticore – if it came to a contest between himself and a dangerous creature, with death as the prize for coming second, he had a feeling that the smart money would be on the fire-breathing, scale-armoured, razor-clawed professional killer, not on Mrs Carpenter's little boy who came over all faint at the sight of needles. True, Benny Shumway was going to train him, but in his heart of hearts he felt that that probably wouldn't be quite enough. Groaning pallets stacked high with sows' ears aren't unloaded every morning at the gates of the silk-purse factory.

Paul frowned into the two millimetres of froth at the bottom of his glass. Officially, he no longer cared. He'd just lost the only girl he'd ever loved (correction: the only girl out of the hundred or so he'd loved who'd ever loved him back), and accordingly his life was without meaning and worthless, and any dragon who relieved him of it would be doing him a favour. Officially. In his heart of hearts, however, Paul wasn't quite so sure about that. And besides: what if the dragon didn't kill him outright but left him horribly chewed up and burned, blinded, imprisoned in a wheel-chair, only able to communicate with the outside world by wiggling his ears in semaphore? Somehow he knew instinc-tively that he wouldn't like that at all.

He turned the problem over in his mind as he dragged home on the bus. The answer came to him in a flash of pure white light while he was in the bath. It was blind-ingly obvious and brilliantly simple.

Take, for example, a kamikaze pilot. First, he has to do his basic training: this is how an aeroplane works, this is how to read a map, this is how you take off and land, this is how to make the aircraft go left or right, up or down. Months of classwork and one-to-one tuition later, he's ready. He's passed the written tests and the practicals, clocked up his thirty solo hours, attained the exacting standard required of a fighter pilot. He climbs into the cockpit, and never comes back. Meanwhile his slow-witted, cack-handed class-mate who flunked navigation and turned his flying instructor's hair prematurely grey by bouncing down the runway like a rubber ball, survives the war and goes on to found a multinational electronics corporation. Moral: it doesn't always pay to do your very best.

With that comforting thought to snuggle up with, Paul fell asleep as soon as his briskly towelled head hit the pillow. He dreamed.

He dreamed that he was back in the wilds of rural

Gloucestershire, in the dark and the rain; and here are the strange children, fixing his car. Here is Carrot-top, handing him the bill, as Monika purrs contentedly on the floodlit forecourt. Here is Paul, explaining that he didn't have that much cash on him, but—

'Doesn't matter,' says Carrot-top, looking up at him with round, violet eyes. 'On the house. Least we could do, seeing it's you.'

A moment, while the penny drops. 'Me,' Paul repeats, suddenly wary. 'What about me?'

Carrot-top smiles. 'You're him,' she says.

'Oh,' says Paul. 'Am I?'

"Course you are,' interrupts another child, all golden hair and missing front teeth. 'We knew it soon as we saw you. You're Paul Carpenter, aren't you? Him. The chosen one.'

Oink? Paul thinks. 'I'm not sure I quite—'

'Hang on a sec,' says Carrot-top; and she darts back into the workshop, while all the other children – there's rather a lot of them, apparently – come out of the shadows and stand round him, all staring at him as though he is the answer that's been inadvertently written up on the blackboard instead of the question. Then Carrot-top comes back, lugging along with her a huge calf-bound book, as big as the office-procedures manual, if not bigger. 'Here you are, look,' says Carrot-top, and she thrusts the book at him, open somewhere near the middle.

'I don't actually—' he starts to say; but there on the page right under his nose is a picture of a good-looking, clean-cut youth, and underneath it the words—

PAUL CARPENTER
The Chosen One

'Oh,' he says; and then, feeling a right prawn for not knowing, 'Chosen for what?'

One of the other kids, a mop-headed brunette with glasses, clicks her tongue. 'To lead your people to the chosen land, of course, silly. Here, look, it tells you all about yourself in the book. Pages 256 to 312 inclusive.'

'Gosh,' Paul says. 'Can I have a look at that, please?' So they hand him the book; and it's written in normal English letters, and he can see his name repeated over and over again, but the rest of it's in French, or Italian, or possibly Spanish, and although he can make out about one word in ten, that's not enough to give him the sense of it; and just as he comes to a bit in Turkish (which apparently he can understand) they take the book away from him and close it with a snap.

'See?' they say. 'That's you, that is.'

'Yes,' he's forced to admit. 'That's me. But what about me? What am I supposed to—?'

They're scowling at him. 'You shouldn't make fun,' they're saying. 'That's rude.'

So Paul turns to Monika, who's still quietly idling away behind them, and he asks her what they're talking about. And she says, it's obvious, it means that you're the *gepriesener Freiheitsbote*, even a *dummkopf* like you ought to know that — But he doesn't catch the rest of what she's saying, because the kids are grabbing hold of him and lifting him up off the ground, carrying him on their shoulders round and round the courtyard, shouting, waving their arms, setting off the fire alarm, cheering like crazy. This is ridiculous; they couldn't be more pleased with him if he was Lawrence of Arabia *and* he'd just scored the winning goal in the World Cup final, but at the same time they seem to know exactly

who he is, so surely they ought to know he's just an immature waste of space who's just been dumped by the only
girl—

Paul opened his eyes. Not the fire bell after all; just the
persistent tweeping of his alarm clock. He'd always had the
impression that it didn't think very much of him. This
morning it sounded more than usually outspoken in its
disapproval. *You, some kind of Messiah or something?* it seemed
to be saying. *Yeah, right. In your dreams.*

On Paul's desk was a memo:

> *To: PAC*
> *From: BS*
> *Re: Supplies*
> *Your first job for the department. We're running low on basic*
> *supplies. Check the enclosed stockbook against the inventory*
> *and make out purchase requisitions for anything we need.*
> *   BS*

He read the note twice, just to be sure. *Could be worse,*
he thought; *if I can spin this out for long enough, maybe I won't
have to die today.* He opened the file that came with the
memo. It was all pretty straightforward.

Four hours later Paul had discovered that they were almost
out of sulphur candles, yellow 12-volt detonators, .50-calibre
Browning machine-gun ammunition and cyanide gas, and
they could probably do with topping up on spare bear-trap
springs, chainsaw oil, two-way radio-battery charger packs
and SlayMore dragon pellets. He checked the unit prices in
the suppliers' list, remembering to deduct the 5 per cent
trade discount, and filled out two copies of the blue

requisition forms and the yellow cashier's slip. It occurred to him that maybe heroism wasn't quite so bad after all. Lunchtime already, and not a drop of blood spilt or shed.

Lunchtime—

There hadn't been anybody on the reception desk when he'd arrived that morning, but he'd been on the doorstep at one minute to nine, so it was reasonable to assume that she'd got in a little bit later than him, and . . . He caught himself at it. Somehow, in the last thirty-six hours, *she* had stopped meaning Sophie, and now meant Melze. *Here we go again. One small step for a lemming, yet another giant leap for lemmingkind.*

Nevertheless. Paul jumped up, grabbed his coat, and raced for the front office like a Pamplona bull who hasn't realised it was that time already. He very nearly made it; but Benny Shumway suddenly stepped out in front of him and called, 'Hey, you.'

Paul knew it was Mr Shumway by his voice and by the thickness of his spectacle lenses; otherwise, he'd have had trouble recognising him. His face was bright red, his beard had shrivelled down to charred wisps, and his suit was covered in white dust. His hands were red, too; not quite red, more of a sort of terracotta brown. He didn't look at all well.

'First-aid kit,' he said. 'In my office, left side of the desk, second drawer down. I'll be in here,' he added, and stepped back through the open door he'd appeared from. Paul vaguely remembered it was the closed-file store.

For some reason, he ran up the stairs instead of just walking. There was a white tin box in the second drawer on the left, though it felt empty. He grabbed it, and ran back.

Paul had never been in the closed-file store before, and under other circumstances he'd have found the time to gawp. It was a huge room, so vast that it looked like it had mirrors on all four walls and the ceiling, and it was crammed with wooden shelves overflowing with identical large, fat buff manila envelopes. At the most conservative estimate it had to be about the size of Westminster Abbey; put another way, many times larger than the whole of 70 St Mary Axe.

But there wasn't time to think about that. Mr Shumway was sitting on the floor, his back against a rack of shelves, his head slumped forward on his chest until Paul came in; whereupon he looked up and whispered, 'Got it?'

'Yes,' Paul replied. 'Look, are you—?'

'I'm fine,' Mr Shumway snapped. 'Fetch that box over here.'

When the box was opened, there was nothing in it except some dried leaves, a tiny glass bottle with a few purple dregs at the bottom, and a small, thick, tatty book. It was the book that Mr Shumway wanted. He seized it, flipped to the index at the back and turned forward till he found the page he wanted. He read a few words aloud, following the text with one stubby, brown-stuff-caked finger. Then he dropped the book back into the box, leaned back and sighed.

'Takes a while,' he said wearily. 'Thanks,' he added.

'That's all right,' Paul replied. 'Look, what happened? Should I call a doctor or an ambulance or something?'

Mr Shumway grinned. 'No need,' he said. 'Let's see. I've got second-degree burns to most of my face, two – no, sorry, I tell a lie, *three* cracked ribs, I've been inhaling hot sulphur fumes and God knows what else, I've grazed all the skin off both knees and I think I've pulled a muscle in my left shoulder. The last thing I need is to be mauled about by one of the butchers you people call doctors. Besides, I'm a dwarf. We're impervious to X-rays, we've got rather more internal organs than you monkey-derivatives and we don't keep 'em in the same places, and our kidneys are soluble in aspirin. When we get messed up, we fix ourselves.' He held up the tatty book. 'Like this.'

Paul stared at the dog-eared cover. It looked just like an ordinary paperback, but the writing on it wasn't in any alphabet he'd ever come across; the nearest he could get to describing it was an extremely violent hand-to-hand battle, drawn by L. S. Lowry. 'Runes,' Mr Shumway explained. 'It just says *First-Aid Manual*. Bloody useful, though. Healing charms for all occasions.'

'Healing charms,' Paul repeated, his tone of voice translating that as *snake oil*. But then he noticed that Mr Shumway's face wasn't looking nearly so scorched and raw, and his beard had grown back at least half an inch. 'Bloody hell,' he said.

Mr Shumway smiled and shook his head. 'Before you ask,' he said, 'no. Doesn't work on your lot; and even if it did, it's only good for a fairly limited range of injuries – broken bones, burnt skin, stuff like that. We can cure colds, though,' he added smugly. 'And we've got stone teeth, so toothache isn't a major problem.'

Paul nodded. This was degenerating into weirdness, to which he'd carefully taught himself to turn a blind eye. 'But what happened?' he asked. 'Were you in a fight or something?'

'You could say that,' Mr Shumway muttered; something was happening to him that apparently hurt. 'No big deal, mind. Just a dragon.'

'Just a dragon,' Paul parroted.

Mr Shumway nodded. 'Twelve-year-old doe, seven and a half feet, about three hundred pounds. Damn thing'd got itself nicely dug in down in the stacks of the V&A. Cunning little bitch, I'll give her that. Got hold of a sack of cement from somewhere and rolled in it, then went and stood in a corner, nice and still. It'd been there six months before they realised it wasn't just another statue, and then they only found out because it sneezed.' He sighed. 'I tried smoking it out, but they didn't like that, reckoned it'd damage the paintings and stuff. Couldn't use explosives, obviously, or the fifty-calibre; and they wanted rid of it PDQ, so poison was out. Meant I had to get rid of it manually, what Corporal Jones would've called the old cold steel.' He stretched his back and winced. 'I'm getting too old for all that,' he sighed. ''Course, young Ricky, he loves all that shit. But he's not here, is he?' Mr Shumway growled. 'Off prancing around with Gren— with this special project,' he amended abruptly. 'And you aren't fit to be out on your own yet, which just leaves me. Just as well I got this book, because I've got bank reconciliations to do this afternoon, I can't afford a week off flat on my back having skin grafts.'

Paul didn't say anything. He had no idea what colour he'd turned – white, or green – but he hoped it wasn't too obvious.

'Anyway.' Mr Shumway's beard was back to its usual length, and he was wriggling his shoulder to see if it was working properly again. 'Thanks,' he said. 'Didn't feel like dragging up three flights of stairs. Where were you off to in such a hurry, anyhow?'

Paul squirmed a little. 'Oh, just lunch,' he said.

'Lunch.' Mr Shumway grinned. 'You mean, you wanted

to get down to reception before that new bird had a chance to get away. Quick off the mark, I'll give you that. But you'll just have to tie a knot in it for today. We've got training to do, remember?'

'Training,' Paul said.

Mr Shumway nodded. 'Which means,' he said, 'you missing lunch for a week or so. Which is cruel and harsh and a bloody fucking tragedy of epic proportions, but never mind. I'll be missing lunch too, and you won't see me crying my eyes out over it.'

'Oh, that's fine,' Paul said, bright and brittle. 'Doesn't bother me. Um, thanks for giving up your lunch hour, it's—'

'Don't crawl,' said Mr Shumway. 'If the Good Lord had intended us to crawl, he'd have given us a hundred legs and an exoskeleton.' He stood up. Apart from the white dust on his clothes and the (let's not kid ourselves) blood-stains on his hands, he looked perfectly normal. 'My office,' he said, putting the tatty book back in the box, 'five minutes. You have, of course, read all that stuff I told you to read?'

'What? Oh, sure.'

'Very sensible.' Mr Shumway grinned at him. 'Because if you hadn't, it would've been unpleasant, I'm telling you. That old survival instinct'll pull you through every time.'

Chapter Three

Paul didn't enjoy the next ten working days. In the morning, there was paperwork: all the admin and procedural stuff that every true hero gets some other poor bugger to do for him. There were applications in triplicate for Section Fifteen exemptions, incident reports, written notifications of intention to use restricted weapons in built-up areas, stores requisitions, expenses vouchers and mileage allowance chits (Mr Wurmtoter got ninety-five pence a mile for his winged horse; Benny Shumway got thirty-five pence a mile for his D-reg Suzuki jeep, but mostly seemed to take the Tube), time sheets and invoices and credit control printouts and a whole bunch of other stuff you won't find mentioned in the Norse sagas or the *Morte d'Arthur*. But the mornings were better than the lunch hour, because between one and two he was either in Mr Shumway's office being lectured or shouted at, or in the closed-file store, which doubled as an assault course, firing range and tournament lists. The experience helped Paul discover things about himself that he hadn't appreciated before: that Semtex brought him out in a rash, for example, and firing anti-tank rockets from the shoulder gave him a headache, and his fear of needles also extended to hand-and-a-half *katzenbalger* broadswords. His cunning plan of deliberately doing so badly at everything that Mr Shumway would despair of him and get him transferred to another department turned out to be a non-starter; mostly because he didn't need to pretend. Even when Mr Shumway yelled at him so ferociously that he gave it his very best shot out of sheer terror, he was still uniformly hopeless at everything. His fuses spluttered and died; he couldn't hit a barn door at point-blank range with the .50 Barrett; he consistently failed to remember the right proportion of SlayMore to water; and the only way he'd ever hurt a dragon or a gryphon with a sword would be if the unfortunate creature was standing directly behind him when he lost his grip on the handle. This, unfortunately, was precisely what Mr Shumway seemed to expect of him. 'Don't worry about it,' he'd sigh, as Paul's dummy hand-grenade bounced off the opposite wall and landed at his feet for the sixth time in a row. 'It just takes practice, that's all. Another couple of weeks and you'll be just fine.'

Lunchtimes, then, were bad enough; but they were a week at the seaside compared to the afternoons. In the afternoon, Paul helped Mr Shumway with the banking.

The first time had been the worst, because he'd had no idea. 'Little job I'd like you to do for me,' Mr Shumway had said, poking his head round the door of Paul's office. 'Won't take a minute.'

Of course Paul had said, 'Yes, right, of course,' like the fool he was, instead of 'No way', or 'Over my dead body' – though, in the event, the latter would've been a very silly thing to say, because—

Just inside the door of Mr Shumway's office was another, smaller door. It was decorated with six bolts, four dead-locks, two Yale locks and a chain you could've anchored an aircraft carrier from – curious in itself, because the door was just standard office chipboard, with an aluminium handle.

Paul had noticed it the third or fourth time he'd been in Mr Shumway's office, but compared with some of the other fixtures and fittings he'd come across at 70 St Mary Axe, it was prosaic to the point of brain damage, and he'd ignored it. This time, however, Mr Shumway was busy with a bunch of keys that must've weighed three pounds. 'I'll go first,' he sang out cheerfully. 'You follow on with that satchel on the desk there.' He was referring to a shabby-looking leather case, the sort of thing Just William carried his schoolbooks in. Paul picked it up; it felt as though it was empty.

'Um,' he asked, as Mr Shumway shot back the fourth bolt, 'what are we doing, exactly?'

'Just nipping to the bank,' Mr Shumway replied. 'Paying in some cheques, drawing petty cash, handing in some TT forms. Usual stuff.'

Paul nodded warily. He knew TT stood for 'telegraphic transfer', which was when you sent large sums of money by fax or Internet or something. Why *usual stuff* needed two of them, with Mr Shumway going first, he wasn't sure he wanted to know.

'Ready?' Mr Shumway had finished with the bolts and all but one of the locks. 'Okay, then, on three. One. Two. Three—'

He turned the key in the last of the deadlocks, grabbed the door handle and pushed outwards. He hesitated on the threshold, not letting go of the handle, as if checking to make sure that it was safe. Then he took a step forward and disappeared.

Seriously unnerving stuff. Paul could distinctly see Benny Shumway vanish – made no sense, but that was what he saw. First Mr Shumway's left hand, then the rest of his left arm, his shoulder, then his head and torso, finally his back and right heel, and then he was gone. *Bugger this*, Paul thought, *no way I'm—*

'Come on, then,' called Mr Shumway's disembodied voice. Paul shut his eyes, and followed.

When he opened them again, everything had gone dark. Panic flooded through him and he shuffled backwards towards where he remembered the door being—

'No.' Mr Shumway again, calm but urgent. 'Don't do that, you've got no way of knowing where it'll take you. It's complicated,' he added, 'I'll explain later. Just follow my voice, OK?'

Paul tried to say something, but his words turned into a little trembly squeak. He stuck his left foot out; it was rather like trying to take the last step off an escalator with your eyes shut. Nothing bad happened, apparently. After that, it was very slightly easier.

'Keep up,' Mr Shumway called back at him. Paul did his best; but each time Mr Shumway spoke after that, his voice sounded further and further away. 'And don't look round, whatever you do,' was another helpful piece of advice. 'Come on, we're nearly there. And don't worry, all right? This is just something you have to get used to.'

The lights came up gradually; first a faint grey gleam round the edges, then a glow that seeped into the darkness like ink soaking into blotting paper. Not that it helped much, because there was nothing to see; nothing to right or left, nothing up or (very worrying) down. Paul was a little animated cartoon figure walking across a blank grey screen—

And there was someone walking beside him. He didn't notice at first, so he had no idea how long he'd been there. It was only when he glimpsed movement out of the corner of his eye . . .

'And don't talk to *anybody*,' sighed a faint echo of Mr Shumway's voice. 'Not *anybody*, got it?'

Just in time; because Paul had been on the verge of saying, 'Is that you, Uncle Mike?' He'd only hesitated because it was such a silly thing to say, given that Uncle Mike had died ten years ago.

'Course it's me, you prat, said a memory of Uncle Mike's voice inside his head. *And look at me when I'm talking to you.*

('Don't turn round,' Mr Shumway had said.)

What's wrong, Paul? It's me, Mike. Aren't you glad to see me after all this time? (Paul wasn't hearing the words, because there was no sound. Someone had hit the mute button, and he couldn't hear his footsteps on the lack-of-floor, or his own breathing or anything. But he could distinctly *remember* Uncle Mike saying the words, at some unspecified point in the past.)

He didn't look round, because he'd been told not to; but Uncle Mike had gone, and there was someone else. *Hello, Paul mate*, he remembered, *haven't you grown? Here, what's the matter? Haven't you got anything to say to your old grandad?*

(Which was cruel; because Paul had so much to say, starting with, *Sorry I missed your funeral.* He'd pretended he'd had a migraine, but that had been a lie. He'd always hated funerals, anyhow.)

This is daft, son, we never had a chance to say goodbye. Don't just walk away, Paul. Please. (Wherever this was, Paul decided, he'd rather be somewhere else. 'This way,' Mr Shumway was calling, but Paul wasn't sure whether he was hearing him or remembering, the dwarf was too far away. *Don't look round*, he ordered himself, *don't say anything.*)

Then, quite suddenly, he could see Mr Shumway. He was kneeling down on the absence-of-ground, and he was reaching into his pocket. He pulled out a folded, tatty old baseball cap, opened it, reached in and pulled out (*Why am I not surprised?*) a white rabbit. In his other hand he was holding a knife. With a deft, quick movement—

(*Don't say anything*, Paul commanded himself; because what he wanted to shout was 'No!', at the top of his voice)

—Mr Shumway cut the rabbit's throat, and its blood splashed on the empty space where the ground ought to have been, and disappeared, just as Mr Shumway had when he'd walked through the door. The rabbit stopped twitching in his hand; blood was still gushing out over his wrist, through his fingers. Now, however, where it stopped falling, there was ground; a flat, grey surface of dust, as though that was what the rabbit had had in its veins.

'It's life, see,' Mr Shumway was muttering. 'Where it lands—' He hesitated. 'You do know where you are, right? Don't answer,' he added quickly. 'In case you haven't figured, this is death.'

Fine, Paul thought.

'It's all right,' Mr Shumway went on. 'It's only a magic rabbit, it never really existed. But the blood's real blood, so it does the job. Just about enough for what we've got to do.' He dropped the carcass, which vanished. 'Right, you can talk now. But only to me, and *don't look round*. They'll say anything to make you talk to them, and you really don't want to do that. Trust me.'

Implicitly, Paul thought. He had a nasty feeling that right behind him was a substantial crowd, all people he knew, relations mostly, all of whom he'd never expected to see or hear from again. He tried to concentrate on Mr Shumway, a tiny figure in a cheap suit standing on a minute patch of dust.

'Greetings.' The man appeared almost out of nowhere, but not quite. Actually, he shot up out of the dust, like one of those shorts they show on television occasionally when something's broken down; a film of a plant growing from a seed, speeded up thousands of times. He was Chinese, about seventy years old, in a long blue silk gown with enormous sleeves. He had a wrinkled face and a lovely smile.

'Afternoon,' Mr Shumway replied casually. 'How's death treating you, then?'

'Very dull,' the Chinese gentleman replied. 'Yourself?'

'Can't grumble. Paul,' Mr Shumway added, 'over here. This is Mr Dao, the chief cashier. This is Paul Carpenter.' Short pause, significant. 'He's with me.'

Mr Dao nodded politely. 'Of course,' he said.

Then Mr Shumway turned round. His face was as white as paper. 'It's okay now,' he said, 'you'll be all right now they know you. Give me the bag, and then we can get out of here.' Paul handed him the satchel; he opened it. 'These cheques to pay in,' Mr Shumway said to Mr Dao, 'and these TTs; if you can get them out today that'd be a great help.'

'No problem,' said Mr Dao, with a faint smile.

'Thanks. Oh, and here's the cash slips.' Each time Mr Shumway handed something to Mr Dao, there was a moment between Mr Shumway letting go of it and Mr Dao taking it. The cheque or form or chit didn't fall to the ground – obviously gravity was optional here. Equally obviously, if the two of them both touched something at the same time, something unpleasant would happen.

Mr Shumway passed the bag back to Paul and nodded at the Chinese gentleman. 'Seventeen thousand, four hundred and sixty-five pounds sterling,' said Mr Dao. Paul, holding the satchel open, felt a very slight tug on his hands, as something he couldn't see dropped into it. 'Nine thousand and forty-one US dollars.' Another tug. 'Eighteen thousand, nine hundred and forty Swiss francs. Seventy-two thousand Tajikistani roubles. Nine hundred and sixty Bulgarian lev.' And so on, through Moroccan dirhams and Haitian gourdes to Comoros francs and Korean won, wealth beyond the night-mares of avarice. The temptation to grab the satchel and run off with it was, however, no trouble at all to keep in check.

'Right,' Mr Shumway said at last, 'that's the lot, thanks. Same time tomorrow, then.'

'Indeed.' Mr Dao bowed graciously, then glanced quickly at Paul. 'But perhaps, if you aren't in too much of a hurry, you might care to stop for a cup of tea? Your friend—'

Suddenly, Paul realised that he'd never felt so thirsty in all his life. A cup of tea, yes. He could really do with—

'No, thanks,' Mr Shumway said abruptly. 'Paul,' he added, as if calling a dog to heel.

'But—' Paul said; but Mr Dao was looking away, ever so slightly shamefaced. 'My apologies,' he was saying. 'It won't happen again.'

Was that compassion on Mr Shumway's face? 'It's all right,' he muttered. 'I understand. But we'd better go now.'

'Of course,' Mr Dao said. He vanished, and the patch of dust with him. Mr Shumway breathed out slowly.

'Turn round,' he said. 'Gently does it. Now we're going straight back. Follow me, and no looking back or talking. Don't answer, just nod.'

For some reason, it seemed to take twice as long to get back as it had to get there, wherever 'there' was. All the way, Paul kept his eyes fixed on the back of Mr Shumway's head, as if it was the most fascinating thing he'd ever seen in his entire life. At times it seemed like they were both wading knee-deep through something heavy and sticky – toffee sauce or cake mix – and Mr Shumway's progress gradually got slower and more laborious with every step. The memories raged in Paul's head like a snowstorm, so many of them, all of them so hurt, so disappointed, angry, because he just walked on past them and wouldn't even look them in the eye. He realised that he hadn't taken a breath since they'd met Mr Dao; but he didn't feel strained or uncomfortable. At last, Mr Shumway stopped, though Paul couldn't see anything to stop for. He was panicking about that when a tall rectangular hole appeared in the darkness, and the savage brilliance of the shaded hundred-watt bulb in Mr Shumway's office scorched him like a laser cannon.

'On balance,' Mr Shumway said, closing the door behind them and leaning on it, 'I think I preferred it when we used to use Nat West.' He reached behind him and shot the top bolt. 'But the BOTD's long-term deposit rates are pretty much unbeatable, and their business-account charges are two per cent less.' He turned round, supporting himself against the door frame with his left hand, and locked up.

Paul managed to get as far as the desk before his knees gave way. His eyes were full of sweat, and now, suddenly, he was out of breath and freezing cold. 'Mr Shumway,' he said.

'Benny,' Mr Shumway replied without looking round. 'I guess you can call me that, after—' He shrugged. 'I got to do that every day, five days a week. You can see why, far as I'm concerned, dragons and vampires are a pleasant change.'

'Benny,' Paul said. 'That – man.' Not the right word, but *was* there a right word to describe Mr Dao? All in all, he rather hoped there wasn't. 'When he offered me a cup of tea. What would've happened if I'd—?'

Benny shook his head. 'Nothing you'd have enjoyed,' he said. 'Same as if you'd looked round, or answered Them when They talked to you.' He turned to face Paul. His eyes were very round behind their three-eighths of an inch of glass. 'You've got to remember,' he said. 'On the other side of that door, there's nothing. Nothing at all. Not people, or things, just—' He shrugged. 'Well, you know, you've been there now.' He walked slowly to the desk, like a drunk trying to stay upright, and flumped into his chair. 'Look, Paul,' he said, 'I'm sorry for not warning you. But if I had, you wouldn't have come with me. And—' His shoulders sagged. 'Just once in a while, it's good to know that there's something alive in there, apart from just me. It's supposed to be all right, now that they know me, I'm the accredited representative of JWW, and the bank people've guaranteed my safety. But.' Benny sighed, and his head went forward onto his folded arms. 'But they never stop trying, you know? Just little sneaky things, like the business with the tea. If they get you, you see, they get just a little bit of life, a couple of seconds maybe, and then it's back to—' He yawned; he was exhausted too, Paul realised. 'So you can't blame them, really. I mean, you'd be the same. Will be one day, of course, but it doesn't do any good thinking about that.' He raised his head. 'You OK?'

No, of course not. 'Yes,' Paul said. 'I'm fine. Only—'

'Yes?'

'Only,' Paul said, 'do I have to do that again? I mean—'

Mr Shumway looked at him. 'No,' he said. 'Like I told you, I just wanted the company. No, you don't have to go.'

I don't have to go, Paul thought; and then he looked at Mr Shumway, bloodless and empty-eyed. 'It's OK,' Paul said. 'I don't mind.'

Just a very faint smile, because anything more would've needed more strength than Benny Shumway had just then. 'Thanks,' he said. 'Doesn't mean I'm going to be nice to you, mind,' he added. 'You don't get your lunch hour back or anything.'

Slight disappointment, because Paul was only human. For now, anyway; grateful for small mercies. Whatever it was that had been whispering in his mind's ear back there, it hadn't been human at all. 'I know,' he said. 'It's all right.'

'Fine.' Mr Shumway shrugged off the whole experience like someone shuffling out of a wet coat. 'In that case, tomorrow we're going to make a start on intermediate nitro-glycerine.' His trade-mark feral grin flashed for the first time since they'd gone through the door. 'Just something for you to think about between now and then,' he added.

That night, Paul had a rather unpleasant dream. In it, Sophie had become an incredibly famous and glamorous movie star, and he'd stood in line to get her autograph for hours and days and weeks, only to find when eventually he got to the head of the queue that she'd died in her sleep, and Countess Judy di Castel'Bianco had taken over from her.

The next time was worse.

On the way to wherever it was they went to, there were even more of Them; dead aunts, uncles, cousins, relatives Paul had never even heard of, names scrawled in brown ink on the backs of curling photographs, all reproaching him bitterly for his total lack of compassion. It'd have been worse if he'd ever been under the illusion that any of his relations liked him

And when they got there, and Mr Shumway had produced his old baseball cap, stuffed a big silk handkerchief into it, shaken out half a dozen milk-white doves and blasted them out of the air with the Remington 870 pump-action shotgun he drew out of his top pocket (now that, Paul had to admit as the sixth pathetic white corpse spiralled out of the air, is *conjuring*); this time it wasn't grave, venerable Mr Dao who sprouted up out of the bloody dust at his feet. This time it was a heartbreakingly lovely young girl, who smiled at him and said that her name was Miss Wa, and could she be of any assistance? Even Benny Shumway had to take a couple of seconds to pull himself together; and when, their business concluded, she smiled again and asked if they'd like to stop for a cup of tea – because, she explained, she hadn't had anything to drink since 1723, when she'd died in the arms of her husband on their wedding day—

'That,' Benny admitted as he slammed the door shut and leaned on it, 'was too bloody close.'

'Yes,' Paul said.

'Too bloody close,' Benny elaborated as he turned the keys, 'by half, or maybe even five-eighths.' He shook his head and pocketed the keyring. 'I've been doing this run for two years now and they never tried *that* on me. In fact,' he added, favouring Paul with a sour frown, 'my guess is, it was laid on for your benefit. They know about you, see. About all of us. They can spot your weaknesses soon as you step through that door.'

'Oh.' Paul could feel his face going red. 'I'm not that bad, am I?' he mumbled.

Benny Shumway looked at him for a moment or so before he answered. 'They know,' he repeated. 'I guess I'm lucky,' he added, 'because they don't have Westerners working for the Bank, and my problem's always been redheads. And blondes,' he added, after a brief pause. 'And brunettes. Not that I've got anything against your Oriental types, come to that, but I never could resist a redhead.'

'Um,' said Paul.

'Don't you go all thoughtful,' Benny said. 'Like I told you, they know; so it's pretty obvious where you stand on the issue. Nothing to feel bad about, either,' he added. 'I've never felt bad about it, me. If there's such a thing as re-incarnation, I want to come back as a Maidenform bra. But letting them see it — that's something else. You've got to find a way of dealing with it.'

'Right,' Paul muttered.

'Me,' Benny added, dropping into his chair, 'I always think about goblins.'

'Goblins?'

The Shumway grin. 'You've come across Dennis Tanner's mother, right?'

It was, Paul had to admit, a valid point. 'I'll try that,' he said. 'Thanks'

'No charge.' Benny looked at his watch. 'Well,' he said. 'It's a quarter past five, and by rights you've got just enough time to help me write in these yellow slips. But,' he added, pulling his wire tray towards him across the desk, 'I reckon I probably owe you one by now, so you piss off and I'll do it. I happen to know,' he added to nobody in particular, 'that she rather fancies seeing the new Mel Gibson film. Odeon Leicester Square, programme starts at ten past six, but you won't mind missing the trailers.'

Maybe, Paul thought as he ran down the stairs, *it's a dwarf thing*; or maybe it was so bloody obvious that even dead bankers could read it in his face. That said, Benny Shumway had been right on the money. Ever since that serendipitous lunchtime, Paul hadn't had a chance to say more than a quick, clipped 'Hello' to Melze on his way past the front desk, and that was a situation that he badly wanted to set right.

Melze reckoned that it wasn't a very good film. It went on twenty minutes too long, she said, and she didn't really like effects-fests anyhow. Paul had no opinion whatsoever about the movie; he couldn't remember a thing about it, since his attention had been elsewhere. The flickering light of the screen had been bright enough to highlight the curve of her cheek and the curl of her ear lobe. He'd noticed them during the last trailer, and by the time he'd managed to drag his attention away from them, there was nothing on the screen except the names of assistant cameramen.

'Mostly I like his films,' she was saying, 'though the endings are usually a bit of a let-down. This one, though, I started fidgeting halfway through.'

He knew. He'd noticed. She fidgeted divinely. Bizarrely, he hadn't been aware of how gloriously she fidgeted when he'd sat behind her at Laburnum Grove primary, but he put that down to being a late developer, or profoundly stupid. 'You're so right,' he was about to say, but instead he sneezed.

'Bless you,' Melze said promptly; then, 'Looks like you've caught it now.'

Paul looked up; so she'd guessed. Only a matter of time. 'Sorry?'

'The office cold,' she explained. 'Been going round for a week or so. I'm lucky,' she added, 'I never get colds, or flu. Not for want of trying – at my last job, I'd have given good money for a really sure-fire flu bug that'd have kept me at home for a week. Everybody else got it, not me. Life can be really unfair sometimes.'

He had no idea what she was talking about, but of course it didn't matter. What mattered was that she was sitting at the same table as him in the Pizza Hut in the Strand, and she didn't seem to mind one bit. Bizarre; but he wasn't going to argue. Suited him just fine.

'So,' he was dimly aware of saying, 'you like the pictures, then?'

'Love them,' Melze replied promptly, apparently not noticing how fatuous his remark had been. 'In fact, it's crossed my mind to see if I can put in for a transfer. You know JWW's got an office in Hollywood?'

Something crumpled inside Paul's head. Yes, he knew that very well. Somehow he'd managed to forget, just temporarily, but now she'd reminded him. So kind of her. 'You don't want to go there,' he said, before he'd realised it.

'Oh?' She just looked intrigued. 'What's the matter with it?'

'Earthquakes.' He tried to ignore the fact that he despised himself for being an unimaginative buffoon. 'Very dangerous area, because of all the, um, seismic activity. I was reading somewhere, one of these days that whole part of California's going to disappear down a huge crack in the ground.'

Melze giggled. Most young women over seventeen don't do giggles well, but she had the gift. 'I see,' she said. 'Well, if I do get a transfer, I'll be sure to take a parachute. Seriously, though, is there something I should know?'

Paul hesitated, then nodded. 'I've heard — well, a few things,' he said awkwardly.

'Really?'

'A friend of mine.' Why so much guilt, just because of his choice of words? But he felt as though he'd just given the order for all his most cherished memories to be dragged out and shot. 'Friend of mine,' he repeated, 'got posted over there just recently. Apparently it's no fun at all. Not glamorous or anything, just plain boring.'

She frowned, then her face lit up. You could have taken a photograph down a mine shaft by the glow. 'Oh yes,' she said, 'I heard something about that. The clerk who used to work with you. Someone told me her name—'

'Sophie. Sophie Pettingell.' There, he'd done it. The ultimate betrayal, like finally throwing away your childhood teddy bear. 'I, um, got an e-mail the other day. She says she can't wait for her three months to be over so she can come home.'

Melze was looking at him. She didn't need to say, *Didn't she use to be your girlfriend?* 'Well,' she said, 'maybe I'll give that a miss, then. I suppose three months is a long time to be away, anyhow.'

He'd done it; but in spite of that, or maybe because of it, they weren't alone at the table any more. Next to Paul, just on the extreme edge of his vision, was a hole where Sophie wasn't, a palpable presence – it put him in mind of the patch of nothing where the blood fell, and suddenly a dead clerk jumped up. It occurred to him that the two effects were essentially the same. Mr Dao and Miss Wa were – what, ghosts? But a ghost's just a heavy-duty memory, which can only be revived and called back with a splash of someone else's life. He thought of the memories that had mobbed him as he'd walked across the empty place with Benny Shumway. Would Sophie be with them tomorrow?

No matter how good you are at multitasking, you can't really brood on guilt and death and flirt at the same time. Melze seemed very slightly disappointed when, ten minutes later, Paul explained that he had a bit of a headache and he'd better go home now. But she replied that it was probably the cold, and she was sure he'd be better in the morning. A hot Lemsip and two paracetamol, she suggested. She did rather make it sound like she cared. Infuriating, how something like that can be truly wonderful and an absolute disaster at the same time.

'It's okay,' Benny Shumway announced at 2.15 p.m. on the eleventh day. 'I can see to the banking myself.'

Paul could have wept with relief, except— 'No, I don't mind, really,' he said. 'I'm sort of getting used to it,' he added, truthful as Bill Clinton. 'It's not so bad once you know what to expect.' But Benny shook his head. 'I'm not being nice,' he replied. 'But there's a rush job come up, and one of us's got to go and see to it.'

'Oh.'

'Quite.' Benny pulled a face. 'Because if you were to ask me, do I think you're ready to be let out on your own doing heroism, the answer'd have to be no. But one of us has got to do it, and one of us has got to nip out to the bank. Do you see what—?'

Paul nodded.

'Actually,' Benny went on, 'I think you can probably handle this one okay. I mean, you know all the theory and procedures and stuff, and it's only a titchy little job. I guess,' he added, with a total lack of sincerity, 'it'll be good experience for you. I mean, better to cut your teeth on something small like this rather than get chucked in at the deep end.' He was scribbling something on a blue stores requisition. 'You'd better take a taxi to get there,' he said. 'Some of the stuff's quite bulky, and none of it's really the sort of gear you can take on the Tube.' Paul, glancing over his shoulder, caught sight of the words *35mm anti-tank grenade* and decided it was nice that there was something that he and Benny could agree on.

As it turned out, all the kit fitted quite easily into a large suitcase; and it wasn't far, in any case. The job, according to the file Benny handed him, was to dispose of a small but moderately vicious wyvern that was nesting in a Cashpoint machine at the Piccadilly Circus end of Oxford Street. So far, it had confined itself to eating customers' cards, which wasn't a problem since they were used to it and therefore didn't suspect anything unusual. Inside the file, Paul found a note in Benny's handwriting: *Suggest 50 ml SlayMore mixed 25:1 w/tap water delivered by plant mister through slot; failing which use your discretion and try not to blow up any bldgs*. It was more helpful than some of Benny's other suggestions, but not by much.

When Paul got there, he found that the bank people had already put out orange plastic cones and a yellow-and-white tape; a better invisibility magic than anything he'd come across in the office-procedures manual. He put down his suitcase, took out the dummy cashpoint card he'd been issued with, and very gingerly fed it into the slot. As anticipated, it went in and didn't come out again. The little wisp of blue smoke that drifted up from the slot afterwards was so slight that he wouldn't have noticed it if he hadn't been looking for it.

Unfortunately, although he'd brought the plant mister and a bottle of Evian, he'd forgotten the SlayMore. The thought of going back to the office and explaining didn't appeal to him. Nor (rather to his surprise) did the idea of taking a life. True, killing a fellow life form wasn't something he'd ever choose to do, but in his list of priorities getting the job done without making a total bog of it would normally have towered over mercy like an overgrown Alp. Possibly it was all those trips to the bank, seeing at first hand what it was like on the other side of the final curtain; anyhow, he didn't want to do it, and maybe there was another way. He'd read enough broadsheet newspapers to know that violence is always the problem, never the solution, and that a sword is a piece of steel with a victim at either end; the way of peace, however, will always prevail, if only enemies can be made to talk to each other. Which would be fine, if he could speak Wyvern.

Communication; that was the key. All Paul had to do was figure out how to get through to the little scaly horror, and everything would be peachy.

Communication: communication begins with information, and information is about the only thing the twenty-first century's good at. In his wallet, Paul had a whole deck of little plastic rectangles which held, in digital form, every single bit of information about him in the whole world. He pulled them out: Visa card, social-security card, video-library card, mobile-top-up card, Boots bonus-point card – a Tarot pack containing his entire past, present and future – and began stuffing them into the slot, one after another. Puffs of smoke came out like on a really bad day at the Vatican. As the last one vanished into the black hole, he stood back and waited. Inevitably, the wyvern would by now have a complete picture of Paul Carpenter, his station in life, his obligations, resources, passions, habits. From these, the canny creature would realise that Paul wasn't its enemy, just a friend it hadn't met yet. It would come out, they'd exchange expressions of mutual respect in sign language, and nobody would have to die or get their fingers bitten.

He waited. Nothing happened. Then, just as Paul was starting to wonder what had gone wrong, the slot burped at him.

Shit, he thought.

He spent the next ten minutes trying to fish around inside the slot with a plastic ruler, until that got eaten too. He tried kneeling beside the machine and singing into it: music is a purer form of communication than words — whales sing to each other, and you never read about mugged whales. Then he tried pleading, and threats.

Come along, Paul urged himself, this is pathetic. What would Jean-Luc Picard do? But it occurred to him that every time Jean-Luc found himself at the mercy of an unseen super-intelligent adversary, it turned out to be a lost, frightened little orphan who really only wanted to go home. Suddenly, the idea of a stiff jolt of SlayMore made a lot of sense. Unfortunately, he had no cash for a ride back to the office, and the bloody machine had swallowed his card.

What would Benny do? Well Paul knew the answer to that, it was on the little bit of paper he'd so recklessly ignored. What would Mr Wurmtoter do? Or Mr Tanner, or Professor van Spee? He considered these questions for a while, and then realised that he was asking the wrong questions. The right question, of course, was: what would Paul Carpenter do, assuming Paul Carpenter's IQ was at least double his shoe size?

'Having problems?' said a voice to his left.

He jumped up – he'd been crouching on the ground so that he could whisper into the slot without having to crick his neck – and looked round to see who'd spoken. There was a beautiful girl standing next to him – tall, willowy, natural redhead, lovely smile that almost managed to conceal the fact that it had only just evolved from a rather distinctive grin—

'You,' Paul growled. Then he remembered. 'I thought you were off on maternity leave or something.'

'I am,' the flame-haired beauty replied. 'Been for my check-up. Harley Street, just over there.' She waved a hand in some direction or other. 'Only goblin gynaecologist in Western Europe.'

'Right,' Paul said. 'And I suppose that – *skin* you're wearing is just some old thing you found at the back of the wardrobe.'

'I like to look nice,' Mr Tanner's mum replied. 'What's wrong with that? I mean, which would you rather look at, this or a six-months-pregnant goblin?'

Paul shrugged. 'Anyhow,' he said, 'the answer to your question is yes.'

Mr Tanner's mum took a step towards the bank machine and sniffed. 'Let me guess,' she said.

'Wyvern, right? And you've been feeding it plastic.'

Paul nodded. 'That's a mistake, isn't it?'

She smiled. ''Fraid so,' she said. 'Only two ways to shift wyverns, short of high explosives: gas 'em or starve 'em. Me, I'd have gone for fifty mil of SlayMore mixed twenty-five to one—'

'Yes, I know,' Paul interrupted. 'But I haven't got any bloody SlayMore, have I? And I can't go back to the office to get any, because—'

'Right.' She was not-sniggering. 'Well, in that case, you're left with Plan C.'

'Plan what?'

She twitched her nose at him; probably a goblin thing. 'Best summed up in the words of the late Richard Nixon: when you've got 'em by the balls, their hearts and minds will follow. Lucky it's a doe and not a buck.'

'Is it? How'd you know that?'

'Tut,' replied Mr Tanner's mum. 'Who hasn't done his reading assignments, then? Page 774 of the office-procedures manual; it's wyvern breeding season, as you ought to know but obviously don't. What you've got there is a broody young doe. Probably got half a dozen eggs. Crisp new Bank of England tenners are their preferred nest material.'

'Oh,' Paul replied, and for some reason he blushed. Mr Tanner's mum had the knack of making anything remotely concerned with procreation sound totally obscene. 'How does that help?' he added.

She gave him a pitying look. 'Shut up and keep perfectly still,' she said. 'At this point I'd usually say it won't hurt a bit, but I read somewhere that lying makes you fat.' She snapped her fingers, and—

Paul managed to keep from a forced landing on the hard pavement by flapping his wings. That was fine, except that it made him think, *Wings? What wings?* and that interfered with the instinct that was keeping him airborne. He tried to remedy that by flapping harder, but all that achieved was to zoom him fast and head first into the wall.

That hurt; also, it hadn't done anything to solve his gravity problems, which were starting to get urgent again. He flapped wildly, but all he was managing to do was hang in the air, like the cat in the cartoons when it's just run off the edge of a cliff. *Help!* he tried to shout, but all that came out was a terrified kitten-like mewing. Then, as if that wasn't enough to contend with, a monster came rushing at him, a vulture-beaked, leather-winged feathered dragon, swooping through the air with its talons flexed and its claws out—

—Which grabbed him by the scruff of his neck and lifted him into the air, yelling, *How many times have I told you, you're not to play outside without asking first* in some form of speech that didn't need words. The expression *maternal instinct* had just formed inside his mind when a Himalaya-sized Mr Tanner's mum swatted the monster with a rolled-up newspaper, volleying both of them to the ground in a confused and painful heap.

'Ow!' Paul yelled, and realised he'd yelled it in English; also, he was sitting on the monster, which had suddenly shrunk down to the size of a small King Charles spaniel.

'Get up, you're squashing it,' commanded Mr Tanner's mum, pulling him out of the way and placing her stilettoed heel firmly on the wyvern's neck. She'd shrunk, too, which was something. 'If there's one thing I can't be doing with, it's cruelty to animals.'

Paul flopped against the wall. 'What did you *do* to me?' he gasped.

'Turned you into a baby wyvern, of course,' Mr Tanner's mum replied calmly. 'It's a well-known fact, mummy wyverns in the nesting season can't tell their own offspring from strangers. So, soon as it heard a baby in distress, it was out of there like a ferret up a Yorkshireman's trousers.' She beamed at him. 'Job done. Mind, it'll be a bit pissy when it wakes up, so if I was you I'd kill it now.'

Paul scowled at her. 'No,' he said. 'Absolutely not. You can't go around killing things just because they're inconvenient—'

The wyvern woke up, and bit him in the leg.

After that, things got a bit confused, what with Paul trying to stamp on the wyvern's head with a foot he'd have been better off using to stand on. It was probably falling on it that made it let go of his leg, though Mr Tanner's mum insisted that she'd felled it with a well-aimed kick from her steel-toecapped Roland Cartiers. By the time he'd staggered to his feet again, everything had gone quiet.

'See?' said Mr Tanner's mum. 'You changed your tune pretty quick.'

'But—' Paul hadn't bothered looking at the wyvern to see if it was all right. But it didn't matter, because one glance at it told him there wasn't any rush.

'Poor little cow,' Mr Tanner's mum said. 'Still, that's the pest-control game for you.'

Paul waited to see if it moved, but it didn't. 'It's dead,' he said. 'Isn't it?'

''Course it's dead,' Mr Tanner's mum said. 'You were sitting on its windpipe for about half a minute. They may be fierce little bastards, but they're fragile. It's like I always say, in seven cases out of ten the bum is mightier than the sword.'

Paul's knees had gone wobbly, and it probably wasn't due to the pain from his savaged ankle. 'I killed it,' he said. 'I wasn't going to do that.'

Mr Tanner's mum grinned at him. 'Drat,' she said. 'Still, there you go. Omelettes and eggs. Talking of which,' she added quickly, 'you'd better get a wriggle on if you want to nip inside and make them open the vault.'

'Why would I want to do that?'

'The eggs, stupid. Wyverns' eggs. They're solid gold with a diamond shell, worth an absolute bomb. You don't want some light-fingered cashier getting to them before you do.'

'No.' The authority in Paul's voice surprised him. 'I've just killed the poor thing, I'm not going to steal its eggs too. Maybe if they're left alone they'll hatch—'

'You bet they will,' said Mr Tanner's mum. 'And then there'll be five wyverns in this cash machine instead of just one.' She hesitated. 'Actually,' she said, 'that's not a bad idea, because then we'll get called in to get rid of them. Five wyverns at a grand a time; our Dennis would love that.'

Paul sighed. 'What we'll do,' he said coldly, 'is rescue the eggs and take them somewhere remote where they can hatch out in safety. Maybe we could call the RSPCA— What's so funny?'

Mr Tanner's mum's grin had a very faint soppy look to it. 'You,' she said. 'Crazy as a barrelful of ferrets, but funny with it. They're *wyverns*, dumbo. Soon as they're old enough to walk, they'll head straight for the nearest accumulation of wealth and start making nuisances of themselves. They're small and fragile, but they can *kill*. And they do. Really,' she added, shaking her head, 'even for a human, you're weird. What else do you want us to do? Knit little jackets for orphan vampire bats, and put out a saucer of milk for stray cholera bacilli?'

There didn't seem any point arguing with her; besides, Paul's attitude seemed to be having the ghastly side effect of making her feel fond of him, something he wanted to avoid at all costs. Tough on the baby wyverns, of course, but their mum had just eaten all his personal plastic.

'Fine,' he said, 'we'll go and get the eggs. What'll happen to them?'

Mr Tanner's mum looked sad. 'They belong to the Bank,' she said, 'so they get the money. But we get ten per cent, which'll please our Dennis. Or,' she added, 'we could keep them. Two for you, three for me – we'd be rich. Very rich.'

Paul's turn to hesitate. If the baby wyverns were doomed anyway, and if the blood money was going to go to JWW and the Bank . . . If he was rich, there were all sorts of things— But where would be the point in that? He was still bound to JWW by the terms of his contract, money couldn't change that. And there was also a small matter of having to live with himself.

'I don't want them,' he said. 'You can have them, if you like.'

Mr Tanner's mum stared at him. 'Bloody hell,' she said. 'Why?'

Paul shrugged. He wasn't sure himself. 'Better you than the Bank, I suppose. Anyway, it was you who got rid of the wyvern, so I guess . . .' He'd run out of things to say.

'Thanks,' Mr Tanner's mum said quietly. 'Nobody's ever given me anything like that before. Not that I need the money, mind,' she added, 'but it's the thought that counts.'

It occurred to Paul that he'd probably just done a very stupid thing. 'This doesn't mean—' he said quickly.

'I know.' The very lovely girl who Mr Tanner's mum was being at that moment smiled at him, and there was no trace of a grin. 'That's what makes it – well, unusual, because you *don't* fancy me rotten. Anyway,' she said, suddenly brisk, 'let's get the eggs and get out of here.'

Twenty minutes later, they had the eggs. They were heavy, but small enough to fit in the suitcase that Paul had brought along to hold his dragon-slaying gear. They wrapped up the dead wyvern in a black dustbin liner they'd begged from the Bank staff; Mr Tanner's mum hoisted it up onto her shoulder, saying she had a use for it. Paul didn't want to know what that might be.

'Well,' he said awkwardly, 'thanks. I'd better be getting back.'

'You're trying to get rid of me,' Mr Tanner's mum replied (accurately). 'But I've got cash for a cab fare, and you haven't.'

Paul smiled weakly. 'That's all right, then,' he said.

Mr Tanner's mum had no trouble finding a taxi; she raised her arm, and there one was. If it was magic, it was probably the simple, bitterly unfair kind that looks after pretty young women and leaves gormless-looking young men to fend for themselves. As they walked into reception together – Mr Tanner's mum was holding Paul's arm, and he was too preoccupied to make her stop – Melze looked up from whatever she'd been doing and stared at them. Correction; she stared at Paul and *scowled* at Mr Tanner's mum. It took Paul a moment to figure out that Melze wouldn't know who the lovely young female beside him really was.

Gosh, he thought.

Then Melze looked away, her body language explaining to Paul that he didn't exist. He felt a powerful urge to explain ('It's not what you think, really she's this incredibly ugly goblin. Go on, turn back into a goblin so Melze can see . . .') but resisted it manfully and pressed on towards the fire door. He wasn't looking, but he had an idea that Mr Tanner's mum was smirking.

'Don't know what you see in her, anyway,' she said, as they climbed the first lot of stairs. 'Mind you, she's an improvement on that bony little cow who dumped you. Still, you want to make sure you keep her away from the cream cakes and the choccy biccies.'

'Shut up,' Paul replied. 'Please.'

'Whatever.'

As Paul had hoped, the closed-file store was deserted. He shut the door, opened the suitcase, and handed over the wyvern's eggs. They were still, he realised guiltily, quite warm.

'You sure about this?' Mr Tanner's mum asked, as he held out the first pair to her. 'If you've changed your mind—'

'No, really.' Mostly he just wanted rid of them. 'You have them, just get them out of my sight.'

'All right.' Mercifully, she took them and loaded them into a cardboard box that she'd found on the floor. 'Now you bugger off,' she said. 'I may see you later.'

Paul fled.

First, he checked to see if Benny was back yet from doing the banking. But his office was empty, and the small door was ajar. Paul made a special point of not looking through it. Instead, he went back to his own office and looked up 'wyvern' in the office-procedures manual's index. There were lots of references, mostly to do with statutory limitations on when, where and with what they could be killed. In fact, he'd broken at least six laws that afternoon, not that he cared too much about that. Nowhere in the legislation did it say *Thou shalt not kill wyverns*; the message that came across was more along the lines of *Thou shalt not kill wyverns the easy way*, which wasn't the same thing at all.

Paul was just checking out the commentary on section 665(ix)(2) of the Small Dragons (Extermination) Regulations 1997 (wyverns may not be shot with a mechanical crossbow exceeding 9 feet in width on Sundays between 15th June and 3rd November, except in Scotland, the Channel Islands and the Isle of Man) when the door opened. This time, Mr Tanner's mum had reverted to her goblin shape. On balance, Paul decided, trying not to stare at the finger-long tusks, the chin bristles, the little dribble of slaver, he preferred her that way. Less intimidating.

'Got something for you,' she said.

She opened her hand, and something fell onto the desk in front of him: a single red gemstone about the size of a tiny nugget of coal.

'Thank you,' he said automatically. 'Um, what is it?'

Grin. 'You don't want to know.'

'Tell me anyway.'

She shrugged. 'It's a wyvern's third eye.' Paul winced while managing to keep perfectly still. It was a knack that he'd acquired since he'd been working for JWW. 'It was a right bitch getting it out. Broke two screwdrivers.'

'Fine,' Paul said. 'What does it do?'

Bigger grin. 'Pick it up.'

Paul hesitated. Clearly Mr Tanner's mum thought he'd be too squeamish. Not so wide of the mark, at that, but he picked it up anyway. 'Well?'

'Very good. Now look at it.'

He looked at it, focusing on the sharp, straight facet-lines. 'I'm looking at it,' he said. 'It's a small red stone, big deal—' Something turned off his speech at the mains.

It was like staring at a very small television through a dusty keyhole; but he could see a desk, and behind it—

'In case you haven't guessed,' Mr Tanner's mum said, 'it shows you stuff you can't normally see. If you practise, you can learn to see useful things. Otherwise, it just shows you your own true love, so it's a bit wasted on you. I mean, who needs a fantastically rare stone when all you've got to do is nip down the stairs to reception? Still, it's traditional: your first dragon – wyverns count as dragons, see, just about – you get to keep its eye.' She clicked her tongue; Paul was still gazing into the stone, as if nothing else existed. 'Well,' she said, 'I'll leave you to it, then. Really, if I'd known you had this thing about fat women—'

At some point, she must've stopped talking and gone away, because when Paul finally managed to look up, she'd gone. He blinked a couple of times, then looked back at the stone, just to make sure—

—And saw a thin, dark young woman with large eyes. She was picking her nose with the cap of a biro, and behind her head, through a window, Paul could just make out a hillside with big white letters on it.

Funny how, when you're fairly sure that at least one segment of your horrendously complicated life has finally fallen into place, even though everything else is still screwed up beyond any remote possibility of redemption, something will come along and twist everything through ninety-five degrees—

His own true love, apparently. Sophie.

Chapter Four

'Not bad,' said Benny Shumway, holding the little red stone up to the light. 'And I had this feeling when I first saw you that your arse was probably the deadliest weapon in your armoury. But you should've used the SlayMore, like I told you. Keep it simple and you won't go far wrong.' He handed back the stone, which Paul dropped into a matchbox and pocketed. 'Who told you about this, by the way?'

For some reason, Paul had left Mr Tanner's mum out of his report. 'I must've read about it somewhere,' he replied unconvincingly. 'Is it right that you can use them for scrying and stuff? Only I'm supposed to have a knack for that sort of thing, so I thought—'

Benny Shumway nodded. 'Can do, yes,' he said. 'With a lot of patience, self-discipline and training, you can get to the point where they're almost an acceptable substitute for a laptop and a mobile phone. Personally, I could never be bothered. Better things to do with my free time.'

'Oh,' Paul said. 'Well, anyway. What are we going to do today?'

Benny was silent for a moment. 'By way of vocational training, you mean? Nothing. Finished,' he explained. 'We've covered it all. As far as I'm concerned, you now have all the knowledge and resources that you need to be a genuine, practical hero.' He grinned. 'Doesn't that make you feel a whole lot better?'

'No,' Paul said.

'Thought not. Truth is, the theoretical side isn't really worth spit, you've got to pick it up as you go along. Assuming you live long enough.'

'Fine,' Paul said, frowning. 'I thought I was going to be doing this for three months.'

'Call it parole. Time off for mediocre behaviour. You complaining, or what?'

'No, absolutely not,' Paul said. 'I mean, it's been, um, interesting, but I don't really think it's my cup of tea somehow. I was better at finding bauxite, that's for sure. So now what?'

Benny laughed. 'So now, you'll be delighted to hear, you're officially released from this department, and you move on to the next one. Since you've already done your time with Dennis Tanner, that'll probably mean either Effective, with Countess Judy, or Practical with Theo van Spee. Don't envy you either of those,' he added. 'But after that you'll be ending up doing civil engineering with Cas Suslowicz, and that'll be an absolute doddle in comparison. I always say it's best to get the nasty stuff out of the way first.'

'I see,' Paul said. 'But what I actually meant was, what do I do *now*? Do I go back to my office and wait for someone to send for me, or should I go and find someone and tell them I've finished here?'

Benny shrugged. On the wall behind him, Paul noticed a framed print – three white kittens – that hadn't been there before. Neither, now he thought about it, had the wall; it was where the little door had been, but it had vanished. 'Depends on how much of a hurry you're in,' Benny said. 'If it was me I'd spend a day or so lurking in one of the empty offices upstairs, where nobody's likely to come looking for me. Flask of coffee and a good book, you could stay hidden for a week before anybody noticed.'

If Paul could've been sure Benny wasn't joking, he'd have been sorely tempted. 'How'd it be if I went and asked Julie?' he said. 'She generally seems to know what's going on.'

'More so than anybody else in the building,' Benny confirmed. He yawned. 'Well, thanks for all your help. I won't pretend you've got enough aptitude for pest control to line a small thimble, but it's been nice having someone to deal with all the crummy paperwork.'

'My pleasure,' Paul replied. 'When's Mr Wurmtoter likely to be back, then?' he added, not that he was particularly interested.

'Any day now,' Benny said. 'Can't be more specific than that; a job takes as long as it takes, and besides, he's got this habit of skiving off for a day or so once he's finished and then pretending he's been stranded in the desert or held captive in the dungeons of the Dark Lord. Really, of course, he's been off seeing the sights, lounging by the pool, going on coach trips. But he's a partner, so you can't say anything.'

As Paul had predicted, Julie knew exactly what he was supposed to do next. 'The Countess will see you in her office at 2.15,' she said. On the opposite wall, the clock showed seven minutes to one. 'You might as well take an early lunch,' Julie said, as though conferring on him the freedom of the City.

Actually, Paul was in two minds about that. What he really wanted to do was hang around reception and see if Melze wanted to come out for lunch. If it hadn't been for the vision he'd seen in the annoying little red stone—

Sort of a subconscious compromise; he hung about in the corridor agonising about whether it'd be the right thing to do until 12:59, then sprinted for the front office before they locked the street door. He got there just in time, and Melze was on her way out.

'Long time no see,' she said, smiling at him like a searchlight. 'I was just heading for that sandwich place round the corner. You coming?'

Easy as that. 'Yes, all right,' he replied. Like Benny had just told him: keep it simple and you won't go far wrong. Indeed.

'So,' she said, as they sat opposite each other across an old formica table. 'What've you been up to, then?'

If only, Paul thought. It'd be so easy to get along with Melze. When he'd been with Sophie it was all jagged pauses and unbridgeable silences; you had to be a mountaineer to get from one end of a conversation to another without falling down a crevasse. Before he'd met her, he'd been under the impression that love was everything, that once you'd acquired or attained love you were free and clear, and the world owed you happiness as a reward for valour. But now his own true love was in California, and here he was with someone he could talk to, if only—

'Finished heroism,' he replied with his mouth full. There's no elegant way of eating a brittle-shelled ham roll. 'Not sure what I'll be doing next. Either glamour or wisdom, I think.'

Melze laughed. 'Was it fun? Heroism?'

He shook his head. 'Filling in forms, mostly,' he replied. 'And I sat on a dragon. Small dragon,' he added. 'Squashed it, poor little bugger. But apparently they're a real pain in the financial sector, so I'm not to lose any sleep over it. Also I had to read a lot of stuff about weapons and poison gas and blowing stuff up. Not my scene at all.'

'Good,' she said. 'So, what've you got to do for glamour? Or don't you know yet?'

Paul grinned. 'I'm hoping it'll just be more filling in forms. It may be boring, but I can handle that. Did I tell you about the time—?' He hesitated. He'd been about to say *the time Sophie and I had to catalogue the strongroom.* 'The time I broke down out in the wilds somewhere, and there was this garage run entirely by kids.'

Melze looked suitably intrigued. 'How do you mean, kids?'

'Kids. None of them was older than twelve, I don't think. But they knew what was wrong with the car and fixed it, just like that. Spanners and screwdrivers and the hydraulic ramp and everything. Of course,' he added – was he showing off? Apparently. 'Of course, it's not exactly a normal car.'

'How do you mean, not normal?'

So Paul explained to her about Monika, and how she bossed him about in German, and how she'd originally been an agent for one of JWW's deadly rivals and how she'd been caught spying. 'For all I know,' he went on, 'she's not the only one. I mean, why spend money on office equipment when you can turn your enemies into it for free? You know about the photocopier, don't you?' he added.

She didn't, so he told her; and this gave him the opportunity to explain his part in the overthrow of Humphrey Wells and the rescue of old Mr Wells, the rightful senior partner. Somehow, Sophie didn't figure much in this version of the story. Nevertheless, Melze seemed to find it all quite fascinating.

'I can see why you like it here,' she said.

'But—' Paul was about to object that he didn't, not in the least; that he only stayed out of mortal fear of Dennis

Tanner's malevolent sense of humour. 'Well,' he heard himself say, 'it does have its moments.'

She sighed. 'I wonder,' she said. 'Do you think there's any chance they'd take me on as a clerk? I mean, there's a vacancy, isn't there? At least, until the other clerk comes back from the States. I don't know if I could do the magic and stuff, but I could do the filing and sorting and paperwork and things.' *Like you*, her eyes said. *With you. It'd be fun.*

'I don't know,' he said awkwardly. 'You could ask, I suppose.'

She frowned. 'I don't know,' she said. 'They probably wouldn't agree, because I can't do the magic.'

'Maybe you can,' he said. 'Have you tried?'

She shook her head. 'I wouldn't know how to,' she said. 'Neither did I.'

Melze was looking at him. 'How did you find out you could do it?' she said. 'Did they teach you, or did it just suddenly come, or what?'

Paul didn't answer straight away. The truth was, he'd got drunk out of wretchedness, been thrown out of a pub, and found himself forcing a policeman who was trying to arrest him to eat his own truncheon. 'It's hard to say,' he said. 'I suppose it was like suddenly remembering something you've forgotten for a long time. It didn't suddenly come so much as suddenly come *back*, if that makes any sense at all.'

'I think so,' she said. 'But now, presumably, you can do magic any time you want.'

'Well—' *Well*, he thought, *I suppose I can, yes. But I never seem to want to unless I've got to. Why is that, anyhow?* 'Sometimes,' he said. 'But I'm still a beginner. That's why I'm doing the time in each of the departments. Except there wasn't much magic in pest control; mostly it seems to be basic chemistry and use of power tools.'

There was a look in Melze's eyes. 'Do some magic now,' she said. 'Go on.'

Bad idea, a voice in his head pointed out. *Very bad idea.* 'Well—'

'Doesn't have to be anything spectacular,' she was saying. 'Just a little bit, so I can see what it looks like. Please?'

He stalled. 'I can't think of anything,' he said.

She looked round. 'Can you turn that empty cup into a mouse or something?'

'No.' Paul had an idea. 'But I can make it wash itself up, that's easy. Look.' He considered the cup, identified the fact that it was dirty and ought to be clean; and then it was. 'See?'

'Cool.' Her eyes were actually shining. 'That's so amazing. Do it again.'

'I can't. Someone'll see.'

'Please?'

It was, just as his mother had always told him, the magic word. 'Oh, all right then,' he said magnanimously, and cleaned another cup.

'That's amazing,' she said again.

'Well.' Paul shrugged. 'Fairly amazing. But you can do it just as well with a J-cloth and Fairy Liquid.'

Melze didn't seem to have heard him. 'Can you teach me to do that?' she said eagerly.

He shook his head. 'Truth is,' he said, 'I haven't got a clue how it's done. I just look at the cup and realise that in an ideal world it wouldn't have brown rings round the inside and an eighth of an inch of cold coffee in the bottom.'

'Oh.' She leaned across to the next table, said, 'Excuse

me' to its rather startled occupant, and took his empty cup. 'All right,' she said, 'I'm looking at it. Yes, I can see what's wrong. This cup is very dirty, it's an absolute disgrace.' Behind her, Paul could see the waitress turn her head.

'No,' Melze announced sadly. 'No luck. Look, still dirty.'

Paul smiled weakly. 'I think it's one of those things,' he said. 'Actually, I've thought about it a lot, and my theory is, it's – well, this sounds really silly, but it's all to do with how you look at things, things that've gone wrong. I mean, if you look at them and you say to yourself, Oh well, that's life, I guess, only to be expected, and there's nothing I can do about it, then I don't suppose you can do magic. It's what I said just now about in an ideal world. I suppose that deep down you've got to believe that there's an ideal world out there somewhere, and you believe in it strongly enough that you can sort of swap: one little bit of our rotten old real world for one little bit of the ideal one.' He tailed off and looked at her hopefully. 'What do you reckon?' he asked.

'I think you're right,' she said.

'Really?'

'Yes. I think you were spot on, about it sounding really silly. Because,' Melze continued, as a stray flicker of annoyance crossed Paul's face, 'that'd mean that in order to do magic you'd have to be, what's the word? You'd have to be an idealist. And, well, I've met the partners, and presumably they're all very good indeed at magic, and they don't look like a bunch of starry-eyed dreamers to me. No way. If you met them in the street, you'd think they were probably lawyers.'

She had a point there. 'I suppose,' he said. 'But—'

'And then there's you,' she said. 'No disrespect, in fact

quite the opposite, because I wouldn't put you down as a bleeding-heart pacifist whale-saver. You're too—'

'Selfish?'

Melze shook her head. 'It's not that,' she said. 'I imagine that if you ever found yourself in a situation where you could save a whale, you would, provided there weren't loads of people standing around watching. But that's not the issue; you're more the sort of person who's convinced that he could never save a whale, because it's probably too difficult, and you're not brave or clever enough. You'd say, no point me trying to end acid rain or Third World debt when I haven't even got a girlfriend. Right?'

Paul didn't say anything; whereupon Melze came over all remorseful, as though she'd just trodden on a kitten's tail. 'Sorry,' she said, 'I didn't mean to get at you particularly, all I meant was, I think you've got to have an ego the size of Mount Rushmore if you're going to be an idealist, because you're saying to yourself, here's this problem and I'm just the person to do something about it. And that's not you, is it?'

Paul shrugged. 'No, it's not,' he said. 'I'm a coward and selfish. No point pretending otherwise.'

That seemed to make Melze angry. 'No, you aren't,' she said. 'I know you aren't, because you rescued that Mr Wells who got turned into a stapler; and that was very dangerous and you didn't have to get involved, but you did it anyway. But I think you did it because you thought, it must be really horrible being a stapler for a hundred years, not because you were on some sort of idealistic crusade to stamp out illegal shape-shifting. Do you see what I mean?'

'Yes,' he said, mostly because he wanted to change the subject. 'I guess so. Anyhow,' he went on, 'that's all I can tell you about how to do magic. Not much help, I guess.'

'Doesn't matter,' she replied, smiling brightly. 'Presumably I just haven't got the knack. No big deal. And I won't persecute you about doing magic any more. And I do think it's really clever of you, and so cool.'

In retrospect, Paul decided later, that was probably the moment that Cupid decided to stop mucking about with bows and arrows and went in with the old cold steel. In the past, people had occasionally told him that he was kind of sweet, but that was about as far as it went. Even Sophie hadn't said nice things about him. Praise and flattery came his way about as often as claret and foie gras did to someone in prison. Probably he mumbled something by way of reply, some sort of denial or half-hearted rebuttal, he couldn't remember. Love he'd just about learned to handle. Admiration, on the other hand, was as new, strange and intimidating to him as photography to a Trobriand Islander, and deep down he was afraid that it just might steal his soul.

Paul could remember pointing out that it was getting late and they'd better get back to the office; and Melze had looked slightly sad, because their time together was almost over. To someone whose relatives had been known to put their clocks forward an hour to hasten his departure, that was dangerously rich, too. All in all, when he knocked on Countess Judy's door at a quarter past two for their sched-uled meeting, he felt as though he'd just drunk a pint of champagne far too quickly: light-headed and blown up like a balloon.

'I expect you've been wondering,' Countess Judy was saying, 'about how magic works.'

Paul gulped so sharply that he almost gave himself

hiccups. 'Well,' he said, 'it's crossed my mind occasionally, yes.'

She nodded, just a little, like a nodding dog in the back window of a Cortina abandoned in the desert. 'It didn't occur to you to ask, of course. Instead, you preferred to try and figure it out from first principles. Maybe a rather strange way of demonstrating your commitment to your chosen career.'

Suddenly he was in trouble again; but he was used to that. Having spent so much of his life in the wrong that it counted as his domicile for tax purposes, he could slip as effortlessly into guilty mode as a cat through a cat flap. 'Sorry,' he said.

She didn't react. 'At the very least,' she said, 'you could've come and asked me for a book about it. There are several, you know. But instead, you think about it. And no doubt you've reached a conclusion.'

It took Paul a second or two to realise that she was asking him a question. 'Well, sort of,' he said. 'Only now I'm pretty sure it's wrong,' he added.

'Let me be the judge of that.'

So he explained, for the second time in sixty minutes, how he thought (had previously thought) magic worked. When he'd ground to a halt, the Countess looked at him for a moment, then went on as if he hadn't said anything.

'Magic,' she said, 'falls into two distinct categories. There is practical magic, and effective magic. So far, you've experienced a little practical magic. I'm concerned almost entirely with the other kind.'

Pause. Paul knew better now than to give in to the urge to fill these silences with inane chatter.

'Practical magic,' the Countess said, 'is magic that does

something. It cleans a dirty cup, for example, or shifts a mountain a metre to the left. Effective magic, by contrast, creates an effect. It makes you believe something that may not be true – like, for instance, a love potion. You'll shortly come to learn that a great deal of magic which you believe is practical is in fact effective, for the simple reason that it's often easier and cheaper to make someone *believe* something is true than actually to make it so; and we are, after all, in business to earn a living. Are you with me so far?'

To his surprise, he was. He nodded.

'I'll give you an example,' she went on. 'Imagine, if you will, a young and immature magical practitioner, who gets drunk and meets a policeman in the street. The policeman is about to arrest him, so he forces the policeman to eat his own truncheon. Would that be,' she asked, vulture-eyed, 'practical or effective magic?'

Practical, of course, since it was making someone do something. It was so obvious it had to be a trick question. 'Effective,' he said.

'Very good. Why?'

Paul looked at her. 'Don't know,' he confessed.

'Clearly,' the Countess said. 'Effective, because the young magician, untutored and untrained, will not have mastered the exceptionally difficult and abstruse skills required to practice telekinesis on human nerves and muscle. It'd be very difficult. I could do it.' *Yes*, Paul thought, *I bet you could*. 'But I would find it difficult, and the effort involved would be out of all proportion to the benefits to be gained. Instead, the young magician would simply persuade the policeman that what he most wanted to do in all the world at that exact moment was take his truncheon and bite it as hard as he possibly could, until his teeth started to snap off. And that,' she added casually, 'is very easy. So easy, in fact, that humans with no talent whatsoever can sometimes be trained to do it. You've heard,' she said, 'of hypnotism.'

'Yes.'

She dipped her head, as though acknowledging that he wasn't completely stupid. 'And of course you've heard of love.'

For a moment Paul assumed that she'd used a technical term taken from a foreign language. 'Did you say love?' he asked.

'That's right. Love is effective magic; but it's so common-place that nobody notices.'

'Oh,' Paul said. He thought for a moment. 'Really magic, or just — well, song-lyric magic?'

'Really magic,' Countess Judy said. 'Effective magic. Or, if you prefer, an optical illusion. *Trompe l'œil.*'

'Excuse me?'

'A French term,' she explained patiently, 'for a style of painting that tricks the eye into mistaking something false for something real. Love,' she went on, 'is much the same sort of thing; *trompe le coeur*, if you'd rather.' She smiled thinly at her own joke, which slipped past Paul like a cheetah in a hurry. 'You may care to think about it,' she said. 'Love is an optical illusion that makes you believe that the object of your affection is the most beautiful person in the world. You believe this; although you also know that it's not true, because if you look at your girlfriend and then leaf through either the latest edition of *Vogue* or, depending on your personal standards, a Pirelli calendar, you'll quickly see that she isn't; there are more perfect lips than hers, more flaw-less complexions, more limpid eyes—' She paused. 'And, of course, bigger boobs. But your belief overrides the truth, and you see what you're determined to see. And that's magic. Effective magic.'

'Right,' Paul said after a moment or so. 'But everybody can do it.'

'Quite so. It's built into the human mechanism, because it's necessary. Essential, for the survival of the species. Humans have got to love, Mr Carpenter, or they'd be extinct in no time. Think about it. Human young have a nine-month gestation period, towards the end of which the female is so grossly distorted that she can barely move; she can't fend for herself, hunt or gather food. She needs to be provided for. Then follows a period of fifteen years, often longer, during which the child is too immature to be let out on its own. It needs, as well as the bare essentials of nourishment and warmth, the care and attention of two parents. In consequence, a substantial proportion of human life is sacrificed to the thankless task of rearing young. Other animals don't put up with it; other animals are still only animals, as a result. But the task *is* thankless; it's a sentence of hard labour, and humans are intelligent crea-tures, they know that there are so many other wonderful things they could be doing, if only they weren't tied to a boring job and a school run and early-morning feeds. If it wasn't for the magic, nothing would induce them to mate and procreate. But the magic forces them, Mr Carpenter, they're enchanted, and they can't see the reality, even though deep down they know it for what it is, a cruel confidence trick that they play on themselves.' The Countess leaned forward a little. 'The magic, of course, is beauty. What proverbs do you know about beauty, Mr Carpenter?'

'Um,' Paul said. His mind had, of course, gone blank. *'Beauty and the Beast?'*

'I said proverbs, not animated films.'

He ran his memory through the mangle of concentration. 'It's only skin deep,' he remembered. 'And it's in the eye of the beholder.'

'Correct.' Her cold grey eyes awarded him two notional marks. 'It's the eye of the beholder that creates beauty, because of course it doesn't really exist. True, there are features that are traditionally considered beautiful; but that's a misapprehension. Name three of them.'

'Excuse me?'

'Name three things that make a woman beautiful.'

Oh God, Paul thought. 'Well,' he said. 'Um, nice eyes.'

'And?'

'Nice, er, skin?'

'And?'

He could feel his face burning. 'Well, sort of, a nice figure.'

'Very good.' One more mark, for effort. 'Now, look at me.'

Paul didn't have much choice in the matter; because Countess Judy changed. Or rather, she didn't change at all. Her face stayed the same upside-down isosceles triangle, her eyes carried on being grey, her chin was just as sharply pointed. But suddenly he noticed for the first time how incredibly, bewilderingly lovely she was.

'I said look at me, Mr Carpenter, I didn't say salivate. Am I beautiful?'

Oh God. Oh God. 'Yes,' Paul squeaked.

'Thank you. Why?'

'What?'

She sighed. 'Please explain to me,' she said, 'why I'm beautiful.'

'I—' He had no idea. 'I don't know,' he said.

'Really.' She nodded again. 'Well, let's consider the three aspects we identified earlier. If you'd care to refresh my memory?'

Judy di Castel'Bianco was incredibly lovely, but also really annoying. 'Nice eyes,' Paul said.

'Nice eyes,' she repeated; and her eyes glowed like moonlight shining through mist. 'Like this?'

'Yes,' Paul croaked.

'Next.'

'Nice skin,' he said; and for a moment it was all he could do to stop himself reaching out and touching, because her skin was so very soft—

'Very well. And the third aspect was—?'

'Nice figure,' said Paul, in a very small voice.

He tried very hard not to look. He succeeded for at least a sixtieth of a second.

'Fine.' It was as though the Countess had vanished and been replaced by a plain middle-aged woman who looked exactly like her. 'Now, let's see. The eyes were nice because they were—?'

'Huge,' Paul said dreamily, in spite of himself. 'And shining.'

'And the skin?'

'Soft and smooth.'

'And the figure?'

'Sort of round and curvy and, um—'

'Big.'

'Yes,' Paul admitted, his flesh crawling. 'Big.'

'I see,' she said. 'Like this.'

For a moment, Paul thought he was looking at a goblin. Countess Judy's eyes were like fried eggs, and they were glowing with a creepy, Borg-like light. Her skin clung to her like cold, lumpy custard in a plastic bag. As for the rest of her – boiled down and refined into lamp oil, she'd have lit a large city for a week.

'I haven't changed, Mr Carpenter,' she said; and suddenly she was back to how she'd been when he first walked into the room. 'Do you understand what happened?'

Paul couldn't speak, but his neck still worked. He shook his head.

'The technical term,' she said, 'is glamour. Glamour is, if you like, an information virus; it affects the part of your brain that interprets the signal it receives from your eyes – and also,' she added, in the sexiest voice he'd ever heard, 'your ears, and the rest of your basic senses. The same data comes in, but your brain processes it differently. That's all. Instead of decoding the numbers in base ten, it reads them as base eight, or base twelve. Because it's so simple, it's exceptionally effective; even a trained professional who knows what to expect and who's had time to prepare has extreme difficulty resisting it. To the unsuspecting layman – well.' She smiled bleakly. 'You will appreciate,' she said, 'the industrial implications.'

Paul looked up, as though she'd suddenly started talking in Sanskrit. 'The what?'

'Multibillion-dollar business,' she said. 'The sale and purchase of human beauty. The process whereby a commonplace forty-year-old woman with limited intelligence, few talents and a debilitating alcohol- and substance-abuse problem can be passionately adored by millions of men – and women – who've never even met her, and never will. It's glamour, Mr Carpenter, that makes movie stars and pop idols, supermodels and media personalities; women and men who you'd pass in the street without even noticing them, because they look like this – ' she leaned two degrees forward. ' – but whose faces and bodies are insured for more than the value of an oil tanker because they look like *this*.' She leaned back again, and Paul only just managed to stop himself crying out for pure love, because she was so beautiful, and so obviously the only girl in the world for him . . .

'As you were, Mr Carpenter,' she said; and he was looking at the normal Countess Judy – instinctively he'd thought of her as the *real* one, but that, he realised, was a totally unwarranted assumption. 'Now, I trust, you understand. Why famous men and women, multinational corporations, even governments, are willing to pay very large sums of money for what we have to sell. Well?'

Paul nodded.

The Countess studied him for a moment; apparently he was satisfactory. 'And that,' she went on, 'is just one small part of the science of effective magic. Put another way: if effective magic was mathematics, what you've just witnessed is learning how to do percentages. Easy, and trivial.' She looked away. 'For me, at any rate. For you, however—'

'Yes?'

She looked back at him. 'Impossible,' she said. 'Unless, of course, you have the aptitude.'

'Oh.'

'But.' It was like trying to play tennis blindfold. 'I have reason to believe that you may not be entirely devoid of that. The incident with the policeman, for example.'

'Oh,' Paul said. 'That.'

'Quite,' she said. 'Clearly, when you did that, you were making use of a latent natural ability. It seems most likely, for the reasons I mentioned, that you were using effective magic. It's remotely possible, however, that you have a latent but extremely powerful natural talent for practical magic, and that you made the policeman eat his truncheon by exercising telekinetic control over his basic motor functions. What I have to do now,' Countess Judy said, 'is find out which it was.'

'Oh,' Paul said. 'Um, right. Will it hurt?'

The look in her eyes was so deep, so far away, so remote that for a moment he was scared. 'Mr Carpenter,' she eventually said, 'a truth that few people appreciate is that, at the root, *everything* hurts.' She folded her hands on the desk in front of her. 'There is only one way that a human like yourself could be able to do effective magic,' she said. 'It's a matter of blood.'

Paul didn't like the sound of that one teeny little bit. 'Um,' he said.

'Not like that,' she said impatiently. 'If you prefer, it's a matter of descent. Lineage. Ancestry. You see, effective magic – *deliberate* effective magic, which can be controlled and used – is a monopoly of my people, the Fey. And we,' she added, rather superfluously, 'aren't human.'

'Ah,' Paul said.

'But,' the Countess went on, 'from time to time, we have crossed humans with our kind, and bred specimens who have some of our abilities. It's possible that you are descended from just such a hybrid; in which case, you may have the knack.' She opened a desk drawer and took out a blank sheet of A4 and a Biro. 'Write down the names and dates of birth of the last twelve generations of your family.'

'Sorry?'

'Your family tree,' Countess Judy explained, saying the

words *loudly* and *clearly*, as though he was a *foreigner* or something. 'Write it out for me, please.'

'But—' He shrugged. 'I can do as far back as my grandparents,' he said. 'Not dates of birth, though, because I'm rubbish at remembering birthdays. Apart from them—'

Her eyes scoured his face like sandpaper. 'I see,' she said. 'That's rather inconvenient, but it's all right, I can find out for myself. Until then—' She shrugged. 'I suggest you go back to your office and find something to occupy your time until I send for you. Good afternoon.'

Before he realised that he was doing it, Paul had stood up and started towards the door. He stopped himself. It took a distinct effort. 'Er,' he said.

She looked up, faintly surprised that he was still in the room. 'Well?'

Deep breath, not that it ever seemed to help. 'Can I, um, ask you something?'

'Of course.' Straight off, no hesitation. 'What's on your mind?'

'Goblins,' he said. 'When they change shape, is that effective magic? Only you said—'

She shook her head. 'Practical,' she said. 'Their bodies dissolve for a split second into their component molecules, and then recombine in the required shape. It's horrendously difficult, but they can do it by light of nature. Of course, they have no idea *how* they do it.'

'I see,' Paul said, thinking about Mr Tanner's mum. 'Well, that was all, thanks. I'd better—'

'Good afternoon.'

The door slammed in his face. It was three whole seconds before he remembered that it'd been him who'd closed it.

*   *   *

Find something to occupy your time, Countess Judy had said. As Paul traipsed through the tortuous corridors towards his office, he tried to think of something he could do for two and a half hours, until it was legal to go home. The only thing that came to mind was the office-procedures manual; perhaps it had a section on glamour and beauty and all that stuff the Countess had been waffling on about.

Waffling . . . While he'd been in there with her, of course, it had all made perfect sense. Once he was away from those piercing grey eyes, however, he had real problems remembering what had been so convincing about it all. There'd been some rather lame biology, some stuff about movie stars; but it was slipping away fast, like those wonderful ideas for new inventions that you get in dreams, ideas which evaporate ten seconds after you wake up.

There was indeed a section in the procedures manual; in fact, there were six chapters about effective magic, four pages of one of which he was able to read before his eyes refused to stay open any longer. He leaned back a little in his chair; at some point, he felt the book slip from his fingers, and heard it go *thump* on the floor. No matter; he'd pick it up in a moment—

Paul was, he realised, back at school, in the playground at Laburnum Grove primary. It took him a moment to remember that this was, of course, where he was supposed to be, given that he was only eight years old. Then something cracked across his knuckles, and he looked up. He and Melze were playing conkers.

'Ow,' he complained. 'That was my hand.'

She glared at him. 'Keep still,' she said. 'We can't play if you don't keep still.'

'All right,' he replied grumpily. 'But watch what you're doing.'

'Wimp,' she said, squinting carefully down the line of the string. 'Three, two, one, and—' His conker shattered into half a dozen chunks, leaving one small yellow nugget dangling sadly from the string. 'I win!' Melze yelled, holding her hands high in the air. 'Beat you,' she added, just in case there was any lingering ambiguity.

'Cheater,' Paul muttered. 'I know what you did. You soaked it in superglue – that's why it's so hard.'

'Did not,' she replied blandly. 'Go on, say it. You promised you'd say it if you won.'

'No,' he growled. 'It wasn't fair, you cheated.'

'Say it,' she warned him, 'or I'll bash your head in.'

He tried killing her by sheer glarepower, but it didn't work terribly well. 'Come on,' she said. 'Say it.'

He looked away. It'd be easier if he said it to a distant bush. 'I'm a little flower fairy,' he mumbled.

'Louder.'

'I'm a little—'

'*Louder.*'

'I'M A LITTLE FLOWER FAIRY,' Paul bellowed, and kids from all parts of the playground turned and stared. 'All right?' he snarled.

Melze nodded smugly. 'Yep,' she said. 'And I didn't cheat,' she added, 'so there.'

'Let me see your rotten conker,' he said. She shrugged, and dangled it in front of his nose.

'There,' she said. 'Satisfied?'

He nodded grudgingly. 'All right,' he said. 'One last game. Go on,' he pleaded as she shook her head. 'Go on.'

'All right.'

Paul reached in his pocket and found the string of his last conker. *I'll get her this time*, he promised himself, as the conker swayed gently in front of his nose. The horse chestnut was dry and wrinkled and smelt of vinegar. He sneezed, wiped his nose on his sleeve (remembering as he did so that he'd never done that when he was a kid; in fact, the only person he'd ever known who did that was Sophie –) and stood by to receive incoming—

The stone of the knowledge of good and evil lies hidden inside the conker of self-doubt.

The voice was so loud and clear that he looked round to see who'd said it. Nobody there, apart from Melze, who chose that moment to lash out, her arm coming forward with the dreadful power of a medieval siege engine. Their conkers met; hers shattered like glass. 'There!' he crowed. She burst into tears.

'That's not a conker,' she was saying, 'that's a *stone.*'

'That's right,' Paul heard himself say, 'it's the stone of knowledge.' This made him look to see exactly what he'd got on the end of the string he was holding. They'd both been right. Instead of a conker—

'That's ours,' Melze snarled through her tears. 'That belongs to us. Give it back.'

As the string twisted, it swung round; a bright yellow unblinking eye with a black pupil that looked into him and then at her as it swung to and fro. 'No,' he said firmly. 'It's ours. We won it, and we're going to keep it.' Paul stuffed it back in his pocket before she had a chance to make a grab at it. 'Now,' he said, 'your turn. Go on, say it. You've got to.'

She gave him a look of pity and contempt. 'I'm a little flower fairy,' she enunciated disdainfully. 'Right, *now* give it back.'

'No.'

'Give it *back*,' Melze repeated. 'Or I'll tell my aunt.'

'You tell her, I don't care,' he replied, but he knew he was lying. Melze didn't have a mummy or a daddy (some people didn't, apparently) but she did have an Auntie Judith; and nobody in his right mind would want to tangle with her. She came from the same place where the nightmares come from; she was huge and fierce and very, very stern. On the other hand, Paul remembered, she wasn't likely to get involved in a trivial conkers dispute. Auntie Judith didn't approve of conkers, or children, or anything much.

'I hate you,' Melze said. She was about to do more crying; which was unusual, because Melze wasn't like that. All the other girls went for tears like gunslingers in a Dakota saloon, especially if a teacher was nearby, but Melze only blubbed when she was *unhappy*. The thought disturbed Paul. It wasn't exactly ideal, having a girl for your best friend, but he figured that it cut both ways. It didn't seem right, making her unhappy over a silly old conker.

Except that it wasn't a conker. It was an eye, and they don't grow on trees. And she had no right to it; none of her side had any right to it, and it wasn't fair for them to want it. She was his friend, but if she was really a friend, she wouldn't have asked. She'd have known.

'I hate you too,' he said. 'So there.'

Her eyes were suddenly hard, and strange, and very old. 'Right,' she said. 'I'm telling my aunt about you.'

The fear was real enough, but she was wrong and he was right. Surely no harm could come to him if he was in the right, or else how could the world possibly keep going?

'Don't care,' he said. 'You tell who you like, you still can't have it.'

Melze didn't reply; instead, she opened her lunch box and drew out a long, thin sword, silvery-white like an icicle. It was much longer than the box, but then, there were a lot of things in life that Paul didn't understand, even when he was awake. 'I hate you,' she repeated (and behind her, the rest of her side were lining up; they had swords like hers, and spears and bows and double-headed axes) and stabbed the sword at his face—

Paul jerked back so hard that he nearly fell out of his chair. 'Melze?' he said aloud, but of course there wasn't anybody in the room except him. He sat quite still, just in case, but nothing happened.

The stone of the knowledge of good and evil lies hidden inside the conker of self-doubt.

Coffee, Paul said to himself, *it must be coffee. Pity the decaffeinated stuff tastes so yucky. Still, if it can do things like that to a person, no more caffeine from now on.* He leaned forward and picked up the book, closed it, hesitated and slid it back onto the shelf. One good thing about his peculiar dream, it had helped pass the time. His watch said ten past five; twenty more minutes and he was out of there. Just as well; it'd been a long and gruelling day. It occurred to him that if he nipped down to the front office (realistically, of course, nipping wasn't possible in the JWW building; the distances involved were too great for nipping, you had to plod or trek instead) he could casually mention to Melze, assuming she wasn't busy with a client or answering the phone, that he didn't have anything much planned for this evening, so maybe they could go and see a film or something. He could do that. Probably she'd say

'Yes, I'd like that.' There was no reason why it couldn't happen.

Paul frowned. He'd like that, wouldn't he? He'd like that more than anything else he could think of. Wouldn't he?

Well, of course. It'd be silly not to.

Right, then.

He stayed where he was. It had absolutely nothing to do with the strange dream (which was entirely due to coffee; purely a chemical reaction, meaningless). It wasn't that debilitating, limb-cramping fear that he'd learned to associate with talking to girls. It wasn't anything. Just—

Of course, he knew about all that stuff, he'd seen chat shows and read bits in magazines in waiting rooms. He knew about how men reach a point in a relationship where the road forks, commitment or escape, and their natural instinct is to run like hares. He knew too that he was still healing from the trauma of getting dumped, so naturally he was scared of getting back into the ring. There were plenty of reasons why he wouldn't want to stroll down to reception right now. Loads of them. Absolutely certainly and for sure, it wasn't anything to do with the crazy dream.

Twenty-five past five; Paul stood up, reached for his coat, put it on, stopped. There were many excellent reasons for not being in the office once they locked the front door, all of them goblins; but he stayed put, studying the second hand of his watch. Mr Wurmtoter would be back any day now, according to Benny Shumway. Paul had no idea why but he found that thought reassuring. Not because he had any naive notions of Mr Wurmtoter being on his side or anything like that; Ricky Wurmtoter was a partner, and therefore a part of the weirdness. But he was also a hero, which meant that it was his job to fight the forces of darkness and save the innocent from mortal danger. Paul found the thought of that mildly reassuring, until he remembered that he was now a hero too. The criteria obviously weren't particularly stringent.

A little scrap of worry was niggling him, but he didn't know what it was; it was like being irritated by the feel of a raspberry pip jammed in the crack between two teeth you'd had pulled out years ago. Five-thirty. He pushed the door open and set off down the corridor as quickly as he could go without actually running.

In theory, the front door was shut at five-thirty but not actually locked until a quarter to six; also in theory, the goblins stayed lurking in wherever it was they lurked during the day until the front door had been locked and the duty partner had checked the building to make sure everybody had gone home. In theory—

'You.'

Paul heard it, but it sounded strange; a human word spoken by something inhuman, like a phrase repeated by a mynah bird. Best to ignore it, he thought; but then whatever it was spoke again.

'You. I'm talking to you.'

He stopped, looked round. He was standing outside the closed-file store, whose door was ajar. Wondering why in hell's name he was doing such a very stupid thing, he pushed the door open with the tip of his forefinger and looked in. Nobody there; just a million buff envelopes on shelves, and somebody's old bicycle.

'Yes, you,' said the bicycle. 'Look at me when I'm talking to you.'

He wasn't even sure how he knew it was the bicycle talking; it wasn't staring at him with its headlamp or frowning with its handlebars. He just knew.

'Sorry,' Paul said. 'Can I do something for you, or—?'

'Shut up and listen,' said the bicycle. 'You've got to let her go, do you understand? You've got to. It's not right.'

?, Paul thought. 'Sorry,' he repeated, 'I don't understand. Who do you mean?'

'Let her go,' the bicycle said. It was old, and green, and the white vinyl of its seat was cracking. 'Otherwise, so help me, we'll kill you. Do you understand?'

'No,' Paul said, and waited for a reply; but the bicycle was now nothing but a bicycle, incapable of human speech. Paul sighed. 'Look,' he said, though he was fairly sure there wasn't anybody there to hear him, 'if you don't tell me what you want, how can I be expected to do it? Be fair. Please?' Just an old bicycle, with a black oily chain and bits of chrome flaking off the pedal stems. 'Screw you, then,' Paul said bitterly, and left the room.

Something was following him. Eloquent testimony of how strange Paul's life had become, that he hoped it was just goblins and not an enchanted push-bike. He turned a corner and collided with something; something short and very chunky.

Fuck, he thought, *goblins*; but it turned out to be Benny Shumway, who scowled at him and asked him what he thought he was playing at.

'Sorry,' Paul said. 'I was just on my way out when a bike started threatening me. In the closed-file store. Do you know anything about that?'

Benny shrugged. 'Nothing that goes on in there would surprise me any more,' he replied. 'I'd stay well clear of it if I were you. Come on, I'll see you to the front office. I don't suppose the goblins'd pick on you, because of Dennis Tanner's mother, but you never know. They can get rather boisterous sometimes.'

'Thanks,' Paul said, realising that he was in fact rather more scared than he'd appreciated. 'So,' he went on, making conversation, 'do we know when Mr Wurmtoter's due back yet?'

'Any day now,' Benny replied. 'Thank goodness. It's been a real pain, doing his work and mine as well. So,' he added, 'what did you make of your first afternoon in Glamour?'

Paul thought before answering. 'Interesting,' he said. 'But I don't think I'll be any good at it. I mean, *glamour*. Not my thing, you know?'

Benny looked up at him and grinned. 'What makes you say that?'

'Well—' Wasn't it obvious? 'I mean, it's all about beauty and charm and all kinds of stuff I wouldn't know about.'

'Because you're awkward and shy and your ears stick out like wing-mirrors?'

'Yes.'

'Valid point. But you've got to know about it, even if you can't do it yourself. I suggest you do your time and then ask to be put in with Cas Suslowicz. You'll like his department, it's – well, almost normal. Civil engineering, like I said – can't get more down to earth than that.' Benny frowned. 'Actually, that's a bad choice of words, given that what Cas is best at is building rainbow bridges and castles in the air. But it's still all about planning permission and quantity surveying and snagging lists and subcontractor scheduling. Not much magic, is what I'm trying to say.'

Paul agreed that that would suit him far better. 'And no talking bicycles,' he added thoughtfully.

'That's really bugging you, isn't it?' Benny laughed. 'Listen, don't worry about it. Probably someone's idea of a joke, like a whoopee cushion or a bag of flour balanced over a door. It's a safe bet that it was meant for someone else, anyhow.'

They did bump into a party of goblins, in the corridor leading to the fire door behind reception; but as soon as they saw Benny, they scowled and turned away. 'They're no bother really, if you stand up to them,' Benny said cheerfully. ''Course, it helps if you're a dwarf, like me. We've got a lot of history with goblins, mostly stuff they'd prefer to forget. You get on,' he added, 'it's my turn to lock up. See you tomorrow, then.'

As the door closed behind him, Paul felt an unusual surge of relief at being outside, in the normal, safe street. Mostly, being in the office didn't spook him any more, not the way it had done at first. He'd got used to it, like the people who build villages on the slopes of active volcanoes. This evening, however, had reminded him of just how flimsy the partition was between the monotonous daily routine and the stark terror of it all. A bit like being an estate agent in a war zone.

It was only when he'd got home and was defrosting a frozen pizza for dinner that he suddenly realised what had been preying on his mind, ever since he'd woken up from his dream. He darted across to the bookshelf and pulled down Sophie's copy of the office-procedures manual. At the back, just before the index, was a page that he'd flicked past without reading several times. He found it, ran his finger down the list of names till he came across the entry for the chapters he'd glanced at earlier –

EFFECTIVE MAGIC by Otto Nijsbakker, Contessa Judith di Castel'Bianco, Professor Kajikawa Yosobie & Dr Ernest Carpenter

Ernest Carpenter. Ernie Carpenter. Uncle Ernie.

Cohere, Paul ordered himself. *Not the most uncommon name in the world. Probably — no, almost definitely someone else, a complete stranger.* Nevertheless; Uncle Ernie, whom he hadn't seen or heard about since he was a little kid. Not since he was at junior school, in fact. Hadn't his name come up in some conversation recently? He wasn't sure. He made a mental note to ask after him next time he heard from Mum and Dad, assuming he could get that many words in edgeways.

The microwave pinged; dinner was served. Paul slapped the pizza onto a plate, found a clean fork and knife, made himself a strong black coffee, switched the telly on and flopped down on the sofa. He'd apparently hit the news, but he couldn't be bothered to get up and change the channel. He munched pizza through various small wars and other melodramas, and was chasing a stray olive round the plate when he heard something that made him look up—

'. . . *Reports just coming in of an explosion in the City of London.*' Shaky hand-held footage of a red glow behind silhouetted buildings; a fire engine, men with hoses. '*The blast wrecked offices in St Mary Axe, causing extensive damage, though as yet there are no reports of casualties.*' Paul jumped to his feet, dropping the plate and scattering fragments of pizza crust. Irritating helicopter shot, could be anywhere; then, unmistakable, the frontage of JWW. There was the brass plaque on the wall, but the door was gone and so was a large chunk of the masonry. '*Police have not yet commented on the cause of the explosion, but are not ruling out the possibility of terrorist involvement. Finally, Larry the ring-tailed lemur who escaped from London Zoo two days ago has been found after a—*'

Paul said something vulgar about Larry the lemur and

switched the television off, thinking: *a bomb? Surely not.* A bolt of lightning, maybe, or even a direct hit from a fire-breathing dragon; but ordinary mundane old high explosive would be beneath the dignity of trade rivals, and nobody else knew who JWW were so why would they blow them up? Unless it was an accident; goblins having water-balloon fights with Benny Shumway's private stock of nitro-glycerine, perhaps, or playing chicken with a gas main. Unless it really was a dragon, and the news people were just—

Then someone grabbed him from behind, and he felt claws digging into his neck.

Chapter Five

'It's all right,' hissed a horrible voice in Paul's ear, as the claws bit into his skin. 'Nobody's going to hurt you.'

Fibber, Paul thought; but the grip was too tight to allow him to put his thoughts into words. He decided to hold very still indeed, and pass out as quickly as possible. On balance, if he had to die, he'd rather be asleep when it happened.

'Mum,' said a voice in the distance, 'not so tight, all right? They're fragile, you'll break it.'

The grip relaxed slightly, and Paul could feel something huge on his shoulder, turning him as though he was a page in a book. He'd closed his eyes when the pain was bad; now he opened them again. Injudicious. He shuddered.

'*Mum!*'

'It's no use saying "Mum" at me like that,' said the horrible voice. 'How do I make it stay still?'

'Let it *go*, for God's sake. You're probably hurting it.'

'Oh. Right.'

The thing, the hideous, terrifying, *ugly* thing, was huge, like a grizzly bear or a monster gorilla, but it wasn't any kind of creature that Paul had ever seen or heard about. Its skin was fish-belly white and coarse as sandpaper; its head was completely spherical, with slits for ears, eyes and mouth, and sat on top of a gross sack of a body like a golf ball balanced on a dollop of weightless custard. Paul could feel how very strong it was, but where it kept its muscles was anybody's guess. He didn't even bother trying to peer over its shoulder for a look at the owner of the other voice.

'Mum.'

'Sorry? Oh, yes.' The thing appeared to be concentrating, as if about to try something difficult. But it relaxed its grip a little, which was nice. 'Now then, dear,' said the thing. 'Can you understand what I'm saying?'

Dear? 'Yes,' Paul mumbled. 'Um, who are you?'

'See, Mum, I told you. They can understand everything we say.'

'Yes, all right.' The thing frowned, a neat trick since it had no eyebrows. 'Hello,' it said, then hesitated. Tongue-tied? A shy monster? 'Now then, there's nothing to be frightened of, I'm not going to hurt you. Are you all right?'

'Yes,' Paul gasped.

'You won't try and run away or anything?'

Paul shook his head. 'Promise,' he added.

'All right,' the thing said, and let go of Paul's throat completely. He staggered back and landed in his chair, the one he'd been sitting in watching television before his life got all cluttered up with monsters. 'That's right,' cooed the thing approvingly. 'You settle down, and we'll have a nice chat. Would you like that?'

No, Paul thought, *absolutely not*. 'Yes,' he said, feverishly maintaining eye contact. 'That'd be great.'

'See?' said the other voice smugly. 'They're just like people, really.'

The thing didn't sit down, mostly because it had nothing – at least, nothing *specific* – to sit down with. Rather, it sort of coagulated on an area of carpet. 'I hope we didn't startle you,' it said.

'No, not at all,' Paul said.

'That's all right, then. Now, I expect you're wondering who we are.'

Tact, Paul thought. 'Well, a bit,' he said.

The thing nodded. 'I don't think we've actually met before.' Behind its shoulder, another round, featureless head bobbed politely. Paul tried to smile, but his face had gone numb. 'We know you, of course, but you don't know us.'

'Sorry,' Paul said, 'but how do you know me? I mean, I'm not famous or anything.'

For a moment, Paul was sure the thing was about to bite him, but it was just a smile. Its teeth, he couldn't help noticing, were brown. 'The thing is, dear,' it said, 'we're here to help you. That's right, isn't it, pumpkin?'

'That's right,' the other one said, which seemed to clear that up.

'Good,' Paul said nervously. 'How, exactly?'

The thing's face reshaped itself into a kind of soggy pout. 'I'm afraid you're in great danger,' it said.

That, in Paul's view, was stating the obvious. 'Oh yes?'

The thing nodded again. 'We can't tell you very much, unfortunately, so you'll just have to take our word for it. But—' It was thinking again. 'Well, you saw just now on your talking-box thing . . .'

A sigh from the middle distance. 'Telegraph, Mum. They call them telegraphs.'

'The place where you work,' the thing went on, 'got blown up. Remember?'

'Yes,' Paul said. He'd forgotten. Being strangled by nightmare monsters can do that to a person. 'I saw it on the news.'

'The what, dear?'

'Sorry, the telegraph. There was a report about it.'

'Well.' The thing appeared to have lost its thread. 'Anyway, that explosion. It was in your room, the place where you sit all day. It was – I'm sorry to have to tell you this, but it was meant for you.'

'Oh,' Paul said.

The thing's narrow yellow eyes clouded slightly. 'It was a – what's the expression? A burbly-trap. Someone connected up the exploding thing to the handle of your big metal box for keeping things in, so that next time you opened it, you'd be blown up. But the goblins must've gone in your office and played with it, and set it off by accident.' The thing looked grave. 'I'm very sorry,' it said. 'This must be rather a shock for you.'

You betcha, Paul thought. 'Well, yes,' he said. 'Um, can you tell me who did it?'

Now the thing was looking very sad. 'I'd tell you if I knew,' it said. 'But I'm afraid it was probably one of us. I'm so sorry,' it added. 'But you see, some of us are very frightened.'

'Frightened,' Paul repeated.

'That's right. And when they're frightened, people can do some very silly things. It's this dreadful war,' it went on bitterly. 'If we're not careful, it'll ruin everything. But they don't see that, of course. All they can think about is trying to beat the other side. Quite ridiculous, the whole thing.'

'Excuse me,' Paul interrupted tentatively, 'but what war?'

The thing looked shocked. 'You don't know about the war?'

'Sorry.'

'Oh.' The thing pursed its palpable absence of lips. 'They haven't told you about the war. Oh dear.'

'It's all right,' Paul said. 'They don't tell me anything. What war?'

'The civil war,' said the thing wretchedly. 'Us against

them. Or really, us against us, which is why it's so sad. The point is,' it continued, lowering its voice, 'we aren't doing at all well, and you – well, you're the hero, strictly speaking. Until the other hero gets back, the blond one with the nice eyes. So really, it's just self-defence. Well, self-defence in advance, anyhow. They wanted to get you before you got them, is what I'm trying to say. Do you understand?'

Paul dipped his head. 'Sort of like a pre-emptive strike, you mean?'

'A what, dear?'

'You think the enemy's going to get you,' Paul explained, 'so you get him first. Like Pearl Harbor, that sort of thing.'

'Pearl what?'

'This war,' Paul persevered. 'Who's fighting who? And what's it got to do with me? I'm no threat to anybody, I can't even squash spiders.'

The thing looked gravely at him. 'Now that's not quite true, is it?' it said reproachfully. 'You're a Dragonslayer, I can smell its blood on your hands. At least,' it added thoughtfully, 'I can smell its blood.'

'A—' It sounded so *silly*, put like that. The thing had even pronounced the capital D. 'It was an accident,' he said. 'Honest. And I'm not a – what you said, I'm an assistant trainee.' He broke off. The thing was still gazing at him. 'What?' he said. 'Really and truly, it was an accident. Mr Tanner's mum—' His voice dried up. Goblins fooling about, she'd said; some goblins had opened the filing-cabinet drawer, and got themselves blown up. In which case, they'd be dead. And he knew a goblin; not that she was his friend, more like an unmitigated pest, but he knew her, and she couldn't be dead, could she? Things like that didn't really happen—

'Until the nice-looking one gets back,' the thing was saying, 'you're the senior hero in this area. And we're monsters,' she said sadly. 'Which means it's your job to kill us, if someone comes along and asks to have one of us killed. And you slew the dragon—'

'I *sat* on it, for pity's sake,' Paul protested.

The thing shook its head. 'Doesn't make any difference,' it said. 'But we haven't come here to argue, we just thought you ought to know. You're in danger, and so's your—' The thing's bleached skin coloured faintly pink. 'Your female,' it said. 'She's in deadly peril too.'

'Oh,' Paul said; and realised that his first thought had been *Melze*. But. 'Um,' he said, 'which one?'

Now the thing looked shocked. 'Sorry, dear?'

'Which, um, female do you mean? Only . . .'

He knew that expression. 'Oh,' it said. 'My mistake. Only, I'd got the impression that humans mate for life. It says so in the encyclopedia.'

'Ah.' Paul wilted slightly. 'Well,' he said, 'they're supposed to, I guess. But it doesn't always . . .'

'I see.' The thing had no lips to purse, but pursed them anyway. 'Well, anyway. I don't know which female they're on about, but I have it on very good authority that she's in terrible danger, and we thought you ought to know. And now we'd best be going.'

They were looking at him again. 'Goodbye, dear,' said the Mum thing. 'Do take care.' Then he felt as though he was falling through the air; which turned out to be true, though in the event he only fell a little way, from his chair to the floor. He opened his eyes.

'Bugger,' he said.

No trace of any things; just the TV, burbling quietly

to itself, and the clock, reading 1.25 a.m. He'd fallen asleep in his chair. Had a bad dream. On the table next to his chair he saw the empty pizza plate and coffee mug. Caffeine and mozzarella cheese; just plain biochemistry, nothing more.

Yes, but. Paul thought for a moment, then got up and went to the bathroom. In the mirror, he could see the red claw-marks on his neck, plain as anything.

Bloody hell, he thought. *If I show up at the office with marks on my neck, people are going to think* . . . And then he remembered. Explosion. What office?

Seven and a half sleepless hours later, Paul stood on the pavement opposite a hole where 70 St Mary Axe should have been. All in all, he thought, he was getting sick and tired of holes.

Strictly speaking, it wasn't a hole. During the night they'd rigged up hoardings; in fact, this being London, the hoardings were already covered in red, yellow and green fly-posters. There was also a white-and-yellow police tape, a crowd of people staring, and a TV crew. A power-dressed female was talking earnestly to a camera, while a couple of kids tried to sneak behind her shoulder and wave. *Curious*, Paul thought; *last week, if someone had told me JWW was going to get blown sky-high, I'd have grinned like an ape.* No JWW, no employment contract, no more doing bizarre and scary things for fear of being tortured by Mr Tanner. Free. But now, standing looking at the scaffolding poles and plywood sheet, he felt a surge of anger, and a tiny voice inside his head saying, *Welcome to the war*.

War. And what fucking war would that be?

'Mr Carpenter.' Paul spun round so fast that he nearly

knocked Countess Judy over. 'I tried to telephone, but I guess you'd already left.'

She looked exactly the same as when he'd last seen her, except for a very faint green glow right at the back of her eyes. He tried to think of some way of asking the obvious question.

'Actually,' she said, 'this is rather fortuitous. You may recall what we were talking about yesterday.'

Yesterday; he could just remember that far back, if he tried. 'Effective magic,' he said; then looked round sharply, to see if anybody was listening. But none of the gawpers or media types was interested in them.

'Quite so,' Countess Judy replied. 'And here's an excellent example of it in action.'

Paul frowned. 'Sorry,' he said. 'I don't follow.'

She raised an eyebrow. 'Come with me,' she said. 'Don't worry,' she added, 'nobody'll see us.'

She walked straight in front of the TV camera, past the crowd, not over or under but *through* the yellow tape and into the hoarding. *Oh well*, Paul thought, and followed her. Sure enough, as he got close to them, they seemed to shift, like the end of a rainbow; and he was standing outside the front door of the office. As far as he could tell, it looked perfectly normal.

'Effective magic,' the Countess explained, pushing the door open. 'Simple glamour; they think they can see a hoarding and an incident line, and that satisfies their curiosity – they don't expect to see more. Well,' she added, 'come on. It's perfectly safe.'

The door felt real enough; and inside, reception was just as it had been the day before. And there, behind the desk, was Melze, and she was smiling at him. 'So really,' he said, 'there wasn't a bomb?'

A cloud passed across the Countess's face. 'Oh, there was a bomb,' she said, with unmistakable anger in her voice. 'And the damage was quite extensive. Mr Suslowicz was here most of the night repairing it. But everything's back to normal now.' She paused, standing directly in front of the reception desk. 'You're aware, I take it, that the bomb was placed in your filing cabinet.'

Paul nodded. 'I—' How would he have known that, though? It hadn't been on the news; Mum the thing had told him. 'Was it?'

'Yes.'

'Oh,' Paul said. 'I mean, why? Why would anybody want to kill *me?*'

The Countess frowned. 'You're assuming it was meant for you personally,' she said. 'Do you have any grounds for that assumption?'

'I—' Paul shrugged. 'I suppose I just jumped to conclusions,' he said. 'So you don't think—'

Her face was completely neutral. 'It's too early to form a reasoned hypothesis,' she said. 'However, you'll be relieved to hear that nothing was damaged.'

It took a moment for that to sink in. '*Nothing?*'

'Nothing.'

'But – not even the cabinet? What about the files and stuff inside? Surely they must've been . . .'

'Nothing,' Countess Judy said again. 'It's not this firm's policy to allow acts of petty vandalism to disrupt our work. Accordingly, we take precautions, as a matter of course. You will find that everything is precisely as you left it last night.'

Colour me impressed, Paul thought. Backing up files was one thing, but an entire building and its contents— 'Well, then,' he said feebly, 'that's good. No harm done and nobody hurt, that's—' He stopped short. There had been a flicker in her face when he'd said *nobody hurt*. 'Nobody *was* hurt, were they?'

She didn't answer. Instead, she moved away from him and picked up some letters from the front desk. 'Ah,' she said, 'excellent. Your family history. Please wait in your office until I've had a chance to look at this. I'll send for you.' She walked out, leaving Paul standing.

'What,' Melze said, 'was all that about?'

He'd forgotten she was there. 'Search me,' he replied. 'Look, I'm not dreaming, am I? It was on the news last night, this place getting blown up?'

Melze shrugged. 'Well, I thought so. And I was thinking, oh well, back to job-hunting again, and then Mr Tanner rang me at seven o'clock this morning. Just said be here as usual, and here I am.' She looked around, then added: 'Doesn't look all that blown up to me. Like, for instance, everything's exactly where I left it on the desk last night – you'd have thought that *something* would've got moved. But what was all that about it being your office that the bomb was in?'

Paul hesitated before answering. 'You heard what she said,' he replied.

'Makes sense, I suppose,' she replied. 'After all, your office is pretty much in the centre of the building.'

'Is it?'

Melze looked at him. 'Well, yes. And I don't know anything about demolition, but I suppose if you want to blow somewhere up, in the middle's probably the best place to plant your bomb.'

'Right,' Paul said. That hadn't occurred to him, of course, mostly because he still had only a very sketchy idea of the geography of the place; he knew that if he went up such and such a staircase, turned right then left then left again, nine times out of ten he'd find himself outside his office door. For all that told him about the layout of the building, however, it might just as well have been transdimensional folds in hyperspace. Paul had long since faced up to the fact that when he died, he'd probably manage to get lost inside his own coffin. 'Well,' he said, 'that explains that, then.' He broke off. Melze was looking at him, her head slightly sideways. Her nose twitched. *Oh buggery*, he thought, *she's looking at my neck*— 'See you later,' he mumbled, and fled.

He stood in the corridor outside his office for maybe a full minute before he found the courage to go inside. If they'd been right, and the bomb had been set off when an over-inquisitive goblin started poking about inside his filing cabinet, then it stood to reason, surely, that at least one goblin must've died there last night, in a particularly flamboyant manner. Paul had never seen a dead body, or been in a room where someone had recently died; death was something that happened to superfluous relatives he hardly knew, in distant hospitals. He was aware that the partners were very clever at magical cleaning and tidying (or was it just effective magic, making the place *look* spick and span after the nightly revels of Mr Tanner's relations?) but he didn't relish the thought of spending time sitting in a chair that had recently been misted with a fine spray of vaporised goblin.

But there was nothing to see, no faint lingering smells, no tell-tale stickiness on the chair vinyl or the desktop. As Paul sat down, he reflected on how little he actually knew about goblins. Was it a safe assumption that getting blown up did actually kill them? Quite possibly not; in which case, he was curling his toes and puckering his guts for nothing. Mr Tanner's mum would probably tell him, if he happened to run into her at some point. Assuming, of course, that she'd survived the blast—

'Mr Carpenter.' Countess Judy was standing in the doorway. He hadn't heard her approach. 'Follow me, please.'

She led him along corridors and up and down staircases that he couldn't remember having seen before, to a small windowless room at the end of a long passageway. His sense of direction told him that they were down in some kind of basement. The room was bare-walled, uncarpeted, and empty apart from a plain pine table and two plastic stacking chairs.

'I've only had time to glance at this,' she said, holding up the paper she'd shown him earlier, 'but it would appear that you're qualified by birth to practise effective magic.'

'Ah, right,' Paul said. Apparently he'd passed, then. What joy.

'However,' Countess Judy went on, 'an emergency has arisen requiring urgent input from a member of the pest-control division. Right now,' she added mournfully, 'you're the only representative of the division on the premises.'

'Am I?' Paul said, startled. 'But, what about Benny? I mean Mr—'

'Mr Shumway,' the Countess said grimly, 'is currently indisposed.' She hesitated, then added, 'And that, in fact, is the emergency. Mr Shumway has been abducted and is being held hostage; most probably by the same terrorist group that planted the bomb.'

Fuck, Paul thought. It was a good, flexible, one-size-fits-all reaction covering a variety of issues, including genuine horror at Benny's plight, and even more genuine terror at the thought that Paul himself was now, by implication, duty hero. 'That's awful,' he said.

'Indeed. But not,' she went on, 'entirely unexpected. I sent Mr Shumway to find Mr Wurmtoter.'

'Ah,' Paul said.

'Mr Wurmtoter,' the Countess said, 'should have returned from his assignment three days ago. I suspected that something might be amiss, and last night I asked Mr Shumway to investigate. This morning, just before six o'clock, I found this outside my door.' She produced — Paul didn't happen to see from where — a long, narrow grey cardboard box. Inside was something that looked vaguely like the stuffing out of an old-fashioned sofa. 'Mr Shumway's beard,' the Countess explained. 'I fear there can only be one explanation. Mr Shumway has fallen into the hands of an enemy.'

More fuck, Paul thought; *fuck with double buggery, a cherry and a little red-and-white-striped umbrella*. 'I see,' he said. 'But what—?'

'So it's fortuitous,' the Countess went on, 'that you've completed your vocational training in pest control and are equipped to deal with this situation. Feel free, of course, to make use of whatever resources you need. Mr Shumway's safe return is, needless to say, our top priority.'

Yes, but— 'Countess,' Paul said nervously, 'that's absolutely fine, but really, I haven't got any experience or anything like that, all I've done so far is a load of paperwork and sitting on one small dragon. Couldn't someone else go instead? I mean, what about Mr Suslowicz, or Professor van Spee? They're — well, proper wizards. I'm just a clerk.'

She looked at him for a very long time, and he came to realise that there are worse things in the world than chasing off after dangerous lunatics; high on the list of such things was being stared at by Countess Judy. When at last she spoke, her voice was as cold and hard as a VAT inspector's heart. 'We have no definite leads,' she said, 'only suspicions. However, in the light of the current situation, it's hard to see this as a coincidence.'

What situation? Then Paul remembered; something about a war, us and them, dreams and nightmares. 'You mean the war?' he hazarded.

'Precisely.'

He nodded, then asked: 'Excuse me, but what war?'

She raised both eyebrows at him, a truly alarming sight. 'The war, Mr Carpenter. The armed conflict among the Fey. Don't you *ever* read memos?'

There's a time for lying and saving face. 'No,' he said. 'At least, I thought I did, but apparently not. Will you please tell me: what war?'

A tiny little sigh; then the Countess said: 'It's not so much a war as a rebellion. A dissident separatist faction among my people has seen fit to make a unilateral declaration of secession. It's this faction that we believe is behind the bombing attempt and Mr Shumway's abduction. It'd take too long to brief you on the issues involved. You'll just have to take it from me that the separatists are callous, ruthless criminals who will stop at nothing to further their cause. Hence the need to retrieve Mr Shumway as quickly as possible.'

Paul slumped a little. If Benny really was in danger, and if Paul was genuinely the only person who was qualified to go and rescue him, there was no point trying to wriggle out of it; and if Benny's captors were these dissident Fey, they were by definition the enemy, and to hell with any issues. 'It's all right,' he said, 'I'll go.' He stopped, then added: 'Um, go where?'

Quite unexpectedly, Countess Judy laughed. 'Now you're

actually beginning to sound like a hero, Mr Carpenter. Most encouraging. I was sure my faith in you wasn't misplaced.'

Well, he'd walked into that one, like a plate-glass window. 'Really,' he said, 'I'm not quite sure . . .'

'But I was.' Her eyes were as cold as steel. 'At your interview. You may recall that there were other candidates, and very impressive some of them were, too. I had to argue long and hard on your behalf with some of my partners. But I was right. And besides, you did answer the questions correctly. There was no other choice.'

Um, Paul thought; *that's not the way I remember it. But what the hell.* 'Thanks,' he muttered. 'Now, what've I got to do?'

There's heroism, which is basically just killing wildlife and retrieving missing persons and lost property, and there's courage. Courage is setting sail into the turbulent currents of the North Circular Road, alone in a Volkswagen Polo, at the height of the rush hour.

For some reason, the Countess had insisted that Paul should drive to High Wycombe rather than catch a train or a coach. He couldn't imagine why, unless it was pure malice on her part. He wasn't a very good driver and he had a mortal fear of roundabouts. The car wasn't helping, either. 'Pay attention,' barked Monika's voice from the car radio. 'You could have gone then, but now it is too late . . . *Dritte Pferdegeschirr*, third gear, for the love of the Almighty. Now look, you are in the wrong lane. No, this is wrong, *links, links fahren* . . .'

He'd tried switching the radio off, but it didn't work; neither did ripping off the faceplate, or stuffing digestive biscuits into the tape slot. 'Not now,' he pleaded. 'Shut up, Monika, *please* . . .'

Eventually he cleared the Hillingdon roundabout and the M40 enfolded him in her strong arms, sweeping him effortlessly out towards the setting sun. Once they were on the motorway, Monika seemed to calm down a little, which was a blessing. 'I am studying here the map of High Wycombe,' she announced crisply. 'I have located Grasmere Drive, it will be very simple to find. First, we shall need to follow the signs for Marlow and Maidenhead.'

Paul tuned her out and went back to asking himself: *What am I doing here, for crying out loud? Think about it; if Benny was sent out here and he got captured, what sort of a chance am I going to have? Lamb to the*—

'You have no self-confidence,' Monika interrupted. 'You should be positive. It is not good to dwell on the likelihood of failure.'

That was the last straw and a half. 'Fucking hell, Monika,' he snapped, 'can you read what I'm thinking?'

'*Natürlich*,' she replied calmly. 'I was before my transformation a fully qualified *Seelritter* – I do not know what it is in English. In Germany it is taught as a core skill. We are very methodical,' she added proudly, 'in our vocational training, not like in this country, where you must pick it up as you go past.'

Unfortunately, he'd run out of digestive biscuits some time ago. 'Fine,' he said. 'Would you mind terribly *not* doing it? Especially,' he added, 'when I'm driving.'

'I am trying only to help,' Monika said, offended. 'To me it is no pleasure, seeing inside a mind like—'

'Thanks,' Paul said, very firmly indeed. 'Look, is this our junction?'

'*Ja*. Follow the signs for the town centre until we reach a double roundabout, then left—'

Finding Grasmere Drive wasn't quite as straightforward as Monika had predicted, and it was pitch dark by the time they got there. The headlights revealed a row of pebble-dashed bungalows, white-weatherboarded, hedgeless, each with an Audi or a pristine four-by-four standing outside like stone sphinxes guarding a pharaoh's tomb. 'You sure this is the right place?' Paul asked again.

'Of course I am sure,' Monika replied impatiently. 'There is in High Wycombe only one Grasmere Drive, and here is number seventy-four. You should get out and ring the doorbell.'

Paul sighed. 'Yes,' he said, 'I suppose I should.'

It'd have been just a little bit comforting, he thought, if he'd brought some equipment with him. Not that he really had the faintest idea how to use any of it – Benny had shown him how to wave the swords and load the guns and prime the bombs and all the rest of it, but he knew he wouldn't be able to remember complicated technical stuff like that if anything actually *happened* – but at least he'd have had something to hold on to, like those poly-styrene floats when you're learning to swim. Walking down the front path of a bungalow that's supposedly a portal to the Land of the Fey armed with nothing deadlier than a single manila wallet file takes more than courage. You have to be really courageous – brave as two short planks, fear-less as a hatter – to do something like that.

He still wasn't sure he'd come to the right place, though. In the middle of the lawn was a clump of those carved wooden mushrooms, surrounding the water feature, and the sign hanging from the porch read *Brooksmeade*. As if that wasn't enough, the door chimes played *Què Viva Espana*.

'Hello,' Paul said as the door opened. The man who'd opened it was elderly, bald, wearing a fawn cardigan with frayed elbows. 'Excuse me,' Paul went on, 'but I'm looking for the portal—'

The man nodded. 'Hold on,' he said, 'I'll fetch her.' He turned and shouted over his shoulder, 'Vee, it's some bloke about the portal.'

The television that had been burbling in the background cut out abruptly, and the man was replaced by a woman of similar vintage, wearing a lilac jumper and curlers. 'You here for the portal, love?' she asked. Paul nodded.

'Right you are, then,' she said. 'Watch the step.'

Paul duly tripped over the step, nearly flattening her, and followed her down a long, deep-carpeted hall. A small dog, possibly a Yorkshire terrier or some similar brand, yapped behind him as he trudged. She showed him into a sun-lounge, in the centre of which was a wagon wheel converted into a coffee table.

'Here you go,' she said. 'Won't be a tick.'

She left, leaving Paul alone with the table, a large straw donkey wearing a Spanish hat, and the small yappy dog. It was some time before Paul realised that the dog had three heads.

He stared. It was still a small, yappy dog, and round the place where its three necks met was a tartan flea-collar. One of its mouths held a small rubber ball, and its tail was wagging. *Christ*, Paul thought, and kept perfectly still until the woman came back.

'You done this before?' she asked. When Paul shook his head she smiled reassuringly (Paul wasn't reassured) and said: 'There's nothing to worry about. All you got to do is drink this, sit down in the chair and close your eyes. Nothing to it, really.'

Whatever *this* was, it came in a mug inscribed *The World's*

Best Grandad. It tasted like cold, sweet tea. There was also a plate of mixed biscuits, but apparently they weren't compulsory. The chair was one of those canvas-and-steel-tube loungers, and the dog seemed to think that Paul was trespassing when he sat in it; it growled at him, but its tail was still wagging. *Soon as I close my eyes*, he thought, *the bugger's going to lick me to death*—

But by then his eyes had closed anyway; and at that juncture, things took a turn for the worse.

It'd have been harder to handle if he hadn't been to the Bank with Benny Shumway. The landscape was different – a vast brown heath stretching out as far as the eye could see – but the lighting and general ambience were pretty much the same. It was bleak and cold; it seemed to say that creatures who breathed weren't welcome here. It was probably safe to assume that there were no public toilets.

'We had better be going.' Paul looked up in surprise, and saw he wasn't alone. Standing next to him was a tall, dark-haired woman in a smart suit. She was maybe five years older than him, handsome rather than pretty, with glasses. Also, a marked German accent.

'Monika?'

'*Natürlich*. You see me as I was before I was transformed.' She hesitated, and her manner suggested that hesitation wasn't something that came naturally to her. 'We must hurry,' she said awkwardly. 'But I do not know the way.'

'I—' What he wanted to say was that he was really, really glad she was with him; not because he expected her to do all the heroism, or even map-read, though he'd be prepared to bet money that she'd be better than him at both; but because this wasn't a place where he wanted to be alone. 'Neither do I,' he said. 'Let's go that way.'

Paul wasn't even aware in which direction he was pointing. 'Why?' Monika asked, puzzled.

'I don't know,' he replied. 'But it's a four to one chance, and perhaps we'll be lucky.'

'That is a very bad reason,' Monika replied. 'However, you are in charge. We should go.'

She sounded braver than he felt. Lion-hearted as a brush. 'Fine,' he said, and started to walk.

'But you are going west,' she objected behind him. 'You said to go north-east.'

'Whatever.' He shivered. 'I have a feeling that it doesn't greatly matter. Where we need to go will probably find us. Unless,' he added with feeling, 'we're really lucky.'

'That does not make sense,' Monika objected, scampering a few steps to catch up with him. 'This is not how we are accustomed to do such things in my country. First we research thoroughly the geography of the place we are going. Do you have a map?'

Paul shook his head. 'I don't think this place would fit on a map,' he said. 'I don't think it's that sort of—' He stopped dead. A nasty thought had just struck him. 'How do we get back?' he asked.

She was staring at him. 'You don't know?'

'No. How about you?'

'I have never done anything like this before,' Monika admitted. 'I do not know the approved procedure. You should have researched it before you left the office.'

Paul shrugged. 'Don't suppose it's going to matter much,' he said gloomily. 'You know what?' he added, as he pulled his foot out of a pool of black mud. 'I think this is even worse than the Bank.'

She frowned. 'I do not understand,' she said. 'My father

works for the *Rhenische Stadtsbank* in Stuttgart. It is nothing like this.'

'No kidding.' He stopped again and looked round. Nothing to be seen for miles and miles except desolate moorland, with here and there a black, stagnant tarn or a cluster of granite rocks. Suddenly Paul felt tired, as though six months of weariness had only just caught up with him. *Showing off*, he said to himself; *effective magic; either they can hurt me or they can't, but I haven't got the time or the energy for all this stupid ambience.* 'Bugger walking,' he said. 'Let's just wait here and see what happens.'

'But—' Monika began to object; and then she stopped talking and stared at a low, grass-covered mound, no more than ten yards away to her left. 'That was not there before,' she said quietly.

'No,' Paul agreed. 'Told you all we had to do was stay put and be patient. Ah,' he added, as a door opened in the side of the mound, leaking pale green light. 'That'll be for us, I expect. Well, come on. We haven't got all day.'

'Paul, wait.' Unless the German for Paul was *scheisskopf*, she'd never called him by his name before. 'We cannot go in there, it is not safe.'

He shook his head. 'It's all right,' he said, 'it'll just turn out to be a dungeon or a tomb or something. Or maybe a really amazing hall with torchlight and pretty furniture. Makes no odds, one way or another. You coming, or what?' Without looking round to see if she was following, he stepped through the door into the green light.

In spite of his new and hard-won cynicism, Paul was impressed. It was as though Peter Jackson and Laurence Llewellyn Bowen had been hired to make over Hell, with a long list of product placements to fit in wherever possible.

A long green fire ran the length of a broad Hollywood-medieval hall, oak-panelled and hammer-beam-roofed, painted and gilded. Polished tables and carved benches flanked the hearth, and the walls were masked by acres of richly coloured tapestries, a grotesque combination of flowers, wildlife, court and battle scenes. Though the flames from the hearth were taller than he was, the place was icy cold, like a flame-effect electric fire with the elements turned off. Paul yawned ostentatiously and called out, 'Hello? Anybody home?'

'You should not shout like that,' Monika hissed beside him. 'It is not respectful. We must not anger them—'

Paul grinned and walked down the hall towards the high table that crossed the T at the end. He'd have been more impressed if he hadn't seen it all before; in his mind's eye, when he was twelve and they'd had to read Tolkien at school. True, he hadn't imagined it in quite such detail; the quaint carved bosses and misericords, for example, with their funny little faces and cartoon-like monsters and dragons. He'd been rather vague about how the beams actually kept the roof up, whereas whoever was responsible for this lot had done his homework, read up about plates, purlins, studs and ties. Still, the overall design was simple plagiarism, and they were going to have to do better than this if they wanted to get his disbelief suspended.

As if on cue, a side door opened and a small child came in: a girl, about ten years old. 'There you are,' she said. 'Like it?'

Paul shrugged. 'Not bad,' he said. 'The gilding's rather tacky and the green fire is probably a mistake, but you're on the right lines. Now, if it's all the same to you, I'd like to see the manager.'

Paul could feel Monika tensing up next to him, but the girl just grinned. 'You sure you want to do that?' she said.

'No,' Paul replied, looking past her at a tapestry of silver unicorns on a field of golden flowers. 'But it's not up to me. Can we get on, please? I'd like to be home in time for *Buffy*, if it's all the same to you.'

The girl raised an eyebrow. 'We're impressed,' she said. 'We were expecting a snivelling little wimp. If you've suddenly come over all brave, it could save us all a lot of time.'

'Not brave,' Paul replied. 'Just bored. Scared stiff too, of course, but not impressed, if you see what I mean. I'm guessing that the scary stuff is what I can't see. Would that be right?'

The little girl didn't answer; instead, she swept him an exaggerated curtsy, and went out the way she'd come in. Nothing much happened for a while, and Paul sat down on the nearest bench.

Monika was horrified. 'You must not do that,' she said. 'We do not know what dreadful enchantments there might be.'

Paul sighed. 'Don't worry about it,' he said. 'This is all strictly industrial light and magic, while they're figuring out what to do next. Or else they've already figured it out, and it takes a while to get everything ready. In any case, nothing bad's going to happen to us yet. Sit down, take the weight off your tyres. We could be here for some time.'

Monika hesitated, then sat down beside him. 'Mr Carpenter,' she said gravely, 'there is something I would like to know. But it is personal.'

Paul picked a dried bulrush off the floor and held the end of it in the green fire. As he'd expected, it didn't even char. 'Go ahead,' he said.

'Well—' She frowned, reminding him vaguely of someone or other. 'I have to say it, you do not seem to be behaving normally. Your manner is different. I do not understand.'

Paul felt the end of the bulrush – quite cool – and threw

it away. 'You're right,' he said, 'and I don't understand either. I think it was when we walked through the door, or maybe a little before that. I suddenly realised I didn't feel—' He stopped. 'I was going to say, I didn't feel frightened any more, but that's not true at all. It's more—' He shrugged. 'I think the word I'm after is *intimidated*. Sorry,' he added, 'I haven't got a clue how to say that in German.'

'No problem,' Monika said, 'I know what is intimidated. You do not feel inferior and out of place.'

Paul nodded. 'That's it,' he said. 'It's like I've been here before. Actually, it's more than that. This is going to sound pretty weird, but it's almost like I feel at home here. But not in a good way,' he added. 'Like it's familiar, but I don't like it much. It feels like – I don't know, sort of like Heathrow airport, or some big government office if I worked there. And that's strange,' he added thoughtfully, 'because obviously I've never been in a place like this before, ever. The fire's a fake, by the way. No heat or anything. I think where they went wrong was making it green – it's unconvincing. It's like they have a vague idea what I'm expecting to see, but they don't understand. Like words copied out of a book by someone who doesn't know the language.'

Monika shivered. 'It is very cold,' she said. 'I do not like it here.'

'Me neither. Is there a bell we could ring or something? It's just psychology, making us wait around like this, but I'd rather get to the next bit.'

'Excellent.' Paul looked up to see who'd spoken. The little girl was back, and apparently she'd brought her friends. He wasn't sure if they were the same kids he'd come across at the garage in the middle of nowhere, or whether they just looked very much like them.

'Excuse me?' he said.

'You're doing well,' they said – they all spoke at the same time, but Paul could only hear one voice. 'Better than we expected, anyhow. We think you're ready to move on. How about it?'

Monika had grabbed Paul's arm as if to warn him, but he took no notice. 'I'm up for that,' he said. 'What's involved, exactly?'

'That'd be telling,' the children replied. They were all, he noticed, wearing either sky blue or lilac, and identical blue-and-white trainers. 'But since you're being a good sport, we'll give you a clue. This is—' They giggled. 'This is child's play. Now we're going to take you somewhere a bit scary. Do you want to continue, or have you had enough? If you want to back out now, that's fine.' At the far end of the hall, a small dog was barking. It wore a tartan flea-collar, and it had three heads. 'You can go back the way you came, and no hard feelings.'

Paul thought for a moment. There was, after all, absolutely no reason why he should go on, was there? He'd got this far, made an effort, and he'd never wanted to be a hero in the first place. Honour was satisfied; except that Countess Judy had told him that they were holding Benny Shumway hostage, and there wasn't anybody else who could get him out of there.

Wasn't there? Bullshit. There was Professor van Spee, who was supposed to be some sort of really high-powered wizard; or Mr Suslowicz, who was a giant; or couldn't Dennis Tanner come bursting in with an army of goblins? Or why couldn't Countess Judy do it herself? Wasn't she supposed to be the Queen of the Fey? It didn't make sense, what she'd said. If Benny hadn't been able to deal with these creeps, what possible chance had Paul got?

On the other hand; there was a lot he didn't understand about the firm's business, mostly because nobody had bothered to tell him. Maybe he really was the only one who could save Benny Shumway. And Benny was—

His friend? Hardly that. Benny Shumway was just some very strange short guy who'd once been grateful to him for coming with him to the Bank. That was hardly a life debt.

'I think we should go back now,' Monika said quietly.

But Paul shook his head. The gesture surprised him; he was under the impression that he was still making up his mind. Apparently not. 'No, thanks,' he told the children. 'I'm ready when you are.'

The children grinned at him. 'Excellent,' they said. The lights went out, and almost immediately came back up again.

The shock hit Paul like a hammer.

The mood he was in, he could probably have handled something strange and unfamiliar, since that was what he'd been bracing himself against. What he saw when the light came back was the very last thing he'd been expecting. It was also so familiar, so *ordinary*, as to constitute his mental default setting. *That* was scary.

He was sitting on a bed. His bed. The duvet was dark blue, with red polka dots; he'd always hated it, from the day his mum brought it home from Marks' sale, but she'd never taken any of his hints to that effect. Above him, a cluster of dusty Spitfires and Messerschmitts dangled from bits of fishing line. From the poster on the wall opposite, the crew of the starship *Voyager* smiled blandly over his head. He was home.

Chapter Six

'You watched *Voyager?*' Monika said at last. '*Gott in Himmel.*'

It should have been a momentous occasion, to be celebrated ever after with fireworks and a military band: the one and only time there'd been a girl in this room, even if she was really a Volkswagen Polo. But Paul hadn't noticed. All the fatalistic confidence had drained out of him, like oil from a British motorcycle. He was home. *Eeek.*

In the main conference room at JWW, there was an enchanted table. It was polished to a mirror finish, and the technical term for it was 'imp-reflecting'; a goblin masquerading as a human or a shapechanger would show up in it as it really was – all teeth and claws and tiny yellow eyes. Maybe the Fey had similar technology, Paul thought; because this room had the exact same effect. They'd unmasked him, caught him out, a stupid little boy pretending to be a grown man in a suit four sizes too big for him. This room no longer existed, of course. When his parents had moved to Florida, the house had been sold: everything that he couldn't fit into two suitcases and a dozen supermarket cardboard boxes had gone to the charity shop or the tip. These posters, this duvet, those plastic aeroplanes were long gone; but the room was for ever, and he'd never left it. He was trapped in it for ever.

'No,' Paul said. 'Well, yes, the pilot episode and some of

the first series, but then I gave up. My mum bought me the poster for Christmas one year. I had to put it up, or she'd have been hurt.'

The thought made him shudder. His mother had always been so vulnerable to unintentional slights. The smallest thing could cut her to the quick; and he couldn't bear the thought of hurting her, naturally, so he'd always had to be so careful . . . Standing here again, surrounded by things he'd hated but put up with for years and years and years, he realised (consciously for the first time) that hurt and offence had been his mother's sheepdogs, to herd him into the small, sparse pen she'd built for him. His mother's sensitivity and his father's contempt kept him here like chains.

'Excuse me,' Paul said. 'Hello?'

At once, a small child materialised in front of him: a small boy in scruffy school uniform, shirt-tails trailing, tie askew and tightly knotted, sitting at the desk by the window with an exercise book open in front of him. 'Is that you?' Monika whispered.

Paul nodded. 'When I was twelve,' he replied.

'You were – shorter,' she said awkwardly. 'You've grown.'

'By eighteen inches,' Paul replied. 'Nice to think I've achieved something in the last ten years, even if it's something a tree could've done much better.'

What she hadn't needed to say was, *Apart from that, you're exactly the same.* Well, at least she had a degree of tact. *Vorsprung durcht Technik*, and all that. 'Well?' said Little Paul, looking up at him, with an expression on his face that Paul had never seen in any mirror. 'Here we are, then.'

'Yes,' Paul said.

'Not quite so cocky now, are we?'

'No.'

Little Paul shrugged his thin shoulders. 'Warned you it'd be scary, but you wouldn't listen. Full of it, you were. Serves you right, don't you think?'

'Yes.'

Little Paul smirked, and stood up. 'You people,' he said. 'Read a few books, learn which end of a rifle the bullet comes out of, and you think you're bloody Siegfried. Your real hero, now, this wouldn't phase him at all. He'd be all pissy because there's no blue plaque and guided tour.'

'I didn't want to be a hero,' Paul mumbled. 'I only did the lessons and stuff because I've got to do three months in each department.'

Little Paul laughed. 'It's all right,' he said; and despite the height differential, he might as well have been patting Paul on the head. 'It's not your fault, you're just going where you're sent. But it's pretty bloody obvious, isn't it? You aren't cut out for this sort of thing. They should've let you carry on dowsing for bauxite. You're good at that.'

'Am I?' Paul's eyes widened a little. 'Really?'

'Really. Everybody's good at *something*. Just like everybody can't be good at everything. It's OK. You just go back to your office, and we'll say no more about it.'

That was so kind, so unbelievably generous that Paul wanted to cry. It was just like when he was small; people had always forgiven him eventually, no matter how thoughtless and inconsiderate he'd been, and he could never figure out why, he'd never deserved it. 'Thank you,' Paul said, suddenly remembering his manners. 'I'm sorry,' he added reflexively.

'That's all right. You've learned your lesson.'

Something was snuffling round his ankles, and he could smell dog. Ten to one on that it was a tiny Yorkshire terrier with a tartan collar and three heads. He'd always been frightened of dogs, even small ones (especially small ones) but this time he was glad it was there, because it meant he could go back—

'*Herr* Carpenter. Paul.' Monika's voice. 'I do not understand. What is the *matter* with you?'

Herr Carpenter; with a jolt of shock, Paul realised that she meant him. 'Sorry,' he said. 'What?'

'It is only a small boy,' she was saying. 'There is nothing to be afraid of. Why are you looking like that?'

Just for a split second, Little Paul gave Monika a look that ought to have turned her to stone. But when he spoke, that crushing drawl was back. 'You want to go on? Fine, you go on. I'm warning you, though. This is ice cream and peaches compared to what's next. You might care to think about that, before your four-wheeled friend here gets you into something you might regret.'

Worse than this? Impossible. But, quite unexpectedly, Paul wasn't quite so sure any more. True, he'd been here; he'd been here a very long time, and he'd only escaped because Mum and Dad had decided they'd earned their place in the sun, and had only taken with them the things they really wanted, like the mahogany chiffonier and Aunt Clara's china dogs. He'd escaped because he wasn't worth taking, he knew that. But he'd escaped.

Suddenly he thought of Melze. When he'd started at senior school, his parents had told him that he didn't really want to see his old friends any more; he'd be making new friends, nice boys and girls, not like the ones from round here ... There had been a day when he'd been up here, with the polka dots and the perpetually tailspinning Hurricanes, and there'd been a knock at the front door. He'd heard Melze and her brother Jason: did Paul want to come out to play? And Mum had said, 'Sorry, but Paul's not here right now'; and her voice had told them that Paul would never be there if they came asking for him again, and they'd gone away and had never come back. The nice boys and girls at senior school had seen him as a target, or not at all (and that had been his fault, for not being outgoing and confident and charming, like he was supposed to be), and so he'd stayed here instead, in his room, with his books and his models, and Paul is such a disappointment to us, in some ways. But now Melze had come back, and she'd smiled at him—

'If it's all right with you,' he heard himself saying, 'I think I'd like to go on now, please.'

Little Paul looked at him blankly for a moment, then shrugged. 'Fine,' he said, 'if you think you can hack it. No skin off our nose.'

'Thanks,' Paul said; and almost before the word was out of his mouth, the faint glow of light outside the window had burst in and flooded the room. Paul shut his eyes, as though he'd carelessly looked straight at a welding torch. When he opened them again—

It was an office; a very beautiful, very expensive office. Even the walls were carpeted, and woven into the pile was a monogram, *JWW* intertwined like wrestling snakes. Somewhere a telephone was ringing, and Paul noticed that it was making one long purr, American style, instead of the querulous British *beep-beep*. Through the window he could see the flat roofs of lesser skyscrapers, and beyond them, a rocky hillside decorated with huge white letters.

Oh *no*, he thought.

A small girl wearing a Friends Forever T-shirt stood up

from a luxurious leather armchair in the corner, and curt-
sied mockingly as she pointed across the room. There, in
matching chairs across a low, broad glass table, sat a lean,
bronzed, surfer-type young man and a dark, thin girl. He
was drinking iced tea through a straw. She was absently
reaming out her ear with her little finger. Paul only knew
one person in the world who'd do a thing like that.

'Welcome to Hollywood,' whispered the Friends Forever
child maliciously.

'Where is this place?' Monika was asking, but Paul ignored
her. If he kept very still and quiet, he could just hear what
the surfer and the thin girl were saying—

'And after I broke up with him . . .' said the thin girl.

Paul swung round, looking for the child, but she'd disappeared. Reluctantly, he turned back. The surfer was laughing
at something apparently very funny.

'Sounds like a total loser,' he said. 'Excuse me, but your
taste in guys—'

The thin girl smiled bleakly. 'Oh, it gets better,' she said.
'After him came Paul. My God.' She looked away for a
moment, as if regaining her composure.

'That bad?' said the surfer.

'Worse. Really, really worse.'

'Jesus.'

'Absolutely. I mean, you've heard of Peter Pan, the little
boy who didn't want to grow up.' The surfer was nodding
gravely, like a plastic novelty Aristotle. 'Like, talk about
immature, Paul was Beaujolais Nouveau. And trying to talk
to him was like juggling with custard.'

The surfer's lips thinned. 'Scared to commit, huh?'

The thin girl sighed and shook her head (and Paul thought:
Her hair never swayed like that when she was with me . . .) 'I

still don't know how I stuck it out for as long as I did. Like, I remember reading once, this thing about an army officer; and in his report, someone had written: *His men would follow him anywhere, but only out of curiosity.* I think that's maybe how I put up with Paul all that time. I mean, it was fascinating to watch, in a sick sort of a way. And it was my fault too, let's be honest.' She pulled a face. 'There was this love potion – it's a long story. And for some stupid reason I thought that maybe I could change him, if I really loved him enough.'

'Ah yes.' The surfer grinned. 'The famous JWW love philtre. But I thought that was, you know, for ever—'

'That's what it says on the bottle,' the thin girl replied. 'And I read up about it, and it'd never failed before. But then, it never had to contend with Paul Carpenter.' She laughed. 'They should bottle him and market him as the antidote. Actually, maybe that's why they hired him in the first place. I mean, there has to be a reason.'

The surfer's chuckle was deep and somehow very distasteful, or so Paul thought. 'Sounds like there's not much chance of you guys getting back together again,' he said. 'But maybe I'm missing something here. If the guy's such a dork, why did you drink the love potion?'

The grin she gave him was sad and guilty. 'Because I'm pathetic, I suppose. I mean, I'd just broken up with the other creep – no, wait, I'm losing count here. It was after the *other* other creep turned out to be a goblin in disguise.'

'Bummer,' whispered the surfer.

She nodded. 'Actually he was a sort of off-relation of Mr Tanner, our mining and mineral rights partner; he'd disguised himself as a human and, well—' Her ears and the tip of her nose pinkened. 'Seduced me, I guess. And it wasn't even because he fancied me, it was just part of some stupid office politics thing. You can imagine, that didn't do my self-image a whole lot of good. And – well, there was Paul, following me round like some kind of pathetic lost puppy; and I thought, the hell with it, let's be practical. I knew Paul was absolutely besotted with me; and if I took the potion, well, that'd be that taken care of and out of the way. I'd be in love with him for ever and ever, I'd be able to cross finding true love off my list of things to do, it'd be one less pressure on me—' She shook her head sadly. 'My parents' fault, to a certain extent. I think they probably do love me, but they were always giving me that sad look – when are you going to settle down, find yourself a nice young man; it's so much *hassle*, having to deal with that day after day after day. That's why the love philtre's such a great idea. Like arranged marriages, I guess, only you can have the convenience and the not-fussing, and true romance as well. Anyhow, that's why I did it, and probably it wouldn't have been such a bad idea, only it didn't work. I had to choose the one man in the universe who's such a colossal waste of space and resources, even a love philtre can't make him tolerable. So I dumped him and came over here.'

Paul looked away. Mostly, he felt cold, as though he'd been lying in the snow for an hour. 'Hey, you,' he said quietly. 'Elf.'

At once the small girl was standing beside him. 'We are not elves,' she said angrily. 'Elves are Santa's little helpers. We are the Fey. Please bear that in mind if you enjoy breathing.'

Paul pulled back his lips in a poor imitation of a smile. 'Oh be quiet,' he said. 'I just wanted to ask you, is there any reason why we've got to stay here, or can we get on? Only there's other things I could be doing, and—'

If the look on the child's face was anything to go by, she was genuinely impressed. 'You want to go on?' she said. 'After hearing that?'

Paul shrugged. 'I don't see what that's got to do with why I'm here,' he said.

'Are you stupid or something?' The child raised her eyebrows. 'Look, maybe you're missing the point here. You've seen what we can do to you if we want to, and you still want to carry on. Either you're really, really brave, or—'

Paul smiled grimly. 'I know what I am,' he said. 'Beating me up like this – well, I'm not exactly enjoying it, but you won't stop me this way. All you're really doing is telling me what a pathetic mess I am, and I knew that already.'

'Oh.' The child seemed rather taken aback. 'So, she told you, did she? About taking the potion?'

Paul shook his head. 'But I'd guessed it had to be something like that. I mean, I had an idea she'd drunk the stupid thing. I thought it was by accident, but apparently not. Broad as it's long. So, can we press on now, please?'

The child pulled a face. 'Talk about a piece of work,' it said. 'All right. But if you think this sucks—'

'You should've stuck with dragons and stuff,' Paul interrupted. 'I'd almost certainly have run away from dragons. All this –' he waved a hand vaguely towards the corner where the thin girl sat '– this is just stuff I live with every day.'

'Very brave,' the child said mockingly. 'On the other hand, I've got a dictionary at home which says that "brave" is just another word for too stupid to get out of the way.'

Paul couldn't be bothered to reply. It wasn't as though

any of it mattered, anyway. He'd known why Sophie had left him the moment he'd seen her letter. If this was the worst that the Fey could throw at him—

That business with the light again. He opened his eyes, and then closed them and opened them once more. Made no difference. Either it was very dark indeed wherever this was, or he'd gone blind.

'Hello?' he mumbled.

'Paul? Is that you?' Benny's voice; but sounding uncharacteristically subdued. 'Over here.'

Paul tried to walk to where the voice had come from, but something caught his foot and he staggered clumsily to his knees. 'Benny?' he called out. 'Is it dark in here, or—?'

'Yes,' Benny replied. 'Stay where you are, it's not worth trying to move about. What the hell are you doing here, anyhow? Please don't tell me you're trying to rescue me.'

'Well,' Paul said, 'yes.'

'Fuck,' Benny replied. 'Whose stupid idea was that, then?'

Paul didn't answer that. 'What's happening?' he asked. 'Where are we?'

'Dungeons,' Benny said gloomily. 'And that's about all I know. I asked you a question. Who sent you?'

'It was my idea,' Paul said.

'Liar. Who was it? Was it Ricky Wurmtoter? Did he manage to get out somehow?'

'Sorry,' Paul replied. 'I mean no, I haven't seen any sign of him.' He remembered something. 'Isn't he supposed to be in here too?' he asked.

'Don't know,' Benny replied. 'I came down here to rescue him, but I've been here so long I'm losing track of everything. You do realise, don't you?' he added, suddenly urgent.

'We're stuck here for good. We aren't ever going to get out.'

Paul was still too disorientated for that to mean anything. 'What makes you say that?' he said. 'I mean, they know we're here. The partners, I mean. The Countess and—'

'So *she* sent you.'

'All right, yes, she sent me. Which means,' he plodded on, 'when I don't come back—'

He tailed off. It was a moment before Benny spoke. 'When you don't come back,' he said, 'that's it. After that, there's nobody left. Haven't you got it yet? If Ricky Wurmtoter's still in the cell next door, it means the whole fucking department's down here. All of us. There's nobody left up there to come after us.'

A small, detached portion of Paul had to admit: *Well, yes, actually, a hell of a lot better than dragons.* 'But what about Mr Tanner? Or Professor van Spee, or—?'

'You clown,' Benny snapped. 'They can't do this sort of stuff, they aren't heroes. They couldn't get past the portal, even if they wanted to, which they wouldn't. Haven't you worked it out yet? If any bloody fool of a sorcerer could do this job, we wouldn't be needed. It's a specialisation. Not everybody can do it. In fact, only a tiny handful.'

Long silence. 'I don't understand,' Paul whimpered.

'Fine. Then I'll explain.' Paul took a step backwards. Even though it was pitch dark, he could feel Benny's anger building rapidly, like a motorway tailback. 'In order to do this bloody ridiculous stuff,' he said, 'you need a hero, right?'

Paul nodded, then remembered that Benny couldn't see him. 'Right,' he said.

'And you're a hero, it says so in your personnel file, right after where it says *no initiative, not a team player, attitude leaves much to be desired.* So it's a fact. Now you're thinking,' Benny went on, 'that it can't be true, you're not the hero type. And that's where your total and complete lack of a fucking clue betrays itself.'

'But it *can't* be true,' Paul almost pleaded. 'Come on, I should know—'

'You don't know *anything*.' He could hear Benny forcing himself to calm down. 'Nobody ever said you were a great hero. Obviously you're not. You're a little tiny one; you know – faster than a speeding second-class letter, leaps very small buildings in a single bound. But what the hell. A Pekinese is still a dog, right?'

Paul thought fleetingly of the little Yorkshire terrier with its three heads. 'All right,' he said. 'I still don't quite see—'

'Then shut your face and let me tell you.' Silence; Benny marshalling his thoughts. 'Where you go wrong is, you don't know what makes someone a hero. You think it's probably bulging muscles, superior weapon skills, trivial stuff like that. Well, you couldn't be more wrong if you tried. A hero's only got to be two things: brave, and good. That's all.'

In comparison, Paul thought, *beating my head against a brick wall would be both productive and agreeable.* 'But I'm not either,' he whined.

'Fuck you, Carpenter, if I say you're good and brave, you're good and brave. Do you want me to explain, or don't you?'

'Sorry.'

'So you should be. And you are. Right, where was I? Good and brave. Well, brave you can probably get your head around, but how about good? Do you have any idea what "good" means?'

'I used to think I did,' Paul muttered.

'Well, you don't. Here's something for you to think about. Would a good person deliberately do something that'd mean unbearable lasting pain for those who love him most?'

'Um,' said Paul. 'No.'

'Thank you, now we're getting somewhere. How about "brave"? Can you do brave for me?'

Paul nodded. 'Facing danger,' he said.

'Good. Nearly right, anyhow. Brave is facing up to stuff that you know is dangerous, because, obviously, if you don't know that it's dangerous it doesn't count. So a brave guy is someone who does something even though he knows he could get killed, right?'

'I suppose so.'

'Fine.' Paul had never heard Benny sound so harsh, even in his manic drill-instructor mode. 'So you're a brave man, and you face the terrible danger, and you get killed. So what about people who love you? Family and kids and wives and girlfriends? Obviously you're going to have to use a little imagination here, Carpenter; but how do you think they're going to feel when they hear you didn't make it this time? That you went chasing off to fight evil against overwhelming odds, knowing full well that you didn't have a chance, knowing full well there're these poor fools who love you, and you got yourself killed. What does that make you?'

Paul thought about that. 'A bastard,' he said.

'Exactly. You just did something that'd mean unbearable lasting pain for those who love you most. You put saving the world from some nebulous evil overlord, who's probably so crazy or so thick he'd have blown himself up anyway if only he'd been left alone, above the feelings of the people you owe most to, because they loved you. You thought more of saving a poor lost kitty stuck up a rickety tree than ruining the lives of everybody who ought to matter most to you. Are you a good man, or are you a reckless little shit? Rhetorical question,' Benny said, 'because there can only be one answer. Which is why,' he went on, 'Cas Suslowicz can't come and rescue us, because he's got an invalid sister who depends on him; and Theo van Spee's got children and grandchildren, and Countess Judy's got a couple of dozen ex-husbands who'd self-destruct if anything happened to her, and even Dennis Tanner's got a mother. But the three of us—' He laughed suddenly. 'Us three sad bastards. Ricky Wurmtoter's an orphan, and you can imagine why he has problems with lasting relationships. I've outlived all my relatives who were on speaking terms with me by a couple of centuries. And you – well, you don't need me to tell you. At your interview, the moment they set eyes on you, they knew. Because who the hell would ever be upset if you went off one day and never came back?'

It occurred to Paul to wonder whether the small child was somewhere in the cell with him, in the shadows where she couldn't be seen, grinning evilly and mouthing, *Told you so*. It'd be a pity if she wasn't, and missed all the fun. 'Right,' he said quietly. 'I think I see what you're getting at. But you're wrong.'

'Really? You think so?'

'Yes,' Paul said firmly, 'I do. All right, Sophie may have dumped me, and she never cared about me anyway. And my mum and dad went off to Florida, and they never had much time for me, and— But that still doesn't mean they don't love me; I mean, don't love me *at all*. After all, I'm their son. And if anything happened to me—'

He wondered if he'd just said something funny; an unintentional pun, maybe *son* was the Dwarvish word for turnip or something. 'I'm sorry,' Benny said, 'didn't mean to burst out laughing like that, I guess the stress is getting to me or something. But obviously you don't know, do you?'

Paul sighed. Not again. 'Apparently not,' he said. 'What is it this time?'

'Oh for – well, can't do any more harm, I suppose. Like, it's not as if either of us is ever going to get out of here, and pretty soon we'll have other things on our minds beside the fact that—' Paul waited while Benny sorted out his train of thought. 'What I mean to say is, if there was any chance that we'd escape and go on to lead normal, happy lives, then I wouldn't tell you this, because it'd screw you up permanently. But since we're irretrievably fucked in any case, you might as well know. To cut a long story—'

But Paul wasn't listening. 'Shut up,' he snapped. 'Please,' he added, remembering his manners. 'There, can you hear it?'

'Hear what?'

'Sort of panting, snuffling noise.'

'Oh. I assumed that was you.'

Couldn't be bothered replying to that. 'It's the dog,' Paul said. 'The little dog with the tartan flea-collar.' He could feel the grin flooding across his face. 'They're letting us go—'

'Doubt it,' Benny said, but Paul was down on his hands and knees, feeling for the source of the noise. He wasn't quite sure how it was supposed to work; would the dog open a door for them or lead them to the exit, or did he have to grab hold of it, or what? But hope, the one thing he'd felt sure he'd never feel again, was sloshing about inside him like too much cherryade. If only he could find the dog—

He found something, but he was pretty sure it wasn't the dog. Then someone slapped his face, very hard.

'Oh,' he said. 'Sorry.'

Then someone called him something in German. He didn't have to be a linguist to get the general meaning.

'Monika?' he said. 'Is that you?'

'*Ja*. And if you do not take your hand away *now*, I will—'

'Oh.' He shoved his hand behind his back, where he devoutly hoped it'd be out of the way.

'Monika, thank God. Have you come to rescue us?'

Silence.

'Oh,' Paul said again.

'It was my intention to rescue you,' Monika said stiffly. 'However, I do not think I have succeeded. I think I have been captured too.'

It didn't help that Benny started roaring with laughter. It was too dark to see to kick him, however, so all Paul could do was hiss, 'Shut up!' in what he hoped was the right direction. 'Sorry,' he went on, now thoroughly confused as to where everybody was. 'It was really nice of you to try, though.'

'It was nothing,' Monika replied. 'It was my duty. I have failed.' And then the snuffling noise started again, and Paul realised that it hadn't been the dog; just Monika, crying.

Marvellous, he thought.

'Serves her right, though,' Benny was saying. 'That's the other complete bitch about love. Not only does it really hurt when the irresponsible bastard goes off and gets killed, it makes people do really stupid, dangerous things, like trying to rescue the loved one from the dungeons of the Fey. Stupider than which,' he added savagely, 'it's impossible to get, outside of a general election.'

For a moment, Paul didn't understand at all. It didn't make sense. For one thing, Monika was a *car*. 'You mean,' he said, in a rather wobbly voice, 'you came here just to try and save—'

'*Ja*. What else could I do?' Snuffle, whimper. 'I could not just leave him here.'

'Monika—' Paul started to say, and then the incongruous pronoun hit him like a meteorite. Unless, of course, she'd been talking to Benny, in which case – *Fuck total darkness*, he thought bitterly, *it makes everything so bloody complicated*.

'And now,' Monika went on, 'it turns out that he is not even here. That is correct, yes?' she added.

'Um,' Paul said. 'Who do you mean?'

A snort from the middle distance. 'Ricky Wurmtoter, you clown,' Benny said. 'You don't think she came all this way just to keep you company, do you?'

Well no, Paul thought, *I suppose I didn't. Not in the part of my mind that deals with reality and stuff*. 'Mr Wurmtoter,' he repeated. 'He's your boyfriend.'

Howl of outrage, with a pronounced German accent. 'He is not my boyfriend. He is my brother.'

Shit, Paul thought; and he wanted someone to blame, since it looked like he was now doomed to spend all eternity in a small, dark place with someone he'd mortally offended. The only person he could think of to blame was Ricky Wurmtoter, for not having mentioned it. But, he was forced to admit, it wasn't the sort of thing that'd crop up in casual conversation: *Oh and by the way, my sister's a two-door hatchback.* His nerves were now so thoroughly jangled he couldn't even apologise; and as far as Paul was concerned, saying 'Sorry' came slightly more naturally than breathing. 'I didn't know that,' he said.

'It is quite all right,' Monika said, with a lack of sincerity you could've carved into a second Mount Rushmore. 'He does not talk about it. He is ashamed. It is understandable.'

Paul, however, wasn't paying attention. Something about what he'd just learned was bothering him; a detail that didn't fit. He couldn't quite figure out what it was, but it was itching, a raspberry pip of doubt under his mind's dental plate.

'Now perhaps,' Monika said, 'we should leave.'

This time, Paul was sure that Benny was going to do himself an injury, he was laughing so much. 'That's right,' he gasped between roars, 'let's leave. Why didn't I think of that? It's such a good idea—'

'Mr Shumway,' Monika said sternly, 'your behaviour is most inappropriate. It is not good manners to laugh so, and besides, I do not see what is so amusing. This is a serious matter.'

That more or less finished it, as far as Benny was concerned; Paul could hear his boots clumping against the wall as he rolled on his back. 'I do not think Mr Shumway is well,' Monika said, raising her voice so as to be heard. 'Perhaps it is the stress. I think maybe that you and I should be the ones to deal with this problem.'

Paul was beginning to see the joke himself. 'Fine by me,' he said. 'What did you have in mind?'

Pause. 'I was hoping you might have an idea,' Monika said awkwardly. 'You are, after all, a qualified *Ubermensch*. Surely this situation was covered in your basic training.'

'Not really,' Paul said. 'Mostly, it was more to do with

killing things and stuff. How about you?' he added hopefully. 'I mean, someone told me you were a proper sorceress before you got – before you, um, joined the firm. What sort of thing did you do?'

'My field of specialisation, you mean? Herbal remedies and ecological magic. In Germany, I was the leading authority on turning disused industrial facilities into flower-carpeted meadows.'

'Oh,' Paul said. 'I mean, that's really great, and I bet you were good at it. But before that: did you do all the trying-out-in-various-departments thing?'

'*Ja.* I received vocational training in alchemical transformation, intermediate healing and maintenance and repair of electrical and mechanical appliances. Also, I have an international baccalaureate in—'

'Fine,' Paul said. 'So, nothing that's going to be any help at all. In that case, we're screwed.'

'I can make a light,' Monika added hopefully.

'What? Right, that's good.'

'You would like me to make a light now?'

'*Yes.*'

He heard her mutter something; then the shock of the burning amber glow made him feel dizzy, and he had to shut his eyes and look away. When he turned back, however, there was only a small glow, as if someone had lit a match.

'That's it?' Paul asked.

At least now he could see Monika nod. 'The darkness in this room, it is very *dicht*; very dense,' she amended, 'or maybe tight, I am not sure which is the best word. It takes a very great effort—' Then she yelped, as though the notional match had burned her fingers, and the light went out. 'I am sorry,' she said.

'It's all right,' Paul said. 'You did fine, really.'

'Maybe in an hour, I can try again—'

'No, really.' No point, after all; the little pool of light had shown him nothing except her face, pale and drawn, and alarmingly worried. He'd suspected ever since he'd found himself in the cell that there was rather more to the darkness there than a simple absence of light. He could almost feel the pressure of it on his skin. 'Like I said,' he went on, 'we're screwed.'

Pause. 'You do not know how to proceed?'

'No.' He laughed. 'Well, that's not true, actually, I know exactly what to do. All it'd take would be for me to find the wall, by feel, and then get out the Acme Portable Door and set it up, and then we could just walk out of here back to 70 St Mary Axe. Only, I haven't got it any more.'

Silence. 'That,' Monika said, 'is unfortunate.'

'Yes,' Paul replied.

'This door – do you know where it is?'

'Sort of. I lent it to—' He stopped suddenly, before he could finish the sentence. *I lent it to your brother*; your brother who's still missing, presumed captured. Fat lot of good the Door did him, then. 'Anyway,' he said, 'we can't use it.' A surge of panic rose inside him, but he managed to fend it off. 'Benny,' he said, 'Mr Shumway. Any ideas?'

Benny giggled. 'Nope,' he said. 'Well, one. We can stay here till we die of old age, unless they aren't planning on feeding us. In which case, we'll be out of here in just over a week.'

Paul didn't follow. 'You mean, we slim down until we can crawl between the bars or something?'

'I was more thinking of starving to death,' Benny replied. 'But they'll feed us, or they've put some hex on this place so we don't need to eat. Letting us starve to death would be downright humanitarian, far as they're concerned. Which describes them pretty well, of course.'

'Really?'

'Oh yes. Great humanitarians, the Fey. Like, if you eat vegetables, you're a vegetarian. If you eat—'

'Mr Carpenter,' Monika interrupted. 'Who did you lend the Portable Door to?'

Panic. 'Um, I can't quite remember offhand. It was someone at the office—'

'Did you lend it to my brother?'

Fuck, Paul thought. 'Yes.'

'Ah. Then it is all right. If Dietrich has the Door, he will have escaped, which explains why he is not here. Once he finds out that we have come here, he will return and rescue us. So there is nothing to worry about.' She sounded perfectly calm, as though she was holding a signed contract with God's signature on it. 'We will wait for Dietrich to arrive, and everything will be fine.'

At that, Benny Shumway started howling like a wolf. 'Ignore him,' Paul said through gritted teeth (he'd never gritted his teeth before; it was actually a lot easier than he'd imagined). 'I'm sure you're right. Sooner or later—'

'Ah,' Monika interrupted. 'That will be him now.'

Benny broke off in mid-howl. Sure enough, something was happening; they could all hear a very faint buzzing noise, high and light and metallic, like an elven dentist's drill at the end of a long corridor.

'What the hell is that?' Benny muttered. Paul and Monika shushed him simultaneously. The sound was definitely getting gradually louder, and now there was another noise as well: the muffled yapping of a small, angry dog.

'Dietrich,' said Monika smugly. But Paul thought, *That can't be right, the Door doesn't make a noise, or at least I can't remember anything like that.* On the other hand, he'd never been in a place into which the Door opened, he'd always been the one going through it. So maybe—

The noise was very loud now; painfully loud, in fact, though whether it was the volume or the pitch that was making his head swim, Paul wasn't sure and didn't really care. He started shuffling on his backside away from the wall. That turned out to be a smart move a few seconds later, when it imploded.

Paul had no idea what hit him, though his best guess would have been either a brick or a chunk of stone. Whatever it was, it connected with the point of his left elbow, and it packed a solid punch. He couldn't hear himself scream over the clatter and thump of flying masonry, but he was fairly sure he had, and why not? If God hadn't meant us to scream, he wouldn't have given us horrendous pain.

Then the noise stopped, and there was a moment of intense, eerie silence. It was still as dark as a bag, even though the wall had been taken out; there was absolutely nothing to see apart from the faint glimmer of a pair of red eyes—

'Dietrich?' Monika said nervously. '*Bist du da?*'

Red eyes, Paul thought; then someone sniggered.

If Paul had had a pound for every time he'd heard that snigger, he could've afforded to quit work and join his parents in sunny Florida. In the past it had always been profoundly annoying and mostly at his expense. This time, though, it was the loveliest sound he could possibly imagine.

'Mrs Ta— Rosie?' he called out. 'Is that you?'

Repeat snigger; the sound of a heavenly choir telling

dirty jokes behind the celestial tabernacle. 'Well, it's not that soft git Ricky Wurmtoter,' said Mr Tanner's mum. 'Heroes,' she added scornfully. 'Couldn't bust their way into a bunny hutch with dynamite and jackhammers.'

For a moment Paul thought Monika was going to start a fight (which was probably, Paul reckoned, why Mr Tanner's mum had said it in the first place). But she confined herself to 'Dietrich is not with you?'

'Hell as like. Here, will one of you cop hold of this stupid dog? It's just peed all down my arm.'

Paul felt something wriggly and wet kicking against his chest. Fortunately, he overrode his instincts and grabbed it. It bit him. Thrice, simultaneously.

'How does this thing—?' he shouted, as a snowstorm of white light caught him up and spun him away.

Paul opened his eyes. Then someone smacked him round the face.

He was getting used to that, so he didn't let it get to him. Besides, his attacker had also snatched the dog out of his arms, and that was definitely a good thing. The light hurt worse than the smack or the dog bites.

Meanwhile, someone was calling him various names. 'Did the horrible man hurt mummy's baby, then?' she was saying. 'Nasty man.' He looked up and saw the woman whose house the portal was in. She was scowling at him and holding the little three-headed Yorkie, which was twisting and writhing in her arms, clearly frantic to get at him and bite him some more. Not that he minded.

Bugger me, he thought, *I escaped. I—*

Bad pronoun. Not I, we. Where are the others? 'Sorry,' he said. 'Um, have you seen my friends? A short bloke and a—' The woman wasn't paying attention. Paul looked round the room, which seemed to be pretty much the same as when he'd left it; wagon-wheel table, straw donkey, steel and canvas chair, even the empty mug he'd drunk from (except that the writing on it had changed from *World's Best Grandad* to *Dog-Hating Bastard*). But there was nobody else in it apart from himself, the woman and the dog.

Hell, Paul thought. 'Excuse me,' he said, over the dog's low growling, 'but I've got to go back. My friends, you see. They should've—'

But the woman shook her head. 'Portal's closed,' she snapped. 'Doesn't open again till nine tomorrow morning. And *you*'re not using it again, not after what you did to Twinkle.'

There didn't seem to be any point in arguing. Even if he kicked up a fuss or (unthinkable) tried to use force, he didn't know how the stupid thing worked, so hijacking it was out of the question, and the woman didn't look the sort who'd be amenable to sweet reason or pathetic pleading. Also, he'd had about as much of the woman and her horrible little dog as he could take. Nothing for it but to go back to the office in the morning and hope that somebody there would know what to do. He felt awful about it, but at least failure was something he understood. He stood up, mumbled a further, unheeded apology, and left.

Outside, as he'd expected and dreaded, there was no sign of a maroon Volkswagen Polo. Paul stood for a while staring at the place where it had been, then started to walk. He didn't know the way, of course; he had a rotten sense of direction, and Monika had done all the map-reading to get them there. He knew that there was a railway station in High Wycombe, but not where it was. Taxis, presumably, didn't happen out here. Some hero he'd turned out to be.

'Want a lift?'

She hadn't been there a moment ago. This time, just for a change, she was a drop-dead gorgeous redhead (usually she was a blonde or a brunette) and she was sitting in the driver's seat of a fireapple-red Porsche convertible. In spite of that, Paul was overjoyed to see her. 'You're all right,' he shouted. 'I thought—'

She grinned; and although her eyes were a bewitching emerald green, Paul realised that he much preferred them red. 'You do a lot of that,' she said. 'Just as well I'm always there to save your arse. You want a lift or not?'

He stayed where he was. 'The others,' he said. 'Benny and Monika. What happened? Where are they?'

Her eyes chilled a little. 'Three guesses,' she said. 'I had my work cut out getting you past the defences, and I've only got one pair of claws. And before you say it, no, I'm not going back.'

'But you've got to.'

'No, I fucking haven't. I haven't *got* to do anything – I'm a goblin, we're shallow and self-centred. Also,' she added, 'we're not bloody *heroes*.' She made the word sound faintly obscene. 'Have you got the faintest idea where you've just been?'

Still Paul didn't move. 'We can't just leave them there,' he said.

She scowled, and the beautiful girl turned into a goblin. Even the Porsche turned into a Lada, albeit a Lada convertible. 'You ungrateful little shit,' she said. 'For two pins I'd let you go back, only the portal's shut, so you can't. Where you've just been—' Her green skin paled to khaki. 'I don't even like thinking about it, and I'm a fucking *goblin*. You can get in, or you can walk home. Doesn't matter to me.'

It occurred to Paul that he was being truly obnoxious. 'Sorry,' he said. 'And, um, thanks. It was really—'

'Nice of me?' She leered at him. 'Just enlightened self-interest, that's all. Because one of these days—'

Paul managed to keep the shudder from showing, and opened the car door, glancing swiftly at the fuel gauge as he did so. The old running-out-of-petrol-in-the-middle-of-nowhere trick was hardly subtle, but neither was she. 'Thanks, anyway,' he said. Time to change the subject. 'So where was that? That place.'

Mr Tanner's mum started the engine and drove off. 'I guess it's something of an honour,' she said. 'Not many people end up in the dungeons of the castle of Grendel's Aunt. And nobody gets out again, ever. Except you.'

'Grendel's—?'

She nodded, and turned into a platinum blonde; probably absent-mindedness, though Paul knew she never gave up trying. 'Like in *Beowulf*, yes. Grendel's mum's sister, the only one of the family that's left now, apart from a couple of distant cousins in Canada somewhere. Presumably she's got a name of her own, but everybody just calls her Grendel's Aunt. Must be really annoying for her.'

Quite, Paul reflected; like being thought of as Mr Tanner's mum. 'But how does she come into it? Why was Ricky Wurmtoter—?'

She shrugged. 'Hero stuff, I suppose. Don't ask me. Maybe it's something to do with this stupid Fey civil war thing, or maybe it was just business. Nobody tells me anything, and I can't be arsed to find out. Now, how about stopping off somewhere for dinner? I know this really nice pub just outside Beaconsfield—'

'No,' Paul said quickly. 'Thanks,' he added. 'But really,

I'd just like to get home, if that's all right. I'm really tired, and—'

'And you've got a headache coming on,' said Mr Tanner's mum. 'Yeah, right. Why do I get the idea that you just don't trust me?'

'Because I don't trust you,' Paul said. 'Sorry.'

She grinned. 'You're a fool to yourself, you,' she said. 'But that's all right. When you get to my age, there's nothing gets the juices flowing like a challenge. Besides,' she added, 'you could probably do with an early night. After all, you'll have to explain to our Dennis in the morning how you managed to lose a company car.'

'Um.' Paul hadn't thought of that aspect of the matter. 'He'll understand, though, won't he? I mean, compared with losing Benny and—'

She shook her head. 'Where it costs the firm money, our Dennis never understands. If you're lucky, he'll just stop it out of your wages; in which case, you might be able to afford a cup of tea some time in the mid-2040s. Or he might get upset about it, you never know with our Dennis. Still, even that's better than being marooned in those dungeons.' She hesitated for a moment. 'Yup,' she said, 'on balance it's got to be better. Less cramped, for one thing.'

She was just kidding. Paul fervently hoped she was just kidding. Wasn't she? 'It'll be all right,' he said firmly. 'Once they go back and rescue Monika and Benny—'

'Dream on,' Mr Tanner's mum said. 'You're hopeless, you are. Probably why I like you,' she added, carelessly missing the gear lever with her hand and finding his knee instead. Paul yelped, and she let go. 'A romantic, I think the word is. Latin for idiot. No wonder they reckoned you'd make a good hero.'

Paul looked out of the window. 'That's not what Benny told me,' he said. 'He told me they chose me because you can't be a hero if anybody'd miss you if you died.'

'Is that what he said?' Mr Tanner's mum shrugged. 'I suppose I can see the sense in that. Me, though, I always thought that a real hero's the sort of person who does all the risk-taking and sword-fighting and death-defying because he enjoys it. Part romantic, like you, and part borderline psychopath. Only,' she added, 'your honest-to-God psycho enjoys killing 'cos he likes the blood or the screams or whatever, and that's not really the case with most of the heroes I've met; and I've met plenty, believe me. There's no real malice in them, no rage or anything like that. They just like the swirly capes and the white stallions and the jewel-hilted swords.'

'Ah,' Paul said. 'More in Zorro than in anger, you mean?'

Mr Tanner's mum sighed. 'You want to walk back to London from here, you carry on. I'm trying to have a serious conversation.'

'Sorry.'

'I was trying to explain,' she went on, 'why I don't think you're really cut out for the hero business; not as a vocation, I mean. But I think you could be up to doing hero-type things, if you absolutely had to. Just not in cold blood, nine to five-thirty, three weeks' holiday a year. I'm sorry I raised the subject, really.'

Paul was quiet for a while; then he said: 'Benny also told me he knew something really bad. Something about my mum and dad, I think. But he didn't get around to it.'

Mr Tanner's mum frowned. 'Lucky escape, then.'

'But if it was something I ought to know—'

She pulled a face. 'I know a bad thing about your parents.

They had a moron for a son. Bloody hell, why would anybody *want* to hear something like that?'

'Academic, really,' Paul replied. 'If Benny's stuck in there for good, I guess I'll never know.'

'Ignorance is bliss,' Mr Tanner's mum said sagely. 'Actually, I can think of a *lot* of things that're bliss, and ignorance doesn't even make the top one hundred, or even the top one hundred that don't involve live animals and raspberry jelly. Anyhow, the point is, you can pretty well guarantee that you're better off not knowing. Trust me.'

That word again. 'This civil war business,' he said, as casually as he could manage. 'You wouldn't happen to know what it's about, would you?'

She laughed. 'It's the Fey,' she said, 'they don't need a reason. I'd stay well clear of them, if I were you. Stick to goblins; so maybe we kill a human or two once in a while, and hollow out their skulls for chamber pots. We don't mean anything by it. The Fey, though; it's different with them. It's always *spite* where they're concerned. Jealousy, and not liking that everyone else has got what they reckon they deserve. I heard someone say once that the Fey think insult and injury go together like balti and naan; the one's just not quite right without the other. They give me the creeps, if you want to know.' She shrugged. 'Like it matters,' she said. 'If the little fuckers want to have a war, bloody good luck to them, and I hope they wipe each other out.'

'You don't like them much, then.'

'Not a lot, no. But hey, there's worse things.'

Paul could believe that, though it wasn't a comforting thought. 'I just wish,' he said wearily, 'that I didn't have to get involved, that's all. I've got enough problems as it is— I don't need things like that in my life.'

'Chicken,' Mrs Tanner's mum jeered. 'You don't know how lucky you are. Most men your age, they've got really scary stuff to contend with: mortgages and pensions and commitment and the patter of tiny feet. All you've got to worry about is dragons and the Fey.'

She dropped Paul off in the street outside his flat, and he managed to stop her following him in without using actual violence, which was progress of a sort. It was only when he'd kicked off his shoes and flopped down on the sofa that he began thinking about some of the things he'd seen and heard that evening. Somehow, the absence of Sophie was worse than ever; he wanted to shout at her for the things she'd said, or burst into tears and snivel, but he couldn't. When he climbed into bed and turned off the light, he felt for a moment as though he was back in the dungeon cell; except that this time he was alone. He stuck it as long as he could, then switched the light back on and looked round for a book. Unfortunately, the only one he could reach without getting out of bed was the copy of *Beowulf* that Benny had lent him, and he really wasn't in the mood. He got up and made himself a cup of tea; no sugar left, and the milk had things floating on the top. *Some hero*, he thought.

Some time after two a.m. he fell asleep on the sofa and dreamed restlessly about three-headed dogs and maroon Volkswagens, and a hospital ward full of sleeping children who wouldn't wake up.

Chapter Seven

'**M**r Carpenter,' said Countess Judy.

Delivered with the full force of the eyes, the most devastating modulation of the voice, it should have been enough to freeze him like a packet of sweetcorn. It explained why the Fey were reduced to fighting civil wars, since no external enemy would dare take the field against them. It was the Goddess in her triple aspect as Headmistress, Unapproachable Ice Princess and Aunt. It didn't work.

'But you can't just leave them there,' Paul protested, so loudly that they could probably hear him in the corridor. 'You've no idea what that place is like—'

'Actually,' she said, 'I have. I've been there myself.'

That was enough to shock him into silence. 'Oh,' he said, after a brief toe-curl of acute embarrassment; then he rallied and continued: 'In which case, you know how really, really bad it is in there.'

'Exactly.' Apart from her mouth, the Countess didn't move at all. Come to that, Paul could never remember having seen her blink. Not once. Like a painting. 'Which is why I sent you to rescue Mr Shumway. And now,' she went on, calm as a sea of mercury, 'you tell me that you were captured and barely managed to escape. Since you are the only member of the pest-control team still at liberty, we would seem to have run out of options. I take it that you're not volunteering to try again.'

She had him there; because, he realised with a pang of shame, nothing on earth would make him go back. The full force of it had only hit him when he'd woken up that morning; it had been dark, and for a split second when he opened his eyes and couldn't see anything he thought his rescue had just been a dream and he was still down there. He'd been so scared, he hadn't been able to move for about fifteen seconds.

'Well, it shouldn't be up to me,' Paul said, defensive as a child who knows it's in the wrong. 'I'm only a trainee, I haven't got a clue how you're supposed to go about breaking out of magic dungeons. But you, and Mr Suslowicz, and Professor van Spee—'

Still Countess Judy hadn't moved. At any other time, that would've been enough to freak Paul out on its own. 'You should know by now,' she said, 'that heroism is entirely species-specific. Humans can be heroes; so, under certain circumstances, can dwarves, like Mr Shumway. Giants, goblins and the Fey, however, are explicitly excluded. On account,' she added, with the ghost of a smile, 'of being officially classified as creatures of darkness; in other words, the enemy. That rules out Mr Suslowicz, Mr Tanner and myself; and Professor van Spee is four hundred and sixty-two years old, and suffers from chronic asthma. It's you or nobody, Mr Carpenter. I'm sorry, but there's nothing we can do. Mr Shumway knew the risks; likewise Mr Wurmtoter, although I notice you haven't mentioned him. In case you'd forgotten, he too is missing in action. As for Ms Wurmtoter – your car – she was a fully qualified practitioner before her transformation, and doubtless entirely aware of the perils of her chosen career. Professionals, Mr Carpenter, all three of them. We should honour their sacrifice and move on.'

Paul's anger didn't shrivel away, as it would normally have done. To his great surprise, it crystallised into cold, hard determination, and he hid it in the back of his mind, where even the Countess couldn't see it. 'All right,' he said. 'I see. Fine. I'm sorry for coming barging in here like this . . .'

A very slight shrug, maybe one and a half degrees per shoulder. 'That's quite all right, Mr Carpenter. Your reaction was entirely understandable and shows a laudable concern for the well-being of your colleagues. We pride ourselves on our team spirit here at JWW. And now,' she said, 'I must ask you to put your recent experiences behind you. As will be obvious, the loss of our pest-control department and our cashier places us in a most unfortunate position. We shall, of course, start advertising in the trade journals for suitable replacements; in the meanwhile, however, I'm hoping very much that you will agree to mind the store, as I believe the expression is.'

It took a couple of seconds for that to sink in. 'Me?' Paul whispered. 'Do the heroism *and* be the cashier? But I can't. I don't know how—'

Countess Judy raised her hand. 'My partners and I have every confidence in you,' she said. 'Mr Shumway was of the opinion that you were competent to practise as a pest-control operative, or else he'd never have released you early from your in-service training programme. We shall, of course, not undertake any major new commissions in that department until a full-time replacement has been found. However, I shall expect you to service all existing contracts in the interim, and deal with emergencies for our regular clients. As for the cashier's job, I appreciate that you will require an assistant; I thought perhaps that our new receptionist, Ms Horrocks, might be suitable. She has broad experience of office procedures, according to her résumé, and I'm sure Mr Tanner's mother would be prepared to cover for her on reception. I'm aware that officially she's on maternity leave, but if she's fit enough to break into the dungeons of the Traumburg, she ought to be up to sitting behind a desk for a week or so.'

The outright refusal died on Paul's lips like a microwaved slug. Working with Melze, the two of them together . . . Admit it, he told himself, it'd be fun. It'd be – well, like old times, when he was sharing an office with Sophie, and that had been enough to make him want to get up and go to work in the mornings, even though he knew perfectly well that what awaited him there was weirdness, goblins, bewilderment and fear. And Sophie – as he admitted it to himself, he squirmed – Sophie had never been half as much fun to be with as Melze, she'd never really been his *friend* – On the other hand, even he wasn't so naive as to think that Countess Judy would suggest something that he'd like without some ghastly, exploitative ulterior motive. On the third hand (pretty soon his train of thought was going to have more hands than Shiva, but what the hell) did that matter? Did it hell.

'All right,' Paul said. 'Yes, I think that's a great idea. After all,' he added, 'it's only going to be for a week or so.'

'Maybe a little longer,' Countess Judy said softly. 'Clearly we'll be taking our time, making sure that we find the right people. You can't rush really important decisions, like who you're going to be working intimately with for the foreseeable future.'

Paul looked up and stared at her, then looked away in confusion. She had a way of saying *intimately* that made him feel like a twelve-year-old boy trapped in a changing room with thirty extremely tall strippers. 'Um, yes,' he said. 'I think you're absolutely right there. So, let's do that. Fine.'

There was triumph and malice in her smile; not bad going, to fit so much into something so small. 'Perhaps you'd do me a favour and sound Ms Horrocks out on the idea,' she said. 'Though I'm sure she'll have no objections.'

Well yes, Paul thought, as he hurried down the corridor towards the front office. *Yes, I've been suckered into doing two difficult, horrible jobs, for no extra money. And yes, she was blatantly obvious about it, using Melze to bribe me with. Cool.*

(And Benny? And Monika, and even Ricky Wurmtoter, who was as weird as a blenderful of hummingbirds but who'd always been sort of nice to him? He shooed the thought away with the fly swatter of fatalism; if Countess Judy reckoned nothing could be done for them, she ought to know. They'd just have to stay there; locked away, along with Sophie, in the dungeon in the basement of his memory where he stashed all the inconvenient guilt. *I can't believe I'm doing this*, he told himself; but himself was remembering the last time he'd had lunch with Melze, the way she licked crumbs off the corner of her mouth, and thus wasn't in the mood to listen.)

She was answering the phone when he got there; she looked up and smiled, then carried on telling whoever it was that Mr Tanner was out of the office at the moment but would call him or her (or, since it was Mr Tanner and possibly a personal call, maybe it) right back as soon as he returned. Paul stood fidgeting, unable to decide on the exact choice of words; and as he waited, it suddenly occurred to him that maybe Melze wasn't going to be thrilled to bits and pieces at the thought of being stuck in the cashier's office all day, or at the prospect of working (*intimately*) with him. Hadn't thought of that; and neither, now he mentioned it, had Countess Judy. But it was a possibility, a distinct possibility—

'Hello, you,' Melze said, as the phone clicked back on its cradle. 'Haven't seen you to talk to for ages.'

She was smiling, and the warmth in her eyes hit Paul like a chocolate bullet. He'd seen smiles like that (mostly aimed at other people; pointed at *him* usually only when he was asleep) but this one was right up close, you could toast muffins over it. 'Been busy,' he mumbled. 'Bloody work, you know. How are you getting on?'

She shrugged. 'It's all right, I guess. I mean, everybody's really nice and I'm not rushed off my feet and stressed out, it's okay. But – well, it can get a bit boring sometimes. I'm not complaining, but it'd be nice if there was a bit more to it, you know?'

Paul gawped at her for at least two seconds before he managed to figure out how his voice worked. 'Odd you should say that,' he mumbled. 'How'd you fancy helping me out in the cashier's office?'

She squeaked. 'Great,' she said, 'I'd really like that.' Then she frowned, very slightly. 'What're you doing working in there, though?' she said. 'I thought you were supposed to be learning about glamour and stuff.'

'Change of plan,' he croaked. 'Benny Shumway's – on holiday for a bit, so I'm covering for him; and Countess Judy thinks I could use some help, which is absolutely true—'

Melze's eyes sparkled; they were saying, 'Thank you for choosing me,' and of course he couldn't tell her otherwise without sounding totally rude and ungracious. 'Fantastic,' she said. 'Who'll be doing reception instead of me? Oh, let me guess.' She twitched her nose. 'Old Red Eyes is back.'

Mr Tanner's mum, who'd snatched Paul out of the dungeons of the Fey; he really ought not to snigger about her behind her back. He sniggered. 'That's all right, isn't it?' he said.

'Absolutely,' she said. 'Rather her than me. When do I start?'

Melze was good at it, too, though Paul was hardly surprised at that. She knew which box file the pink requisitions had to go in after they'd been stamped, and how to reconcile the green inter-office transfers with the end-of-day print-outs, and which forms to use to record unused second-class stamps left over at the end of a VAT quarter. When he'd asked her how the hell she knew about that, she just grinned and said, 'Magic.'

Paul spent the whole of the morning in the cashier's office. He justified it to himself by saying that he was hiding there, in case some client turned up downstairs wanting a dragon slain or a vampire staked; but he'd never had much luck with lying, least of all with lying to himself. Just spending time with her was wonderful, in a way that being with Sophie had never been. He felt relaxed, unguarded, happy; he could almost be himself and not have to worry about how woefully inadequate that made him feel.

At five to one Melze shut the ledger he'd ostensibly been explaining to her (though the flow of information had been going in entirely the opposite direction) and said firmly: 'Lunch. Not that Italian sandwich place. I'm buying.'

'Fine,' he murmured. 'Where were you thinking of?'

She pursed her lips slightly. 'Didn't you say there's a great little Uzbek place just round the corner? The one you went to with Mr Wurmtoter.'

'Yes, but—' *Yes, but it's fiendishly expensive and really crowded, you haven't got a hope of getting a table unless your grandfather booked one for you on the day your father was born, and I can't remember offhand where it is, either—*

'I like Uzbek food,' she said briskly. 'Let's go.'

Paul led the way to the best of his recollection, until eventually Melze grabbed his sleeve, took him back the way they'd just come, and kept going until they got there. As he'd anticipated there was a queue almost out into the street, but she swept on past it, straight to a corner table, where the head waiter was waiting to take their order.

She ordered *behili palov* for two with *kalinji* bread and a pot of Tashkent black tea, and while they were waiting for it to arrive, she brought Paul up to date with her life story. Most of it, apparently, seemed to be about boring jobs and useless boyfriends; it surprised Paul that someone who had so much going for her should have had such a rotten time. Surely, if you were good-looking and bright and fun to be with, shouldn't the world do exactly what you wanted it to, like a well-trained dog? That had always been an article of faith, as far as he was concerned; his life had been a rolling sequence of disasters because he was an unsatisfactory mess, and if only he'd been better-looking/smarter/cooler/more tanned/better dressed, things would have been entirely different. He hadn't objected to the system particularly, once he'd figured out how it seemed to work. On the contrary, knowing he'd never really stood a chance had been a comfort, an excuse for not trying. But if there was no such system, no such rules, things suddenly became alarmingly arbitrary; and by implication, if he hadn't managed to get the things he wanted, it was somehow *his fault*, rather than the responsibility of his parents and remoter ancestors, for landing him with a set of genes and a station in life that meant there was no point in bothering to aspire— While these fraught issues were whizzing through his mind in a sort of frantic Brownian motion, he kept nodding and making little sympathetic noises as Melze embarked on an account of yet another disaster. Apparently he was doing the right thing, because as she talked, she was looking at him with a warm, thoughtful glow in her eyes, like a predatory angel.

'And basically, that's it,' she said; and Paul, looking up with a mouthful of *behili palov*, concluded that the briefing was complete. 'So,' she went on, 'that's all my gory details. How about you?'

He shrugged and swallowed rice. 'Oh, nothing to tell, really. I mean, like I told you, I've been here about nine months now and I suppose I'm sort of getting used to it. Split up with my girlfriend just before you arrived – she reckoned that she couldn't stand the sight of me any more, and I guess I can see her point. That's all, really.'

Melze pulled a face. 'You'll have to do better than that,' she said. 'Like, what are your plans for the future, where do you reckon you're going, all that sort of thing. And don't say you don't know, because I don't believe you. I know what you're like, always the quiet one with loads going on just below the surface. For instance, I don't believe you just sort of drifted into this magic thing by sheer fluke and then found out you had the gift or whatever you call it, straight out of the blue. Something like that, you must've known all along that you were different, special.'

The correct answer was, of course, 'No.' It wasn't the

answer that Paul gave. Instead, he found himself hinting, implying, suggesting; in fact, if the impression he was giving was anything to go by, he was a pretty enigmatic and fascinating piece of work. *Effective magic*, commented a tiny little voice somewhere in the back of his mind; *see, you can do it if you try*. He was telling her what she wanted to hear, though, and surely that was a good thing.

And then there came a moment when neither of them were talking. His hand was on the table, he wasn't sure how it had got there; and slowly, deliberately, she reached out her hand toward it. He saw it and looked at her; she was staring, no, gazing at him, and he was caught in her regard like a rabbit in headlight beams.

The pain shot up from his wrist into his elbow, from there to his shoulder. It was like various sorts of pain he'd actually experienced, and others he'd only imagined – toothache, crushing, slicing, burning, stinging, electrocution, tearing, stabbing. It punched the air out of his lungs and stopped his heart for a second, until a reflex cut in and made him pull his hand away. The pain stopped immediately, though the shock lingered. His hand and arm were numb for a couple of seconds, and then the pins and needles set in.

'What's the matter?' Melze said, and her voice was slightly panicky. 'Are you all right?'

'I'm fine,' Paul snapped. 'I don't— Sorry, I just got this pain in my hand, like a twinge or something.' Inside him, a little voice protested that if that had been a twinge, the First World War had been a slight difference of opinion. 'Cramp,' he said. 'That's all.'

'Oh.' She laughed; it sounded like a stone falling down a well. 'That's all right, then. I thought I'd – well, upset you, or something.'

It was only then that he realised she'd touched his hand. *Shit*, he thought; *what a way to react, how unbelievably romantic.* 'No, no, no, no, really,' he bleated, 'like I said, it was just cramp, I get it sometimes. Really,' he added, in case there was any lingering ambiguity.

'That's awful,' she said sympathetically. 'Sounds like one of those repetitive strain things. You should see a doctor.'

He did the martyr's can't-be-bothered shrug. 'It's not so bad,' he said.

'It looked pretty nasty,' Melze replied, looking slightly sideways at him. 'If it *is* repetitive strain whatsit, you can have physiotherapy, they give you this sort of brace to wear. My aunt had it, and they cleared it up in no time.'

'Ah,' Paul said. 'I'll have to give that a try, then.' He was painfully aware that he was blushing like a beetroot. 'I'm really sorry if I startled you,' he said.

'That's all right.' She made a show of looking at her watch. 'Damn, it's ten to two, we'd better be getting back.' She looked up, and at once the waiter materialised, like a Romulan cruiser decloaking, and handed her the bill. She produced a card, apparently out of thin air, and he went away. 'Well,' she went on, 'thanks ever so much for showing me the ropes this morning.'

'My pleasure,' he said. 'Thanks for lunch.'

Melze nodded. 'We must come here again,' she said. The waiter came back with her card and the receipt for her to sign, and a moment or so later they were outside on the pavement. Paul's legs still felt distinctly wobbly, but he ignored them.

He came with her as far as the door of the cashier's office, then muttered something about some bits and pieces he had to see to, and turned away. 'See you later,' she called after him. He stopped, but didn't look round. 'You're coming with me to the Bank, remember.'

'Oh, right. See you, then.'

He'd forgotten about that little chore. Not something to look forward to; not terribly romantic. Even he couldn't visualise himself strolling hand in hand with her through the featureless darkness of the Kingdom of the Dead. Still—

Paul realised that he'd stopped, for some reason he couldn't fathom, outside the door of the closed-file store. It was a spooky sort of place at the best of times, and ever since the weird episode with the bicycle, he'd steered well clear of it. Now, however, he felt an odd urge to push the door open and go in. He fought it down, but as he walked away he was aware of a feeling both familiar and unexpected: guilt, as though he'd just turned his back on a friend in need.

Having nowhere else to go, he went back to his office. The door was open. Countess Judy was sitting at the desk, in Sophie's old chair.

'There you are,' she said, frowning a little.

'Sorry,' Paul said automatically. 'Um, have you been waiting—?'

A tiny head gesture on her part indicated that it wasn't important. 'Presumably you've been briefing Ms Horrocks about running the cashier's office.'

He nodded. 'That's all right, isn't it?' he added. 'You said—'

'Perfectly all right,' she replied. 'Thank you. However, if you have a moment—'

Bugger, Paul thought. 'It's not dragons, is it?' he said quickly. 'Because I think I've done something to my hand, and—'

She shook her head. 'Not dragons,' she replied, with a

faint smirk. 'Nothing like that. Christine needs someone to help her move a filing cabinet, that's all.'

'Ah.' It was a mark of how jangled Paul's brain had become that it took him a moment to remember who Christine was: Mr Tanner's secretary, efficient woman, talked a lot. 'No problem,' he said, 'I'll get on it right away.'

'Splendid.' Countess Judy stood up. 'And when you've done that, you might care to spend a few minutes reviewing the chapter in the procedures manual about baiting chimeras. A client faxed us this morning asking for advice on how to deal with them. And don't forget,' she added, 'about the banking.'

No, mum, Paul thought, and set off for Christine's room.

'Mind the paint,' Christine said for the seventh time. Paul nodded, too exhausted to apologise. The cabinet was heavy, he wasn't used to hard physical labour, and the room was too damn small anyhow. 'No, doesn't look like it's going to fit. Try it the way you had it the first time.'

He'd assumed it'd be easy, now that he could use magic; but it wasn't allowed. Apparently, the cabinet had been festooned with filing charms, so that all you had to do was open a drawer at random and drop in a piece of paper, and when you looked for it next, it'd be in the right folder, in alphabetical order, neatly tagged to the rest of the bundle. The charms didn't work, of course; no force on earth, natural or supernatural, can keep stored paperwork from reverting to a state of chaos. But once they'd been applied they couldn't be removed, and they didn't mix well and play nicely with any other forms of magic. Using telekinesis on a charmed cabinet would assuredly have all sorts of bloodcurdling side effects. Hence the need for boring old human muscle.

'That'll have to do,' Christine said eventually. 'Right, thanks, you'd better get on and do the banking. Don't want Mr Tanner getting all upset, do we?'

Too bloody right we don't, Paul thought, and he scampered down the stairs to the cashier's office.

While he'd been playing with office furniture, Melze had sorted out the overcrowded in-tray, done all the reconciliations, fed all the totals into the computer, tidied the windowsill and done something subtle but effective with her hair. Paul didn't understand that sort of thing, but the net result made him forget what he was going to say and walk into the edge of the desk.

'Is it that time already?' Melze looked at him, and he saw a shadow of apprehension in her eyes. 'It probably sounds a bit feeble, but I'm not looking forward to this.'

Paul grinned. 'Me neither. But it's not nearly as scary as it looks. Just – well, do as I do, and don't look round. Oh, and don't talk to anybody except Mr Dao, he's the cashier; and whatever you do, don't let them get you a cup of tea. That's really important. Okay?'

She nodded. 'I think so,' she said.

'Ready?'

'As I'll ever be.'

'Fine.' Paul started flipping back bolts and turning keys. 'You'll soon get the hang of it,' he said in a hollow voice. 'All right, then, on three. One, two—'

He took a long, deep breath, checked his pocket to make sure that the baseball cap was there, and stepped through the door. On the other side was that same total absence of light and colour that he remembered so clearly – odd, that the essence of nothing could be etched so vividly into his mind. This time, though, it was perceptibly colder. He could feel pain in his knuckles and toe joints, and a harsh pressure on either side of his head. He didn't dare call out, 'This way' or 'Keep up', let alone turn round to see if Melze was there. That made him feel bad, because surely it was his duty to protect her. But, he rationalised, it wouldn't do either of them any good if he broke the rules and got trapped in here for ever.

At least the dead seemed glad to see him. Distant cousins and venerable friends of the family who'd never had a civil word for him while he was alive came bustling up through the darkness to greet him. Ignoring them was easy enough, since he'd never had anything to say to them while they'd been alive. After a while they gave up and drifted away. He didn't like to think what Melze was going through; for all he knew, she'd lost people she genuinely cared for, which would make ignoring them very hard indeed.

Today's blood sacrifice was the usual: rabbit-out-of-a-hat. Paul had tried his best not to think about it all day, and that had only made it worse. He'd never actually tried doing the conjuring trick, since that would've involved admitting to himself that at some stage he was going to have to do this terrible thing. A substantial part of him was hoping that when he unfolded the baseball cap and felt inside it, there'd be nothing there; in which case, he hoped, he could just turn round and go back. But as soon as he thrust in his fingers, they connected with soft, sleek fur. *Bugger*, he thought. True, it wasn't the first time he'd killed something: he'd sat on a wyvern, so there was already blood on his hands, or on some part of his anatomy. Even so—

Paul got a grip on what felt revoltingly like a teddy bear's paw and heaved. Out came the rabbit, squealing and thrashing, and he discovered that he was holding it by one hind leg. Cursing himself, the rabbit and the world in general, he fumbled in his other pocket for the knife. It was there, but it had managed to get wedged underneath his bunch of keys, and the keys had poked their way through the pocket lining. *Not now*, he thought bitterly as he tugged, *please not now, this isn't a good time*. Then something whacked him hard on the nose.

He reared back, but not far enough; the rabbit's free hind leg socked him again, this time scrabbling across his top lip. His hands automatically let go, and the rabbit arched its back and kicked furiously in mid-air before landing on all fours and scooting away out of sight. He opened his mouth to swear and thought better of it. Then he recognised a coppery taste in his mouth. Blood. Nosebleed.

'Good afternoon.' Mr Dao was standing beside him. 'Thank you,' he added, bowing gracefully. 'A rare treat. We are most grateful.'

Paul stared at him in horror, as a drip of blood trickled down his chin and fell away. 'I didn't mean—' he mumbled. 'Accident. The rabbit—'

'No doubt.' There was a flicker of amusement in Mr Dao's deep eyes. 'There is a saying on your side of the Divide, I believe: never work with children and animals. You are obviously a brave man.' He licked his lips, like a cat. 'To business,' he said. 'The cheques to be paid in?'

'Right.' Paul shivered, and reached behind him. Someone, presumably Melze, put a wad of papers into his hand, and he passed them over. Mr Dao took them from him and bowed again.

Mr Dao was looking past him. 'Your assistant, presumably?' he said. 'Perhaps you would care to introduce me?'

Cursing himself for his carelessness, Paul muttered,

'Demelza Horrocks, she's standing in for Benny Shumway. I'm just, um, showing her how it's done.'

'Delighted,' said Mr Dao. 'You probably can't imagine how great a pleasure it is for us to see new faces here; especially,' he added with a dignified smile, 'such a charming face as this. Would Miss Horrocks care for a cup of——?'

'No,' Paul growled. 'And I've told her, so—'

Mr Dao shrugged. 'Naturally,' he said. 'You must excuse the lapse. Now, unless there's any further business?'

Paul shook his head, and Mr Dao abruptly vanished, leaving no trace that he'd been there at all. Paul stood still for a moment; he very much wanted to throw up, but he reckoned that he'd been far too liberal with his bodily fluids already. He swallowed a couple of times, then slowly turned round. The feeling of nausea stayed with him until the last bolt had been fastened and the last key turned.

'Sorry,' he said, finally daring to look and see if Melze was there. 'It's not usually that bad. It was my fault, I—'

She was looking puzzled. 'What was bad about that?' she said.

Paul opened his mouth, but no words came out.

'All right,' she was saying, 'it's a bit of a chore, but what the hell, it's out of the office. Why are you looking at me like that?'

'But—' Paul narrowed his eyes. Melze was still looking at him as though there was something she'd missed. 'What exactly did you see in there?' he asked.

The question clearly puzzled her. 'Well,' she said, 'we went through the door, and then we were in this long corridor, with carpet and doors on either side, fire extinguishers, the usual stuff. Then we crossed a courtyard and you knocked on a door, and this nice old Chinese bloke opened it. Then you gave him the cheques, and he asked if I'd like a cup of tea. You said no — which is fair enough, I mean, we've got things we need to be getting on with, we can't sit around drinking tea all day. And then we came back. That's it.'

'Oh,' Paul said. 'That's—' He didn't know what to say. 'That's all right, then. Only, um, I get claustrophobic in long, narrow corridors. I thought you might, too.'

Melze shook her head. 'It's sweet of you to be concerned,' she said, 'but I'm all right like that. It's heights I can't be doing with, so I'm glad there weren't any stairs or anything.'

'You didn't see—' As he heard himself say the words, he wished he hadn't spoken. 'You didn't see any rabbits, anything like that?'

Her expression was a study in bewilderment. 'Rabbits?'

He nodded. 'White rabbits.'

'Oh, I see.' She laughed, a little. 'You mean, great big white ones in waistcoats with watches, saying, *Oh my ears and whiskers*. Yes, it was a bit like that, wasn't it? All those doors and stuff.'

Paul could probably have found an excuse to hang around the cashier's office for a bit; judging by Melze's expression when he excused himself and left, maybe she was expecting him to. But he wanted to get out of there as quickly as possible.

There was, he told himself as he clumped slowly down the stairs, an obvious explanation, if only he wasn't too stupid to figure it out. Clearly she hadn't seen the same things as he had. Perhaps it was a magic thing. Perhaps you only saw the nothingness and the blood and heard the dead relatives if you had the magical knack. Melze didn't, so maybe she saw some kind of interdimensional screen saver, put there so that the paranormally challenged wouldn't realise where they were and start panicking. That made sense, surely—

(Paul stopped; something had caught his eye. He looked round, but everything seemed to be as close to normal as it ever was. Paranoia, he told himself; a great excuse but a lousy lifestyle.)

It made sense, all right; it made sense of a whole lot of things. For the last few hours, he'd been trying hard not to think about the sudden and savage jolt of pain he'd felt when Melze had touched his hand; because there was a limit to how much bewilderment he could handle at any one time, and his instinct was to ignore the thing that disturbed him most. But suppose; suppose it was a condition of this magical stuff that people who had it were confined, where what the TV chat shows call interpersonal relationships are concerned, to their own kind. It wasn't the first time he'd touched a girl, after all; but Sophie had been One Of Us, and Melze wasn't. A great deal might be accounted for in those terms. Wouldn't it be interesting, and convenient, if he could dump the blame for his pathetic record in matters of true love on the sneaky little sorcery gene? If there was some sort of inbuilt defence mechanism in his genetic whatchamacallit to stop him forming attachments with people who couldn't do magic— And he could explain why the defences had lapsed long enough for Melze to get to the point of buying him lunch: she was spending all her time in a magic environment and as far as those pesky genetic watchdogs were concerned she probably smelt of the stuff enough to slip past the perimeter defences. How about that for a theory, huh?

As Paul developed and refined his shiny new hypothesis,

it did occur to him that pretty well every such rationalisa-
tion he'd come up with since joining JWW had turned out
to be hopelessly wrong. Even so; at some point, he was
bound to figure something out right. Question was, did he
want this to be that one time? If it transpired that he couldn't
touch Melze without feeling as though he'd just put his
fingers in a coffee grinder, was that a good thing or a bad
thing?

Good question.

He'd reached the bottom of the central staircase and was
about to turn left down the corridor that led to his office.
Something was wrong.

That wasn't as unusual, or as scary, as all that. Paul knew,
though he'd never actually done a scientific test, that the
number of steps in the central staircase varied; some days
there were more than others. That was fine. The geography
of 70 St Mary Axe was beguilingly flexible. Rooms came
and went, or moved, like sunflowers, to catch the daylight
(with an attendant saving in electricity that no doubt
delighted Mr Tanner). He'd heard it said that Humphrey
Wells, the disgraced ex-partner now serving the firm in the
capacity of Xerox machine, was in the habit of shortening
corridors when he was running late for a meeting, sometimes forgetting to put them back again afterwards. Logically,
if rooms appeared or vanished, the staircases would have to
be edited accordingly, or else they'd overrun or fall short.
Likewise, it was widely rumoured that when Countess Judy
and the creative-and-media department held a meeting with
their opposite numbers from another firm or organisation,
the resulting build-up of superheated glamour had a nasty
tendency to leak into the environment, changing the colours
and textures of curtains, carpets, wallpaper and other

glamour-sensitive fixtures and spontaneously creating Constable prints and trailing maidenhair ferns. All that sort of thing he'd learned to take in his stride or ignore, just as he no longer needed to remember to keep his hands and the end of his tie at least eighteen inches from the teeth of the shredder when it was switched on, if nobody had used it for a day or so. This thing he'd noticed, coming down the stairs and now at the foot of them, was something else. That was probably bad.

Then he saw it. Leaning against a wall, butter-wouldn't-melt-in-its-saddlebags, was the bicycle that had accosted him in the closed-file store. Staring at it now, he began to remember seeing it about the place on other occasions, before it had spoken to him; but of course he'd assumed then that it was just somebody's bike, an ecologically friendly alternative to Tubes and taxis. He thought for a moment, then turned to face it.

'Are you following me?' Paul said.

Silence. *Ridiculous*, he said to himself. *I'm talking to a bicycle.*

'Well?' he said.

'Yes,' the bicycle replied.

He thought about that. It was old and battered, but it was a Raleigh: good, long-established British make, you ought to be able to take its word at face value. 'Why?' he asked.

'You've got to let her go, do you understand? You've got to. It's not right.'

Paul frowned. 'That's what you told me the last time, right?'

'Yes.'

'Oh. Thanks for being consistent, anyway.'

'Don't try being funny with us. Let her go, or we'll kill you. That's a promise.'

'Oh, for pity's sake,' Paul sighed. 'Just for once, can't somebody *explain* around here? Who have I got to let go? Just tell me. Please?'

'You know,' the bike answered sullenly. 'Don't pretend you don't – it won't save you.'

Suddenly, Paul felt very tired. 'Humour me,' he said. 'Look, if you care enough about this person to kill me, surely it's not too much trouble just to say her name. Right?'

Silence. You can sometimes gauge the flavour of silences by how long they last. In this case, it tasted like embarrassment.

'We can't,' said the bicycle.

'Sorry. You can't what?'

'Say names,' the bicycle replied awkwardly. 'We just can't, that's all. But you know who we mean.'

'No, I bloody *don't*,' Paul wailed. 'Come on,' he went on, forcing himself to get a grip, 'don't give up on me, give me a clue. How'd it be if I said some names and you answered yes or no?'

'No names,' grunted the bicycle. Was it, just possibly, scared? 'We don't hold with them. And besides, you—'

'I know, right. Only I don't. Okay, how about descriptions? You know. Old, young, height, hair colour, glasses or no glasses—'

Now the bike sounded palpably uncomfortable. 'That wouldn't help. We do not understand – appearances. We deal only in essentials. We cannot see,' it concluded painfully.

'Oh,' Paul said. 'I'm sorry.' *Hang on*, he thought, *it was threatening me. Where does it say in the rules that I've got to be an equal-opportunities victim?* 'Well, there must be something.

I mean, you can recognise me, right? How do you do that?'

'By essentials,' the bicycle told him, as though it was the most obvious thing in the world. 'We would know you in any place, at any time, in any guise. And if you don't let her go, we will hunt you down—'

'Yes, fine,' Paul snapped. 'Let's try it your way, shall we? What are the, um, essentials of this person I've got to let go?'

Pause, as though the bike was marshalling its thoughts. 'Waterfalls,' it said. 'A suddenness. The urgency dwindles as the perception broadens, but gold is soft under the hammer. A Wednesday, at the end of a long alley of darkness. Her hair, like water lilies. The sharp edge is brittle. A thrice-used tissue, tucked into a sleeve, and then for ever.'

Paul counted to five and then said, 'You what?'

'You heard us,' the bicycle growled at him. 'You must let her go immediately, or she will die and so will you. We will kill you, because you will not suffer yourself to live. You will *ask* us to kill you, and we will oblige.'

'Really?'

'Yes.'

'Great.' Paul took a deep breath, then smiled. 'Jones,' he said.

The bicycle wobbled slightly. 'Do not attempt—'

'Parkinson. Sinclair. Cohen. Ivanovitch. Rashid. Banerji.'

'Traitor! We defy you!'

Paul sighed. 'Lennon,' he said. 'McCartney. Harrison. Starr.' He grinned. 'Rumpelstiltskin.'

With a scream, the bicycle sprang away from the wall and reared up on its back wheel. For a split second Paul was convinced that it was about to charge him; then it crashed down onto two wheels, back-pedalled frantically, and shot away backwards down the passage that led, more often than not, to the stationery cupboard.

Paul was too weary to do anything more energetic than shrug. You had, he decided, to take the broad view in these matters; death threats from a blind push-bike that scarpered like buggery when you recited the names of the Beatles were probably the least of his problems.

Even so. *You must let her go immediately, or she will die.* He didn't really want to have to worry about that, but he had a feeling he was going to. All he'd managed to find out, he realised, was that this person he had to let go was female.

Let go. *But I can't let anybody go, I'm not holding anybody. Am I?*

He thought about that as he sat at his desk, waiting for it to be five-thirty. *Am I holding anybody?* he wondered. *Not in the way you'd normally understand it, but in some other way? Who am I connected to who's female?*

Fortunately, the gender thing made it easier; for various reasons, Paul simply didn't know a lot of women. *Let's see*, he thought. *There's Melze; and Sophie, except she left me, does that count as letting her go? There's Mum, but she's in Florida. Countess Judy? Or what about Mr Tanner's mum? Or Monika — she's being held, sure enough, and where she is there's every chance she could die, but there's absolutely nothing I can do about that. Who else? Christine?* A thrice-used tissue, tucked into a sleeve, and then for ever. *Well, that could be any one of them, obviously.* Unless the thrice-used-tissue bit was some kind of subtle, riddling metaphor. He thought about that and decided he really didn't want it to be. *Yuck*, in fact. He remembered that he was supposed to be reading up on chimeras, and then it was twenty-five past five.

Long day. When he got home, he'd have a leisurely bath

and an early night, because – because it was only yesterday that he'd been trapped in the dungeons of the Fey, with two people he'd somehow resigned himself to never seeing again. He thought about that. *Probably a good thing*, he told himself, *that I can do that, it's probably a knack or a survival instinct. Soldiers in war must be able to do it, when their friends are suddenly killed in the middle of a battle.*

What if I were to quit? What could Mr Tanner actually do to me that'd be worse than this? Turn me into something nasty and inhuman? Seems to me I'm doing a pretty good job of that on my own.

His hand, Paul realised, was in his jacket pocket, and had found something: a matchbox. He wondered what on Earth it was doing there, then remembered; it seemed so long ago now, the day he'd sat on the funny little dragon, and Mr Tanner's mum had scooped the little red jewel out of the poor dead bugger's brains. *It shows you stuff you can't normally see*, she'd told him. *If you practise, you can learn to see useful things. Otherwise, it just shows you your own true love, so it's a bit wasted on you.*

Nearly five-thirty – he ought to be making a move. But he slid the matchbox open and took out the stone. It lay on his palm, glowing faintly red, then green, like a small piece of gravel from the planet Krypton. *If I practise*, he told himself, *I'll learn to see useful things. Otherwise—*

The stone was looking back at him; a neat trick, for something with no eyes. He could feel it, scanning him, downloading his thoughts, deciding something—

Where do you want to go today?

Paul sat up a little bit straighter. 'I'd like to see something useful, please,' he said.

The stone grew, from a loose chipping to a potato to a

basketball to a boulder that filled all the space between floor and ceiling, until it was so big he couldn't see it any more. The green glow was warm, and crackled softly with static. *Please wait.*

I'd like to see something useful, he thought. *I'd like to see if Monika and Benny are all right. I'd like to see why touching Melze hurts so much. I'd like to see what I've become, and why that bloody bicycle's threatening to kill me. I'd like to see why my parents went off to Florida without me, and if you happen to do winning lottery numbers, that'd be pretty useful too.*

The green light went black; so black that Paul thought for a moment that he was back in the dungeon. Before he could work up a really good head of panic, however, light seeped in from the edges, crawled and trickled inwards in white swirls and worm-casts, until the only black left was letters on a page of writing.

Chimeras for Dummies, it read. *Chapter One. Big, scary monsters with teeth, and why they're sometimes bad news.*

'Thank you so much,' Paul muttered, closing his hand round the stone. The writing vanished, the world came back, and he put the stone away in the matchbox and closed the lid.

Chapter Eight

The chimera people turned up at nine-fifteen; two solid, grey-haired, double-chinned men and a thin, elegant woman, who wanted to know how to keep fabulous winged monsters out of the ventilation shafts of their new leisure complex. Paul smiled, tried to look like he knew what a chimera was, and said, 'Chicken wire.' That seemed to satisfy the clients, who thanked him and went away again. Easy peasy.

And that was it; nothing to do till lunchtime. Nothing to do except sit behind his desk and wait for something to happen.

It didn't take long for Paul to realise that he'd misjudged being chased by goblins, tortured by the Fey, threatened by bicycles and sent to the next world for the petty-cash float. None of them were fun, by any means, but they were all a whole lot better than being bored to death. He didn't dare leave the office or read the paper or get out a pack of cards and play patience, for fear that someone would come in and find him. If he went to Christine or Julie and confessed that he had nothing to do, there was every chance that they'd tell Mr Tanner, who could be relied on to find him something truly horrible to occupy himself with. If Sophie had still been there, of course, they could have had one of their brittle, fragmented conversations; but she wasn't. He had the use of a telephone, but he couldn't think of anybody who'd want to talk to him.

This is stupid, he told himself; *this is my lifespan, something I'll never get again, being frittered away like it's not worth anything.* In desperation, he dragged down the office-procedures manual and opened it at random –

Mountains, Movement of: *It is the responsibility of the individual practitioner, not the firm, to make certain that all necessary planning consents are in place before mountains are moved in accordance with clients' instructions. Your attention is specifically directed to approval of reserved matters (access, environmental issues, landscaping &c) which may need to be resolved before work can be commenced. Indemnities should be obtained in advance from the client in respect of curses, blood feuds &c arising from the displacement of troll and goblin colonies caused by mountain relocation. Any buried treasure, abandoned dragon hoards, lost dwarf cities, petroleum, natural gas and other mineral resources uncovered during the removal process remain the property of JWW, not the individual practitioner. In the event that mountain removal awakes a nameless evil from its slumber in the bowels of the earth, it is your responsibility to ensure that the firm's insurers are informed at the earliest possible opportunity.*

The hell with it, Paul thought. *If they fire me, so much the better. If Mr Tanner turns me into an earwig, I'll be better off. Earwigs don't have to put up with this sort of—*

'Mr Carpenter.' He hadn't heard her come in. He dropped the book on the desk and it closed with a snap. 'I hope I'm not disturbing you.'

Paul shook his head and smiled feebly. 'No, really,' he said. 'Um, what can I do for you?'

As usual, Countess Judy looked completely different from

how she'd looked the day before. Today, she was tall, long and almost painfully thin; her hair was bright silver, to match her eyes, and flowed down over her shoulders like lava from an ice volcano. She wore eight rings on her fingers, each ring silver and studded with pale jewels. 'Yesterday you were asking about the possibility of taking action to rescue Mr Shumway and your car. At that time I told you that there was nothing we could do. On reflection, I believe there is a procedure that might be worth trying.'

That was different. Paul sat up; the palms of his hands were itching, and he could feel his heart beating. 'Right,' he said, 'that's great. What do you want me to do?'

The Countess's forehead clouded a little. 'I appreciate your offer, Mr Carpenter,' she said, 'but in this instance I hardly feel that it would be appropriate for you to be directly involved. What I have in mind involves the use of inter-mediaries, to negotiate a settlement with the dissidents.'

'Oh,' Paul said; and then he thought, *Better still. In fact, bloody wonderful, someone else'll have to go and I won't.* 'Absolutely,' he said. 'Great idea.'

'However,' the Countess went on, 'in light of your wish to be involved, you may care to assist in the overall coordination of the project. Unless,' she added, glancing quickly at the closed book on Paul's desk, 'there are other matters that require your attention.'

'Nothing that can't wait,' Paul replied crisply. 'I mean, I saw those chimera people earlier today, so that's all done and dusted; and Me— Ms Horrocks can do the banking on her own if I'm not back in time to give her a hand.'

'Splendid,' Countess Judy said. She stood up, and Paul couldn't help but notice what a perfectly composed picture she made, framed by the doorway behind her. Instinct, presumably. 'In that case, I'll trouble you to arrange an initial meeting with the intermediaries. The address and contact details are in the file.' What file? *Oh*, Paul realised, *that file*: the one on the desk that wasn't there ten seconds ago. 'Please report to me as soon as you've made contact.'

When she'd gone, Paul picked up the file and pulled out a sheaf of papers, neatly held together with a treasury tag. The first thing he came to was a blank sheet of headed notepaper; rather grubby, crumpled and carefully smoothed flat.

EKD AGENCIES

– followed by an address in Bermondsey; a factory or ware-house, by the look of it. There was also a phone number. He braced himself and dialled the number. No reply.

Next in the bundle was a handwritten note; very small, cramped, pointy writing, done with an incredibly fine-nibbed pen. Mostly it was dates and numbers, but at the bottom were a few sentences. It cost Paul much squinting and the foundations of a world-class headache before he could make them out;

> *Do not telephone; personal visit essential. Ask for the boss, who will not be there. Extremely suspicious, secretive, nervous and annoying. Mostly lies, in any case. Wednesday.*

Apart from that, the bundle was mostly old JWW invoices, marked 'Paid': for services; various matters; legal and financial advice; emergency supplement 25 per cent; interim account; for the attention of Derek. The only other thing was a dainty little Victorian silver locket on a chain, loose in the bottom of the file.

Bermondsey, Paul thought; *personal visit essential. Well, why not? Anything to get out of the office.*

He was just walking through the front door into the street when a voice called to him.

'Oh no,' he said. 'Not you. Hey, you're on duty, you shouldn't leave reception.'

Mr Tanner's mum grinned at him. Today she was wearing brunette, with enormous eyes and the sweetest little rosebud mouth you ever— Paul turned away, scarlet as a bus.

'That's what you think, lover,' she replied. 'Velma's going to cover for me while I'm out. Aren't you, dear?'

Paul looked past her into the office. An identical doe-eyed, rosebud-mouthed brunette was waving at him from behind the desk. 'She's hoping that nice young bike messenger's going to call again. She's got this thing about men in crash helmets. You see,' Mr Tanner's mum added in a broad whisper, 'compared to her I'm practically normal. Come on. Where are we going?'

'All right,' Paul hissed. 'But I'm not going out with you looking like *that*.'

Mr Tanner's mum glanced down. 'What, you mean horizontal stripes? Everyone says I can carry them off, but if you'd rather—'

'Not the clothes,' Paul growled. 'You know perfectly well . . .'

'Fine,' Mr Tanner's mum snapped. 'All right. If you want, I'll change into something really frumpy and boring and yetch. Is that what you want?'

'Yes.'

She grinned at him, then turned into an exact replica of Melze. 'Happy now?'

Paul groaned. 'Look,' he said, 'what do you get out of

this, picking on me like you do? Can't you go and persecute somebody else for a change?'

Now she was looking up at him out of Melze's soft blue
eyes. 'That's what I get for rescuing you from the dungeons,
is it? Charming. Not unexpected, but charming.' A tear
formed at the corner of her eye; if it hadn't appeared perfectly
on cue, Paul could've sworn it was real.

'Sorry,' Paul snapped. 'All right, then, wear what you
like. And I am grateful, really. It's just, you can be so—'

'So what?'

My sentiments exactly, Paul thought. So long as she stopped
being Melze, which was gross, it really wasn't any of his
business. And he shouldn't have said that, about persecuting.
'Nothing,' he sighed. 'Let's just go, all right?'

Mr Tanner's mum smiled brightly and turned back into the
rosebud brunette. 'You're a bit strange, though,' she said, as
he hurried down the street; he noticed that she had no trouble
at all keeping up, even though his legs were much longer. He
wondered whether, if he looked closely, he'd see her feet actually touching the ground at all. Looking closely, however,
wouldn't be a sensible move. 'Any normal boy your age would
be thrilled sick to be seen out with something like me.'

'Something,' Paul repeated. 'I think that explains it all,
don't you?'

She just shrugged. 'So you're into humans,' she said. 'I'm
broad-minded – so am I. All right,' she added, as he rolled
his eyes. 'I'll stop it and be good. You didn't tell me where
we're going.'

'Bermondsey,' Paul replied. 'It says Unit 5, Skivers Walk,
so I think it's a factory or—'

'Warehouse, actually.' Mr Tanner's mum smiled. 'Great.
I rather like them, they're sweet.'

'You know where we're going, then?'

She nodded. 'Glad I decided to come now, aren't you? Don't worry, nothing to be afraid of. Not if I'm with you.'

Really, Paul thought. 'According to the timetable, if we catch a 37A to—'

She hit his arm playfully. He was proud of how he managed to stifle the shriek of pain. 'No buses when you're with me, silly,' she said. 'I never go on buses. No privacy.' She whistled and held up her hand. At once, a taxi appeared. Paul wasn't sure, but as he climbed in he reckoned he caught a glimpse of round red eyes in the driver's compartment.

He shuffled along the seat, trying to keep away from Mr Tanner's mum's legs, which seemed to fill all available space. 'Aren't you cold, dressed like that?' he asked sourly.

'Me? Nah.' She twitched her nose at him. 'Think about it. I'm covered from head to foot with thick black fur, it's just that you can't see it under the monkey suit.'

Paul made a point of looking out of the window. 'I wanted to ask about that,' he said. 'How you do it, I mean,' he added quickly, before she could make anything of it. 'Is it, like, effective magic? What the Countess does, I mean?'

She laughed. 'Not likely,' she said. 'That's Fey stuff. Our lot don't hold with that. Fact is, we reckon it's unethical.'

'*Unethical?*' Paul nearly choked. 'That's a bit rich, isn't it, coming from—?'

'Don't be nasty,' Mr Tanner's mum interrupted. 'As it happens, we have a complex and highly developed tradition of moral philosophy. You may think that to us, ethics is a south-eastern English county pronounced with a lisp, but that says more about you than us, if you ask me. But that's all right,' she added, her voice softening. 'You don't know any better, so I forgive you.' Paul felt something scarily handlike on his knee, and shifted in his seat. 'Anyway,' she went on, 'to answer your question, no, we don't do effective magic. When she shift shapes, we shift shapes, it's not just – what is it Judy calls it? – *trompe l'œil*. If you were to cut me open with a knife right now, I'd be solid ape-derivative down to the bone. Just furrier than most, that's all.'

Paul hadn't realised that Bermondsey was such a long drive from the City, though it was possible that something akin to effective magic was interfering with his perception of time. He was, however, extremely grateful when the taxi eventually stopped.

Skivers Walk turned out to be old brown brick, dusty windows and flaking paint; bad camouflage, he couldn't help thinking. If you wanted to hide paranormal activity in modern London, you'd do better with concrete, steel and smoked glass. Maybe they were into Victoriana, or just liked it the way it was. 'Are we here?' he asked.

She nodded. 'We want Number Five,' she said. 'It's round the side, down a little sort of alley. I keep telling them it's too Harry Potter for words, but they won't listen. They've actually got a notice on the door saying *No Callers*, would you believe? Might as well have a sign saying *Suspicious building this way, folks* in flashing green neon. Still, nobody ever said that the little buggers were any too bright.'

Paul knocked and waited. Then Mr Tanner's mum shoved him out of the way and knocked, and they waited. Then they both tried knocking again, and Mr Tanner's mum produced a spike-poll tomahawk from inside her dress and chopped a large splinter out of the door. Then they waited some more.

'It's all right,' she told him, 'they're always like this. Shy.' She clouted the door hard with the side of her boot, making it shake.

'Would you mind putting that away?' Paul muttered, nodding towards the axe in her hand. 'Before someone sees.'

'Fusspot.' The tomahawk vanished from between her fingers. 'Actually, you could set off a bomb on the doorstep and nobody'd take any notice. Glamour, you see. I guess that's how they get away with the bloody stupid decor.'

She clumped the door ferociously with her balled fists, threw back her head and howled like a wolf. Ten seconds later, the door opened on a chain.

'Oh,' said a voice. 'It's you.'

Mr Tanner's mum scowled at the crack between door and frame. 'Let us in, you pillock, or I'll introduce you to my friend here. You want that?'

The door swung open as though blown out by an explosion. 'Get in,' snapped the voice. 'And please don't threaten me again. You know it upsets me.'

Paul stepped in quickly, before the voice could change its mind. The building he found himself standing in seemed vaguely familiar, though he knew for a fact he'd never been there in his life before. Then he figured it out. It was exactly like the warehouse locations they were so fond of using in 1970s cop shows, where Bodie and Doyle shoot it out with the evil masked terrorists. Everything was just so, from the patches of white mould on the bare brick walls to the rusty chains dangling from rickety catwalks overhead. And thus, of course, entirely unconvincing.

'Shhh,' warned the door-opener. 'They're all asleep.'

Paul looked at him. He was short, middle-aged, glasses, thinning on top, in a brown warehouse coat with biros in the top pocket. The only thing about his appearance that Paul was prepared to believe in was the look of fear and disgust on his face. 'I'm sorry,' he began. 'I'm from J.W.

Wells, I'm here to ask you if you'd be prepared to help us out with a job we're—'

The man stared at him through his quarter-inch-thick lenses. 'You don't want to buy anything, then.'

'No. Sorry.'

The tension in the man's face reduced considerably. 'That's all right, then, though you could've said so earlier. You had me worried there for a minute.'

Paul thought about that. 'You don't want people to buy anything?' he asked.

The man shuddered. Over his shoulder, in the vast gloom of the warehouse interior, Paul could see row upon row of wooden packing cases, piled on top of each other a dozen high. 'Too right,' the man said.

'Oh. Then why—?'

'Bastards,' the man cut in savagely. 'They turn up on the doorstep without a by-your-leave, hammer on the door, won't go away, and then they want to buy stuff. And they phone,' he added bitterly, 'and send faxes. If it was up to me I'd hang the lot of 'em.'

As if on cue, a distant telephone started to ring. The man swung round, yelled 'Shut *up*!' at the top of his voice, and wiped his hands nervously on the front of his coat. 'It rings for bloody ages sometimes,' he said, 'minutes at a time. You'd think they had something better to do, wouldn't you?' He shook himself like a dog, then walked away briskly. 'Come on, then, if you're coming,' he called back after them. 'And for pity's sake don't make a noise. They won't thank you for waking them up, you know.'

Mr Tanner's mum's four-inch stilettos made a noise like Fred and Ginger working out on a rickety iron bridge; but it was Paul who got shushed when he tripped over a cardboard box on the floor. 'Who *are* they?' he hissed at Mr Tanner's mum, as the man opened a door in the wall and passed through.

'You mean you—? I thought Judy'd have told you.'

'Well no, she didn't. Who—?'

'Shhh.'

'Don't you start.'

It was dark in the room that they'd been ushered into, dark enough to give Paul a nasty pain in the memory. Happily, the man turned on the light.

'Should be all right,' he said. 'This is the office, nobody comes in here.'

Paul could see why. There was probably a desk, under all that paper; hardly surprising if there turned out to be a seam of coal, too. The floor was similarly elusive under a crust of old envelopes, crumpled newspaper, plastic sandwich boxes and old brown paper bags spotted with mouse droppings. There was a chair that nobody would ever want to sit in, under any circumstances.

'Right,' the man said. 'You sure you don't want to buy anything?'

'Positive,' Paul said, with feeling.

The man glanced at him, frowned, and gave him the benefit of the doubt. 'I had to ask,' he said. 'We had four of them in here the other week. One of them,' he added with a shudder that started at his toes, 'asked to see a catalogue. Just as well it was me here that day – I can take it. What's *she* doing here, anyway?'

'Just being friendly,' Mr Tanner's mum said. The man made a soft spluttering noise and looked away.

Paul took a deep breath. 'The thing is,' he said, 'two – no, sorry, three of our people are sort of trapped in this dungeon.' The man nodded; his manner had changed when Paul said *trapped* and *dungeon*, as though the horrible weird interlude was finally over and they'd got back to the real world. 'Apparently it's something to do with the Fey—'

Now the man was scowling, as if Paul had offended him in some way. 'Oh yes?'

'That's what I was told. Grendel's Aunt, if that means anything to—'

'Oh, yes.' Now he was unoffended again, businesslike, sympathetic. 'And you want them got out of there.'

'Well, yes. If that's all right, I mean.'

'Of course it is.' The man took a biro from his top pocket and pulled the cap off with his teeth as he reached for a piece of paper with his other hand. 'Go on.'

'That's all I know about it, really,' Paul said. 'I was in there with them for a bit, but I didn't really get a good look at where I was or anything.'

The man looked up sharply. 'You were in the dungeon,' he said, 'and you got out?'

'I got him out,' Mr Tanner's mum put in.

'Oh.' The man appeared to lose interest. 'Well, we'll see what we can do for you. Let's have some details.'

Paul nodded. 'Okay. Probably best if I start with some names—'

The man winced as if Paul had burned him. 'Bloody hell,' he snapped at Mr Tanner's mum, 'didn't you tell him? You should've told him before you brought him here.'

She pulled a remorseful face. 'Sorry about that,' she said. 'Only, when he starts chattering away it's a job to make him shut up. No names,' she said to Paul, all school-teacherish. 'They don't like them, it's not the done thing. Perhaps you'd better leave this to me.'

Paul ignored her. 'Just a second,' he said. 'Why no names?'

'Allergic,' the man muttered. 'Tell him to stop, will you, for—'

'Did you threaten to kill me the other day?'

'Threaten?' The man looked blank. 'What do you take me for?'

'Answer the question.'

'Are you accusing me of something, or what?'

Paul breathed out through his nose. 'Answer the question,' he repeated. 'With a statement,' he added. 'Please.'

The man glanced nervously at Mr Tanner's mum, then said, 'No. Satisfied?'

Hardly, Paul thought; but verbal bludgeoning wasn't his style, just as dormice very rarely pull down full-grown elephants. 'Sorry,' he said. 'Only I was talking to someone just the other day, and this business about being allergic to names cropped up. So I wondered, that's all.'

The man opened his mouth, but Mr Tanner's mum beat him to it. 'It's not important,' she said firmly. 'Just trust me, all right? It's no big deal.'

That was disconcerting, to say the least; because, in all matters not involving personal relationships and garment removal, Paul realised that he did trust her. He had no idea why. 'Fine,' he said. 'So, what do you want to know?'

The man was still quivering slightly, but he seemed relatively coherent. 'You say you've got three people needing rescuing from the dungeons. Humans?'

'Well, of course they're—' Paul thought about it. 'Well, no,' he amended. 'One's a dwarf, and another one's a car. Is now, I mean; she used to be human.'

That didn't bother the man one bit. 'Right,' he said, making notes on the back of an envelope. 'One human, one dwarf, one—' He looked up and grinned suddenly. 'One convertible. How long have they been there, do you know?'

Paul glanced at his watch and figured out the time, to the nearest half-hour. 'God only knows what sort of a state they're in by now,' he added. 'I was only in there a few minutes, and I was about ready to crack up.'

'Don't worry about it,' the man said, with actual sympathy. 'You're not the first, won't be the last. And we'll see what we can do about your friends,' he added. 'Not promising anything, mind, but we'll see how we go.'

Paul nodded. He wasn't reassured and he didn't feel better, but at least something had been done, or was about to be done, or might get done at some indeterminate point in the future. 'Is there anything else?' he asked. Suddenly he wanted to be back in his nice safe office.

'I can get you a cup of tea if you like,' the man said, but Mr Tanner's mum shot him a vicious scowl. 'Just being polite,' he grumbled, 'that's all.'

'I think we'd better be getting back,' Paul said, nodding to Mr Tanner's mum. 'I don't suppose your friend's going to want to stay on reception all day.'

'My great-aunt, actually, and yes, she would. Some days you need to prise her out of there with a crowbar.'

They tiptoed back out the way they'd come in, the man poking his head round the door and looking both ways before he let them past into the main warehouse. 'We'll be in touch,' he said as he shooed them into the street. '*Please* don't phone.' Then he slammed the door hard, and they stood listening to bolts shooting home and locks graunching for about thirty seconds. 'Actually, they're all right once you get to know them,' Mr Tanner's mum said, as she flagged down a taxi. 'At least, if you can learn to cope with us, they're not a whole lot worse.'

It was only as the taxi pulled away, and Paul shuffled out of reach of an absently straying hand, that he remembered something he'd seen propped against the warehouse wall, glimpsed out of the corner of his eye. A rickety, shabby, dusty old Raleigh bicycle.

When Paul got home there was a letter waiting for him on the mat. Sure, Paul got letters. Several public companies and government bodies wrote to him at least four times a year, and the bank seemed almost pathetically keen to keep in touch. Letters from *people*, on the other hand, weren't particularly common. What made this one stand out, however, was the American stamp and the handwriting on the envelope.

> *Dear Paul*, it said;
> *Well, the weather here is very nice and your father and I are having a good time. The neighbours are friendly and there are some nice shops. We have bought a big trailer so we can go touring in the fall. However, I am still having trouble with my feet. I am sorry to have to tell you that your Uncle Ernie died last week. I don't suppose you remember him at all, you were quite small the last time he came to the house. The funeral will be in Ireland. I don't suppose you'll be able to get time off work to go.*
>
> *His lawyers have written us that there's a box of his stuff at their office. Dad and I don't want anything particularly, so if you want to go and collect it, you can keep anything you want and welcome. The lawyers are quite handy for where you work, they are in Grays Inn Road. You could*

drop by on your lunch break. I enclose their card, and Dad has written on the back that you can have the box.

Hope you are well,

Mum

Paul picked up the card and looked at it: on one side the firm's name, Messrs Swindall, Frettenham & Shark; on the other, his father's heavy, blunt letters: *Paul Carpenter is my son, he can have Ernie's old junk as I don't want it. D. Carpenter.*

Christ, he thought.

It was, he reflected, the first time he'd ever inherited anything; and since Uncle Ernie only mattered to him because of the remote chance that he might be the Ernest Carpenter who'd written part of the chapter in the office-procedures manual, his death wasn't a desperately harrowing event. The timing of his sudden windfall was something quite other, as spiky with implications as a hedgehog group hug. But his parents couldn't be involved in JWW stuff, could they? And they wouldn't lie to him, or anything like that.

No, Paul decided, he could be fairly sure they wouldn't, in the normal course of things; since in order to lie, you must first communicate. He thought for a moment. He'd had a letter from his parents before – one, enclosing a note for him to pass on to the bank, cancelling his subsistence allowance when he'd got his job. It had been pleasant enough, but laconic to the point of terseness; there hadn't been any of the gushing personal detail that his mother had crammed into this one. Another point he couldn't help but notice was that his Mum's writing style had changed rather, and some of the turns of phrase didn't sound like her at all. He tried to analyse the differences, but the only one he could put his finger on was that when he was a kid, all her sentences tended to start with the word *don't*. That, he admitted, could be accounted for by context. He put the card in his wallet and left the letter on the hall shelf, mostly covered by his library book but with one corner showing.

The woman who collected Paul from the waiting-room introduced herself as Mrs Leary. She was smart, brisk and moderately friendly, which made a pleasant change after a morning helping Christine move more filing cabinets.

'I have to say I never met your – uncle, was it?' she said over her shoulder, as Paul followed her across a savannah of deep, monogrammed beige carpet.

'Great-uncle,' he replied, 'I think. My parents were always a bit vague. You know, everybody was uncle this or aunt that. Anyway, we weren't close or anything like that.'

Mrs Leary took him to a small room with a plain desk and a wall full of prints of Great Nineteenth Century Judges; they gave the impression of having ended up there because there was nowhere else to banish them to, like the Picts. The box of Uncle Ernie's effects was on the desk when he got there. A long time ago, it had contained tinned South African peaches.

'That's it,' said Mrs Leary. 'And here's a note of our charges,' she added, handing him a scary-looking envelope. 'No need to bother with that now, next week will do fine.'

Paul looked at the box. 'You were his lawyers,' he said. 'Can you tell me anything about him?'

Mrs Leary shrugged. 'Not very much, I'm afraid. We were the executors, and actually there was only just enough money to cover the funeral and our costs. The nursing home got rid of the clothes and bits and pieces, apart from this. There's photos and stuff – they didn't like to throw them away without asking.'

Paul hesitated. For some reason, he didn't feel like going through the box at home, or even back at the office. 'Would it be all right if I just sat here for a few minutes and had a look through?' he asked. 'If I'm not in the way or anything?'

Mrs Leary smiled. 'You go ahead,' she said. 'I'll leave you to it, if that's all right. I'm just next door, so when you're finished, just knock and I'll take you back to reception. This place is a bit of a maze, I'm afraid.'

Compared to 70 St Mary Axe it was a Roman road across a desert, but Paul thanked her and she went away. He sat down, composed himself, and peered into the box.

Someone had gone to the trouble of typing out a list.

> 1 *library ticket*
> 1 *Sea Scout badge*
> 1 *pen*
> 1 *watch (broken)*
> 1 *screwdriver*
> 1 *packet coloured chalks*
> 3 *photograph albums*

Flawlessly accurate, you had to give them that. He opened the box of chalks, closed it and put it back; shook the watch just in case; tried the pen, which had run out; flicked through two of the albums, which were both full of black and white photos of people he didn't recognise. Then he opened the envelope, and learned that he owed Messrs Swindall, Frettenham & Shark a hundred pounds plus VAT. That sort of a day, really.

'All done?' Mrs Leary chiruped at him when he asked to be let out. 'Was there anything nice?'

Paul smiled thinly and handed her a cheque. She thanked

him very politely, and held the door for him on the way out, since his hands were full of cardboard box. It was raining outside, and needless to say he hadn't worn his coat.

'Anything in there for me?' Mr Tanner's mum chirped at him as he trudged past reception. He stopped and smiled at her. 'Sure,' he said. 'In fact, you have a choice. Packet of coloured chalks or a screwdriver.'

Her face straightened; the trade-mark smirk evaporated. 'Let me see,' she said.

'Don't be silly, I was only kidding. It's just some junk left to me by some uncle I never met since I was a—'

'Let me see,' she repeated, in such a stern and commanding voice that, for a moment, Paul pitied Mr Tanner for his childhood. 'I may not be the most powerful rune in the charm, but I have got a sense of smell, and that box *stinks*.'

It took a second for the penny to drop. 'Oh,' he said. 'You can smell magic and stuff.'

Mr Tanner's mum sighed impatiently, then froze for a moment, as if she'd been turned to stone. Paul was about to panic and start yelling for help when she exploded with a window-pane-rattling sneeze. Apparently it was her turn with the office cold. 'That's one way of putting it. Take all day to explain, and most of it'd go over your head, you'd feel like a dwarf in a strip club. Let me see that box.'

He shrugged and put it down on the desk. 'As far as I'm concerned, you can keep it. Cost me a hundred quid I haven't got, for one—' He stopped, as Mr Tanner's mum yelped with pain. The Sea Scout badge clattered on the desk. 'What's the matter?'

'That,' she replied, sucking her fingers. 'Bloody thing. Could've done me an injury.'

'What, you pricked your finger on the pin or something?'

She gave him an icy scowl and lifted her hand for him to see. The skin on the pads of her thumb and forefinger had been melted, and blisters had already started to swell. 'Shield,' she explained. 'What did you say your disgusting uncle did for a living?'

'No idea,' Paul replied. 'Well—'

'This shield,' Mr Tanner's mum went on, 'is a really nasty, very rare and expensive piece of specialised kit. In fact,' she added, pushing it across the desk at him with the tip of a pencil, 'I'm fairly sure it's illegal; bloody well ought to be, anyhow.' She paused, sneezed again, then went on: 'It's to protect humans against creatures of darkness.' She scowled at him. 'Like me.'

Paul could feel himself go red in the face. 'I'm terribly sorry,' he said, 'I had no idea—'

'Well, now you know. Look, will you put that bloody thing away? It's giving me a migraine just looking at it.'

He picked it up nervously, but he couldn't feel anything unusual at all. He dropped it in his pocket and pulled down the flap. 'That's what you could smell, was it?'

Mr Tanner's mum grunted. 'I remember you telling me once that your family are a load of bastards,' she said. 'Should've listened. Let's see what else you've got in there, before you accidentally kill the whole office.'

'Sure,' Paul said. 'Look, would you rather I held them up for you to see? In case there's any more dangerous stuff?'

She nodded, and he took out the packet of chalks. When she saw them, Mr Tanner's mum opened her eyes wide, then grinned. 'Stone me,' she said. 'Haven't seen any of them in a long time.'

'What?'

But Mr Tanner's mum just shook her head; still upset,

presumably, because of the shield. 'Put them somewhere safe and forget about them,' she said. 'They'll come in handy one of these days, but they're not something you want to go playing with. Anything else?'

Paul held up the pen, the broken watch and the screwdriver. This time, Mr Tanner's mum gave a low whistle.

'And all this shit used to belong to your uncle, did it?' she said.

'Great-uncle,' Paul replied. 'I think. I never really knew him, to be honest.'

'Count your blessings,' Mr Tanner's mum replied, dabbing at her nose with a Kleenex. 'All right, here's a couple of clues. That watch thing – you've probably noticed, it doesn't go.'

'That's right,' Paul said. 'At least, I assume it doesn't. I tried winding it—'

Mr Tanner's mum opened her eyes wide. 'You didn't try setting the hands?'

'No. Why?'

She smiled. 'That's another truly horrible gadget you've got there,' she said. 'Reason it doesn't go is that it's not meant to. Quite the reverse. If you pull out the little winder thing and set the hands, then wind it up till it starts ticking, it freezes time. Like I said, truly horrible and anti-social. I'd suggest you get rid of it, only that'd be really irresponsible. Imagine: you chuck it away, someone picks it up and tries it to see if it'll go—'

Paul shuddered. 'What would you suggest?' he said.

'Strongroom,' she replied. 'In a sealed box, marked *do not touch*. I'll put it away for you if you like.'

'Thanks,' Paul said, with feeling. 'Is that the lot?'

Mr Tanner's mum shook her head. 'The pen and the screwdriver aren't quite so bad, but you don't want to leave them lying about either. Probably best if I put the whole lot away for you. And the chalks,' she added, maybe a touch too quickly. 'Right?'

'Absolutely,' Paul said. 'Really, I didn't have the faintest idea. How's your hand?'

'Painful,' she replied. 'Hang on, what's that in the bottom of the box? Books?'

'Photo albums. Maybe you could check them out for me. You know, just in case.'

She hesitated, then grunted, 'Oh, go on, then. Give them here, one at a time.'

Paul put them on the desk. She used the pencil to turn the pages. 'Anything?' Paul asked.

'Nah, just a lot of boring pictures of ugly people. Your family, presumably.' She bent her head down and sniffed. 'Can't smell anything, so I'm guessing they're all right. How did you say you came by this lot?'

'I told you, it got left to me. Well, not me, my mum and dad; but they didn't want it.'

She was looking at him very oddly. 'He died, then, this uncle of yours.'

'Apparently. I mean, I haven't seen the body or anything—' He'd meant it sarcastically, but the look on her face startld him. 'What? You think there's something wrong.'

A debate of some kind was going on behind her eyes. No way of knowing which side won; but she lowered her voice and leaned forward a little. 'A suggestion for you. Whatever you do, *don't* let Countess Judy know about this.'

'Why not?'

Her eyes sparkled. 'Because I say not, that's why. Right, you take on the photo albums, I'll deal with the rest of it. Go on, then,' she added, before he could say anything, 'piss off. Shoo.'

That was odd, too; normally Paul had trouble getting away from her. Still, he wasn't complaining. He thanked her once again, and retired to his office. There was a note on his desk, in Countess Judy's tall, slanting handwriting. He dumped the photo albums on the shelf and picked it up.

My office 2.30. J di C-B.

'One damned thing after another,' Paul muttered under his breath, and checked his watch. He had ten minutes to kill, no work to do, and he wasn't sure offhand what day of the week it was. He took the Sea Scout badge out of his pocket, meaning to hide it away in his desk along with the run-out biros and Polo-mint wrappers. It lay in his hand, harmless as a paper clip.

Uncle Ernie, he thought. *My inheritance.*

Just a stupid badge; but he couldn't bear either to hold on to it or put it away. On an impulse that came from a part of his brain that he didn't bother with much, he opened his jacket and pinned it to the lining. Then it was time for his meeting.

Countess Judy looked older and thinner than she'd been that morning, as though she'd had too much on her mind to bother putting her face on. When he walked in she avoided his gaze, which was very unusual. In a way, she looked more *real* than he'd ever seen her before.

'You'll be delighted to hear,' she said, 'that the negotiations have been successful.'

Probably because his brain was still awash with coloured chalks and being parted from a hundred pounds, it took Paul a moment to remember what she was talking about. 'That's fantastic,' he said.

She shrugged. 'There are aspects of the matter that you

aren't familiar with,' she said vaguely. 'Rest assured that the negotiations were long and involved, and also cost this firm a great deal of money. However, the main thing is that Mr Wurmtoter and Mr Shumway, and your car, have been retrieved. Your part in this—' She looked up at him, then abruptly looked away. 'I owe you a debt of gratitude, Mr Carpenter,' she said stiffly. 'Thank you.'

Paul hadn't been expecting that. ''S all right,' he mumbled.

'Also—' The Countess was holding out a small rectangular piece of paper. 'Reimbursement,' she said, 'for out-of-pocket expenses.'

He took the paper: a cheque, for a hundred pounds. 'Thank you,' he said; and then, 'Why?'

She was practically fidgeting. 'Come now, Mr Carpenter, you know what they say about gift horses. Do you want the money or not?'

He looked at it again. One hundred pounds; and drawn on a proper bank, not the Bank of the Dead. 'But you don't have to,' he said slowly. 'I mean, what's it for?'

'I told you,' she snapped. 'It's what you had to pay to get that box from the lawyers. Or have you suddenly come into money, and a hundred pounds is neither here nor there?'

The signature was just a squiggle; pity. He'd have been interested in knowing which of the partners had signed the cheque. 'But it's my stuff,' he said quietly. 'The firm doesn't have to pay for me to get my own things. I mean, it's really kind of you and all that, but I can't take it.'

'For God's sake—' The look on Countess Judy's face was terrifying. 'Just take the goddamn cheque and get out of my office.'

Paul shook his head and put the cheque down on the desk. 'No,' he said. 'I'm very sorry, but I can't. Really.'

For a moment, he thought that the Countess was going to hit him; she stood up, but then it was as though an invisible hand had shoved her down into her chair. 'Very well,' she said icily, 'that's up to you. Far be it from me to lecture you about gratitude. I take it that now you're independently wealthy, you won't be needing the salary review that was scheduled at the end of the month. Now, if you'll excuse me, I have work to do.'

She looked down at the papers on her desk. Paul could feel her willing him to leave; also, he could feel her failing. He couldn't think of anything to say that wouldn't make things worse. He turned, at last, to leave.

'Oh, Mr Carpenter.' He stopped, but didn't look round. 'If you don't have anything else to do, there's always the Mortensen printouts. It's been quite a while since you did anything about them, so there's probably quite a backlog. Julie will bring them down to you if you ask her.'

Quite why that made Paul feel so angry, he wasn't quite sure, but it did. He turned round slowly and faced her. 'Right,' he said. 'Will do. But it's not fair, you not giving me a pay rise.' He realised how ridiculous that sounded; after all, he was pathetically useless at his job, so fairness really didn't come into it. He waited for her to make the point, but she didn't. 'I mean,' he went on, 'just because I wouldn't take your cheque. That's all.'

A look had crept into Countess Judy's eye that he couldn't place; at any rate, she didn't seem quite so apprehensive about looking at him. 'Perhaps your principles do you credit, Mr Carpenter,' she said. 'However, I'd find this display of conspicuous integrity a little more convincing if I didn't happen to know that you have indeed come into money lately. Obviously, it makes a difference.'

You what? Paul thought. 'I'm sorry, I don't quite—'

'Come, now,' she went on – crafty, that was it; she was looking crafty. 'You've been – supplementing your income, let's say – which is why you don't need the money; that's what's behind that little exhibition we had just now. You must have a farily low opinion of our intelligence, Mr Carpenter.'

'I really haven't got the faintest—'

'Indeed. You were sent to deal with a wyvern, on behalf of a client. You dispatched the creature, so I gather, but I don't seem to have any record of you surrendering the eyestone. Did it simply slip your mind, Mr Carpenter? Or weren't you aware how valuable they are? But of course you must be, or else why did you go to the trouble of prising it loose, a squeamish individual like yourself? Clearly, that's where your new-found wealth derives from, and I have to say, it's not the sort of behaviour we expect from our employees. I'm disappointed. However, in light of your contribution to the release of Mr Wurmtoter, we're prepared to overlook it on this occasion. You'd do well, though, not to express your contempt for us in future by brandishing our own money under our noses. Tactless, Mr Carpenter; you should know better than that.'

It was probably just as well that Paul's voice appeared to have been turned off at the mains. Instead of replying, he fished out the matchbox containing the stone (it'd have been rather more impressive a gesture if he hadn't had to turn out both his jacket pockets before he could find it) and tossed it on the desk in front of Judy di Castel'Bianco. Her hand shot out and covered it, then lay quite still.

'That's better,' she said quietly. 'Now, the Mortensen printouts.'

'What?'

'The Mortensen printouts,' she repeated. 'Go and deal with them, please.'

Paul didn't say what he wanted to say; instead, he nodded and left the room. He didn't start shaking until he was halfway back to his office, which was in the wrong direction for Julie's room anyhow.

Cow, he thought. *Horrible, evil, entirely justified cow. Not that I wanted the stupid thing anyway, but getting caught out like that—* He pulled himself together. He wasn't the first person ever, he reflected, to discover the harsh truth that our enemies are never more loathsome than when they're in the right—

That was it; the vague suspicion that he'd been carting around with him for so long had finally slotted into its allotted place, and he *knew*: Countess Judy was, somehow or other, the enemy. Suddenly he remembered the Sea Scout badge, pinned inside his jacket. So that was why she'd been – well, practically afraid of him. Creatures of darkness, and all that. He wondered if it'd burn her hand, the way it had burned Mr Tanner's mum. Only she, for all her faults, wasn't the enemy.

Julie had the Mortensen printouts all ready for him; bundles and bundles of them, all tied up with stationers' red tape. 'That ought to keep you out of mischief for a while,' she said, as he hefted the load and staggered to the door. 'I'll be down with some more when you've done those.'

An afternoon sorting printouts into date order turned out to be exactly what Paul needed: mindless repetitive work to occupy his hands and the superficial areas of his brain, while the rest of his mind slowly chewed over recent events. When going-home time finally drifted by and he set off for his flat, he discovered that he'd reached a decision (and without even trying to).

He'd believed Countess Judy when she'd told him that the prisoners were coming home. Fine. Unaccountably, but probably because he was an idiot, he'd taken it upon himself to assume a certain level of responsibility for them. But that was all over and done with now, so whatever the big thing was that was going on all around him – civil war among the Fey, vague threats from bicycles with Moses complexes, bizarre and powerful artefacts just happening to drop into his lap at precisely the right moment (Paul believed in coincidences, but he'd also managed to believe in Father Christmas until he was nearly eleven, so it was a good bet that anything he believed in was therefore, by definition, untrue) – whatever it was and whoever was involved, it was none of his business and quite definitely not his fault. Not his mess to tidy, not his dishes to wash, not his sink to unblock, not his socks to pair. Screw the lot of them. Because he wasn't allowed to quit, he'd just sit there nice and quiet and sort Mortensen printouts until either he or the partners retired or died. As a plan of campaign (he told himself, as he set his alarm and switched off the light) it was utterly flawless. It would work. It had to.

Paul had been asleep for several hours – he knew that because his left arm had pins and needles where he'd been lying on it – when something disturbed him and he sat up. At first he guessed that he'd fallen asleep with the bedside lamp still on, but that wasn't right, he had a razor-sharp mental image of himself pressing the switch. In which case, where was all this bright stuff coming from?

The answer was sitting at the foot of his bed. It was, by any objective standard, a very nice answer; beyond question the nicest human shape that had ever shared his bedroom with him, regardless of context. Where her short, flaxen hair ended and the pale glow began was hard to say, but the way it reflected off her golden skin was really quite—

'Rosie?' he muttered. 'Bloody hell, can't you find some other poor bastard to—?'

She moved her head a little, and her eyes were like an unexpected brick wall across a railway track.

'You're not Rosie,' Paul said, his throat suddenly dry. 'Mr Tanner's mother, I mean. You're someone else.'

Her perfect chin moved up and down, maybe as much as an inch.

'You aren't a goblin at all, are you?'

She shook her head, but the glow didn't move with her. Now it seemed to be coming from just behind her back, giving the ridiculous impression that she had a pair of graceful snow-white wings. But that was daft, because if she had wings it'd mean she was an angel—

'Look,' he said. 'I mean, who are you?'

She shook her head again. *Fine*, Paul thought; *this no-names business is really starting to annoy me.* On the other hand, she hadn't winced or started when he'd said *Rosie* or *Mr Tanner's mum.* 'I can tell you what I am, if you like,' she said.

(Her voice was like many things; chocolate and milk and rain falling on the roof, autumn sunshine and the soft hiss of waves on a shingle beach, home and safety and Melze when she was nine, and a great many other things that he'd imagined but never got around to experiencing.)

'That'd be nice,' Paul croaked.

Her lips curved round a smile. 'I'm the girl of your dreams,' she said. 'Don't you recognise me?'

Chapter Nine

'You what?' Paul said.

'The girl of your dreams,' she repeated. 'Oh come on, Paul, get a grip. I've been visiting you since you were thirteen, you should know me by now.'

Paul sat up, trying to get a better look at her face, but she shifted a little and the light dazzled him. 'Sorry,' he said, 'but you aren't at all familiar. And I think I'd remember if I'd seen you,' he added awkwardly.

She giggled. 'Silly,' she said. 'That's just you. You always forget your dreams the moment you wake up. Pity,' she added, in a tone of voice that he couldn't quite identify, but which made the hairs on the back of his neck curl. 'Some of them were really – nice. You should dream more often, you know that?'

She'd said 'Paul', he thought – she could say names without doing the whole salted-slug bit. 'I still don't follow,' he said. 'If you're, like, a recurring dream or something, how come I can see you now that I'm awake? I am awake,' he added, mostly to himself. 'I can feel the pins and needles in my arm. Ouch,' he said, by way of vindication.

'Of course you're awake,' she replied, 'that's why you don't recognise me. Nice pyjamas, by the way. A lot of men couldn't get away with red paisley. What happened to the green and brown check? You always looked good in them.'

'They got frayed, I threw them out—' He stopped dead.

'How the hell do you know about my pyjamas?' he snapped. 'You're not – *real*, are you?'

She raised an eyebrow. Paul slowly turned a deep puce colour and pulled the sheet up to his neck. 'Anyhow,' she went on, 'since you aren't going to do the to-what-do-I-owe-the-pleasure bit, I'd better just tell you. Listening?'

Paul nodded.

'Splendid. Right, here goes.' She pursed her lips and took a deep breath. 'You want to know why I'm here, right? Well, we couldn't help overhearing – we don't eavesdrop as a rule, but it was pretty hard to miss, really – you were thinking, why should you get mixed up in all the stuff that's going on, it's none of your business, blahdy-blahdy. And that's *so wrong*, Paul, really it is. It's – oh, this is annoying, what I want to say is, after everything we've been to each other you really ought to trust me, but of course you can't remember, so that's no good. The point is, you really do have to get involved, because it's very much to do with you—' She hesitated, frowned. 'And me too, if you must know, because it's not just you they've got their claws into, it's me as well. Us, in fact. All of us. And that's just not right, because—'

'Just a minute,' Paul said grimly. 'What exactly is that supposed to mean, *all of us*? You mean it's not just—'

Her smirk was plain as anything, even through the blinding glow. 'Not just me, that's right.'

'How many?'

'That'd be telling. Oh, don't pull faces. Several, all right?'

'No, it's not all right,' Paul wailed. 'You make it sound like a – a *harem*, or something.'

She giggled. 'You can be very sweet sometimes, you know that? All right, at least three. Will that do? Anyway, we're doing the best we can, but there's ever so many more of them than there are of us, and sometimes they just don't play fair, and when we're gone – well, we're gone for ever, and I really don't want to talk about that. I shouldn't be having to explain. It's your uncle's fault, for not telling you when you were little. But you've got to be careful, Paul, you've got to *pay attention*, is the main thing. I know you, for two pins you'll let the whole thing wash over you and carry on doing those stupid Mortensen things and never even notice who's not there.' She paused, as if she expected him to react. He didn't. 'Now I expect you're thinking I'm just a by-product of really strong Canadian Cheddar on top of a long, hard week, and of course you're absolutely right; but you're not imagining the pain in your hand, I can tell you that for nothing. I know it's all suddenly started piling in on top of you like a bookshelf collapsing, but there's a reason for that, obviously. I mean, men like your uncle don't up and die just like that; and I know they say *for tax reasons* and everybody assumes they know what that means, but there's a hell of a lot more to it, you take my word for it. It's *war*, Paul, and unless you get off your bum and start pulling your weight, we'll all be really screwed, and then where'll you be? Sleeping alone for ever is where, and that'll be the least of your problems. Do you understand?'

'No,' Paul replied, with flawless honesty. 'I'll say this for you, though. You're an improvement on the one where I'm giving the prizes at Speech Day with no clothes on. But on balance, I think I'd rather get some sleep.'

'Oh, *you*.' She folded her arms and scowled at him. 'You're just going to have to pull yourself together, figure out your priorities and which side your mirror's glazed on. Otherwise it's all going to be a disgusting mess, and it'll all be your fault. Do you hear me?' She leaned forward, and for a moment he thought he recognised her − except she couldn't be two people at once, could she? 'She's counting on you,' she said sternly, 'and there's nobody else who can help her except you. Now we've been to a lot of trouble, all of us. Your uncle even died. You've got everything you need − apart from the Door, of course, but that can't be helped, and you'll be able to cope now, in any case. You're all set. Now it's time for you to stop lolling about feeling sorry for yourself and start *fighting*. Or next time, it won't just be a goblin who gets blown up, it'll be you.' Then she turned off, just like a light; and at precisely the same moment, Paul felt the switch click between his fingers, and the bedside lamp came on.

He thought for a moment. 'Aargh,' he said.

Just a bad dream, after all (it said something about the effects of overexposure to Mr Tanner's mum that his bad dreams featured lovely blondes). He relaxed a little, and reached for his glass of water; for some reason, his mouth was very dry indeed. As he picked it up, he dislodged something on the bedside table.

Paul carried on and drank some water. It was only as he put the glass back that his conscious mind saw it. Between the alarm clock and his watch − a rubber band.

He jerked convulsively, spilling what was left of the water; then he grabbed the rubber band and held it up to the light. Ridiculous thing to do. It was just a plain brown rubber band, such as the postman drops on your doorstep. That was how this particular specimen had entered his life; Sophie had found it there one morning. She'd leaned forward to get it, and her hair had fallen in front of her face. That always annoyed her, so she'd used the band to tie it back, and forgotten to take it out and replace it with a toggle.

For some reason, Paul had commented on it, jokingly said it suited her, and thereafter (until she went away) she'd always worn it in the evenings and at weekends, even though she claimed it pulled her hair and was uncomfortable. When she left, she either threw it away or took it with her, because it hadn't been there; he'd looked for it, sentimental clown that he was, even scrabbled about on his hands and knees in case it had fallen on the floor.

He sat up in bed, with the band stretched around four fingers, staring at it. It couldn't be the same one; it had to be one he'd absent-mindedly pocketed in the office, which had come out with his keys and handkerchief. Except that it wasn't. He knew it wasn't; and just to ram the point home as deep and firm as a vampire hunter's wooden stake, there was a single black hair still trapped inside it. Sophie's colour, Sophie's length.

Fine, Paul heard himself think. *But the girl who was here just now was a blonde.*

That worried him; catching himself at a moment like this trying to figure out the mystery, Hercule-Poirot-in-the-library, instead of freaking out and screaming till they came for him in a plain van, was about as scary as scary got.

It hadn't been there before, but now it was back. Therefore someone must've brought it — we won't go anywhere near the topic of how it came into that person's possession — in which case someone must've been here, either earlier today or — God help us — just now. But in any case; why leave *that*, of all things? Threat? Ransom demand? If people wanted to get in touch with him, why the hell couldn't they just write him notes, instead of cluttering up his life with cryptic artefacts?

He caught sight of the clock. Mental arithmetic: if it's three in the morning in England, what time would it be in, say, Los Angeles?

International directory enquiries gave him the number, and a cheerful voice with a Spanish accent told him he'd reached JWW Associates, and how could she help him? He asked to speak to Ms Pettingell. Spanish-accent was very sorry, Ms Pettingell wasn't in the office right then, but she'd be happy (deliriously so, to judge by her tone of voice) to take a message.

'It's all right, thanks,' Paul muttered. 'I'll call again later.'

Probably just as well. One doesn't call up one's ex-girlfriend on the other side of the world, probably dragging her out of a meeting with Leo's people and Julia's people and the numbers guys from Fox, just to ask her if she knew what had become of a manky old ex-GPO rubber band. Paul didn't need to speak to her to know exactly what she'd say: his first name, caked in enough ice to preserve all the mammoths in Siberia. He could practically hear her saying it right now, her voice was clear and sharp inside his head—

Paul. Help.

He was out of bed and halfway across the room with a turn of speed that would've done credit to a greyhound, only pausing because he'd tried to run through the bedroom door without troubling to open it first. As he lifted his hand to rub his sadly used nose, he noticed that the band was still around his fingers. Frantically he tried to shake it off, as though it was a spider in his hair, but it wouldn't leave him. *Great; not only am I finally losing it completely, I'm going to spend the rest of my life with a rubber band twined round my hand. That's going to play havoc with drinking tea and buttering toast.* Then it occurred to him to use his left hand to peel the band off his right. That worked flawlessly, and he dropped the terrifying object on the floor.

It'd be really nice, he reflected, if he was one of those people who had friends. Just pick up the phone, any time, day or night, and they're there for you. *Sorry to bother you, Philip or Chris or Justin, but just now I could've sworn I heard Sophie calling my name. Really? How fascinating. Did she say anything else? Actually, yes, she did, she said 'Help.' Gosh, Paul, perhaps you'd better come over here and we can talk about it. Better still, stay there, I'll be round in about ten minutes. That*, he thought, *would be really nice. Instead, I have to deal with it on my own. Just me. No friends.*

Paul sat up the rest of the night in the armchair, with all the lights on, plus the TV, the radio and the CD player. They might as well have been unplugged, because all he could hear was her voice. *Paul. Help.* Not the most eloquent of speeches compared with, say, the Gettysburg address or *We shall fight them on the beaches*. Memorable, though. Dead memorable.

He got dressed at a quarter to six, had a slice of toast and a cup of black instant coffee at six-fifteen, then sat by the door waiting for it to be time to go to work. Horribly, he'd rather be there than in his own home, which was no longer safe now that Sophie had come back to him. (*Paul. Help. Yes, all* right, *I heard you the first time*.) He ended up outside 70 St Mary Axe at twenty to nine. The door was still firmly locked, as usual. The memory of her voice was slightly weaker now; he actually had to think of it in order to hear it, but it was like a loose tooth, impossible not to keep fiddling away at it just to see if it was still there. On the other hand, it helped pass the time like nothing else on Earth, because before he knew it, Mr Tanner was standing next to him, shouting, 'I said, a bit keen, aren't you?'

Not the sort of experience you can recover from instantly. 'Sorry,' Paul mumbled. 'Couldn't sleep.'

'So you came here.'

'Yes.'

'In preference to, say, counting sheep.' That Tanner grin; like mother, like son. 'Well, the Mortensen printouts ought to do the trick, but if not, come and see me, I've got some notes of meetings that'd tranquillise a rogue elephant.' Mr Tanner turned his key in the lock and stepped through the door. 'I suppose you might as well come in,' he said, 'you've already met the menagerie, after all. Oh, in case I haven't mentioned it, if you ever do anything to encourage my mother, I'll rip your head off and hollow out your skull for a very small toilet bowl.'

The goblins were still out and about, scampering round reception in full armour, jumping on and off the post table, eating the fax paper and the toner cartridges. Paul managed a wan smile and a faint wave, which (he was vaguely touched to note) they duly returned. And to think; not so long ago, something as homely and folksy as goblins wrecking the front office had been enough to freak him out for days. How far he'd come since then.

Mr Tanner was sifting the post; interestingly, he used a pair of blacksmith's iron tongs for the purpose. 'So,' he asked, not looking up, 'why the insomnia? Indigestion? Bad kipper?'

'I—' *I have no conceivable reason to tell Mr Tanner, of all people, about what I thought I saw last night. Mr Tanner is not my friend Mr Tanner is half a goblin, and my* boss. 'I had this really weird dream,' Paul said.

'I get that a lot,' Mr Tanner said. 'But it doesn't matter with me, because it's all just biochemistry and stuff. What do you get in yours, then?' He made it sound like they were comparing sandwich fillings.

'Girls,' Paul said, before he was ready.

'Right,' Mr Tanner said. 'Serves me right for asking.'

'No, not like that.' *Shut up, Carpenter. Embarrassing yourself to death is a really tacky way to commit suicide, not to mention criminally inconsiderate.* 'It was – well, this girl I knew. She was calling my name and saying, "Help."'

'This girl you knew,' Mr Tanner repeated. 'Correct me if I'm wrong, but you don't know any girls.' He frowned, tongs extended towards a brown window-envelope marked *Inland Revenue*. 'Not any more, at any rate. She dumped you, right? That thin girl.'

'Sophie.'

'Like it matters, but yes.' Mr Tanner put the tongs down on the desk. 'Was that who you heard, then?'

Paul nodded wearily. 'Yes.'

'So—' Mr Tanner broke off, fished in his pocket, brought out a huge blood-red handkerchief and sneezed violently. 'Bloody office cold,' he muttered. 'You had it yet? It's a classic, you'll enjoy it. So you had a dream where Ms Petingell was calling your name and pleading for help?'

Not pleading, exactly. Barking in exasperation for help. 'Yes,' Paul said. 'Well, actually, no, because that was after the dream. When I was awake.'

Mr Tanner looked at him, like an early bird debating whether to send back an unsatisfactory worm. 'Then it can't have been a dream, can it? You only have them in your sleep, it's one of the salient features of dreams. You heard voices.'

'I suppose so,' Paul mumbled.

'Like Joan of Arc.'

'Well—'

'All right, not quite like Joan of Arc. I accept that Sophie wasn't urging you to drive Peter Mayle out of Provence. But you heard her voice, and you were awake.'

Paul dipped his head. 'Yes.'

'I see. Out of interest, why've you got a rubber band looped round your fingers?'

There was a short interlude, during which Paul had rather a lot of trouble breathing. Then he said 'It' a couple of times. Mr Tanner, oddly enough, was nodding his head.

'Hers,' he said. 'Right?'

'Right.'

'Give it to me. No,' Mr Tanner added quickly, 'hold on a second.' He picked up the tongs, used them to grip the band and tease it gently off Paul's wrist, like a detective retrieving a fibre sample from a murder scene. He dropped it in one of the empty envelopes, sealed it with Sellotape and put it away in his inside pocket. 'I'll hold on to that for you for a day or so,' he said. 'You need to get some sleep sooner or later, or you'll be completely useless.' He frowned, then used the tongs to push aside the lapel of Paul's jacket. 'That badge thing,' he said.

Paul had forgotten all about the Sea Scout badge, and its painful effect on goblins. 'Sorry,' he said guiltily, 'I hadn't realised it was still there. I'll put it away—'

'No, don't do that.' Mr Tanner took the tongs away and stepped back as if getting but of range. 'You hang on to that for a bit, you never know.' He paused. Something was making him uncomfortable, as though he had a fishbone stuck in his throat. 'You know,' he said, 'I'm sorry, the way things've turned out for you. I know you don't like it here and you'd far rather pack it in, quit. Unfortunately,' he went on, looking at the frosted-glass front window, 'that's not possible right now. But I just thought I'd tell you, it's not – Well, anyway.'

Paul would have liked to say something at this point, but he had nothing worth making the effort for.

'Quite,' Mr Tanner said. 'Right, you get on with the Mortensens, and let Julie know when you're finished. That's all.'

Paul wanted to fall asleep during the morning, curled up in a soft nest of computer printouts, but he seemed to have lost the knack. (*Can you forget how to sleep?* he wondered. *Do you have to go on special sleep-training courses, where they read you bits of railway timetables and literary criticism textbooks?*) He couldn't even persuade his mind to wander; he was focused, to his absolute amazement, on his work; to the point where he'd have missed lunch if someone hadn't knocked on his door and broken the spell.

'Hi,' Melze said, poking her head round the door. 'Fancy coming out for lunch?' *The hell with it*, Paul thought, *why not?* Last night, during the long vigil, he'd been wishing more than anything that he had a friend, someone he could talk to about what he'd been through in the last week or so. Fool, he'd forgotten about his oldest friend of all – true, the issue was clouded somewhat by the fact that she was a girl and he was (not beyond reasonable doubt, but on the balance of probabilities) in love with her. Stuff like that can clog your mind, like bits of rice and cold pasta gumming up a dishwasher.

They didn't go to the Italian sandwich bar or the little Uzbek place. Instead, they wound up in a Burger King. Somehow Paul felt that this was a bit of the adolescence he'd never had, sitting on a plastic chair drinking a milk shake through a straw with a girl he'd been at school with (though by right, in order to make it canonically correct, they should have been skiving off double Maths); it reminded him of those letters that get lost in the post and are finally delivered thirty years later. 'Something's bothering you,' Melze said, looking at him with her head cocked on one side. 'You've got that bewildered look you used to get when you discovered you'd forgotten your PE kit.'

'That obvious?'

She smiled. 'It's remarkable,' she said, 'how little you've changed. Peter Pan, almost. Makes me feel like it was only a few months ago we were at Laburnum Grove primary.'

Paul thought about that. 'Odd,' he said. 'I was thinking that *you*'re the one who hasn't changed. Well, you have changed, obviously,' he added quickly, 'but what made me think that was – well, how easily we're getting on, like we've picked up exactly where we left off eleven years ago. I didn't think people could do that.'

'Depends on the people,' Melze replied. 'But don't change the subject. Something is bothering you, isn't it?'

Paul took a deep breath. 'Do you really want to hear about it?' he said. 'It's long, and pretty weird.'

'Sounds interesting.'

'Nah.' He shook his head. 'It's got me in it. I'm serious, though. Can I tell you about it? The point is,' he added before she could reply, 'you're, well, normal. In fact, you're the only normal person I know—'

'Doesn't that make me exceptional, then? Sorry,' she added. 'Carry on.'

'Really?'

'Get on with it, for pity's sake.'

Paul paused for a moment, tidying the tumbled sock-drawer of his thoughts. 'Well,' he said, 'I won't start at the very beginning, with me getting the job and everything, because there isn't time and I don't like the sound of my own voice that much. I think this particular wave of bad stuff started when Sophie and I split up.'

'Ah,' Melze said, 'that sort of bad stuff. I've got A levels in that.'

Paul shook his head. 'It was rotten and horrible,' he said, 'no question about it; but it wasn't *weird*. In fact, I'd pretty much guessed it was on the cards for some time. Well, right from the start, basically. I wasn't good enough for her, and that's all there is to it.'

Melze didn't say anything, but she was looking earnestly at him. *Taking me seriously*, he realised with a faint shock of surprise and pleasure. *So that's what it's like.*

'Anyway,' he continued, 'that wasn't weird. She goes off to California; and next thing I know, I'm transferred from general office dogsbody to trainee dragon-slayer.'

She nodded gravely. 'I'm beginning to see where the weirdness comes in. Tell me, if Sophie hadn't got a transfer to LA, would she have been assigned to the dragon-slaying department too?'

Paul acknowledged the merit of the question with a slight dip of the head. 'Don't know,' he replied. 'The idea is, trainees spend three months or so in each department, to find out what they're good at. But Benny – Mr Shumway, the cashier, only he's also a dwarf and a hero part-time – he reckons you can't be a hero unless you're born to it. There was a lot of touchy-feely stuff about the nature of love, but I think the bottom line was that you've got to be such a sad loser that nobody'd miss you if you never came back.'

'Convenient,' Melze said thoughtfully. 'Your girlfriend dumps you, so suddenly you qualify. Did she *want* to go to California?'

Paul nodded. 'Yes. To get away from me, mostly, I think.'

'Oh well.' Melze shrugged. 'Another finely crafted conspiracy theory bites the dust. So there you are, learning to be Conan the Barbarian.'

'Not likely,' Paul said with a faint grin. 'Mainly it's a cross between working in the planning office and the Territorial Army. Very boring, with little nuggets of real shit in it.'

'You didn't take to it?'

'Can you say out of place? Like a slug in a packet of crisps. Not my sort of thing at all, apart from the paperwork and filling in the forms and stuff. That was boring, but at least I could handle it.'

Melze raised her eyebrows. 'But didn't you actually slay a real dragon?'

'Oh, come on. It was about this long.' He enclosed a trouser leg's length of air between his hands. 'And I killed it by accidentally sitting on it. If Saint George ends up in the dole queue, it won't be because of me.'

'How do you know that's not how *he* did it, and they changed the story a bit so as to look good in the paintings? Slaying dragons is slaying dragons, if you ask me. *I* couldn't do it.'

'Yes, you could. Well, you'd probably ladder your tights, but that's about all. Anyhow, no sooner have I sort of got the hang of being a hero, but I get transferred again. Not after three months; more like a few days.'

Melze rubbed her nose with her fingers; and through a small hole in time Paul could see her doing exactly the same thing in the playground, albeit with shorter fingers and a frecklier nose. 'That's odd,' she conceded, 'but not really weird. When you said weird, I was expecting magic and monsters and spoons bending for no apparent reason, not sideways career moves.'

Paul sighed. 'If you want weird, brace yourself because here it comes. First, I get threatened by a talking bicycle who tells me "Free the prisoners or you're dead." Then I find out that my great-uncle Ernie was a magician too, just like the partners; so good, in fact, that they had him write a section in the office-procedures manual. I'm guessing, but I wouldn't have thought they'd have asked him to do it if he wasn't some kind of leading expert. Then I get woken up by monsters in my own bedroom, telling me all sorts of cryptic stuff I don't understand; and then I hear that someone planted a bomb in my filing cabinet, and the whole office gets trashed. And then,' Paul added bittertly, 'the fun begins. Turns out that whoever planted the bomb has kidnapped Benny Shumway and Ricky Wurmtoter, and there's nobody in the office except me who's qualified to rescue them. So I go to High Wycombe . . .'

'Sorry,' Melze interrupted. 'Did you just say—?'

Paul nodded grimly. 'That's the portal between this world and the Kingdom of the bloody Fey, apparently. So there's me, or rather me and Monika.'

'Monika?'

'My car. Mr Wurmtoter's sister, but also my car. We cross into the Kingdom of the Fey, and we end up in this really nasty, creepy dungeon, along with Benny. Just as I'm being drawn to the sad conclusion that this time I'm really and truly fucked, Mr Tanner's mum turns up out of the blue and rescues me. Not Benny or Monika or Ricky Wurmtoter, mind. Me.'

'Just a moment,' Melze said. 'Mr Wurmtoter's sister is a *car*?'

'Yes. At any rate, she is now. Before that, she was this tall brunette. But she got transformed – in the trade, you see – and I'm assuming they haven't figured out how to turn her back yet. Either that or she prefers it, I really don't know. She's a pretty good car, I'll say that for her; forty to the gallon, and her exhaust—'

'Fine,' Melze said firmly. 'Mind you, I think you're breaking the cardinal rule of office survival: don't drive the boss's sister. But you were saying. Mr Tanner's mother—'

'Rescued me.' Paul turned his head away slightly. 'I think I told you, she's got this thing about me, God only knows why, it's a bit sick if you ask me, her being a goblin and all. But she's got her good points, no doubt about it. She helped me with that stupid little dragon, and fetched me out of that dungeon – really, I thought I'd had it that time.'

Melze nodded. 'But she didn't rescue the others.'

'No. Apparently she could only take back one of us. I imagine Benny's going to be fairly conclusively pissed off with both of us when he gets home.'

'You think they'll be able to rescue him, then?'

'Already done, apparently. The firm brokered a deal of some sort through a bunch of weirdos in an old warehouse in Bermondsey.'

'Oh.' Melze looked surprised; more so than when Paul had told her about their capture in the first place. 'Well, that's good. And how about Mr Wurmtoter and whatser-name?'

'Them too, so I'm told. The funny thing, though, is that when I got back from Wycombe, the first thing I did was barge into the Countess's office wanting to know what they were going to do about Benny and Monika, and she down-right refused to do anything. Nothing anybody could do, she said. And now, quite suddenly, they've been released – they're on their way home, apparently.'

Melze thought for a moment. She thought very fetchingly; a slight frown, a wrinkle of the nose. 'Maybe not so strange,' she said. 'Like, these creeps who captured you were the rebel faction in the Fey civil war, right? And the Countess; isn't she the rightful Queen of the Fey? Maybe when she said there was nothing she could do, she was thinking about, you know, the military option: going in there like the SAS and busting them out by force. Then she had a quiet think about it, or maybe these rebels came through with their demands for releasing the hostages. She negotiates, gives them what they want or some of it, and presto, they've got a deal.'

Paul nodded. 'That makes sense. God, that's a change. I'm so used to everything being bizarrely inexplicable, maybe I've just stopped looking for reasonable explanations.'

'Wouldn't blame you if you had,' Melze said sympathet-ically. 'I mean, it's one thing to hear you talk about it. Must be something else actually having it happen to you.'

'For instance, that bloody bike turned up again, for one thing. Luckily, I think I've worked out how to scare it off. Turns out it's allergic to names.'

'Allergic?'

'It's like names hurt it when it hears them, so all you've got to do is say a whole list of them – John, Fred, Clive, Rachel – and it runs away. Curiously,' Paul added, 'the nutters in Bermondsey I told you about were the same way; and I think I may have seen the rogue bike in their ware-house place while I was there. Or,' he added, 'it could just've been, you know, a bike.'

'A non-rogue one?'

'Does seem more likely, doesn't it? Oh, and then there was my uncle Ernie's stuff. Apparently he died—'

Melze was frowning again. 'Didn't I meet your uncle Ernie once, when we were kids?'

'I doubt it. *I* don't remember him at all.'

Her face lit up. 'Got it,' she said. 'I came to tea at your house, when we were very small. Not just me, I think you'd invited the whole class over for your birthday or something. That's it; it was your birthday party, and I was really jealous because you had a real live conjuror. And you told me, it's not like that, we're not paying for him or anything, he's actually my uncle. Your uncle Ernie.'

Paul thought hard. Now Melze came to mention it, he remembered the party, his ninth birthday; and he remembered the conjuror, vaguely, though he couldn't picture the man's face or anything. 'That was him?'

'I'm sure it was. Tall man, very thin, bald, with a big nose and bushy eyebrows. I was scared stiff of him at first because he looked so fierce and sort of wizardy, but then he started smiling and telling very funny jokes, and I wasn't scared any more.'

'Oh,' Paul said. 'I wish I had a memory, it'd come in very handy. So he was actually real, then. I was beginning to wonder whether he wasn't some sort of, well, trick that people were playing on me.'

Melze shrugged. 'So he died, then. He must've been pretty ancient, because he looked to be about a hundred and ten when we were kids. Mind you, grown-ups always look old when you're that age, so he may only have been sixty or something. I'm sorry to hear that, though,' she added. 'He was a really good conjuror, anyhow.'

Paul laughed. 'Maybe he was cheating. You know, using real magic instead of proper sleight of hand. Anyway, the point is, I got this letter from my parents saying that his stuff was with this firm of solicitors. They didn't want it, so if I went and got it, I could keep it. So I did. Bastards charged me a hundred quid,' he added sourly. 'And then, when I got it back to the office, it turned out to be all this really powerful magic gear – anti-goblin charms and a load of things Mr Tanner's mum told me were too dangerous to leave lying around, so she took them off me and put them in the strongroom.'

A curious look came into Melze's eyes. 'Really? Why?'

Paul shrugged. 'For safe keeping, I suppose. So they wouldn't cause accidents or something.'

'You're sure she didn't really want them for herself? If they were dead powerful, I mean.'

That thought hadn't even occurred to Paul. 'I wouldn't have thought so,' he said. 'I mean, the shield thing; she couldn't bear to touch it – burned her, she said.'

'Or perhaps she was just pretending it hurt, so if it got stolen you'd never think it was her that took it. Have you been to check it's all there?'

'As a matter of fact, no. I mean, if she wants it, far as I'm concerned she can have it. The last thing I want is more weirdness.'

'Maybe it's valuable,' Melze said. 'Could be worth a lot of money, if it's rare magic equipment.'

Paul considered that. 'I don't think goblins care a lot about money. I remember someone telling me that they're all filthy rich anyway, because of mineral rights and God knows what. I could well believe her nicking it to do mischief with, but not just so that she could flog it for cash.'

'Well.' Melze scowled. She had a sweet scowl – *dear God*, Paul thought, *listen to me. How can anybody have a sweet scowl?* 'I know it's wrong and I'm probably not really supposed to think it, let alone say it, but I don't like the goblins. Any of them. I think they're disgusting and vicious and nasty. You should see the claw marks on the front desk some mornings; when there's a lot of post to be sorted, sometimes Mr Tanner doesn't do a thorough job of magicking them away. It's *scary*, Paul.'

Paul grinned. 'Did I tell you about the time I faced down a whole gang of armed goblins with nothing but a stapler? That's how I met Mr Tanner's mum, actually. You see, they'd kidnapped . . .' He hesitated. The night when the goblins abducted Sophie, and he'd gone charging off after them, their spears and swords and axes against his anger and fear of losing her, and he'd won – Somehow it didn't seem right telling Melze about that, best friend or not. 'They'd kidnapped one of the staff, and I confronted them, just sort of said "Boo!" and they all ran away. Honestly, so long as you're careful they're the least of your worries.'

'Huh.'

'Really. To tell you the truth, I'm far more frightened of Countess Judy's lot, the Fey. Now *they* give me shivers down the spine.'

'Oh.' Melze looked at him, then shrugged. 'Well, anyway. God, is that the time? We're late.'

When Paul got back to his office, the pile of Mortensen printouts had quadrupled, to the point where he was afraid for the desk they sat on. 'Bloody hell,' he groaned, then saw a handwritten note on top of the pile:

PAC—
JDCB wants these done by the time you go home tonight. If
you can't finish before 5.30, don't worry; she's working late
and will unlock the front door.
   Julie

JDCB? He had to think for a while before he figured it:
Judy di Castel'Bianco. *Vindictive cow*, he thought. There was
absolutely no way he was going to be able to wade through
all that garbage in one afternoon. More to the point, it
looked like he'd be there till midnight, at the very least.
Still, it wasn't as though he had any choice in the matter.
If she wanted to put him in his place by giving him a
double detention, she could do that. *Bugger*.

At half-past five, Paul's attention was disturbed by
scratching sounds at the door. The goblins were used to
having the run of the place once the front door had been
shut. The light on in his office was probably bugging the
hell out of them. He scowled, took out the Sea Scouts badge
and jerked the door open. Sure enough, on the other side
were two or three goblins, crouched down where they'd
been trying to peer through the keyhole.

'Sorry, chaps,' Paul said sternly. 'This office is off limits
for tonight.' When the nearest goblin lifted its head and
growled at him, he stuck out his hand with the badge in
it, and slowly opened his fingers. The result was instanta-
neous and really rather pleasing. He'd heard the expression
falling over each other in their haste many times, but he hadn't
realised before what an amusing spectacle it could be.
Grinning broadly, he shut the door.

Six o'clock; six-thirty; seven. He was tired, and hungry,
and very, very bored, and he was still only just over halfway

through. He felt a yawn bubbling up inside him, like a belch of lava welling up from the magma level into the throat of a volcano. *Can't fall asleep*, he told himself, *can't go sleep, got to finish or be here all night—*

The pile of Mortensen printouts was actually rather comfortable to rest one's head on. The infinite layers formed a wonderful laminated cushion. A bright spark could make money patenting . . .

Paul could see the office very clearly, which was odd since he knew his eyes were closed. He could see himself, zizzing happily. He looked so peaceful like that, he decided, it'd be a crime to wake him.

The door opened; but not the boring old everyday door in the door frame. This door appeared suddenly out of the wall, and it looked rather familiar. *I know that door*, he thought, *I'd know it anywhere*. A door that appears out of nowhere, coming through the wall. When is a door not a door? Easy—

But that was odd too, because he'd lent Ricky Wurmtoter the Acme Portable Door, his wonderful secret get-out-of-mortal-peril-free gadget; and Ricky had got himself captured. Maybe this was Ricky coming home, with Benny and Monika.

Wrong. The door swung open wide; an arm reached out through it, and wedged it open with a thick heavy book, which Paul recognised as the office-procedures manual. It wasn't a particularly frightening arm; it wasn't green and scaly or grey with shrivelled skin clinging to the bone. In fact, it was wearing lilac, with patterns in silver glitter. A kid's arm.

Followed, a second later, by a kid. Paul wasn't terribly good at telling children apart, but he knew this one. The name escaped him, but he remembered that she was a real hotshot with a box spanner and a torque wrench. Behind her came the other half-dozen or so kids he'd seen at the garage in the middle of nowhere; behind them, at least thirty children he didn't recognise. School trip, he assumed, or someone's birthday treat. No grown-ups, though. Still, it was only a dream, so sod it.

Paul could see them looking cautiously at him, checking he really was fast asleep before tiptoeing past him, round the corner of his desk towards the door. The thing that struck him most about them was how very unchildlike they were, in spite of their round pink faces, out-of-proportion heads and scuffed knees. No child that age has lived long enough to have learned how to move so silently, so carefully, so *earnestly*. It was like watching commandos, or the SAS, not a crocodile of truant nine- and ten-year-olds. Not kids; something else, pretending to be human children. *Eeek*, he thought, *creepy. Glad I'm asleep and don't have to see this.*

He counted them: forty-eight.

When the last one had emerged from it, the Portable Door rolled itself neatly into a scroll, fell to the floor and vanished. The children, meanwhile, were sneaking out of the office. The last one closed the door softly behind her. Then Paul woke up.

According to his watch it was nearly nine o'clock. *Fuck*, he thought; *for all I know, Countess Judy's already buggered off, and I'm stuck in the building all night.* One thing was fairly certain: there was no way he was going to finish this pile of printouts now. If he tried, he was certain he'd be asleep again in five minutes. All he could think of to do was go straight to Countess Judy's office, and if she was still there, admit his failure and ask to be let out of the office. If she wasn't there— He'd been rather dismissive of the threat posed by goblins earlier, possibly because at the back of his mind he'd known that he had the Sea Scout badge. Query, however: would the badge, coupled with his fearsome reputation as a scarer of goblins, be enough to save him from having his throat cut in his sleep? Good question, to which he really didn't want to learn the answer.

All in all, he was enormously relieved to see a wedge of light showing under the Countess's door. Paul took a deep breath, and knocked.

No answer. He waited, counted to fifty, knocked again. This time, the Countess's voice snapped 'Come in,' and he turned the handle.

'Mr Carpenter,' she said. She was looking sterner and more intimidating than he'd ever seen her; her cheekbones were sharp as ploughshares, and her eyes were cold and silvery grey. For all that, something he saw out of the corner of his eye distracted him.

'I'm very sorry,' Paul said, 'but I haven't managed to finish the Mortensens you sent down. I promise I'll stay late tomorrow—'

'Yes,' she said, 'you will. And now, I suppose, I'd better let you out. Follow me.'

As Paul left the office, however, he couldn't resist glancing quickly round, just for a lightning-fast peek. When he'd entered the room, he'd seen the drawer of the Countess's filing cabinet – the same one he'd manhandled all over the place for Julie a few days back – twitch, then close silently, all by itself. Now, as he left, he could see it very slowly and tentatively slide open. Furthermore, he had a pretty strong feeling that he wasn't supposed to have seen anything of the kind.

Paul could hardly keep his eyes open on the bus home; but as soon as he unlocked his front door, he felt wide awake. All night, sleep evaded him like the last unpaired sock in the drawer. Counting sheep was pointless, counter-productive even; all he saw when he closed his eyes was a gaggle of schoolkids tiptoeing through a hole in his office wall. He tried turning on the TV, since television hardly ever failed to put him to sleep; but even the Open University, Channel Four arts programmes and reruns of *Martial Law* couldn't do the trick. He drifted off for a few minutes around five a.m. but was jerked awake by a loud bang. For some reason he imagined it was the slamming of a door, but it turned out to be nothing more than generic Arab baddies blowing up something or other in the course of some ineffable thriller. In desperation, he dragged himself to his feet and did an hour and a half of ironing before running himself a consolatory bath.

It turned into the dreariest week of Paul's life. When he arrived at the office, the Mortensen mountain had at least doubled, and on his chair was a terse note from Countess Judy reminding him that he'd undertaken to clear the lot before leaving the building. Unfortunately, his rate of progress soon slowed from pathetic to derisory, as the sleep that had avoided him all night came swooshing back like an angry tide. No matter what he tried – quadruple black coffee from the machine, pinching his arms, stabbing the point of the scissors into the palms of his hands – nothing could induce his eyes to stay open once he focused them on a sheaf of Mortensens. It had to be some kind of self-induced hypnotism, he reckoned – a smart conclusion which, once arrived at, didn't appear to help in the slightest. Three times before lunch, Julie caught him in mid-doze; each time the first he knew about it was the soft click of the door, and there she'd be, standing over him with a look of contempt on her face and yet more bloody printouts.

'You're not making a very good job of this, are you?' she said the fourth time.

Waking up just the conventional once a day was bad enough for Paul, who wasn't a morning person. Being exploded out of slumberland over and over again in the space of a few hours—

'No,' he mumbled. 'Dunno what the problem is, really.'

The click of Julie's tongue was like a Prussian officer's heels on a parade ground. 'Staying up all night boozing and partying, and being in no fit state to come into work,' she snapped. 'Just don't let Mr Tanner catch you, that's all. Otherwise, you'll be looking for a new job by the end of the week.'

Please, Paul thought, *pretty please. Pretty please with pink icing and ribbon.* 'Couldn't sleep last night,' he tried feebly to explain. 'Overtired, probably. Maybe I'm coming down with something.' Julie didn't dignify that with a reply, and Paul couldn't really blame her. If he'd repeatedly walked in and found someone zonked out on the desk each time, he too would've naturally assumed that the burning smell in the air was both ends of the candle, remorselessly incinerated by a hopeless debauchee.

When lunchtime eventually dragged round, he toyed with the idea of nipping out and getting some fresh air, but the ghastly thought of what'd be said to him if Countess Judy dropped by while he was out and found the snow-capped Mortensen range ungarrisoned was more than he could bear. He stayed at his post, struggled, and slept. Occasionally, he caught snatches of dreams (it was a bit like switching on the last five minutes of a film); sometimes there were kids sneaking through doors, sometimes he was in the main boardroom (the one with the imp-reflecting table top) with old Mr Wells, the senior partner, trying to explain the whole wretched business to him but unable to make himself understood because he'd caught the office cold and was constantly interrupted by a barrage of artillery-grade sneezing. In one dream he was in the land of the dead. He'd gone to do the banking as usual but Melze had wandered off and got herself trapped in the dungeons of Grendel's Aunt, he'd dashed off to find help and got completely lost, and now he was being chased across the asphodel fields by a pack of his relatives (led by Uncle Ernie) all howling like dogs and demanding to know why he never answered letters.

'This isn't good enough,' Countess Judy told Paul at eight o'clock that night, when he'd reported in to confess a second day of failure. 'Go home, go straight to bed, get some sleep, and be damned sure you get the job finished tomorrow. That's all I can say.'

But that night was just as bad as the night before, and the night after: no sleep, just aching, intolerable boredom. Paul tried the fresh-air approach at lunchtime the next day, walking briskly through the City until his feet were blistered, but the only result was deeper gloom and further despair; every time he passed a child or a group of children in the street (and either there were an awful lot of them out and about during the daytime or he was noticing them more than usual) he could've sworn blind that he recognised their nasty, grinning faces from his fragmented dreams. He didn't need to be a doctor to figure that one out; sleep deprivation, stress, with a light overall garnish of loathing and terror. Not the best week of his life so far.

Paul's luck broke on Friday night. He'd been given one last chance: work all weekend and get the backlog cleared before it formed a critical mass and screwed up the Earth's orbit, or else. Resigned to not sleeping yet again, he'd resolved to pass the time by painting the living-room ceiling. He'd got the furniture covered in old sheets, set up the ladder and dipped his little squidgy foam mop in white emulsion when quite suddenly his eyes closed, and nothing he could do would induce them to open again. He groped his way to the dust-sheet-strewn sofa – he felt the emulsion tray get kicked over en route, but there wasn't anything he could do about that – and flopped down with the mop still in his hand. When his eyes eventually opened, the room was full of light and his watch said 9:15.

Paul just made it to St Mary Axe by ten, which was his appointed time. He was still wearing Friday's clothes, stylishly though eccentrically enhanced by a big white rectangle on the left knee of his trousers. Countess Judy gave him a very quick glance, held the door open for him and went away without a word. Even the goblins gave him a wide berth; as he approached, the little knots and gangs of them he encountered in the corridors and on the stairs immediately went very quiet and backed hastily away, which he reckoned was a bit much. Needless to say, none of them came anywhere near him all day.

But, at a quarter past eleven that night, Paul carefully laid the last printout on the last pile, taking exaggerated care to line its edges up perfectly with the sheet underneath. He could feel his brain trying to force its way past his eyes and eardrums as it boiled and seethed with boredom, but he'd got the job done and he hadn't fallen asleep once. In spite of everything, he couldn't help feeling – yes, dammit, actual genuine pride. Something ludicrously pointless and stupid attempted, something done. Go tell the Spartans, and all that.

He stood up – his legs appeared to have forgotten how to do the standing-up business, and it was a second or so before it came back to them – and spent a whole two minutes just gazing at the vast array of neat, orderly paper bundles. *Thank God*, he thought, *that my office hasn't got a window, because this is precisely the moment in every comedy film ever made where a sudden gust of wind scatters the lot—*

Not wind, sure; but goblins. Goblins with the run of the place, dozens or even hundreds of malignant scampering non-humans who most of all just wanna have fun, preferably by breaking and spilling things. The mental image was more than he could bear. But, just as Paul had resigned himself to standing guard until Monday morning, inspiration struck. He took his Sea Scout badge, gave it a quick buff on his lapel, and laid it on top of the bundle nearest the door.

Joy, he thought. *Joy isn't anything I've imagined it to be over the last twenty-odd years. It's not Christmas or true love or chocolate ice cream or even getting out of the dungeons of the Fey. It's finishing this.* Something so simple, yet so unspeakably wonderful.

Paul was just about to turn off the light when he stopped, went over to the long blank wall opposite his chair and studied it, inch by inch. Nothing there, needless to say. No goblin scratches, no faint warmth to the touch, no slight clamminess where something had adhered to it by suction, no faint lines or cracks in the plaster to indicate a cunningly hidden seam. Another aspect of this overriding joy: by Monday he'd be healed – he wouldn't see doors in walls or be convinced that he knew the face of every bubblegum-chomping brat he passed in the street. All he'd have to put up with would be talking bicycles, extortionate lawyers' fees, the Bank of the Dead, his own shortcomings as a human being, and Mr Tanner's mum. And he'd have Sunday off, as well.

Joy.

Paul shook his head, closed the door gently to avoid making a draught, and went home.

Chapter Ten

Sunday dissolved into dreamless sleep; no kids, no girls, no talking bicycles or bossy cars or chatty transport of any kind. When the alarm went on Monday morning, Paul tumbled out of bed feeling brighter and livelier than he could remember. He had a feeling that something horrible was now over, and he wouldn't have to go back there again.

The Mortensen piles had vanished from his desk; it was clear, apart from a page torn out of a small notebook, with a few words scribbled on it in Countess Judy's preying-mantis handwriting:

> PAC—
> Work satisfactory. See Christine, regards office management
> assignment.
>   JDCB

Fine, Paul thought. He knew what office management meant in JWW-speak: shifting furniture, or helping with the photocopying, or replacing the starter motor in the fluorescent lighting tubes. Any one of the above was vastly preferable to sorting Mortensen printouts, so he fairly sprinted up the stairs to find out what he had to do.

'That filing cabinet,' Christine explained.

Paul nodded. 'It's in Countess di Castel'Bianco's office now, isn't it?'

Christine frowned. 'Yes,' she replied. 'Fancy you knowing that. Anyhow, it's got to come out of there and go into the cashier's room. You won't be able to manage it all by yourself on the stairs, though.'

'I could try,' Paul said, trying to sound feeble and undernourished.

'What, and chip all the paint in the stairwell? No, I'll give Mr Suslowicz a ring, he might have a minute or two.'

Much to Paul's relief, Mr Suslowicz wasn't there. Paul had only spoken to him a few times and on each occasion he'd found him unnervingly pleasant, for a partner; but he was still The Boss, not to mention a giant (albeit a rather short one). 'Damn,' Christine said. 'Usually I get Benny Shumway to help with this sort of thing. I'd help you myself, but I did my back last week at aerobics, and it's an enchanted filing cabinet, so you can't just magic it, you'd probably blow up the building.' She tutted for a moment or so. 'This is a pain – the Countess told me to get it shifted this morning, priority.'

If it occurred to Paul to wonder why moving a filing cabinet into the cashier's office was so important to a senior member of the partnership, he didn't dwell on the issue. 'How about Mr Tanner's— Rosie,' he amended quickly. 'I mean, she's a – They're quite strong, aren't they?'

Christine arched an eyebrow at him, but swivelled round to her phone and keyed a number. A minute or so later, the door opened and a petite, fragile-looking Chinese beauty walked in, wearing a pale blue silk dress and four-inch heels. Christine looked at her and clicked her tongue. 'Thanks for helping out,' she said tersely. 'You might want to change, though. Wouldn't want to risk you straining something.'

Mr Tanner's mum's laugh was like the distant tinkling

of silver bells in the still air of morning. 'Get stuffed, Chris,' she said. 'I could carry a titchy little thing like that balanced on my nose.'

Paul edged sideways an inch or so. 'In that case,' he muttered, 'maybe you won't be needing me after all. Perhaps I should just—'

'No you don't, lover,' chirruped Mr Tanner's mum. 'I've been wondering what you'd look like all sweaty. Talking of which, has some joker turned the heating down? This place was like a fridge all yesterday.'

Christine shrugged; nothing to do with her. 'I'll leave you two to it, then,' she said. 'If you go now, the Countess is downstairs with clients in the boardroom – you won't have to disturb her.'

The thought of going into Countess Judy's office bothered Paul, but he couldn't very well say anything; furthermore, all the way down the stairs and through the maze of corridors he had to put up with Mr Tanner's mum leering at him, in a way that elicited at least one snigger from a passing secretary.

'Have you got to do that?' he muttered, as she licked her lips for the third time in as many minutes.

'For crying out loud, Paul, I'm a goblin,' she snapped. 'It's like cats with bits of string, it's not a conscious decision or anything. You don't think I'm not sick to the back teeth chasing about after you?' She sighed. 'It's practically a duty. The sooner I've dealt with you, the sooner I can get on. It's like those computer games, where you've got to beat the dead boring level before you can move up to the interesting ones.'

Even with the door closed, Paul could tell from the outside that Countess Judy wasn't in her room. It was the difference between a light bulb turned on and off. Even so, he knocked on the door and counted to thirty before cautiously turning the handle and going in.

'Bugger,' he said aloud. 'Are we in the right room?'

Behind him, Mr Tanner's mum laughed. 'Think about it,' she said.

Bare walls, plain wooden floorboards, a ratty old chipboard desk, a plastic stacking chair and the filing cabinet. Paul couldn't help standing in the doorway and staring. 'But it wasn't like this the—'

'I said think about it,' Mr Tanner's mum repeated. 'Like the old Fey proverb: who needs a coach when you've got a pumpkin? So long as she's in the room, it's like Versailles – or,' she added, 'a tart's boudoir, depending on your aesthetic standards; any kind of decor, soft furnishings, Old Masters on the wall, you name it. When she's not in it, why should she care? It's the old light-inside-the-fridge paradox; that's basically what the Fey are all about.'

Paul nodded. That made sense; except that the filing cabinet looked exactly the same as it had when he'd caught a glimpse of it the other night. The crummy old government-surplus desk had looked like priceless Louis Quinze. 'Can we not hang about in here any longer than we need to?' he said. 'Sounds silly, I know, but—'

He tailed off. For once, Mr Tanner's mum wasn't grinning, leering or fluttering so much as a single eyelash. 'You know,' she said, 'there are days when you aren't quite as dumb as you look. You grab the top end, and let's get out of here before I throw up.'

Paul took hold of his end of the filing cabinet and, when Mr Tanner's mum got to 'three', he tried to lift. 'Bloody hell,' he said, straightening up in pain, 'that thing's *heavy*. What's she got in it, for pity's sake?'

Mr Tanner's mum scowled at him. 'There are also days,' she said, 'when you make depleted uranium look like gossamer. Trust me, you don't want to ask questions like that in a place like this.'

Paul was puzzled. 'Depleted uranium?'

'As in dense.'

'Oh, right. So you don't think we should try taking the drawers out first, make it easier to carry?'

'No.'

Whatever else Mr Tanner's mum might have been, she surely was strong. Once she'd taken the weight at her end, all Paul really had to do was help steer, and open the cashier's room door with his spare hand once they'd got there.

'Oh, great,' Melze sang out as they backed the cabinet through the doorway. 'I've been waiting for that. Can you put it there in the corner, just next to the bookshelf? Thanks.'

Just a moment, Paul thought. 'You've been waiting for it?' he asked.

'You bet. I hate having little piles of paper littered all over the floor.'

Paul straightened up, trying to ignore the chorus of protests from his back. 'You're going to keep stuff in here?'

Melze looked at him. 'Paul, it's a filing cabinet. You put papers in them, you don't teach them the flute or take them on walking holidays looking at interesting old churches.'

'But it's full.'

Melze laughed, and pulled open a drawer. 'No, it's not,' she said. 'Look, empty. Unless you count very old dead spiders.'

Paul looked at the empty drawer, then back at Mr Tanner's mum who lifted her shoulders in a tiny little shrug. 'Well, anyway,' Paul said, 'there you go. I hope you're very happy together.'

'Actually, it's not just for me, the top three drawers are for those Mortensen things. I gather you had a really fun time putting them in order.'

'Yes, but you'll never get all of them in just three drawers. There were mountains of them—' He paused. Melze was stuffing armfuls of familiar-looking papers into the top drawer of the cabinet. 'There,' she said, 'all done. Unless you've got a few more you've been keeping back for a rainy day.'

'That's *all*?' Paul gasped, but Melze just shrugged. 'It's got nice big drawers,' she said (and, to Paul's surprise, Mr Tanner's mum didn't say a single word). 'So,' she added, perhaps a bit too casually, 'you free for lunch today?'

Paul was about to say something – *yes*, probably – when Mr Tanner's mum pushed past him and stood between him and Melze. 'Sorry,' she said, 'but he's taken. There'll be another one along in a minute.'

'For God's sake,' Paul spluttered. But he didn't get any further than that, because Mr Tanner's mum elbowed him, very subtly and very effectively, in the solar plexus. He took a couple of steps back and thought about things for a bit, while Melze and Mr Tanner's mum stared at each other like a couple of multinational companies playing hostile takeovers. It was Melze who broke eye contact first. 'Fine,' she said. 'Tomorrow then, maybe.'

Mr Tanner's mum's jawline had gone all Mount Rushmore; now it relaxed into the classic grin.

'In your dreams,' she said; and, for some reason, that seemed to bother Melze; she turned her back on the pair of them and muttered something about having work she had to get on with. Mr Tanner's mum clamped her hand round Paul's elbow with a grip like a mole wrench and steered him out of the room.

'Don't say anything,' she said, and you could've sharpened carbon steel on her voice. 'Not one word, got it?'

Paul was still too deeply interested in when it was going to stop hurting to argue; he'd explain it all to Melze later, he decided, when the little red and green lights had stopped flashing behind his eyelids.

Neither of them spoke as Mr Tanner's mum conducted him down the stairs; the only thing missing, Paul reckoned, was the raincoat over their wrists. She let go of his elbow when they reached the ground floor. 'All right,' she muttered, 'so maybe I shouldn't have hit you so hard. I'm a tad out of practice with my gentle hitting these days. But you've got to promise me; just this once, and it's only for the next few days or so, try thinking with your brain instead of your—'

That was rather more than Paul could take, coming from her. 'Please,' he said, with what he hoped was chilling courtesy, 'just leave me alone, will you? For ever?'

She shook her head at him. 'I don't know,' she said. 'Why've I always got to pick the feckless, pathetic ones?' She walked away before he could think of anything to say.

The rest of the week was almost disturbingly calm. A string of trivial pest-control enquiries filtered through from other departments; Cas Suslowicz sent Paul a memo asking him to find out how to evict a bad-luck dragon from the site of a multibillion-dollar mall development in Singapore (the answer was, surprisingly, surrounding the perimeter with ordinary garden twine soaked in creosote, the smell of which bad-luck dragons can't abide); Mr Tanner sent Christine down with a client's file and instructions to research cost-effective methods of dealing with an infestation of water nymphs in the swimming pool of a holiday camp on the north Lincolnshire coast (Paul spent three hours vainly searching for water-nymph references in the office-procedures manual; finally, in frustration, he scribbled *Sharks?* in pencil on the cover of the file, and went out to lunch; when he got back, the file had gone and in its place was a hand-written note from Mr Tanner saying, *Good idea, thanks*); Professor van Spee himself, no less, summoned Paul to his office and asked him to draft a letter to a client advising on which varieties of garlic were most suitable for repelling which categories of vampire. Fortunately, Paul recalled having seen a Suttons seed catalogue in Benny Shumway's desk drawer, with Post-It notes sticking out of the pages; he waited till Melze was out of the room (for some reason), then sneaked in and got it. As he'd hoped, Benny had scrib-bled copious notes in the margins, and he was therefore able to advise the professor's client that Fleur de Lys and White Pearl were both equally good against ordinary night-stalking vampires, but Mersley White or Sultop were preferred in areas known to be infested with the rarer daywalking variety.

'Excellent,' the professor said, when Paul took him the draft. 'You seem to have mastered a notoriously difficult discipline in a short time, which suggests a natural aptitude. You might consider specialising in pest control once you've completed your trial periods in the other departments.'

The unexpected praise had hit Paul harder than Mr Tanner's mum's elbow, and all he could do was grin feebly and shake his head. 'I don't think I'd like that,' he mumbled. 'Thanks all the same. Too much – well, killing and stuff. And I don't think I'd really cope with the mortal peril terribly well, either.'

'You think so?' The professor seemed almost amused. 'It seems to me that you've been handling it admirably over the past few weeks.'

It took a moment for that one to sink in, by which time Paul had already started to say, 'Well, it's the killing that really bothers me, so—' He stopped short and his mouth flopped open, like the tailgate of the lorry off the back of which good things fall. ''Scuse me,' he said.

The professor raised an eyebrow. 'Come now, Mr Carpenter,' he said. 'You know perfectly well what I mean. And,' he added, lifting his glasses and rubbing his eyelids, 'I have to admit that I'm not sure if I'd have been able to display such fortitude had I been in your position. You may have doubts about your courage, but I don't. Good afternoon.'

Somehow, staying in the professor's room once you'd been dismissed was simply impossible, like defying gravity. Paul stumbled back to his office in a daze, and spent the rest of the afternoon staring at the door, trying very hard not to think about what he'd been told.

Of course, he reflected bitterly, *it would have to be bloody Friday today; now I'll have the whole weekend to skulk timidly in, won't that be fun? At least while I'm here I've got work and stuff to keep me occupied, and maybe just possibly someone would come and help me if I was attacked and started screaming the place down. At home, though—*

Quickly, Paul applied his mental handbrake. *Don't be silly,* he told himself, *it's all taken care of* – thanks to dear, good, brave, wise, thoughtful Uncle Ernie, who'd gone out of his way to make sure that Paul inherited that spectacularly useful Sea Scout badge. If something nasty did come for him in the middle of the night, all he'd have to do would be to wave it under their noses (assuming they had noses, of course) and they'd be off like rats up conduits. To think: he'd been worrying himself to a frazzle, and all the time the answer to his problems was right there, in his pocket.

Or rather, it wasn't.

Brief panic break, followed by detailed search of pockets, floor, desk drawers, pockets again. He was feeling his jacket lining just in case it had slipped through a small hole when he remembered the last time he'd seen the badge; he'd put it on top of a pile of Mortensen printouts, to keep the goblins off them until they were collected. That was a week ago, and he hadn't seen or even thought about the badge since.

There was a remote chance it had fallen on the floor and got kicked under the desk, but Paul disposed of that hope fairly quickly. The obvious conclusion, therefore, was that someone had taken it – either casual kleptomania, or because they wanted it, or because they didn't want him to have it. No prizes for guessing which hypothesis he inclined towards.

The journey home that night was little short of terrifying. People kept coming up behind him; not that unusual for London in the rush hour, but Paul had no way of knowing whether any of the scurrying lemmings squashing past him on the pavement or crushing against him on the bus was a disguised goblin or a shapeshifting Fey assassin or even an unusually tall dwarf. To cap it all, the light bulb on the stairs had blown, and he had to creep up to his flat through shadows thicker and more menacing than anything he'd had to face on any of his trips to deposit the takings at the Bank of the Dead. When at last he was able to close his front door on the outside world and he'd conducted an inch-by-inch search of the flat, torch in one hand, his most lethal weapon (which happened to be a cheese knife left over when his parents moved to Florida) gripped in the other, he locked, chained and bolted the door and flumped bonelessly onto the sofa.

Ten minutes later he'd stopped shaking, and was starting to feel just a little foolish. It hadn't occurred to Paul before that maybe Professor van Spee had simply been winding him up. True, the professor didn't look like he had a sense of humour, just as lions don't appear to have pink wings; but wasn't that a much likelier explanation than that someone was prepared to go to all the trouble of killing him? Who'd want to do that? Why murder someone who'd never really mattered in his entire life, a mere Mortensen-collator and part-time filing-cabinet-shifter's assistant? Exactly. No motive. Getting into a state over a joke that had fallen flat and his own pathetic cowardice. Stumbling wearily into the kitchen, Paul traded the cheese knife (ought to give it a suitable name, now that he'd adopted it as his personal sidearm; Edam-cleaver, maybe, or Cheddar's-bane) for a can opener, and fixed himself a rather indifferent dose of beans on toast. Then he sat down to watch the news.

Just ordinary, everyday stuff: mundane scandals, normal crimes, the reassuringly familiar lies of politicians. Nothing about a civil war among the Fey, or werewolves in Surrey, or the release of hostages from the dungeons of Grendel's Aunt. No big deal—

The sitting-room window exploded in a snowstorm of broken glass. Something large and heavy tumbled through;

it was alive, caught up in the curtain like an arena victim in a gladiator's net. The curtain rail and pelmet came away from the wall, and the writhing bundle crashed down on Paul's relatively new Ikea coffee table, crumbling it into dust and fragments. Paul was on his feet before he knew it, stumbling backwards until he couldn't go any further because of the goddamned interfering wall. The thing was bouncing up and down on the floor like an incompetent escapologist, fighting with the curtain and only succeeding in tangling itself further; then it stopped moving for a whole second and a half – enough time to run away in, provided your legs work, which Paul's didn't. Then a tearing, slitting noise, and a bright steel tongue poked through the white curtain lining, like the beak of a baby chicken pecking through the eggshell. Paul stared in horrified fascination as the blade sawed its way along the length of the bundle. He'd seen a score of sci-fi movies where the alien monster fights its way out of its glistening cocoon before springing up, alert, gigantic and ready for instant mayhem. He hadn't realised that they were really nature documentaries.

But the thing that crawled painfully out of the cloth chrysalis wasn't a multiple-eyed black-carapaced nightmare. It was Ricky Wurmtoter, dressed in faultless evening dress but no shoes or socks, and holding a sword. He struggled to his knees, looked up, saw Paul and grinned.

'Thank goodness for that,' he panted. 'I couldn't remember if your flat's 36 or 38.' Then he closed his eyes and slowly toppled over, taking out the footstool as he went.

'Mr Wurmtoter?' Paul whispered.

'Ricky, please.' He reached out with his left hand, groping for the sword, which he'd dropped. 'How's things? Haven't seen you in a—'

'Are you all right?'

Ricky Wurmtoter took a moment to answer. 'Actually,' he murmured, 'no. Bump on the head, probably two busted ribs, couple of extra holes in places where there shouldn't be any, and there seem to be three of you, going round and round like a windmill. Other than that, bloody awful. How's yourself?'

'Fine, thanks,' Paul answered automatically. 'Look, should I call a doctor? I mean, no, sorry. Stay still, I'll phone for a—'

Ricky shook his head. 'Please don't,' he said. 'Don't like hospitals.' He lifted his head, and Paul could see five ragged parallel lines of caked blood across his cheek. 'Afraid of needles, actually,' he said. 'I'll be fine if only I can get to a repair kit. You wouldn't happen to have one lying about, would you?'

'Sorry,' Paul said. 'All I've got is aspirin and plasters. There used to be some cough mixture in the bathroom cabinet, but I think it must've been Sophie's, because she took it with her when she walked out on me. Oh bugger, I'm talking drivel again.'

Ricky laughed as he picked small needles of glass out of his hands. 'Doesn't matter,' he said, with a slightly hysterical edge to his voice that Paul found rather frightening. 'What I really need is about a gallon of really strong black coffee.' He paused, and a look of genuine terror filled his eyes. 'You have got coffee, haven't you?'

'I think so,' Paul said.

'Real coffee, not decaff?'

'Um,' Paul said. He'd met coffee snobs before, the sort who looked at you like you were a cowpat or something just because you didn't have Lavazza Double Espresso or

Jamaican Red Mountain grown on the southern slope of the hill facing the sea. 'It's only instant,' he said. 'Nescafé,' he admitted, in a very small voice.

'Perfect,' said Mr Wurmtoter, visibly sagging with relief. 'Tell you what, you just lead the way and I'll make it myself.'

Ricky's idea of the proper way to make decent coffee turned out to be filling the cup half full with coffee powder and adding just enough cold water to turn it into syrup. 'Thanks,' he sighed after his third dose. 'I ought to be all right now.'

'Pleasure,' Paul said. 'Um, it's nice to see you again.'

Ricky leant against the kitchen worktop, then slid slowly down onto the floor. 'Do me a favour,' he said. 'Just nip and fetch my sword, would you? Only, I don't really feel like getting up, just for a moment.'

Rational explanation, Paul said to himself as he picked the sword up, using forefinger and thumb, as though retrieving a cigarette butt from a pint of milk. A bloke smashes in through the window in evening dress, cuts himself to ribbons but appears impervious to pain, falls over and demands very strong black coffee. Sherlock and Hercule and the boys wouldn't have had to work very hard to figure that one out: Mr Wurmtoter has been out celebrating his release with the aid of intoxicating liquor, and is not feeling well. But Paul had seen enough happy drunks to fill a Students' Union, and Ricky wasn't drunk. He glanced at the sword, and shuddered. It was a remarkably sword-shaped sword: plain steel, smeared all over with some kind of reddish-black gunge, with several large chunks bitten out of the cutting edge. He held it away from himself at arm's length as he returned to the kitchen.

'You're probably wondering,' Ricky mumbled, 'why the evening dress.'

Actually, Paul had been wondering just that. 'You were on your way somewhere?' he said.

Ricky nodded. 'Couple of weeks ago? Can't remember how long. You lose track of time, understandably. I was going to some bloody stupid awards ceremony – hell of a lot of them in the hero business, as you'd expect, always some pest in a tux chasing after you with the *Which Armour?* Lifetime Achievement Award for Manticore Management or some such garbage. Anyhow, I was just getting out of the limo, smiling for the cameras and all, and I suddenly felt terribly sleepy. Shit, I thought, here we go again; and when I came round, there I was, in the dark, rats shuffling, water dripping, that whole scene.' He laughed shrilly. 'I hate that, it makes you feel such an idiot, you know? Anyhow, I thought about it, had plenty of time for thinking, came to the conclusion that someone must've slipped a Mickey in my tea back at the office. The thing is, though, who? There's only two people it could've been, and I can't see either of them . . .' He frowned, shook his head as if to clear it. 'But on balance,' he went on, 'out of two really, really unlikely candidates, you're just about the more believable, by a tiny margin.' Moving so fast that Paul couldn't follow how he did it, Ricky sprang to his feet and flipped the point of the sword up under Paul's chin. It pricked. 'Was it you?' Ricky said.

What Paul actually said was 'Squeak,' rather than *Of course not, don't be bloody ridiculous.* He hoped very much that Mr Wurmtoter was fluent in inarticulate noises.

Two seconds, maybe three; then Ricky lowered the sword and flopped back down onto the floor like a bag of bones.

'It couldn't have been you,' he said quietly. 'In which case—'
The sword slipped out of his hand and clattered on the tiles.
'In which case, I must be wrong about the Mickey. I just
can't believe he'd do that . . .' His eyelids were drooping,
his head lolled sideways. 'Please,' he whispered, 'help me
stay awake. This is really quite important.'

'Sure,' Paul mumbled. 'Um, how?'

'Cold water. Splash. Please.'

Paul filled a saucepan from the tap, thinking, *Well, how
often does the boss ask you to drench him in cold water?* He
poured.

'Thanks,' Ricky said, shaking himself like a wet dog.
'That's much better. You're being a great help, you know
that? Carry on this way, you'll be in the frame for Best
Sidekick at next year's Percies.'

'Gosh,' Paul said neutrally. 'Um, Ricky, do you think you
could possibly tell me what's going on? Only—' He hesitated, intrigued beyond endurance. 'Percies?'

'Parsifal awards,' Ricky said. 'Scunthorpe Heroism
Festival. Generally regarded in the trade as a good indica-
tion of form for the Freddies, but I never bother going
unless I'm shortlisted.'

'Right,' Paul muttered.

Ricky Wurmtoter yawned. 'Do you think you could make
me some more coffee?' he said. 'A bit stronger this time,
if that's OK. Only, I think the last lot's starting to wear
off.'

There was only enough coffee powder left for four more
cups, but Ricky announced that that would probably be
enough to keep him going, at least until Starbucks opened
in the morning. 'Mustn't fall asleep again, see,' he explained.
'Vitally important. Life and death.'

Ah, right, Paul thought; *only*— 'Are you sure you should be drinking that stuff?' he said. 'Isn't caffeine terribly bad for concussion?'

Ricky looked at him as though he hadn't got a clue what Paul meant; then he laughed. 'Believe me,' he said, 'concussion's the least of my problems right now. No, reason I mustn't fall asleep is, mustn't dream. No more dreams, not ever, if I can possibly help it. Had enough dreams to last me.' He looked up. 'You *do* know about dreams, don't you? Dreams, the Fey, the whole shooting match?'

There comes a point when striving to cope and being a brave little soldier cease to have any meaning. 'Dreams,' Paul repeated. 'You mean, like when you're asleep?'

'Of course that kind of dream,' Ricky said, frowning. 'Bloody hell, didn't anybody tell you when you joined the firm? You mean to say,' he went on, his anger growing steadily, 'that you've been happily getting into bed and going to sleep and having dreams as though there was nothing to worry about, and you don't know even the basic safety precautions?'

Paul stared at him. 'Is there something to worry about?' he said.

'Are you kidding? Dreams, for God's sake. That's like saying, does it really matter if you dive into a swimming pool full of nitroglycerine holding a lighted stick of dynamite? I don't know, of all the bloody stupid irresponsible—'

'Oh, come on,' Paul couldn't help saying. 'Yes, I get some pretty weird dreams these days, but that can't hurt you, can it? I mean, it's all just stuff getting played back in your subconscious, isn't it? How can you possibly come to any harm if you're just sleeping peacefully?'

For a moment, Ricky had trouble making his voice work.

When he finally spoke, he was scarily calm. 'Tell me,' he said. 'How do most people die?'

Paul didn't like the sound of that. 'Old age?' he ventured. 'Illness?'

'Most people,' Ricky replied quietly, 'die in their sleep.' He turned his face away for a moment, then looked back. 'Sleep's a bit like water, it's fine so long as you don't try breathing it. Listen,' he said. 'I'm a pretty courageous guy. You don't have to take my word, I've got a shelfload of gongs and stuff to prove it, from *Hero Monthly* Bravest Newcomer of 1987 right up to my 2003 Freddy for Best Daredevil.' He paused for a moment, simpering ever so slightly, then went on: 'But you know what? There's one thing that scares me so much I can't bear thinking about it. I'm afraid I'll die in my bed, with my eyes shut, sleeping. I know the Fey, and I trust them about as far as I could sneeze them out of my ear. Now do you understand?'

'No.'

'Oh, for crying out—' Ricky pulled himself together with an effort. 'All right, let's take this a step at a time. You know about the Fey, right? What they are. Where they come from.'

Paul thought about that. 'No,' he said.

'Fine.' Ricky settled his back more comfortably against the side of the fridge door, then went on: 'The Fey are dreams, Paul. That's the very essence of what they are. They start to exist when one of us, a real person, sees them in our sleep. And normally, that's the only place they can exist, inside our dreams. In a way, it's a good existence: they don't need to eat or sleep or work, they never get old or sick, they don't have to bother with relationships or office politics or guilt trips or even being bored out of their skulls; once we've created them, generally speaking they can be whatever they want, inside the dream. But they can't exist outside that little cartoon speech bubble we make when we're asleep; and they've got to have someone to dream them, carry on dreaming them, or they just go pop! and fade away. In a sense they're like the dead; you know about them, they can only keep existing so long as someone remembers them. But the Fey never existed at all, they've never been solid or real, just pictures in somebody's mind. That's why they're so resentful; and it makes them dangerous.'

'Oh,' Paul said. It seemed the only appropriate comment in the circumstances.

'Dangerous,' Ricky repeated – he was talking mostly to himself now, Paul thought. 'Which wouldn't matter, only they're so goddamned clever and resourceful. They found out, a long time ago, that if one of us dies in the middle of a dream, if they're really quick they can slip through the gap and change places with the dying guy; they become sort of real, the dying guy's stranded in the Kingdom of the Fey. You wouldn't like it there, Paul. I've been there. It's not so good.' He swallowed and took a couple of deep breaths. 'You know why my Viking ancestors were all so dead keen on dying in battle? You can't fight in your sleep. It's so much safer getting your head split open with an axe.'

'I see,' Paul lied. 'So that's why it's dangerous going to sleep.'

'Part of it,' Ricky said, shaking his head. 'There's more. I said that if they sneak out when someone dies, they can sort of exist. Very much sort of. They still need someone to dream them, see; it's just that while they're being dreamed, they can walk about and talk and do stuff over here, in real life.' He paused for breath, then continued: 'Which means that whoever's dreaming them can't be allowed to wake up, or they go straight back to where they came from, and no chance of ever getting through again. So, you see, the ones who've managed to get through are completely ruthless. They'll do anything to anybody to keep from getting sent home. And if it means getting hold of some poor bastard and putting him to sleep for the rest of his life – like a coma, I suppose, only it's worse, because you can feel what's being done to you, all the time – well, they don't give a damn. That's what the Fey are, Paul. They're parasites and predators, and if they get their hooks into you, it's far, far worse than being dead, believe me.'

'But that's —' Paul shook his head slowly. 'That's awful. Hang on, though. The Countess: she's one of them, isn't she?'

'She's more than that. She's the boss, the Queen of the Fey. Says so on the headed notepaper, in case you haven't looked.'

'Bloody hell,' Paul said. 'But if she's that bad, that dangerous, why the hell don't you all do something about it? Stick a stake through her heart or something.'

Ricky grinned feebly. 'There are several reasons,' he said. 'I guess the main one is that she brings in about seven and a quarter million dollars in fees every year. We're running a business, after all, and the overheads just keep on shooting up. I mean, take business rates—'

Paul made a sort of strangled noise, then made himself stay calm. 'All right,' he said. 'Now I know about the bloody Fey. But that doesn't explain why it's so dangerous to go to sleep. I mean, why would they be after me, particularly?'

'You can dream,' Ricky replied. 'In fact, you do it rather well. My guess is, that's why Judy was so dead keen to hire you, when you came along for interview. She can smell a good dreamer upwind a hundred miles away. Now there's things you can do to keep safe, charms and talismans and stuff, but nobody seems to have told you about them. That bothers me, you know?'

'It bothers you,' Paul echoed.

Ricky nodded. 'Don't get the idea they're a hundred per cent bulletproof, by the way,' he added. 'Because they aren't, or else I wouldn't have needed to drink all your coffee. But they're like a burglar alarm. Most of the time they're enough to make the Fey decide you're more trouble than you're worth, so they go away and pick on someone else. But if they're determined to get you, it's pretty hard to keep them out. It's like putting the chain on the door when the bad guys have a battering ram.' He yawned again; such a huge yawn, he could've swallowed a cross-Channel ferry. 'I have to go,' he said. 'It's not safe for you while I'm here – actually, let's be honest, it won't be a hell of a lot safer for you after I leave, but it's worth clinging on to those few probability points – and anyhow, I've got a whole load of stuff I need to do before I show up at the office on Monday.' He frowned, his face reflecting the struggle he was having trying to focus his mind. 'By the way,' he said, 'how did you get on with that wyvern? In the cash machine.'

'I sat on it.'

Ricky nodded vaguely. 'Way to go,' he said. 'Best foot forward, and if feet aren't going to cut it, use what it takes to get the job done. Is there a back door or a fire escape?'

'No. I mean, I don't think so. I've never seen one, but—'

'Forget it. You got any rope?'

In the end, Paul knotted his dressing-gown cord to his spare belt to the extension lead for Sophie's hairdryer (she'd taken the dryer but had forgotten the lead), and hung on for grim death as Ricky scrambled down from the bathroom window onto the flat roof beneath. The last Paul saw of him was a quick wave of the hand before he vanished into the darkness.

Jesus, Paul thought, and, since he was all out of coffee, made himself a cup of tea. Clearly there were enough implications in what Ricky had told him to scare him to death fifteen times over. The sensible course of action, therefore, was to think about something else. Also, it was imperative that he stay awake for the rest of his life. Absolutely no question about that. Whatever else he did or didn't do, closing his eyes, even for a split second, was out of the question. Sleep-free zone. Just say no.

Zzzzz.

He dreamed that he was sitting at his kitchen table, his head cushioned on his arms, fast asleep, with an untouched cup of strong sweet tea six inches from his left elbow. He dreamed that as he slept, Countess Judy di Castel'Bianco walked in through the shattered window, and behind her followed a dozen or so very tall, very blond children, cloaked and hooded and carrying strange objects that he didn't recognise but which he knew were various kinds of weapon. *It'd be really nice if I could wake up now*, he thought, as Countess Judy stood over him, grabbed his hair and pulled his head up; *how the hell can I sleep through all this?* he wondered. *That thing with the hair has got to hurt like buggery, you'd have thought I'd wake up screaming right now*. No such luck, though; he watched as Judy tilted his head over to expose the side of his neck, and held out her other hand, into which one of the tall children silently placed a long, thin knife. What was it Ricky had said about people dying in their sleep? Judy was positioning his head just so, with what looked like the skill that comes with an awful lot of practice; she was looking for the whatchamacallit vein; because his head was full of dreams, Paul couldn't think of the right word – not arterial, because that was roads, not vernacular, that was slang, not judicial, that was laws and stuff. *Jugular, that's it, looking for the jugular vein.* Didn't take her long. The knife looked like it was plenty sharp. That was a good thing, right? *Won't feel a thing. Promise.*

Pity, he thought. *My life's been like a book you borrow from the library but never get around to reading until it's due back, and in a second or two it'll be over. Not that I'd ever have got around to doing anything with it, justifying my existence, making the world a better place. It was just a life, and most of the time it was either boring or horrible. Even so; I hadn't finished with it yet*, and already here was the waiter to clear away the dirty plates. Pathetic, really. And now her hand was on his shoulder, gripping like a G-clamp, shaking him—

'Wake up,' Ricky Wurmtoter shouted in his ear. 'Wake up, for fuck's— That's better. Now, look at me.'

Paul opened his eyes. 'Am I dead?' he asked.

'Only from the neck up. Bloody hell, Paul, what did I tell you about not falling asleep?'

'It was— Excuse me.' Paul floundered to his feet like a newborn foal and sprint-slithered to the bathroom, where he was sick with spectacular energy, though his projectile placement was indifferent. Then he staggered back to the kitchen. '*She* was here,' he muttered, dabbing at his face and neck with a towel. 'She was just about to—'

'All right,' Ricky said, wincing. 'Spare me the full narrative. Just as well I forgot this and had to come back for it,' he added, showing Paul the sword. 'Oh, and I got you this on the way, from the all-night shop up the road. Doewe Egberts,' he explained, carefully placing a huge jar of coffee granules on the table top. 'Since you'll be pretty much living on the stuff for a while, I thought you might as well have a brand that doesn't taste of bitumen dissolved in piss. In fact, if I were you I'd get a proper cafetière and some Whittards Mocha. False economy is not your friend.'

Paul nodded. 'Thanks,' he said. 'I – I believe you now,' he added. 'But why would she want to kill me? I never did her any harm.'

Ricky was looking at him oddly. 'Are you sure about that?' he said. 'Or maybe it's the other way around entirely. Maybe you did her a really good turn, something very useful indeed. In which case,' he explained, 'that makes you an accessory.'

Paul frowned. 'You mean like a belt or a handbag?'

'All right, accomplice. At the very least, a witness. The Fey are red hot on attention to detail. Have you been doing much for her at the office lately?'

'As a matter of fact, yes. She had me sorting those Mortensen printouts for the best part of a week.'

'Mortensen printouts,' Ricky repeated. 'That doesn't make any sense. Why would she bother killing you if all you've done is the filing? Oh well, I guess it's just that she doesn't like you very much.' He yawned, like a lion at the dentist's. 'You should be all right now,' he said. 'Now she's been rumbled it's not likely she'll be back tonight, but a couple of pints of that coffee ought to make double sure. What you really need, of course, is something like a seventh-level shield; I've got a spare back home that I could lend you, but I won't be going that way for a couple of weeks.'

'Just a moment,' Paul said. 'What's a whatever-it-is-level shield look like?'

'It can be anything,' Ricky replied, shrugging. 'Pencil, watch strap, scruffy old paperback book. The usual thing is a badge of some sort; something inconspicuous you can pin inside your jacket.'

'Would it scare goblins?'

Ricky laughed. 'Scare 'em?' he said. 'Just being in the same room'd fry their tiny brains. Touching it'd physically burn them, too. Why?'

'I think I've got one already,' Paul replied thoughtfully. 'At least, I did have, but I left it on my desk at the office and now I can't find it.'

Ricky was impressed. 'Where'd you – no, don't tell me now, I really do have to get a move on, run errands, see to chores. If we're both alive and conscious on Monday, you can tell me then.' He frowned. 'Far be it from me to dictate how you run your life,' he said, 'but in your shoes I'd fix that window before anything else nasty comes through it. It's a little-known fact that the Fey have real difficulty getting in somewhere if the doors and window are shut. Properly shut, mind. If they're only open a teeny crack, that'll do.'

For a moment Paul had no idea what he meant. 'It's all very well saying that,' he said mournfully, 'but where am I supposed to get a pane of glass at this time of night? Not to mention putty and—' He stopped. 'Oh,' he said, 'I see. I'd forgotten I can do that sort of stuff.'

Ricky grinned at him. 'Give it a try,' he said.

Of course, Paul didn't really know how to use magic,

just as nobody knows how to fly, but falling from an aeroplane just comes naturally. 'How do I start?' he asked nervously. 'Is there something I should say, or—?'

Whatever else Ricky might have been, he was impressively patient. 'Just think,' he said. 'Think about how the window looked before it got smashed. Then reflect on how a smashed window is inherently wrong, whereas an unsmashed one is how things should be, in an ideal world.'

'Yes, but,' Paul started to say; but Ricky shushed him and pointed at the window. Paul saw both their reflections in the unblemished glass.

'You did that, didn't you?' Paul asked.

Ricky shook his head. 'All you really need is confidence,' he said. 'You've got the basic skills, you just need to convince yourself that you can use them. Now then, remember: door closed, windows shut, curtains drawn and last but not least, toilet seat *down*. You can probably chance it and get some sleep tonight, or what's left of tonight, but if you want to play it absolutely safe, your best bet is a couple of handfuls of stale crumbs in the bed and lots and lots of coffee. And now I really have got to go.' Sword in hand, Ricky crossed to the door, opened it a crack and peeked out. 'Good luck,' he added, and slipped away, closing the door quietly behind him; just as Paul realised what he'd just said and called out, '*Why* have I got the basic skills?', whereupon the Yale catch clicked firmly home.

Once upon a time, Paul remembered as he waited for the front door of 70 St Mary Axe to open, weekends shot past so fast that bystanders were sent flying by the slipstream. As soon as you stumbled out of bed on Saturday morning, it was time to go to bed on Sunday, so as to be up bright and early for work the next day. He remembered mentioning this effect to Benny Shumway, who confirmed that time got distinctly odd around the sixth and seventh day, and went on to tell him about an early prototype time machine that JWW had built in the late 1890s, based on exactly that principle – by stacking up a series of artificially generated weekends, the designers reckoned, it ought to be possible to accelerate the would-be time traveller several years into the future. The project had foundered only because the return mechanism, which was based on the extreme nostalgia of looking at photographs of old school chums, was too erratic to be relied on, with the result that at some point in 2007, the firm was going to have to pay out a hundred and nine years' worth of accumulated back pay to the junior associate who had piloted the first manned test launch.

The previous couple of days, by contrast, had crawled by like hourly-paid snails. Between boredom, exhaustion and caffeine poisoning, Paul was practically on his knees. Only the thought of what he was going to say to Countess Judy at around two minutes past nine on Monday morning had sustained him through the ordeal. He'd had plenty of time to choose his words; eventually, he'd pared his speech down to two words (and one of those was a pronoun). He wasn't looking forward to the interview, but for once he was absolutely determined to follow it through.

The two words were, 'I quit'; and he got them out without corpsing, stammering or mumbling.

'Excuse me?'

'I said, I quit,' Paul repeated.

'You quit what? Smoking?'

'I resign,' Paul explained. 'I don't want this job any more. I'm leaving.'

'Oh.' She had the sheer effrontery to look surprised. 'Really? Why?'

Paul was now seriously over budget on words, but this wasn't a time for parsimony. 'You know why,' he said.

'No, I don't.'

'Yes, you do.'

'No, I don't.'

'Yes, you bloody well *do*.' Paul banged the Countess's desk with his clenched fist. 'Ouch,' he added, as the stapler flew across the room, leaving a staple embedded in the side of his hand. 'You tried to kill me.'

'Did I really? When was that?'

'You know perfectly— Friday night, when I fell asleep at the kitchen table. You got into my dream and you were going to kill me, only Ri— only somebody woke me up,' he amended sloppily. 'You had a fucking great knife, and you were going to stab me or slice me open.'

'Oh,' Countess Judy said, shrugging. 'That. There was no harm done, though. And I found someone else, another donor, so you're no longer at risk. Nothing to worry about, you see.'

It was just as well that there weren't any itinerant haber-dashers in the building at that moment, since for two pins Paul would've punched her in the face. 'No harm done,' he repeated. 'You were going to— Hang on,' he said, 'you found another donor. You mean, you killed someone else.'

She shrugged again. 'Hardly killed,' she said. 'I managed to locate a donor who was terminally ill; in fact, we arrived when he was on the very point of death. Salvage, you see, not homicide. We do have certain ethical standards.'

The anger was making it hard for Paul to speak. 'I wasn't on the point of bloody death,' he ground out. 'There wasn't anything wrong with me.'

Into the Countess's bright, silvery eyes came a curious glow that Paul couldn't remember having seen before. It sobered him up from white-hot fury to terror in about a fifteenth of a second. 'In your case,' she said, 'there are special circumstances. Rest assured, I would never ever presume to take a life to which I wasn't legally entitled.'

Curious, how some people have a certain knack and others don't. Paul had hoped that his two words would've settled the whole business and left him free and clear – free, to be precise, to change his name, grow a beard and start a new life for himself in Nova Scotia. In the event, they'd proved hopelessly inadequate. Countess Judy's two words, on the other hand, were the oncoming truck, and he was the hedgehog.

'Excuse me?' he said. 'Legally entitled?'

She nodded curtly. 'We have to be most particular about the legal side of things,' she said. 'In our position, unauthorised harvesting could lead to most undesirable complications. In your case, however, no such problems would arise, as we have clear unencumbered title.'

It was like swimming in shark-infested custard. 'Just a moment,' Paul mumbled. 'Simply because I signed your rotten bloody contract when I joined—'

Now Countess Judy was actually laughing; admittedly, not a laugh that had anything to do with humour. 'Of course not,' she said. 'Your terms of employment are strictly limited to your work obligations. I was referring to our legal claim to your life.'

'My life.' Another two words with the stopping power of a ton weight. 'You *own* my life?'

'That's right.'

'Really? How come?'

Now she opened her eyes wide, a show of surprise. 'By purchase, of course. We bought you.'

Three words this time. Paul took a step back, but that wasn't sensible. His legs didn't seem to be functioning terribly well. 'Bought,' he said. 'Who the hell from?'

'Your parents, naturally. Come now, Mr Carpenter, please don't ask me to believe you weren't aware of the fact. You have a certain degree of basic intelligence, even though you often seem to be at pains to conceal it. Do you really believe your parents could have afforded to move to Florida on the strength of your father's savings?'

Chapter Eleven

At some point, some time later, Paul must've been in his office, because Melze came in. She asked about where some forms or other were kept, though what had given her the impression that Paul knew where they might be he had no idea. He didn't answer. He was all out of words.

She repeated the question a couple of times, then said, 'Paul, are you all right?'

'What?'

'I said, are you all right?'

Honesty, the best policy; wasn't that what his mum had always told him? Good joke. 'No,' he replied.

Melze looked concerned, bless her compassionate heart. 'You look awful,' she said. 'What on earth's the matter?'

Cue enormous grin. 'Oh, I just found something out. About me, my life, the world in general. No big deal.'

That didn't seem to satisfy her; in fact, she sat down with a let's-talk-about-this look on her face and said, 'You're acting very strangely, Paul. What's all this about?'

Extend grin. 'You really want to know?'

'I wouldn't be asking if I didn't.'

'Fine.' Paul folded his hands on the desk and sat up straight. 'You met my mum and dad a few times, didn't you?'

'Yes, of course.' A look of alarm occupied her face.

'Nothing's happened to them, has it? They're all right, I mean.'

Funny. 'Oh, they're all right. They're as right as bloody rain. I got told something about them, that's all.'

Just a tiny flicker of impatience in among all that warm-hearted concern. 'What?'

Paul pursed his lips for a moment. Not the sort of announcement you want to rush. 'You know they retired to Florida?'

Melze nodded.

'Well,' Paul went on, 'I just found out where they got the money from.'

'Oh.' She waited, then prompted him: 'Was it something bad?'

'You could say that. They sold something.'

'Sold something? What?'

'Me.'

Melze looked at him as though he'd cracked a tasteless joke at a moment of great solemnity, like a christening or a funeral. 'I don't understand,' she said.

'Don't you? It's very simple. They took money in exchange for me. For my life.'

'But they couldn't have. There's no such thing any more – well, they say it still goes on in India and places, but not here. It's illegal.'

'So are lots of things,' Paul said placidly. 'Murder and stuff. Still happen every day.'

'But—' She scowled at him. 'Don't be so bloody aggravating, Paul. Lose the melodrama. Tell me exactly what happened.'

'I just did.' He sighed, and leaned back in his chair. 'They sold me to the firm. This firm, J.W. Wells and Co. For four hundred and twenty-five thousand US dollars.' He frowned. 'Excluding VAT, presumably, I didn't ask about that. I don't know if people are zero rated.'

'But.' Melze seemed fond of that word suddenly. 'But why, for crying out loud?'

'Why did they sell me, or why did JWW buy me?'

'Both.'

Paul shrugged. 'The first one, because they're utter bastards and they wanted the money. The second bit's rather more complicated, and I don't want to bore you.'

'Paul.'

'Oh, please don't say "Paul" in that tone of voice, you remind me of my mum and that's not tactful. All right, here goes. My uncle Ernie, right?'

'The one who died.'

'That's right, the one who died. Turns out that he was one of them. One of us. Good at magic, strong in the Force, whatever. He was *really* good at it, apparently, and according to Countess Judy, the sort of magic stuff he was best at almost always runs in families. She explained it to me, but I wasn't really listening; seems there's charts and tables and whatnot, you can work it out really precisely, who in the family's likely to have inherited the gift, if that's the word I want. Seems that Countess Judy and the other partners did the maths and decided that I'd be a good investment. So they looked up my mum and dad and made them an offer they couldn't refuse.' Paul grinned disturbingly. 'Not that they tried all that hard, it seems. Countess Judy said she and the rest of the gang got the impression that mum and dad would've settled for a hell of a lot less, like a fiver cash and a bag of dog biscuits, but according to her there's rules of professional ethics that mean they had to make a fair offer to start with. She did tell me how they arrived at the figure, something about thirty per cent of the income they'd reasonably expect me to produce for them, multiplied by two-thirds of the number of years till I retire. I'm sure she was telling the truth. She's got an honest face, among others.'

Melze didn't say anything for a very long time. 'Paul,' she said, 'you're not making this up, are you?'

'Nope. Come on, be reasonable. You've known me for years. When did I ever have that sort of imagination?'

Melze looked like someone had just slapped her round the face with a large sea bass. 'But they can't hold you to it,' she said. 'They can't.'

Paul shook his head. 'Don't you believe it,' he said. 'Look, I told you about how Dennis Tanner made puppets out of Sophie and me when we tried to resign, and that was just on the strength of a contract. Where they've bought you outright, it's far, far worse than that. Among other things, they can kill me, just like that.'

'But the police—'

'Can't arrest them for killing someone who drops dead of perfectly natural causes, like a heart attack or a blood clot in the brain. It's not my body any more, you see; it'll do precisely what they tell it to do. Not that they're likely to kill me just for wanting to quit – I cost them too much money. Besides, all they need to do is tell my body to show up for work every morning and that's exactly what it'll do, whether I like it or not. Pretty cool, huh? Anyway, that's my bit of news. How's things with you?'

'But—'

'Please,' Paul interrupted. 'I know you're trying to be nice, but I'd rather you didn't. I think I've stopped believing in nice for the moment, and if you stay here I'm going to say something really horrible. I know I won't really mean it, but you'd have to take that on trust. Besides, you've got that stupid form to find.'

Melze stayed right where she was. 'Are you sure it's not just Countess Judy winding you up?' she said. 'I mean, she doesn't seem the type, but you never know. Did she – well, give you any proof, or anything?'

Paul stifled a yawn. 'Well, she showed me the bill of sale, all properly signed and witnessed. Do you know, they got old Mrs Bath-Patterson from next door to witness their signatures. I hope they didn't tell her what the document was all about – it'd have fried her brain.'

'But—' Melze was struggling, he could see; trying to find a loophole for him, something to give him a tiny crumb of hope. He should have found it touching and sweet, but all he felt was irritation. 'You told me you saw the job advertised in the paper and went for an interview.'

'True; but the questions they asked me were gibberish. According to Countess Judy, that was to see if I freaked out easily. But no, I just thought I was too stupid to understand what they were getting at. They'd got it all carefully arranged. I only saw that advert because mum and dad told me the best place to look for jobs was that particular newspaper. The whole interview thing was a set-up.'

'But it couldn't have been. They hired that other clerk at the same time. The girl. Chloe.'

'Sophie. I guess they must've set her up too,' Paul added; that hadn't occurred to him before. She'd told him her mum had highlighted the ad in the paper with yellow marker pen so she couldn't miss it. 'Look, I really don't want to talk about this stuff any more. Last night—' He frowned.

'Last night, Countess Judy tried to kill me. She'd have done it, probably, if Ricky Wurmtoter hadn't stopped her.'

'*Kill* you? But why?' Paul shrugged. 'And is she going to try again? Paul, for crying out loud . . .'

'The answer is,' he said, 'I don't know. Don't bother asking me the question, whatever it is. I really do think you should go away now.'

'But—'

'Go *away*.'

Melze left. For a long time, Paul just sat, his mind in neutral. He was trying to remember something that had occurred to him – yes, right; Ricky Wurmtoter had saved his life, apparently; but Ricky was a partner in the firm, he'd been at the interview, so he must've known the whole deal, right from the beginning. Another cheerful thought.

How could they do *that to me? Their own* son?

Not that it mattered. Evil, unspeakable bastards, like every other living thing on the planet. Four hundred and twenty-five thousand dollars; what did that come to in English money, anyhow? Paul shrugged. It sounded like a lot, but hadn't he found all those hidden bauxite reserves for Mr Tanner, just by looking at photos of blank bits of desert? Maybe he'd already earned out what they'd paid for him; in which case, no wonder Countess Judy regarded him as nothing more than a Kentucky fried soul on legs, handily in reserve for the next time she needed a midnight snack.

Talking of which, he was feeling painfully weary. Just ten minutes' zizz was all he wanted, and could it possibly matter now, if he slept and dreamed, and never woke up? Paul thought about the fairy tales that had scared him so much when he was just a kid: stories about young men who get lured into the fairy castle, and wake up to find it's a hundred years later and all their family and friends have died. What was it Ricky had said about people dying in their sleep? Not that he was in any position to believe anything Ricky said, at that.

Ricky Wurmtoter. *I trusted that bastard. I gave him the last of my coffee (and that posh stuff he bought me tastes horrible, too). I ought to be fucking angry about that. Depressing, really, that I'm not.*

(If I went to Florida and killed them both, strangled them with my bare hands, I'd inherit the four and a quarter hundred thousand dollars, assuming they haven't frittered it all away on garden makeovers and soft furnishings. That'd be no more than justice, because that way at least I'd get the money that paid for me. Not that money's any good to me. Besides, killing them would mean having to be in the same room as them, and I don't think I could face that. And I'd have to ask Mr Tanner for time off, and he probably only lets you take your holiday if you're dead.)

Ricky Wurmtoter—

The door opened, and Ricky came in. Today he was well groomed and elegant, Pierce Brosnan modelling Armani; not a hair out of place, no scars or bruises. He had a large black box file tucked under his arm. It wasn't often that Paul felt an urge to use the word 'smarmy'; right now, though, he reckoned that it had evolved its slow, painful way from Anglo-Saxon through Middle English to its present meaning just for this very moment. Ricky smiled and said, 'Hello.'

'Hello,' Paul replied.

'How are you feeling?'

'Tired.'

'Well, that's understandable,' Ricky said, with a viscosity of sympathy you could've poured on flapjacks. 'No return visit, though?'

'No.'

Ricky's frown was so slight that most measuring devices wouldn't have been finely enough calibrated to detect it. 'That's good,' he said. 'I said, didn't I, she wasn't likely to try again right away. I guess that means we've got a little time—'

'She explained about that,' Paul said grimly. 'Apparently, she found someone else to murder, so I'm off the hook for now. I expect you're glad,' he added. 'After all, it's your money too, isn't it? Seventy thousand dollars.'

Ricky looked genuinely confused. 'What about seventy thousand dollars?'

'Six partners,' Paul said. 'Six into four hundred and twenty-five thousand is seventy thousand, five hundred.'

'Eight-hundred and thirty-three, actually.' Ricky pulled a sad face. 'She told you about that, then.'

Calm, always calm. 'Yes,' Paul said. 'She told me.'

'Oh.' He paused, then shrugged. 'You wouldn't care to consider the soccer transfer fee analogy, I suppose.'

'Not really.'

'Thought not. And you aren't flattered, I guess.'

'No.'

Ricky grinned. 'You should be,' he said. 'And if it's any consolation, it's a good sign – for your career prospects.' He put the file down on the desk, and sat in the chair; Sophie's chair, of course. 'Shows how highly the firm values you, and all that.'

'I couldn't give a flying—'

'They only paid twenty-five thousand for me.'

Paul couldn't remember what he was about to say, even though he was in the middle of saying it. Instead, he froze with his mouth open.

'Mind you,' Ricky went on, 'that was when twenty-five

K was worth something — we're going back a few years, to when money was something you could melt down and turn into jewellery. Even so, with due allowance for inflation and the underlying trends in the industry as a whole, I was cheaper than you when I was your age. And I'm sure you know better than to go telling anybody what I just told you. It's one of those deadly men's-locker-room secrets that you don't even share with your best friend.'

Paul was still staring, but his mouth was back on-line. 'They own you too?'

'Not *they*,' Ricky said with a sad smile. '*We*. As you so astutely pointed out just now, I'm one of them, which means that I own a sixth of me. Well, a twelfth, if you take the bank's share into account, but even a twelfth of yourself is better than—' He shook his head. 'For a twelfth of me, I've worked seven days a week, five hundred and forty-seven days a year—'

'Five hundred and—?'

Ricky smiled. 'In a magical environment, the term "time and a half" takes on nuances you couldn't even begin to imagine. The point is, I survived and I'm still here, dragons and vampires and animated skeletons and office politics notwithstanding. If I can do it, so can you. It's tough, but this is a tough business. Besides,' he added, scowling fiercely, 'Judy was entirely out of line trying to cull you like that. Clause fifteen of the partnership agreement is absolutely clear: partners must not use the firm's assets in such a way without formal consent at a properly constituted board meeting.' He glanced at his watch and stood up. 'In fact,' he said, 'this time I think she may finally have gone just too far enough, if you see what I mean. In which case, we've got her. Thanks,' he added graciously, 'to you. Of course, it'd be better if we had something in the way of proof other than your word. Still, it's a start.'

Paul shook his head. 'That's all you're interested in, then. Booting her out of the partnership so that you can work your way up the letterhead. Is that it?'

Ricky nodded. 'Partly. In fact, mostly. There's also the small matter of her trying to have me killed for the past hundred and sixteen years, but I flatter myself that I'm big enough to overlook that.' He paused, hand on the door handle. 'Oh, one other thing,' he said. 'I guess I owe you an apology.'

Quite, Paul thought; *and on the same scale of values, the attack on Pear Harbor was a bit uncalled for.* 'Really,' he said.

'Yup. Your Portable Door. You remember you lent it to me, just before I— Well, anyway, I'm afraid I haven't got it any more. It was taken from me when I was in the dungeons. They gave me back the rest of my stuff when they let me go, but not that. Sorry,' he added. 'I'd replace it if I could, but it's not really the sort of thing you can buy in Lakeland Plastics.'

It was some time after Ricky had gone that Paul noticed he'd left his box file on the desk. Paul picked it up, and a typed memo fluttered out from under the lid.

Paul,

    Thanks for minding the fort for me while I was away. By and large you coped pretty well. However, work has been piling up rather, and I'd be grateful (since you're still officially part of my team) if you'd deal with a few odds and ends for me – routine paperwork, mostly. I'll drop JDCB a memo explaining that you'll be working for me for the next few days, as she's now your nominal head of department.

    Ricky

– and in handwriting underneath:

PS I'd clean forgotten, but today's my birthday; and in case nobody's told you, we've got this corny old thing where on your birthday you buy cakes for everyone in the office. I know you like Uzbek, so yours is honey and nut baklava Tashkent style. Enjoy.

Sure enough, inside the box file, along with half a dozen fat brown envelopes full of papers, was a white paper bag, partly transparent with oil and honey, inside which was some sort of sticky pastry thing with bits on top. Paul couldn't see any reason why it should be poisoned, and he'd missed breakfast, so he ate it, but not in such a frame of mind as could in any way be construed as forgiveness. It tasted all right, though.

Work, Paul thought; *well, why not?* He opened the top envelope: a thick wad of forms, most of which he recognised – Form JX775, application for a special licence to cull banshees on a Site of Special Scientific Interest; Form JK981(B), application to remove a Tree Preservation Order from a rogue Ent; Form JG663, special dispensation to burn the corpse of an Undead in a smokeless-fuel zone. He sighed, reached for his pen, and yawned hugely.

So Ricky had lost the Portable Door. Pity; it had been an amusing toy, at least to begin with. Paul had been able to spend week-long lunch hours in exotic places and had still managed to catch up on his work before the front office opened again. At one point, he'd honestly believed that it had helped him attain True Love, in a confused, untidy sort of a way. Possibly it might have come in handy in his present ghastly dilemma; maybe he could've escaped from

Countess Judy and the Fey through it, next time they came
for him, but he doubted that. You had to be awake to use
it, after all. On balance, it was no great loss. He'd learned
before that the Door's principal and fatal drawback was
always what you took with you every time you stepped
through it: namely, yourself. Paul shrugged and added it
to the list of magical goodies that had recently passed
briefly through his hands, along with the Sea Scout badge,
the wyvern's-brain stone, Uncle Ernie's stash of bizarre stuff
that Mr Tanner's mum had whisked away from him on the
pretext of making the world a safer place. *Yeah, right.* Come
to think of it, he'd lost, given away or mislaid enough
potentially devastating weapons to equip a small but very
nasty army.

If he believed that it probably wasn't a coincidence,
would that make him certifiably paranoid? On balance,
probably not.

Paul finished one lot of forms, and found another lot in
the next envelope (JJ409, application to renew a helmet of
invisibility licence; JF006, statutory notification of intent
to destroy a Ring of Power in an environmentally sensitive
area). Filling them in gradually lulled him into the
Accountancy Zone, that dazed no man's land between sleep
and waking in which nothing seems to matter except writing
the answers to damn-fool questions into cramped little
printed boxes. Even as his mind drifted away into the fog,
he couldn't help wondering if the Fey could operate in this
disputed border country, and at some level he was relieved
and pleased when the phone rang and jerked him out of it.

The phone ringing was something of a novelty in itself.
'Hello?' he mumbled.

'Outside call for you.' Paul recognised Mr Tanner's mum's

voice, wondered vaguely why she was filling in on reception and remembered that Melze was the cashier now, even though Benny was presumably free too . . . 'Did anybody tell you that you're not supposed to take personal calls during office hours?'

'What?' Paul said, but the phone clicked in his ear, and then someone said, 'Hello, Paul?'

'Hello?' He recognised the voice. Of course he recognised the bloody voice – he heard it nearly every day.

'Paul, it's me, Demelza Horrocks. Melze.' Pause. 'You don't remember me.'

Huh? 'Of course I remember you, Melze. What's—?'

'Oh, that's all right.' Giggle. 'I know it's a bit strange, me ringing you out of the blue like this after all these years, but last week I ran into Jenny Wheeler, and she said Neville Connelly had told her you were working at this place in the City, which sounded really sort of grand and impressive, so I couldn't resist ringing you up and seeing how you were. How are you?'

'Melze? Is that you?'

Pause. 'Oh, very funny. Same old Paul. Anyhow, long time no see. Did you hear, I got married? That's right. Well, you remember Damien Turnbull; his sister was going out with this bloke Sean, and then they broke up and I happened to run into him at a party, and—'

Pointless trying to listen, absorb information and have the world blow up all around you, all at the same time. Paul tuned out. It sounded like Melze. Fact was, it sounded a hell of a lot more like Melze than Melze did, and it was dropping all the right names, the people they'd been at school with, the friends of the friends of their friends. But Melze was only a staircase and a few yards of corridor away, so what was she doing ringing him long distance from the deep past?

'Melze,' he interrupted, 'where are you living these days?'

'Saffron Walden,' she replied promptly. 'Well, just after Kevin was born we decided it was time we got out of London, and then Sean got a transfer—'

'Saffron Walden,' Paul repeated. 'Look, excuse me asking a very strange question, but what made you decide to call me? Right now, I mean.'

'Didn't I just tell you that? About running into Jenny Wheeler, who told me Neville Connelly had—'

'Right now,' Paul repeated firmly. 'As opposed to last Friday, or tomorrow week. Did you . . .' Battle-hardened and soul-callused as he'd become, he still cringed as he said it. 'Did you have a dream about me?'

Pause. 'You know, that's absolutely amazing; yes, I did. Not a strange dream or one of *those* dreams, you just happened to be there in it, and it made me think, I wonder whatever happened to Paul Carpenter; and then I bumped into Jenny Wheeler in Superdrug, and she said Neville Connelly—'

'That's great, Melze,' Paul said, 'I'll call you back. Bye.'

He sagged back in his chair and dropped the phone onto its cradle; then he glanced at his watch. Quarter past three – he'd worked through lunch, apparently. At that moment, Melze – must get out of that habit – the *fake* Melze would be at the Bank, paying in the cheques. *Good*, he thought, *I should just about have time.*

As Paul stood up, he felt strangely energised. *Well*, he thought, *at least I've figured out what's been going on around here. The fact that there's nothing I can do about it is another matter entirely.*

*   *   *

It was cold and slightly damp in the strongroom, just as it had been when Paul and Sophie had catalogued the contents, somewhere between three months and a thousand years ago. Much of the register was written in her spiky, difficult, little-girl handwriting, and Paul found that enormously distracting; bad, since he really did have to concentrate.

As he'd assumed, Countess Judy hadn't written register entries for the wyvern's third-eye stone she'd taken from him; nor had she simply shoved it onto the shelves where the catalogued items ended up. On the other hand, he was morally certain that she must've stashed it in here somewhere. Why he was so sure, he had no idea. Logically, she could just as easily have hidden it in her own room somewhere under an invisibility glamour, or logged it somewhere in the post-relativistic vastness of the closed-file store, or in any of the countless hiding places with which 70 St Mary Axe was undoubtedly riddled; or she could've gone for absolute maximum security and stuffed it down the front of her blouse, like a madam in a Western. Logic, though, hadn't exactly been on his side ever since he first walked through the door of this hell-hole. Could a Vulcan survive on the premises for more than a fifth of a second, Paul wondered, before his green brain boiled out through his pointy ears? Almost certainly not. The thing was in here somewhere, he knew it. But where?

When searching for proverbial needles in proverbial haystacks, there's always the robust approach: set fire to the hay, then sift through the ashes with a metal detector. Such an approach wasn't likely to endear Paul to his employers terribly much, but he wasn't really too fussed about that. If they chose to fire him for it, yippee; but they weren't going to, because that would mean kissing goodbye to four hundred and twenty-five thousand bucks. In any event, he placed a slightly higher value on his life than on his job, and pissing off Mr Tanner would be *fun*. He closed the strongroom door behind him, and went to reception.

'Sorry to bother you,' he told the ice-blue-eyed Swedish blonde bombshell behind the front desk, 'but I need a favour.'

Mr Tanner's mum scowled at him. 'You've got a nerve,' she said.

'Several. Well?'

She shrugged. 'What can I do for you?' she said.

'I need to borrow some of your friends and relations for a few minutes.'

'Don't be bloody stupid,' Mr Tanner's mum replied, and she was about to remind Paul of the fundamental deal whereby the goblins stayed strictly out of sight during office hours in return for the run (scamper, slither, crawl, waddle) of the place once everybody had gone home, when he shushed her. 'It's an emergency,' he pointed out. 'I need at least two dozen goblins for maybe ten minutes. Is that such a big deal?'

If she hesitated, it was probably only for show. 'What for?' she said warily.

'Research,' Paul replied.

'Fair enough. Where do you want them?'

Ten minutes proved to be a wild overestimate; Mr Tanner's mum's sisters, cousins and aunts were through the strong-room in four, leaving behind a snowstorm of floating papers, shredded envelopes and viciously abused index cards. Sorting and clearing up was going to be the sort of job that'd have all the king's horses and all the king's men sulking in their barracks screaming for their shop stewards; *not*, Paul thought smugly as he cradled his matchbox in his arms, *my problem*.

'Is that the lot?' asked the boss goblin.

'Yes, thanks.'

'Oh. Pity. We could do upstairs for you, no worries. Five minutes—'

Paul shook his head. 'That'll be fine,' he said.

'Or there's the closed-file store,' the goblin persisted hopefully. 'We aren't allowed in there unless one of you Tall Bastards lets us in. You sure you haven't accidentally lost something in there? A paper clip or a two-pee piece or something?'

'No, really,' Paul said firmly. 'But thanks ever so much for offering.'

The goblin muttered something under its breath, then whistled to its chums. They all glowed electric blue for a split second, then vanished. Paul allowed himself a moment or so to gaze at the majesty of the spectacle before him. According to his parents, his bedroom had been, beyond all possibility of comparison, the untidiest place on the planet. Not any longer. For a connoisseur of the Shambles Beautiful, it was an awesome sight. A small part of him hoped that the clearing-up spell the partners used every morning to straighten up the aftermath of the previous night's goblin frolics would suffice to deal with this mess. The rest of him couldn't care less.

Back in his office, Paul carefully opened the matchbox. There was the stone, still looking uncannily like one of the bits of coloured glass that you get in a flame-effect electric fire. He closed his hand around it, then hesitated and opened his desk drawer. Sellotaped to the side was a list of in-house extension numbers. He found the cashier's office and dialled. No reply. Not-Melze was still at the Bank. *Fine.*

On his way to the cashier's room Paul stopped off at the

closed-file store and headed for the shelves where Benny stored the heavy-duty pest-control gear. Since he was on a roll with wanton destruction, he was tempted by the comprehensive selection of explosive devices and accessories, but in the end he decided to keep it simple and discreet, and helped himself to a crowbar, a hammer, a couple of offcuts of two-by-four and a bag of nails. Plenty enough to carry up two flights of stairs (three if there was an R in the month; offhand he couldn't remember), and not so noisy as to risk attracting unwanted attention. It did cross his mind to see if Ricky Wurmtoter was in his room, but he decided against it. Paul still wasn't sure about Ricky. True, he seemed to be mostly all right, but he was still Management. Paul reckoned he'd be better off on his own.

The first part of his plan wasn't too hard, although woodwork had never been his strong suit, and he caught himself a nasty blow on the thumb with the hammer. That gave him the time he was going to need for the tricky bit, the first part of which was breaking into the filing cabinet.

Tricky was about right. When the crowbar snapped in half like a stick of celery, Paul seriously considered going down to reception and asking for a loan of another six dozen goblins. He dismissed the notion; the partners were bound to have specifically goblin-proofed every bit of office furniture in the place, so even the relentless energy and imagination of Mr Tanner's off-relations wasn't likely to do him any good. There were always the explosives, but by now he had a nasty feeling that the rest of the building was likely to give way long before the filing-cabinet lock. Hitting it with the hammer would achieve nothing beyond a temporary alleviation of his frustrations. Apparently he was screwed after all.

Unless—

Surely not. But what the hell, it was worth a try. Paul opened the top drawer of the desk and looked inside. Sure enough, along with the statutory broken pencils, twisted mess of tangled rubber bands, spilt miscellany of paper clips and whorls of discarded Extra Strong Mint wrappers was a little chrome-plated key. Just for kicks, he tried it in the filing-cabinet lock. It turned, something went *click*, and the drawer slid open as smoothly as a politician lying.

Fine, Paul thought, as he took a deep breath. *Now for the* really *tricky bit.*

Muscles stiffened, teeth clenched, he peered inside.

His first reaction was: *Shit – no wonder the bloody thing was so heavy to shift around.*

A spiral stone staircase, such as you'd expect to see in a church tower or the keep of a medieval castle, led down from the lip of the drawer into a huge, gloomy hall, dimly lit with rush lamps set in wall sconces. Paul hesitated for maybe five seconds; then, brushing aside a file divider marked A-C, he scrambled into the drawer and started to descend. He had the key in his pocket, just in case it'd do him any good if someone came in and slammed the drawer shut; he'd also brought the hammer and half the broken crowbar. If he got trapped down here, would anybody think to look for him? Just possibly, yes. After all, his name did begin with C, and all offices everywhere are founded four-square on the principle of alphabetical order.

It was dark. Paul hated spiral staircases. There were almost certainly rats, not to mention spiders. For the first time, he genuinely felt like a junior apprentice hero. Not that that was any comfort at all. In fact, it was right up at the snow-capped top of the list of things he didn't want to be right now. Nevertheless: just for once, he had a plan – not a very good one, in all probability, but still a plan. All junior apprentice heroes have plans, the way teenagers have spots. He pressed on until he ran out of steps, then stopped. Someone was staring at him – he could feel it.

'You again,' said a vaguely familiar voice.

'Hello?' He hated the sound of his voice at that particular moment: reedy and feeble and indescribably silly. 'Where are you? I can't see—'

'Oh, right. In that case—'

Green light seeped through from all directions, showing Paul a scene that he recognised straight away. A long green fire ran the length of a broad Hollywood-medieval hall, oak-panelled and hammer-beam-roofed, painted and gilded. Polished tables and carved benches flanked the hearth, and the walls were masked by acres of richly coloured tapestries, a grotesque combination of flowers, wildlife, court and battle scenes. At the end of the hall, a high table crossed the T. Paul swung round, but the staircase wasn't there any more, needless to say. 'Idiot,' Paul muttered to himself, 'idiot idiot *idiot*.'

'Now you know where you are,' said the little girl, stepping out from the hidden side door. 'Didn't expect to see you here again. Last time, you couldn't wait to leave.'

Behind her were the rest of the gang he'd first encountered at the all-night garage in the Forest of Dean; the same nightmare blend of cuteness and horror, Stephen King moonlighting as script editor for *The Brady Bunch*. *Great plan*, Paul thought; *now what?*

'Sorry,' he muttered, 'wrong drawer. I was looking for D-E. You couldn't possibly point me in the right direction—?'

A freckle-faced boy grinned at him. 'D as in Dungeon? Sure, we'll take you there if you like.'

'Thanks,' Paul said, 'but actually I was after E for Escape.'

'Then you're out of luck,' the boy said. 'Definitively out of luck, in fact. Please abandon all hope in the receptacles provided.' He took a step forward. 'And if you think your horrible friend with the claws and the little round red eyes is going to burst in and save you again, you can forget it. We've upgraded the security since you were here last.' He pointed to something above Paul's head; Paul craned his neck and saw something small and metallic flashing pale green light, nailed to a cross-beam. The Sea Scout badge.

No need to ask how that had got there. Nevertheless, Paul had a feeling that the loathsome kid had committed a tactical error in drawing his attention to it. Apart from that one step forward, the gang hadn't moved. He was prepared to bet (not that he had any choice) that as long as he stayed underneath the badge they weren't in any hurry to come closer. At best, though, it was a stalemate.

'Not that it matters,' the girl was saying, 'but what on Earth prompted you to come back here?' She giggled. 'Is there anything we can do for you?'

Paul forced himself to smile. 'Actually,' he said, 'there is. You can answer a few questions for me, and you can give me back something that belongs to me. Would that be all right?'

The boy grinned. 'Depends,' he said. 'On whether you've got anything to bargain with. We don't think you have. And don't think you can stay safe for ever just standing under that stupid badge thing. Sooner or later you'll pass out from hunger or fall asleep on your feet. We're patient.'

Paul shrugged. 'Fine,' he said. 'While we're waiting, answering my questions'd help pass the time.'

'But what would be the point? Face it, after you've been here a few days, or months, or centuries, whatever it is that's occupying your funny little mind will have lost any traces of significance long ago. You think you'll care who planted the bomb or who the traitor inside JWW is when the only thing you can think about is how wonderful it'd be if only you could die?'

'Humour me,' Paul said.

The girl rolled her eyes. 'Whatever,' she said. 'Fire away. After all, we don't have to answer you if we don't want to. But in return,' she added slyly, 'you'll have to do something for us. Something we can't force you to do. Okay?'

'There's things you can't force me to do?'

'Some. Not many. What's the first question?'

It took Paul a moment to remember. Maybe Little Miss Poison had a point. Already, none of it seemed particularly important. 'Who's Grendel's Aunt?' he asked.

All the kids except the little girl sniggered. She just looked at him as if he was simple and said, 'You don't know?'

'No.'

'Amazing. All right, then. Grendel's Aunt is the queen.'

'What, of your lot? Countess Judy?'

The girl nodded gravely. 'The Contessa Judith di Castel'Bianco. As you've probably guessed, the Contessa thing is just slumming, like God dressing up as the Pope. But yes, she married some tinpot human nobleman when she first broke into your side of the line. She needed a human cover, and your lot are so impressed by titles and stuff. She reckoned it'd give her more credibility. Before that, she was just a – what's the word for it? Someone who sings in a theatre, along with a lot of other human females.'

'Chorus girl?'

'Like it matters. But to answer your question, she's Grendel's Aunt, and this is her home and principal place of business. And the dungeons are hers too, of course.'

'Thanks,' Paul said politely. 'So who is it pretending to be Melze Horrocks? One of you?'

The girl smiled. 'Queen Judy's niece,' she replied. 'Princess Suzie. Out of interest, how did you find out? We all thought she was doing a really good job.'

'She was. But the real Melze phoned me, out of the blue. Otherwise I don't suppose I'd have known.'

'Interesting,' the girl said, poker-faced. 'That raises some implications we're going to have to consider carefully. But that's our business, not yours. One more question, and that's your lot.'

One more question; and they didn't have to answer if they didn't want to. 'This civil war thing,' Paul said. 'What's it about, exactly? I mean, are there genuine issues or is it just that you don't like each other very much?'

'A bit of both,' the girl replied. 'Yes, two-thirds of us can't stand the other third, and vice versa. But what sparked it all off was the big colonisation debate. The majority like the idea of crossing over to your side and settling there, like when your Europeans came to America. But there's a few fuzzy-minded types who don't hold with stealing territory and exterminating the indigenous wildlife. Mostly they're just a nuisance – there's not enough of them to constitute a problem, and they're way too wishy-washy to do anything effective. The only reason we haven't done the invasion stuff before is that we couldn't get across the line except one at a time every now and again – great for building up our intelligence-gathering network, useless for large-scale troop movements. But then you showed up, and we got hold of that wonderful Portable Door contraption, which means we can finally start a full-scale takeover. All thanks to you, with some help from that clown Ricky Wurmtoter. The irony is,' she continued, 'he only borrowed the Door off you in the first place because he was convinced that it wasn't safe leaving it with you; soon as his back was turned we'd get hold of you and prise it out of your cold, dead fingers. So he took it, thought he'd lie low for a while somewhere we couldn't find him. Not a bad idea, actually, provided you haven't got a mole in your support structure. As it is, we were there waiting for him. Stupid arrogant human, thinking he was a match for us. Once we'd got him in the dungeons, it took us about five minutes before he was practically begging us to take it if only we'd let him go. We agreed. We were lying, of course.' She smiled. 'And that's your third question and I hope you feel much better now that you know the answers. Right now, though, you're feeling very, very sleepy.'

Annoyingly, she was quite right about that.

When Paul woke up, his first instinct was to roll onto his side and reach for the light switch. But there wasn't one; and then he remembered. He wasn't at home in bed, he was in the stronghold of Judy di Castel'Bianco, Queen of the Fey. Again.

He was just about to scream with fear and anger when he remembered something else. Yes, he was screwed; but he had a plan.

So that was all right, assuming he could remember what the plan was.

He couldn't.

It's a miserable thing to have a tea-bag memory, riddled with thousands of tiny holes through which information floods out. Paul had lived with the affliction for so long that he generally managed to rise above it; he wrote things down on scraps of paper, or tied knots in his handkerchief to remind him that he'd tied knots in his other handker-chief, or stuck yellow stickies on doors and VDU screens to remind him to check his handkerchief. Forgetting some-thing as big and important as The Plan was, however, seri-ously careless even by his standards. Assuming, that was, that he'd actually forgotten, rather than having had strangers inside his head editing his memory.

Good point. The impression Paul had got from the kids back in the great hall was that he'd been deliberately put to sleep, as opposed to merely flaking out through exhaus-tion and caffeine deficiency. If they'd put him to sleep, it almost certainly wasn't for the good of his health. Pound to a penny he'd been having dreams while he'd been asleep; and while they'd been inside his head, what'd be easier than wiping the odd memory as they passed through?

Bugger, he thought. But he rallied quite quickly. He had no idea what The Plan had been, but if he'd made it up in the first place, it couldn't have been anything too clever or elab-orate. If he'd managed to invent it before, he'd surely be able to invent it again, from first principles if need be. Piece of—

Unless, of course, The Plan hinged on some specific piece of kit, which he'd carefully brought with him only to have the Fey pinch it from him while he was asleep. That wasn't so easily shrugged off. Paul checked the contents of his pockets: keys, crumpled Switch-card receipts, pen cap without accompanying pen, handkerchiefs (with knots), thirty-seven pence in loose change, wallet, ball of frayed string, his battered old penknife (official Girl Guide issue, his twelfth-birthday present from Auntie Chris), one unwrapped and extremely sordid fruit pastille, one small chunk of what looked like the glass out of a flame-effect electric fire. Fat lot of good—

No; Paul remembered now, he'd been at great pains to get hold of the small chunk of what looked like glass. It was, of course (silly him), the third eye of a Suffolk Round Spot wyvern, prised out of the poor dead creature's skull by Mr Tanner's mum, confiscated by Countess Judy, restored to him by two dozen extremely improbable goblin Boy Scouts. Since he'd incurred so much aggro to get hold of it again, it followed as night the day that it featured substantially in The Plan. But how? All it was good for was research, finding out marginally relevant facts about chimeras. Look in it, Mr Tanner's mum had told him, and you might just see something useful.

Fine, Paul thought. What'd be really useful right now? He grinned sourly. What he needed to know, as a matter of urgency, were the details of The Plan, just in case he'd actually managed to think up some way of—

The stone grew, from a loose chipping to a potato to a basketball to a boulder that filled all the space between floor and ceiling, until it was so big that he couldn't see it any more. *Déjà vu*, Paul thought, with a brief spurt of wild hope. *Cool*. The green glow was warm, and crackled softly with static. *Please wait*.

As before, the glow resolved itself into a shimmering, insubstantial blackboard, on which words started to form like frost crystals on a window-pane.

The Plan.

It occurred to Paul that he hadn't breathed for quite some time; since the stone came on-line, in fact. *Never mind, plenty of time for breathing later.*

Note: since it's likely, certain even, that I'll be caught and my memory will be wiped, I'm taking the small chunk of what looks like the glass out of a flame-effect electric fire along with me. With luck, they won't notice it in among all the other junk in my pockets. Then, when I'm trapped in the dungeon, all I'll have to do is look in it and, with more luck, there'll be a copy of this Plan, and then everything'll be just fine. I hope. Fingers crossed.

Fine, Paul thought. *Clever, resourceful old me. Now, about The Plan—*

Please wait.

Stupid stone. Paul did his very best not to get impatient, but it was hard going. Quite apart from the fact that The Plan was his only hope of not spending for ever in a very small dark room with himself for company, he couldn't wait to see how clever he'd been.

The memory you are looking for is currently unavailable. Your cerebral cortex might be experiencing technical difficulties, or you may need to adjust your physical surroundings. Please try again later.

Aaargh, Paul thought. *Now, about The Plan—*

The Plan.

(Thank you. Thank you so fucking much.)

Paul read the wispy white letters once, twice, three times for luck, a fourth time just in case he was being really thick and had missed something painfully obvious that would explain everything. Then he shrugged. *Of all the people in the world to be forced to trust blindly,* he demanded of himself, *why the hell me? I wouldn't trust me to tell me the time.*

Still. He couldn't think of anything better, or even anything worse; his mind was completely blank, presumably an after-effect of whatever the Fey had done to him while he was asleep. He thought about it for a moment and decided: *Let's go for it. Just because it's a bloody silly idea and there isn't a hope in hell of it working and it'll almost certainly make things very much worse, it doesn't mean I shouldn't do it. It's how governments make laws, after all.*

Step one.

As Paul carried out the preparations for step one, he occupied his mind with trying to remember why he'd come down here in the first place. Not the easiest of riddles to solve; but when all was said and done, he'd achieved something by the exercise. He'd learned who Grendel's Aunt was, he'd confirmed his suspicion that the fake Melze was indeed working for the enemy, he'd discovered what the Fey were actually up to – and how they were doing it, using his Portable Door. It'd have been nice if he could have just asked someone back in the office, or looked it up on a website or something, but apparently it was the sort of information that you had to pay dearly for. And now, at least, he had a general idea of what was going on. What a very pleasant change that made.

Step two. Paul had heard it said that step two didn't hurt, not that he could understand how anybody could possibly know. He hoped very much that the rumours were accurate for once, since he'd long since faced up to the fact that he didn't so much have a pain threshold as a pain cat-flap. *Never mind*.

With his thumbnail Paul prised open the big blade of his Girl Guide pocket knife. It had always been stiff, and as usual he tore his nail getting the blade out. Then he laid his left hand on his knee, wrist uppermost, and grabbed tight on the piece of string he'd looped round his elbow. At the last moment he closed his eyes, locating what he devoutly hoped was the right vein by feel. *This is a bloody stupid idea*, he thought, *but*— But what? Presumably there was a but, or this wouldn't be The Plan. *Oh fuck*, he thought, *I hate having to be me*.

Then, grinning at the irony implicit in that last thought, Paul slashed the arteries of his left wrist.

Chapter Twelve

Dying wasn't so bad. In fact, compared to a bumpy Ferris wheel or flying with Virgin Atlantic, it was relatively relaxing and stress-free. Probably it helped that Paul was in a darkened cell at the time, since he hadn't realised that he was going to bleed quite so much, and the sight of blood had always turned him up rotten.

No need to open his eyes or stand up. Once he'd got over the initial panic, it was actually rather pleasant to be free of his body; something like getting out of the house after being cooped up inside for days. He'd never liked it much anyway: it had always been the wrong size, shape, length, width. He'd never thought much of the face, the hair was the wrong colour, the arms and legs were too thin, the feet were too big and his system always seemed to have a headache or a cold. In the event that The Plan screwed up and he didn't get his chassis back, maybe that wouldn't be so bad after all. A person could really be himself without a stupid body holding him back—

Paul couldn't feel anything. He knew, because of all those trips to the Bank, that there was a floor here, something solid enough to take his weight when he'd walked on it. Not any more, apparently. Presumably that was how astronauts felt, floating in space on the end of a bit of string. Only difference being, no string.

Help—

Paul forced himself to stay calm. The Plan would work. Everything was going to be just fine. Any moment now, he'd do what he'd come to do, and then he could go home. It wasn't like this was going to be permanent. *Stop panicking.*

No string. No sensation of movement, either. In fact, no sensation at all. He was beginning to wonder if this had been such a good idea after all—

'Paul?'

He didn't have to turn round to see her; she was just there, so close that he could have reached out and touched her, if he'd had anything to reach out with. Just for a moment, too, he fancied he could feel something; not a particularly nice something, more a sort of excruciating burning sensation, as though he was much too close to roaring fire. It was, he realised, her body heat. As soon as he'd figured that out, it stopped.

'Paul,' she repeated, 'what the hell are you doing here? And what's happened to the door? I can't get back through to my office, I'm stuck here.' She paused. He could see the fear in her eyes; could sympathise, in spite of everything. The thought of being still alive and stuck down here because the door back to the cashier's room wouldn't open almost made him feel guilty about having nailed it shut. 'Paul,' she repeated, 'are you all right? You look – different.'

Well gee, Melze, thanks for bloody noticing. I'm dead. No sound, no voice; he'd formulated his reply and thought it at her. Apparently she must've received the message somehow, because she said, 'Dead? You can't be, it's impossible. What happened?'

She's the enemy, remember? Don't know. Was sudden. I was asleep, dreaming. Now I'm here. This is a dream, right?

She was the enemy, that'd been established beyond

reasonable doubt; so why the look of horror on her face? 'Paul, I—' Her lips trembled, her eyes were wide with the old Aristotelian double whammy, pity and terror. 'I – I don't think so,' she said. 'I think you're— Oh Paul, I'm so, so sorry.'

Why? Not your fault, is it? No, seriously. This is just a dream. I'll wake up soon. Won't I?

'Paul—' She hesitated; maybe she'd just thought of something, like how it would be if she couldn't find her way home, not ever? Guilt and horror and pity are fine when you've got your return ticket safely nestled in your top pocket. 'I can't get out, Paul. What's wrong? Why won't the door open?'

If he'd had anything to grin with, he'd have grinned like a dog. *Don't ask me, I'm dead, apparently. See you around, whatever your name is.*

'Melze,' she said, as though at some level she was trying to convince herself, or keep from forgetting. 'I'm Melze Horrocks. We were at school—'

Fibber. Have a nice day, now.

Paul withdrew from her faint circle of light; he didn't go away, as there were no places to go to or away from, but she wasn't there any more. Reflecting on their conversation, he wished he hadn't been quite so cocky. If The Plan had screwed up, or hadn't been any good to begin with, he was far more likely to end up stuck down here than she was. How long would it be before someone had occasion to drop by the cashier's office, noticed the boarded-up door and broke it open? *No, wait.* What would they notice first, the nailed-up door or the wide-open filing-cabinet drawer? Depends on who it was. Countess Judy, for instance, would probably be more interested in the drawer, whereas Ricky

Wurmtoter would be more concerned about the door. Sooner or later, though, someone would notice, because the banking had to be done, cheques and TT forms and petty-cash requisitions had to be dealt with. Paul had no idea how long the living could stay down here before going native, but it seemed pretty good odds that her chances were better than his. In which case, screw compassion.

Work to do. Initially he'd been worried that he'd have forgotten the way to the Bank. Silly; like being afraid of dying of thirst if you happened to get turned into a fish. No places down here, therefore no ways to forget. He was at the Bank.

'Mr Carpenter.' Mr Dao, the polite, gracious bank official, sounded genuinely concerned. 'I wasn't aware that you were due to arrive; otherwise I'd have sent someone to meet you, as a courtesy to a valued customer. I trust your journey was not unduly distressing.'

Fine, thanks. 'Fine, thanks.' He hesitated. 'Oh, right, I can talk to you. Is that because——?'

Mr Dao nodded, clearing up a very small doubt. 'Because I'm dead too, yes. I can talk out loud to both the living and the dead; it's one of the minor privileges of my office. I'm pleased to hear that your transition was relatively painless, at any rate. Have you been to Reception yet? The paperwork——'

'Not yet, no. Actually,' Paul said, as casually as he could manage, 'before I check in, there was just one little thing I was wondering if you'd do for me. For old times' sake, you know.'

Mr Dao nodded gravely. 'If I can, of course. How can I be of assistance?'

Difficult to be convincingly casual, at a moment on

which his entire future existence or lack thereof hinged, though it was a comfort not to have to worry about his body language giving the game away. 'My uncle,' he said. 'Ernest Carpenter. I believe – you've got a strongroom, right? Where customers can deposit stuff for safe keeping?'

To Paul's overwhelming relief, Mr Dao nodded. Paul had guessed that there was such a facility, but he hadn't ever seen any hard evidence. 'I am, of course, well acquainted with your illustrious uncle.'

'Great,' Paul said. 'Well, as it happens I'm his, um, legal heir. So I was thinking, before I register, which presumably will make me sort of officially dead as opposed to just dead dead; would it be all right if I had a look to see if Uncle Ernie's got anything stashed away down there? Really it's just curiosity more than anything else, but the family was really surprised when all we found was a cardboard box of old junk; I think they were expecting money and stocks and shares and bonds and all kinds of stuff. My guess is, he burnt it all so it'd come down here. Not being able to take it with you's exactly the sort of rule that Uncle Ernie hated most; I'm sure he'd have found a way.'

Mr Dao was silent for a long time. From the pale glow behind his eyes, Paul was convinced that he'd seen through the lies. Nevertheless, just when Paul had given up hope, the banker dipped his head gracefully and said, 'Of course. I can confirm that your uncle has a substantial credit balance at the Bank, as well as a strongbox in our safe-deposit facility. Since you are the next of kin – I'm sure I can take your word for that without having to check – I can see no objection, in this instance. If you'd care to follow me.'

Clever me, Paul thought; *I didn't just figure out the existence of the Bank strongroom from first principles, I also guessed that*

Uncle Ernie had a box there, so it's a real shame I can't remember how I came to all these wonderful conclusions. Mind you, if it turns out there's nothing in the box except a bundle of porn mags and a fortune in Confederate dollars, won't I be the silly old sausage? I'll probably laugh so much I have to be taken home.

Inside the Bank— There are no places where the Bank is. But there are doors: big, thick, black hardened-steel doors with colossal lever locks, huge bolts, gigantic padlocks in enormous hasps; time-delay locks and combinations locks, locks that only open with a retina scan or a DNA sample or a 108-bit security code or a nice smile and a pretty please. There aren't any walls for these doors to live in, but that doesn't matter. A wall can be bulldozed or dynamited. When the door is surrounded by absolutely nothing, that's security. One door after another, like two mirrors facing; and each time, Mr Dao turned the key or entered the code, then stood politely to one side so Paul could go first. After the hundredth door, or it could have been the thousandth, Paul reckoned it would only be simple politeness to say how impressive it all was. Mr Dao acknowledged his compliment with a tiny nod. 'Thank you,' he said. 'However, when you feel you've had enough, please do tell me. I confess I find this activity fatiguing.'

'Oh,' Paul said. 'I thought—'

Mr Dao smiled. 'The more doors you expect to see, the more there are,' he explained. 'A thief would spend all eternity finding new ones. Nevertheless—'

'That'll do fine,' Paul said quickly, as the latest door swung open. Behind it was one of those bead curtains, very 1970s; and beyond that, a set of shelves; and on the shelves, a row of shoeboxes. Paul braced himself like a diver about to plunge into cold water, and forced himself through the curtain. To his great relief, it parted around him and he passed through it; he was solid again, which was nice.

'Second shelf, third from the left,' Mr Dao said. 'I'll be just outside if you need anything.'

He passed through the bead curtain, leaving Paul alone.

Well, Paul thought, *here we are*. He had to stand on tiptoe to read the names scrawled on the boxes in black marker pen; but sure enough, on the second shelf, flanked on one side by *Drake, Sir F.* and *Presley, E.A.* on the other, was a box marked *Carpenter, Dr E.* He reached up and gently pulled it out, nearly dropping it on the way. It was nice to have arms again, but they felt strange, as though they weren't his size. Resting the box on the edge of the bottom shelf, he lifted the lid and looked inside.

'Hello, Paul.'

Uncle Ernie climbed out of the box like steam rising from a bath. It took him a moment to consolidate. He hadn't changed much since Paul had last seen him; a long, stringy man with a large head and enormous bony knuckles. He was smiling.

'Hello, Uncle Ernie,' Paul replied.

'Well done, by the way,' Uncle Ernie said. 'Pretty smart, to piece it all together the way you've done. Chip off the old block, and all that.'

Paul smiled feebly. 'Thanks,' he replied. 'The trouble is, whatever it is I figured out, I've forgotten it. Or rather,' he added, 'someone's forgotten it for me, if you see what I mean.'

Uncle Ernie nodded wisely. 'I think so,' he said. 'How is Countess Judy these days, by the way?'

'She tried to kill me,' Paul said. 'In my dreams.'

'And that's why you're here, of course.' Uncle Ernie

shrugged. 'You have to realise, it's not because she doesn't like you or because of anything you've done. The Fey are just different, that's all. And dangerous, too,' he added. 'Very dangerous, bless them, though they're great fun once you get to know them properly. Wonderful card players, among other things.'

Paul nodded. He didn't really want to hear about how nice the Fey were really. 'Can I ask you something?' he said.

'Of course.'

'Thanks.' He took a moment to pull himself together. 'Are you really dead?'

'Oh yes.' Uncle Ernie grinned. 'As dead as dead can be. I made very sure of that. Otherwise, I couldn't have come here. And of course, this is the only place where I'm safe.'

'I thought so,' Paul said. 'You died and had yourself put away in a safety deposit box in the Bank, just so as to escape from the Fey.'

'One of my better ideas, though I say it myself. It's a bit dull being inside a cardboard box, but compared to the alternative, what'd happen to me if they got hold of me, it really isn't so bad. And of course,' Uncle Ernie added softly, 'I have one last trick up my sleeve.' He paused, then sniffed like a tracker dog. 'And so have you, apparently, you clever boy. Did you work it out all by yourself?'

Paul shook his head. 'Actually, it was an accident,' he said. 'I was down here doing the banking – JWW has an account with the Bank, you see—'

Uncle Ernie nodded. 'I know,' he said. 'Go on.'

'Well,' Paul continued, 'I was here on business like I said, and I happened to get a nosebleed. Which meant that I left some of my blood behind, when I went back Topside. Which means, doesn't it—'

'Quite right,' Uncle Ernie said, with more than a hint of pride in his voice. 'Very well done. You left a drop of your blood behind, just enough to keep you alive as far as the door in the cashier's office. Exactly what I did, though in my case I pricked my finger with a needle. Here it is in my box, look.' He pointed at a small bottle with a tiny red dot inside. 'Mr Dao will give you yours when you ask him for it. A splendid fellow, Mr Dao, I knew him before he died. It's so good to know there's someone you can rely on.'

Paul thought about that. 'No offence, but how did Mr Dao get hold of my blood? I thought it just fell on the ground.'

'It did,' Uncle Ernie answered. 'And there it lay, for about as long as a fifty-pound note would be left lying around if you dropped it in the middle of Oxford Circus station at the height of the rush hour. Obviously, one of the Dead found it – by smell, probably, or else they felt the heat – found it, slurped it up before anybody else could, and ran away laughing all the way to the Bank. Blood is currency here, you see; that's why you have to perform a blood sacrifice each time you want to pay in or draw money out.'

Paul had to think about that for a moment. 'Bank charges.'

'Essentially, yes. And if one of the inmates gets hold of even the tiniest drop of blood, they pay it into the Bank and have it credited to their account. If they manage to save up enough, they can buy a whole second of being alive again. You simply can't imagine what that means to them, once they've been down here for a while. And, clearly, the Bank's the only place safe enough to store something so indescribably valuable.' Ernie grinned unexpectedly. 'It's what you might call their life savings.'

Don't react, Paul told himself, *it only encourages them*. 'But what makes you think Mr Dao'll give it to me?'

'Oh, he will. Because it's your blood, you see. Even that little drop will be enough to keep you alive long enough to return to your side of the line; and once you're there, of course, you'll be extremely grateful and send him a present. He likes presents very much; and it won't cost you anything, in real terms.'

'It won't?'

Uncle Ernie smiled. 'All my life I've been hopeless at cooking; can't even make toast without burning it. I've scraped enough charcoal off charred bread to smelt a ton of iron ore. Imagine my pleasant surprise when I arrived here, and found that my current account at the Bank stood at over eleven thousand slices of bread. Down here, that makes me Mohammed Al Fayed. A moment's carelessness with a grilled sausage or a slice of bacon will more than repay Mr Dao for his assistance.'

'Oh,' Paul said, slightly stunned. 'All right, then, fine. That's a weight off my mind, anyhow. But—'

'But you didn't go to all the trouble of coming here just so you could figure out – very cleverly, I might add – how to get back again.' Uncle Ernie nodded seriously. 'You came here to see me, because you need my help. Am I right?'

'Yes.'

'Splendid. And you need my help because when I was alive I was one of a tiny handful of humans who knew almost as much about effective magic as the Fey, and because I'm your uncle.'

Paul nodded grimly. 'Partly.'

'Partly?'

'Yup. Mostly, though, because it was you who landed me in this shit in the first place.'

For a moment, Uncle Ernie looked startled; then his face

relaxed into a slight frown. 'You certainly are perceptive,' he said. 'More so than I gave you credit for. Or did someone tell you?'

'Countess Judy.'

'Ah.' Uncle Ernie pursed his lips. 'That does seem to be the sort of thing she would do. A remarkable woman and extraordinarily talented, but with an unfortunate malicious streak; she does rather tend to regard cruelty as an end in itself.'

Beside the point. Paul glared at him. 'So it really is true, then,' he said. 'My parents sold me to the firm.'

'Yes.'

'And it was you who told the partners about me, which was why they made the offer in the first place.'

Uncle Ernie shrugged. 'Simple heredity,' he said. 'You could work it out on your fingers, if you wanted to. And, of course, I needed you. Both of you,' he added, looking away for a moment. 'The Fey have got to be stopped, you see, before they start doing serious damage. As soon as I realised that I was essentially on my own – there was even a traitor inside JWW itself – I knew that I couldn't do what had to be done all by myself. I needed to get out of harm's way for a while, and I needed someone to carry on the work while I was – indisposed. So,' he added, 'after a certain amount of heart-searching and misgivings, I involved you. Then I left.'

'You died,' Paul said.

'As you say, I died. You must understand, I was at the end of my resources. The orthodox Fey, led by Countess Judy, were certain to kill me very soon. The dissident movement that I'd started among the more conscientious Fey had foundered; they weren't prepared to follow me any longer, and I can't say I blame them. I'm a reasonably talented magician, though I do say it myself, but I lack the quality most needed in an inspirational leader: courage. I'm a coward, Paul, I admit it freely. Certainly no hero. You, on the other hand—'

There is only so much a person can take. 'What is it with you people?' Paul said. 'First I'm a natural magician, then I'm a born bauxite-scryer, now I'm the last, best hope of humanity against whoever these Fey are supposed to be. All right, maybe that's true. But for the last time—' He was almost shouting by now. 'For the last fucking time, I am *not* a hero. All I did was fill in forms and sit on a poxy little dragon. I can't do the job and I don't want it. What part of that are you having problems with?'

'You,' Uncle Ernie went on imperturbably, 'on the other hand, are a textbook archetype; if I was still teaching, I'd take you along to lectures and point at you so the class could take notes. You're the accidental hero, the dear little chap with furry feet and glasses who sneaks under the gap in the fence that's too small for the musclebound swordsmen to get through. You should be, after all. I bred you that way.'

Just when you think you've heard it all – 'You what?'

'Bred you.' Uncle Ernie nodded serenely. 'Hell of a job. Our family – your father's side – have all the magic and no balls; your mother's side have the hearts of lions and the brains of plankton. You have no idea how much effort went into persuading your mother even to go out with your father, let alone marry him. Thank God for JWW's patent love philtre, is all I can say; and even then, it wasn't easy. In the end I had to pump both of them so full of the stuff it's a wonder they didn't float down the aisle like a couple of Poohsticks. But that wasn't what you wanted to talk to me about, was it?'

For two and a quarter minutes, Paul couldn't say a word. The cumulative effect was too overpowering. He desperately wanted not to believe a word of it; he'd have given anything for a tiny drop of scepticism, the slightest grounds for doubt. Unfortunately, deep down it was like finally remembering something that's been on the tip of your tongue all day – a name or the missing middle bit of a song lyric – he'd known all this, somehow, and forgotten it a very long time ago. He knew for certain that it was true, though how he knew was another matter entirely. 'You bastard,' he said eventually. 'You complete bastard. How could you?'

Uncle Ernie raised an eyebrow at him, Spockwise. 'I'm going to let you in on a little secret,' he said, 'something that very few people in the whole world know, but it's very important and likely to prove extremely useful to you in later life, assuming you have any. In all human history,' he went on, 'there have been exactly two recorded and verified instances of a genuine coincidence; and there's a considerable body of influential academic opinion that reckons one of them's a fix. Accordingly, whenever you run into something that looks like a coincidence, the first questions you should ask yourself are: who's buggering me about this time, and why are they doing it? There now,' he added, 'I've just given you a gift whose value is beyond rubies, and all you can do is stare at me with your mouth open, like a bad-mannered koi carp. You still haven't told me what it is you want, and time's getting on. We do have time down here, you know, lots of it; quantitatively speaking, the difference between here and Topside is like the difference between the Pacific Ocean and a paddling pool. Even so, I wouldn't leave it too long, if I were you. It'd be an awful bore if Judy figured out what you've done before you get back to life.' He gave Paul a jagged grin, like a rip in the canvas of a smiling portrait. 'You *do* want to go back, don't you?'

'I suppose so,' Paul said weakly. 'Though it's not nearly the same clear-cut issue it would've been a few days ago. All right,' he said with an effort, 'I suppose I've got to do it, whatever it is you want me to do. But—' If he'd been listening to himself at that moment, he'd have been impressed, or thought it was somebody else talking; somebody brave and firm and forceful, a non-taker of crap from anybody; a hero, even. 'But if I manage to get this bloody horrible job done, that's it, all right? No more pulling my strings and secret destinies and little odd jobs that'll kill me and that nobody else can do. The rest of my life's my own. Understood?'

Uncle Ernie laughed. 'You remind me of your father when he was young,' he said, 'only without the colossal stupidity and total lack of charm. Yes, understood. After this is over, any messes you get into will be entirely your own fault. Will that do?'

Paul thought about it, then nodded. 'Fine,' he said, 'I'll settle for that. So, what've I got to do?'

Brief, uncomfortable silence. 'Why are you asking me?' Uncle Ernie said.

'Huh?'

'Why are you asking me? I don't know what's going on Topside, do I? I've been dead for months. You're the one who came down here to ask me questions.'

'Oh,' Paul said. 'But I thought—'

'You were supposed,' Uncle Ernie added sternly, 'to have a Plan.'

'Ah.' *Also*, Paul added to himself, *fuck*. 'Well, I did have a plan, but I seem to have lost it somewhere. Or your friend Judy wiped it out of my mind while I was asleep.'

'You mean—' Uncle Ernie stared at him for a moment as if he'd come across a winged chip snuggled up next to his battered cod. 'You went to all this trouble, *died*, and you've forgotten what it was you needed to ask me?'

'Yes,' Paul said; and if he'd been a really heroic hero, he'd probably have scowled and asked his uncle if he wanted to make anything of it. But he didn't.

'Wonderful. Absolutely bloody marvellous.' Uncle Ernie rolled his eyes. 'In that case, my young apprentice, I have a nasty feeling we're screwed.'

That wasn't really what Paul wanted to hear. 'Hang on,' he said desperately. 'What if I had another look in that stone thing—?'

'How?' Uncle Ernie snapped. 'What with? You're dead. You can't see, and you can't take it with you. I take back what I said just now; you're *exactly* like your father, except possibly not quite as bright. Dear God, how could anybody be so pathetically—?'

'All *right*.' The hero voice again. 'Don't go all to pieces at me now, I can't cope. We'll just have to do the best we can, that's all.'

Under other circumstances, it'd have been interesting watching Uncle Ernie pulling himself together; you could practically hear the nuts and bolts tightening. 'Let's do that, shall we?' he said, with just the faintest of sighs. 'Start at the beginning. You've got my box.'

'Box.'

'*Box.*' Uncle Ernie managed to keep his balance on the edge of hysteria, but only just. 'Cardboard box. I left it with some lawyers. You *did* get it, didn't you?'

'Yes.'

Visible relief. 'Thank God for that.'

'They had the nerve to charge me a hundred . . .'

'Quiet.' Paul had the good grace to shut up. 'Now then, in the box you should have found my personal shield.'

Paul nodded. 'Sea Scout badge.'

'That's right. Now, so long as you've got that, you really haven't got anything to worry about, because—'

'They've got it.'

'What?'

Paul bit his lip. 'The enemy. They've got it now. I, um, left it on my desk, and they've—'

Uncle Ernie closed his eyes. 'This isn't getting better,' he said. 'You've got the rest of it, though. Tell me you've got the other stuff.'

'No. Well, sort of,' Paul added quickly. 'Someone's looking after them for me, but it's all right, I trust her.' He caught the tail end of that and replayed it quickly. *I trust Mr Tanner's mum? I'm prepared to risk my life and the future of my species on the integrity of a nymphomaniac goblin. Bloody hell, I do too. Pretty well says it all, that does.* 'I can get the stuff back any time.'

Uncle Ernie sighed. 'I do hope you're right; otherwise, if Judy were to get hold of it, the only sensible thing would be to stay here and ask Mr Dao to seal us up in our boxes and throw away the box-cutter. But here's hoping. The chalks – you found them?'

'Coloured chalk, yes,' Paul said.

'Burn them,' Uncle Ernie said. 'Find a really good hot fire, like a furnace or a boiler. You should also have my watch, my pen and my screwdriver, yes?'

Paul cast his mind back. 'That's right,' he said. 'The

watch does something silly to the space/time continuum, doesn't it?'

'You could say that,' Uncle Ernie said sourly. 'With it, you can halt the progress of time. Be careful with it, though; it's old and fragile, and if you break the winding mechanism, you're stuck. I wouldn't play with it if I were you.'

'I wasn't proposing to—' Paul calmed down. 'Understood,' he said. 'What about the pen, and the screwdriver?'

'Oh, they're straightforward enough. The pen writes only the truth. It's a clever little gadget, but totally illegal, ever since an ancestor of ours lent one to Gladstone so that he could finish writing an important speech. The screwdriver's probably the single most useful thing; it'll—'

The bead curtain was wrenched back, and Mr Dao came in. 'Apologies,' he said to Paul in an agitated voice, 'but if you wish to leave you must do so now.' From his sleeve he took a tiny bottle. 'I've just been told that the auditors have arrived and are waiting for me in my office. This is highly irregular; they have the power to make surprise visits, but this is the first time they've used that power in twelve thousand years. I suspect that someone who is not well-intentioned towards either of you has arranged this. You,' he went on, nodding to Paul, 'are not yet registered, so they must not find you here; it would embarrass me, and of course it would mean you could never leave, in spite of what is in that bottle. As for you,' he said to Uncle Ernie, 'I suggest that you get back in your box and keep absolutely still and quiet until they've gone. In theory, the contents of safety deposit boxes are confidential. In practice, if they wanted to open a box, I can't see how I could stop them. Now,' he added, reaching out for Paul's sleeve then stopping abruptly, as though remembering something at the last moment. 'Drink the blood and go. The doors should open for you automatically, but try not to imagine them, just to be on the safe side. The fewer of them you can envisage, the better.'

Paul nodded, then turned to say goodbye to his uncle; but there was no trace of him, and his shoebox was back where it'd been on its shelf. Paul looked back at Mr Dao. 'What've I got to do?' he said.

'Drink the blood. Hand me the bottle. Run.'

It felt horribly strange having a body again; like putting on the oldest, smelliest clothes you could imagine, the sort of things a scarecrow would give to a charity shop. He'd never been happier, however, with his previously despised legs. Thin, puny and turkey-like they might be, but at least they worked. In fact, he was impressed at the turn of speed he was able to get out of them as he sprinted across nothing at all in the direction (he fervently hoped) of the door of the cashier's room.

Paul could've wept for joy when he saw it: a faint outline in the gloom, fringed with an almost impossible greyish glow. Sagging with relief, he grabbed the handle, turned it and pushed.

Nothing happened. Then he remembered. Of course it wouldn't open. He'd nailed it shut himself, to keep the fake Melze from bursting in on him while he was making his illicit search of her filing cabinet.

He tried kicking it, shoulder-charging it (ouch), pushing against it with his back, using the muscles of his legs (scientific approach; useless), swearing at it and asking it nicely. He tried prayer, tears, and calling for his mummy. He tried bribing it. He broke the blade of his knife trying to cut through it, one shred of wood fibre at a time. He was just about to try crouching down beside it in a huddle and sobbing hysterically when somebody said his name.

He looked up. 'Oh,' he said. 'You again.'

'Paul?' The fake Melze was standing over him, looking concerned and vaguely maternal. 'Is that you?'

'Yes.'

'Are you okay? You look – Paul, last time I saw you, I thought you were dead.'

Paul nodded. 'I was. I probably still am. Long story.'

'Oh.' She frowned. 'What did you mean a while back when you called me a liar?'

'What I said. You aren't the real Demelza Horrocks. I don't think you're even human.' He swore, and kicked savagely at the door, thereby damaging his other foot. 'Now look what you made me do.'

'Paul, I don't know what you—'

'You're one of them, aren't you? The dream creatures, Countess Judy's lot.' He looked up at her; her eyes were deep and full of pain. Why? Because— 'She *made* you, didn't she?'

Slowly, the fake Melze nodded. 'That's right,' she said. 'Somebody told you, right?'

'No, just for once I figured it out for myself. Actually, I had help; the real you phoned me. Apparently she's living in Saffron Walden, wherever that is. But I should've known, shouldn't I? Right from the start. Or at least, as soon as you began—' He hesitated, not wanting to say the word. 'As soon as you started *liking* me. You were only ever bait, or a distraction.'

She made a sort of gulping noise, then started crying messily; tears and sniffs and hiccups all jumbled together. 'It's not my fault,' she said, 'I couldn't help it. That's just the way I was made. I really do—'

'Quiet,' Paul snapped. 'I don't want to hear it. You're not real.'

'But I *am*,' she wailed furiously. 'I'm completely really real, and I completely really love you.' Guilt and anger don't mix well together; the combination made Paul want to smash her teeth in with one hand and hug her with the other. 'Tough,' he said. 'That doesn't alter the fact that you're nothing but a glorified mousetrap. And you're on her side. Well, aren't you?'

She snuffled a couple of times, then nodded. 'She made me,' she said. 'I can't help it. It's not *fair*,' she added, as two fat tears rolled down her cheeks and onto her chin. 'I've got to do what she tells me, I've got no choice at all, but I can still *feel* – That's real enough, I promise you.'

'Oh, for—' Paul shook his head. 'Look,' he said, grabbing her by the arms; she tried to push him away, but not very hard. 'We need to get out of here.'

'I know,' she mumbled. 'But there's something wrong with the door, and I don't know what it is.'

'Um.' Paul let go of her. 'It's nailed shut,' he said, 'from the other side. Two bits of two-by-four battens, with two six-inch nails on each side going through into the frame. I put them there,' he added.

'You? But—' She stared at him. 'Then how did you get through?'

'I died. And now,' he added, 'I'm bloody well stuck, and it's all your fault.'

'My—?'

'I only did it to keep you from coming through the door while I was looking in your filing cabinet. Because you're on their side. I—' He looked at his shoes. 'I guess I didn't think it through properly. This is all *my* fault really.'

'That's all right,' she said automatically. 'I've got to say that,' she added with a faint smile. 'I can't be angry, or think, *Jesus, what a total loser*, even though I really want to; I've got to be forgiving and supportive and tell you it's all right, you couldn't be expected to think of everything.'

Paul looked at her. 'That's awful,' he said. 'I'm sorry.'

'Yes, well.' She was blushing, or else crying had turned her face bright red. 'There's got to be some way we can get out of here. How about if we both try charging it?'

They tried. No dice. 'Ouch,' she said, rubbing her shoulder. 'I never realised you had such a flair for DIY.'

'Sometimes I surprise myself,' Paul replied sourly. 'These days, the queue of people wanting to be my worst enemy tends to stretch back halfway down the hall, but I'm still quite definitely at the head of it.' He turned his head and looked at her. 'I don't suppose there's anything *you* can do, is there?'

'No, of course not. If there was, do you think I'd still be here?' The fake Melze frowned. 'It'll be all right, though,' she said doubtfully. 'I mean, sooner or later they're going to notice what you did to the door. Or someone'll realise that we're missing and come looking. And eventually someone's going to have to come, because they need to get the banking done.'

'Of course,' Paul said. 'The question is, when? You've already done today's. I don't mean to sound downbeat, but do you really think either of us is going to last down here until tomorrow? You, maybe, I don't know what level of ambient weirdness your lot can put up with. Me, definitely not. I'm living on borrowed time as it is. Literally,' he added, with a marginally unbalanced grin. 'I can't be specific, but unless I can get out of here very soon, I'm stuck. And before you ask, no, I haven't got any ideas. Or a plan.'

'That's—' She turned her head to one side. 'That's a nuisance,' she said. 'You see, I think that if you die – die completely, I mean, not whatever it is you did just now – then I sort of stop being, too. Nobody ever tells me anything and it's not really the sort of thing you can ask, particularly with Countess Judy, but I kind of get the impression that I'm – well, I'm coming from inside your head, like a dream, only when you're awake. A daydream. That's how I know how to be exactly what you want me to be,' she added bitterly. 'It's because there's a part of you that's telling me what to do, what you want from me. If you die—' She shrugged. 'Not that it's any big deal, it's been a really shitty life anyway. No offence,' she added. 'But being your idea of what the perfect girl for you is like—' Suddenly she grinned. 'Admit it, Paul. You understand women the way a chimpanzee understands quantum theory. Which is why, with the best will in the world, it hasn't been easy.'

'Oh *God*.' Paul slumped against the door and let his face slop into his hands. 'I'm sorry,' he said. 'Look, would it help if I changed my mind, decided what I really like is strong, assertive women who don't give a damn what I think?'

The fake Melze giggled. 'Not really. Now, if you suddenly developed a fetish for East German lady weight-lifters, that might be quite handy. I could probably smash this door down just by sneezing at it.'

Paul pulled a face. 'Sorry,' he said. 'Couldn't do that to save my life.'

'So it would seem.' She sighed, and sat down next to him. 'It could've been all right, you know,' she said. 'We could've – I don't know, settled down, got married, bought a flat somewhere and spent our weekends choosing curtains and putting up pelmets together. I don't know; is that what people do? I've never been one.'

'I have,' Paul replied, 'sort of. Actually, Sophie and I seemed to spend a lot of the time arguing, or sulking.'

'I know. Oh, don't look at me like that. I probably know more about you two than you do; half of me's just like her, the other half's the exact opposite. I have to say,' she added, 'God only knows what you ever saw in her.'

Paul looked at her. 'What I saw in her?'

'That's right. Miserable, self-centred cow, if you ask me. Mind you, I'm biased. Being made to be half of somebody'll do that to you every time.'

Paul thought about that for a moment. 'I think we'd better concentrate on getting through this door,' he said. 'We can tear each other into little shreds later, when we've got five minutes.'

She nodded. 'I don't suppose your friend with the red eyes and the long nails is going to come along and save us, do you?' she said.

Paul shrugged. 'I wouldn't have thought so,' he replied. 'She's unpredictable, to put it mildly. Besides, she's on reception till five-thirty, and she doesn't know we're missing.'

'What about Mr Wurmtoter? He knows Judy's up to something, maybe he'll notice you're not in your office.'

'Maybe. But he's a busy man, rushing about slaughtering big lizards. I don't think we can rely on him, or on anybody else for that matter. I think we're on our— What're you staring at? I can't see . . .'

'Look.' The fake Melze pointed; and a moment later, Paul could see it too. Wobbling towards them through the darkness, making a very faint creaking noise that implied unoiled bearings and untightened sprockets, was an ancient, rider-less bicycle. When it was a mere two feet or so away from them, it stopped.

'You ought to be ashamed of yourself,' it said.

A moment later, it added, 'Perhaps you'd like to share the joke. You may've noticed, we're not laughing.'

Paul wrenched himself back together with an effort. 'I'm sorry,' he said. 'It's just – well, really. I don't know who or what the hell you are, or why you've got it in for me, but honestly, you do pick your moments.'

'Idiot,' the bicycle replied. 'Feckless, irresponsible clown. God only knows what you thought you were playing at, killing yourself like that when she's relying on you. No consid-eration. And now you're snuggled up here nice and cosy with this ... this *creature*, all because of a stupid door that you yourself saw fit to nail shut. A fine last, best hope you turned out to be,' the bicycle added nastily; then it reversed, backed up ten yards, and shot at the door like an arrow.

Steel is ever so much harder than lead. Even so, a soft lead bullet will bust its way through a steel plate if it's travelling fast enough, but there won't be much left of it by the time it comes out the other side. The same prin-ciple applies to bicycles and substantial pine-board doors. In general terms, the door didn't come out of it too badly; it was still in one piece and sitting on its hinges. The bicycle, on the other hand, had quite obviously come to the end of its long, eventful life. Its front wheel was bent almost double, its slim, elegant structure of spokes tangled like a crushed daddy-long-legs; its forks, handlebars and frame were hopelessly buckled, one pedal had snapped off and the other one stuck out at a disturbingly abrupt angle. When it spoke, its voice was soft and hoarse.

'Get that fucking door shut,' it whispered, 'before they start coming through.'

Paul just stood and gaped; he'd been away so long that the cashier's office seemed improbably unreal, like something out of a dream. Fortunately, the fake Melze still had her wits about her; she slammed the door and wedged it shut with a chair.

'Thanks,' Paul said.

'What? Oh, it was nothing,' the fake Melze said; but Paul hadn't been talking to her. He was kneeling beside the dying bike, and for some bizarre reason there were tears in his eyes. 'Thanks,' he repeated. 'How are you feeling?'

'Guess,' the bike sighed faintly.

'You'll be all right,' Paul said, impulsively reaching out a hand, then hesitating. 'We'll get you straightened and welded and whatever—'

The bike's brittle laugh faded into a coughing fit. 'Don't be bloody stupid,' it said. 'And shut up and listen, I haven't got long. And don't think I saved you because I'm noble and brave, or because I like you. I don't. I think you're a self-centred little shit.'

Paul shrugged. 'You're probably right,' he said.

'I *know* I'm right. You're a pathetic little toad with a mental age of twelve, and God only knows what she sees in you. But she loves you, so I didn't have any choice. Which means you're safe and I'm dying. Call that justice? Because I don't.'

'Hang on,' Paul said. 'Who loves me?'

The bike groaned. 'You're not helping,' it said. 'You're not making me feel better about giving my life to save you. I mean, sad wimpy loser's bad enough, but why have you got to be abysmally stupid as well? You know perfectly well who loves you, moron; or if you don't, then I really have fucked up. Come on, three guesses. And don't say your mum, or so help me I'll get up on my hind wheel and run you over.'

It was a palpably empty threat; the bike's back wheel wasn't in much better shape than the front. 'I don't know,' Paul wailed. 'I mean, *she* doesn't, she's not even real so she doesn't count. And Sophie—' The bike shuddered; Paul had forgotten that it was violently allergic to names. 'She doesn't love me, or she'd never have buggered off to Ca— the New World,' he amended desperately. Luckily, that didn't seem to count as a name; that, or the bike was in so much pain already that it didn't notice. 'So who does that leave?'

'What are you talking about, buggered off?' the bike said. Its voice was pitifully weak now, but it could still just about convey utter contempt. 'She never went anywhere. She's still here.'

Paul shook his head. 'No, that's not right. She got a transfer to the Hol— the office in the place where they make films. Just so that she could get away from me.'

'No.' The bike's death rattle was a faint graunching of gears. 'Never left. Still here. Up to you now, must find—' With a feeble twitch, the bike slumped. The back wheel spun for a couple of slow revolutions, and then was still.

'It's dead,' said the fake Melze, rather superfluously. 'Poor thing.'

Paul swung round. He couldn't see very clearly because of the water in his eyes. 'Don't—' he started to say, then realised he wasn't sure exactly what he wanted her not to do. Anything, probably; after all, she was the enemy, wasn't she? 'Don't pretend you're sorry,' he said. 'Just don't, right? In fact, it'd be better if you just went away somewhere.'

'I can't.' She sounded very stiff, almost formal. 'I can't,' she repeated. 'This is my office. There's work I ought to be doing.'

'Don't be ridiculous,' Paul snapped. 'You can't stay here like nothing's happened, not now. For God's sake, you're not even human.'

'Maybe not.' Her voice was like small chunks chipped off a large, dangerous iceberg. 'But let's see, now. Starting with the partners, we've got a goblin, a giant and the Queen of the Fey. Then there's Mr Shumway, he's a dwarf. And you're a pig, so really it doesn't look like being human's exactly a requirement, is it? In fact, they've probably only got a couple of token humans so as not to get in trouble with the equal-opportunities people. If you want to get rid of me, you'll have to do better than that.'

'Can't be bothered,' Paul said; his mind, slow as Friday night on the M25 but not without a certain tenacity of purpose, was focused on something that the bike had said before it died. 'Why did it say Sophie never left here?' he asked. 'It sounded so certain, it must've known something.'

'Search me,' said the fake Melze.

'Some other time, when I've got a ten-foot pole handy. Come on, I bet you know the answer. Is Sophie in Hollywood or isn't she?'

'How should I know? I've never even met her.'

Paul had no idea how he knew, whether it was something in the voice or the eyes, a slight uneasiness of manner or a tell-tale body movement, but he knew that she was lying, as surely as he knew anything. 'That's not true, is it?' he said. 'You know where she is.'

'No, I don't. Look,' she added, with just the faintest wobble in her voice, 'if it's suddenly so important, why don't you phone the Hollywood office and ask them?'

'Time difference,' Paul said quietly. 'It's the middle of the night over there, they'd all be asleep.' And suddenly he had the answer. 'They'd all be fast asleep, having sweet dreams. So of course,' he went on, looking her straight in the eye, 'now would be the perfect time to call them, wouldn't it? I mean, no good ringing later on, when it's daytime over there and they're all awake.'

'What are you talking about?' she asked, taking a step back. 'Look, you definitely ought to go. What if Countess Judy comes in? You aren't supposed to be here. And look at your arm,' she added quickly. 'You'd better get that seen to, it looks bad.'

Paul couldn't help looking down — at his wrists, which were caked with dried blood where he'd slashed the veins with his Girl Guides penknife. At the time, he hadn't really noticed quite how much blood was coming out of the wound; the state of his jacket sleeves and trousers hadn't exactly been uppermost in his mind. The fake Melze had a good point there. He looked a mess. And what if the cuts hadn't healed? Nasty thought; what if the slightest sudden movement started them off bleeding again? Now that he had something very specific to live for, it wouldn't do to go suddenly dropping dead from catastrophic blood loss, just for being careless.

'You're probably right,' he said slowly. 'What's the time? I took my watch off earlier, for obvious reasons.'

She glanced at the clock on the wall, just above his head. 'Ten past five,' she said. 'We'd both better be going. You wouldn't want to be around those goblins smelling of fresh blood. They're only house-trained up to a point, you know.'

Another valid consideration. Paul nodded. 'Will you be here tomorrow?' he asked.

The fake Melze looked away. 'I don't know,' she said. 'I don't know what's going to happen to me now. Obviously I've screwed up on my main job, but they still need a cashier.'

That was a highly significant remark too, in its way, but Paul filed it away for later consideration. 'Just stay out of my way, all right?' he said. 'If I want to talk to you, I'll find you. Otherwise . . .'

'I understand,' she said, and her voice was empty. 'For what it's worth,' she added, 'I really do love you. And I know it doesn't count, but it's still true.'

Paul looked at her. She was very beautiful, and more like Melze than the real Melze could ever be; because the real Melze would be a stranger, whereas this one had been assembled from bits and pieces of his own mind, like a conceptual MFI wardrobe. 'Like it matters,' he said coldly, and left the room.

Chatper Thirteen

Hospital, Paul thought; but he didn't actually know where the nearest one was, and he didn't exactly relish the prospect of explaining how he'd come by two slashed wrists, either. Ricky Wurmtoter, then; Paul had got the impression that Ricky knew a fair bit about treating wounds, reasonably enough. Besides, he had a certain amount to report, though he wasn't quite sure what to tell and what to leave out. But if anywhere was safe with Countess Judy prowling about, it'd be wherever Ricky was. After all, Ricky was a hero. A real one.

He was so preoccupied with this train of thought that he turned a sharp corner without looking where he was going, and collided with a life form. He couldn't see who he'd run into, but the sensation of his chin crunching on the top of a head told him who his victim was. Mr Tanner. *Shit.* 'Sowwy.' Paul couldn't talk properly with a jarred chin. Mr Tanner took a step back to disentangle himself, and scowled. His glasses were ever so slightly askew, which gave him a small-boy, Just-William look that would've had Paul in a fit of giggles in any other context.

'Idiot,' Mr Tanner said. 'Why can't you look where you're—?'

He tailed off, and Paul guessed that he'd caught sight of all the dried blood. Too late now to try hiding his hands behind his back. 'What the hell have you been up to?' Mr Tanner demanded.

Paul's mind emptied like a department store during a bomb scare. 'Cut myself,' he mumbled.

'Amazingly, I'd guessed that. What on? And if you tell me it's a paper cut, I'll turn you into a rat and let you loose in Crufts.'

Paul thought quickly. It was just as pointless as thinking long and hard, but it wasted less time. 'Desk drawer,' he said. 'There's a sort of jagged edge where the runner's a bit buckled. But it's okay, just a scratch.'

Mr Tanner's eyes bored holes in him. 'Hint for you,' he said. 'Never go into politics or the legal profession. You've got the stupidity, but your lying skills'll let you down every time.' He grinned. 'If you don't want to tell me, that's fine. I was only concerned for your welfare.'

'Protecting your investment, more like,' Paul said, before he had a chance to stop himself. For some reason, Mr Tanner was impressed, or amused, or both. He raised both eyebrows, and didn't grin but *smiled*.

'Very good,' Mr Tanner said. 'Did you figure it out for yourself, or did someone tell you?'

'It wasn't hard to work out,' Paul replied. 'I knew there had to be some reason why you wouldn't let us resign.'

'Is that right? Very shrewd of you. Which reminds me,' Mr Tanner added, reverting to his default grin. 'Bauxite. We think we've got a sniff of some pretty decent deposits in Malawi, but we're having trouble pinning them down. Too many trees in the way, or something. I'll send Christine up with some satellite pics. Try not to bleed on them if you can help it.'

For a moment, Paul wondered whether Mr Tanner's new-found respect for him would be further increased if he told him where he could insert his bauxite. He weighed the evidence and decided against. 'All right,' he said. 'But first I've got to see Mr Wurmtoter.'

'What? Oh, I forgot, you were minding the store for him while he was away.' Mr Tanner shook his head. 'You know, the hero stuff's all very well, but I've got to look at the bottom line, and compared with minerals, the return on expense of time is pretty pathetic. Really, we're only in that sector as a service to our bigger clients. When the time comes for you to choose, I'd forget about it if I were you. Just because you can do it doesn't mean you have to.'

Mr Tanner walked on, leaving Paul staring after him. Was it possible that Tanner didn't know what was going on? Or was he just being his usual obnoxious self? Paul thought about it for a bit, then decided it wasn't important; not compared with, say, whether he'd still be alive at the end of the week.

Almost inevitably, Ricky Wurmtoter wasn't in his office. Paul swore, then trudged down to reception, taking care to keep his hands in his pockets.

'Do you know where Mr Wurmtoter's got to?' he asked the dazzling redhead behind the desk, only remembering at the last moment who she really was.

'Not a clue,' Mr Tanner's mum said, with a click of the tongue. 'Phone's been going for him all bloody day,' she added, holding up a thick wad of While-You-Were-Out notes. 'What happened to you, by the way? Cut yourself shaving, or is that ketchup from a leaky burger?'

Paul sighed. 'None of your business,' he snapped. Then he remembered something else. 'While I'm here,' he said, as casually as he could manage. 'You remember that cardboard box full of junk I got from my uncle a while back? You said you'd look after it for me.'

Her eyes widened slightly; today they were emerald green and very round and deep. 'Vaguely,' she said. 'What about it?'

'I'd rather like it back, if it's all the same to you.'

'Why?' Her mouth tightened a little. 'I thought I told you, that stuff's nasty, not to be played with.'

'Oh, I just wanted to look at it,' Paul said. 'No big deal. I'll give it back as soon as I'm done with it, if it means so much to you.'

Mr Tanner's mum sniffed. 'No need to get all snotty with me,' she said, 'It's for your own good, you ungrateful little toad. You haven't got a clue how to handle stuff like that, and I'm buggered if I'm rescuing you if you get yourself stuck in a Probability Mine or a Butterfield Anomaly.'

Oh, Paul thought. 'That's not likely, is it?'

She snickered. 'That's serious kit you've got there,' she said. 'A bit advanced for you. It'd be like handing a chainsaw to a ten-year-old.'

'I'm not planning on using it,' Paul said, and managed not to add *honest*. 'I just wanted to check something out, that's all.'

'Please yourself.' She opened her mouth, inserted a finger and hooked out what looked like a small lump of chewing gum. 'Only don't blame me,' she added, as she laid it in the middle of her palm and blew on it gently. As it slowly began to grow, she put it down on the desk. Thirty seconds later, it had turned back into the cardboard box, albeit slightly moist and sticky with spit.

'Thanks,' Paul muttered, trying to find a dry bit to catch hold of. 'Really, I appreciate you looking after it for me. I hope it, um, didn't taste too bad.'

Mr Tanner's mum grinned. 'A bit like chicken,' she said.

'Joke,' she added. 'Actually, more like strawberries. Never could be doing with strawberries, mind. In fact, most fruit gives me heartburn. Natural carnivore, see.'

Change of plan. Instead of continuing his search for Mr Wurmtoter, Paul headed back to his office with the box. When he got there, he found that the threatened aerial photographs had already arrived: mile upon mile of identical treetops in black and white, like an Impressionist still life of a ball of wire wool. He put them carefully on one side so that the spitty box wouldn't mark them.

Inside, just as he'd left them, was Uncle Ernie's supernatural junk collection: the busted watch, the screwdriver, the library ticket, the pen and the box of chalks. *Burn them*, he recalled Uncle Ernie saying; that was the chalks, wasn't it? He took them out and slid the lid open. They looked, felt and smelled like your basic schoolroom standard issue. How did you go about burning chalk, anyhow? He shook his head and stowed them, along with the rest of the garbage, in his jacket pocket. In doing so, he found the little glassy stone.

Funny, Paul thought; it didn't seem important any more. He put it down on the desk for a moment while he dumped the cardboard box on the floor in the corner, where he wouldn't trip over it. When he turned back, he noticed that the stone was resting on top of the pile of photographs – and it was glowing faintly.

Mildly curious, Paul picked it up. It felt very slightly warm, but the light inside it was fading rapidly. He put it back on the photo, but the light guttered and went out. Just for the hell of it, he moved it around on the glossy surface of the print, running it up and down systematically, like a scanner. On the fourth pass it started glowing again, and Paul felt the familiar tingling sensation that meant he'd dowsed some bauxite. Automatically he got a marker pen from his drawer and drew a circle round the relevant spot. Then he took a long, considered look at the stone.

After he'd been staring at it for a second or two, it seemed to change. Now it was like looking through a telescope; no, more like a zoom lens, because through it he could see the treetops getting closer, until he could make out first branches, then twigs, then individual leaves. Now he was down below the canopy, zooming in on undergrowth, ferns, topsoil; now he was under the ground, rushing past stones and roots, until he came to a layer of clay, followed by a stratum of rock. That, apparently, was the end of the line; just rock—

Paul sat up straight. *Not* just rock. Bauxite. Needless to say, he wouldn't know bauxite if he got it in a sandwich with onion rings and Branston pickle; nevertheless, he recognised it, because the stone knew what it was, and knew it was what he was looking for. Something useful, Mr Tanner's mum had said; and bauxite was useful stuff, surely, or else why did people bother digging it up out of the ground?

Well, he thought; *pretty cool trick, but actually I don't need the stone to do that, I've got this wonderful gift that means I can make lots of money for other people.* He sat up, and in doing so caught sight of the stack of mouldy old photo albums he'd dumped on his bookshelf, the ones that had been in Uncle Ernie's box, along with all the toys.

I wonder, Paul thought.

Well, no harm in trying. He took down an album at random and opened it at the beginning. Now he thought about it, he realised that he hadn't actually looked in any of the albums himself; Mr Tanner's mum had looked for him, to see if they were dangerous or booby-trapped. She'd said they were safe, just a lot of snapshots of ugly people, presumably his relatives. That had been enough to put Paul off looking for himself. Nearly all the worst hours of his pre-JWW life had been Sunday afternoons, spent at the house of some horrendous elderly female relation, with photo albums. He only had to see one, with its patterned cover and distinctive shiny pages, to tune out automatically. Sort of reverse catnip. It had never occurred to him that there might be anything in them worth spending time on. But he'd have said the same about a screwdriver or a broken watch—

Screwing the stone into his right eye like a jeweller's loupe, Paul examined the first photo.

With both eyes open, he saw a group of glum-looking people gathered round a small plastic Christmas tree. If their appearance was anything to go by – Paul didn't understand about women's fashions, but he could recognise men's flared trousers, fat ties, wide lapels and monster sideburns as the Mark of the Beast – the picture was thirty-odd years old. He didn't recognise any of the faces.

When Paul shut his left eye, however, something very strange happened. It was a variation on the zoom-lens effect he'd encountered when he looked at the bauxite photo – he was swooping down from a great height towards a small table in the corner of the room, well away from the tree and the mob scene. Just when the vertigo was about to knock him silly, his point of view screeched to a jarring stop, and he realised he was looking at a scrap of paper lying on the table top. Now his viewpoint was closing in very slowly, and he could make out handwriting on the paper. A little further in, and he could read what it said—

Hello.

Well, that seemed friendly enough. It was just a scrap of paper in a photograph; maybe a note to say *Gone out, your dinner's in the oven*; or, bearing in mind the context, a child's thank-you letter. Paul read on:

I'm afraid I don't know your name, mostly because you haven't been born yet. I don't even know if you're my great-nephew or my great-niece. In fact, it's possible you may be neither — in which case, Judy, it's a pity nobody ever told you it's rude to read other people's letters.

But; assuming that Donny and Lynn — that's them on the extreme right of the group — get married and have you, welcome to the family. Now I doubt very much whether your parents will have told you about your pedigree — they don't know yet themselves, and I'm in two minds about whether to tell them or not. My nephew Donny has many sterling qualities, I guess; for one thing, he's mostly waterproof, and his fingernails grow pretty well, and he plays an adequate game of canasta. But he's also loud, arrogant, stupid, bad-tempered and so far up himself he's in danger of coming out of his own ear. I don't know Lynn all that well yet, but I have my suspicions she's mostly a waste of valuable resources, and the best that can be said of her is that she can use a knife and fork without putting anybody's eye out. But there it is; you can't choose your parents (I chose them for you; see below) and maybe you'll turn out all right in the end: brave, clever, resourceful, caring and dedicated, like me. Stranger things have happened.

Anyhow, here we go. Our lot, the Carpenters, have had inherent supernatural abilities for at least thirty generations — a thousand years, give or take — and probably longer. I'm the only really outstanding supernatural practitioner we've produced, but over the years we've churned out competent sorcerers and magicians every other generation, and the trend would actually seem to be towards our abilities getting stronger as time goes on. Just think: if that's true, you could turn out to be even better at this shit than I am.

Well, Paul thought, *I'll say this for him, he's got the knack of fitting a long letter on a small bit of paper. That aside, though, I think I'll reserve judgement.*

Allow me to introduce myself, by the way. My full name-rank-and-serial-number is something like Professor Ernest James Carpenter MT FRCMS ZWG (Stuttgart) CSMI blahdy-blahdy; as well as being Visiting Professor of Effective Magic at Cambridge and Reader in Glamour and Enchantment at the University of Chicopee Falls, ID, I'm a senior consultant with J. W. Wells and Co. of 70 St Mary Axe, London. In practical terms, that means that if I want to I can make you think a raddled old boiler looks like Elizabeth Taylor, and that you're a traffic cone. Hot stuff, obviously.

Your mother's family, assuming she becomes your mother in the fullness of time, comes from a long (though frequently pruned) line of heroes, claiming descent from Beowulf on one side and Brian Boru on the other. How heroes come to have a long line beats me, since what they're best at is dying young; however, it has to be said that what they're second-best at is breeding like rabbits. Anyhow, your mum is the outcome of a millennium and a half of peerless swordspersons, brave dragonslayers, champions of the oppressed and similar pests. This means, I sincerely hope, that you will grow up to be both a hero and a magician – brave and clever, though there's excellent grounds for saying the two qualities are mutually exclusive. But what the hell.

My intention is for you to join JWW at an early age, zoom up the corporate ladder like a ferret up a conduit, get made a partner before you're thirty and be fully trained, armed and prepared when the moment comes when I'm either dead, incommunicado or too senile to blow my own nose, and someone has to take my place as leader of the human side in the secret war between us and those incomparable bastards, the Fey. I hope you won't mind too much that I've condemned you to a life of danger, struggle and extreme weirdness without giving you the faintest vestige of a choice. I'm doing it for the best, needless to say. After all, the human race has got to be saved, and if I've been lumbered with the chore, I don't see why I shouldn't make someone else share the misery with me. Of course, you may well not see it like that if you take after your mother's side. Did I mention that the heroic mentality has always been a complete and utter mystery to me?

Anyway, to practicalities. Obviously, I can't predict how the war will go over the next thirty years or so, which means I can't offer you much in the way of concrete, useful advice. By now, you should've worked out that Judy di Castel'Bianco is a truly nasty piece of work and you shouldn't trust her any further than you can sneeze her through a blocked nostril; likewise, that the only way you'll ever win this war is to get rid of her, once and for all. How you're supposed to go about this, I have no idea. She can't be physically killed (tried that; no dice) or locked up or mutilated to the point of effective disability; trying to destroy her mind and reduce her to the level of a gibbering *loon is like trying to drown a fish in water. The only possibility I can think of is to find and eliminate her Source — as you probably know, each individual Fey is no more or less than a dream, dreamed by a sleeping human. If you find the dreamer — the Source, we call them — and wake him or her up, the dream stops and the Fey gets whizzed back to his own side of the line. Mostly, that's not much help; next time the Source goes to sleep, the Fey comes back. But the relatively few specimens who've managed to establish themselves permanently on our side of the line — Judy, for instance — need to be dreamt continuously, without interruption. If their Sources wake up even once, they're banished for good. That sounds encouraging; but understandably enough, the Fey go to enormous lengths to safeguard the Sources of their permanent colonists — they keep them constantly sedated, in a place so secure that no human has ever found it. Even if you were to discover it, I don't imagine you could simply shin up a drainpipe and jemmy open the bathroom window. Fort Knox is most likely a bus shelter in comparison.*

But there you go. Nobody said life was supposed to be easy, or fair, or even a guaranteed minimum length. I wish you the very best of luck, at any rate. By the way, if you're nurturing any romantic notions of having nothing to do with any of this, going as far away as you can get and earning a modest but honest living mending typewriters in Bhutan, forget it. For one thing, I intend to fix it so you can't; for another, even if you succeeded, Judy would almost certainly hunt you down and slaughter you like a Christmas turkey simply because you're related to me. At least if you hold still and do as you're told, she's less likely to kill you on sight and more likely to try and subvert you into being useful to

*her, which would probably add maybe as much as five years
to your life expectancy.*

   Happy hunting!
   Your affectionate great-uncle-to-be,
   Ernest Carpenter

Wouldn't it be wonderful, Paul thought, *wouldn't it be
absolutely fucking grand if Life somehow contrived to let five minutes
go by without dumping some new and incrementally horrible load
of shit on my head from a great height?* He snapped the album
shut; then, on a sort of guilty whim, opened it again at
random. In the corner of the first snap that caught his eye,
a moody study of a small, fat child eating an ice cream on
a park bench, he saw a crumpled-up newspaper poking out
of a litter bin. At once, the zoom business started up, and
a moment or so later he was reading an article on the sports
page, which said;

   *PS: In case I forget to remind you before I die or you read
   this: don't play with the watch, and REMEMBER TO
   BURN THE CHALKS. Regards, EJC*

Paul sighed; all right, already, he'd burn the stupid chalks.
Only, how would you go about doing a thing like that?
Soak them in petrol? Blowtorch? Or would putting them
under the grill and pretending they were sausages get the
job done just as effectively? Of course, if he still had his
Portable Door, he could simply take a sideways journey to
the slopes of Etna or Mount Washington and pitch them
over the edge. But he'd lent the wretched thing to Ricky
Wurmtoter, who'd lost it to the Fey. Suddenly he remembered the times he'd fallen asleep while wading through

the incredibly loathsome Mortensen printouts at Countess Judy's command; how each time he'd nodded off he'd dreamed about a portal in the wall through which platoons of evil kiddies had crept into the world. It all made perfect sense: Judy had the Door, and she'd given him the most boring job in the whole world so that he'd fall asleep right here in the office and dream across her advance guard of hand-picked storm troopers.

All at once, a sort of cold, brittle fury filled Paul. It wasn't so much the disgusting, parasitic way she'd used him, like a fly laying its eggs in an open wound; it wasn't even the manipulation, or the chilling thought of all those hundreds of maliciously grinning children, now safely across the line and poised to begin the task of wiping out the human race. No; what really, *really* ticked him off was that he'd been forced to sort and collate thousands and thousands and thousands of revolting Mortensen printouts, all through the weekend, *in what should've been his free time*, simply as camouflage, a diversion, a ruse. If ever there was a case of a tablespoon of insult with every teaspoon of injury, this had to be it—

Right, he thought. *Fine. If I was born into this stupid bloody war, so be it; but the hell with Uncle Ernie and saving the world and someone having to do the dirty, rotten job, I'm going to make Countess Judy pay through the nose and all other relevant orifices for making me do all that work for nothing.* Silently, he swore a solemn and dreadful oath to himself that he'd get her for that, if (as seemed entirely possible) it was the last thing he did.

So, what'd he got? Go after the Source, Uncle Ernie had said. Find out who's dreaming Countess Judy and her fellow infiltrators, and where they were being stashed. Then wake them up. Simple as that.

Paul pocketed the stone before he lost it, in the process finding the stub end of a roll of Polo mints that he hadn't remembered being there before (but it's well known that stubs of Polo rolls breed in warm, dark, linty places), stood up and threw the photo albums back on the shelf. *Oh*, he thought, *for a Portable Door right now.* All he'd have to do would be to slap it on the wall, tell it to take him to wherever Judy stored her livestock, and that'd be that. But he didn't have the Door any more, thanks to Ricky bloody Wurmtoter—

Ricky. A nasty thought stuck in Paul's mind like a fishbone. Hadn't Uncle Ernie said something about a traitor inside JWW itself? At the time he hadn't thought about it; he'd vaguely assumed that he'd meant Countess Judy, but that didn't make sense. A traitor was a hidden enemy, not someone who paraded up and down in the corridors wearing a fluorescent sweatshirt with ENEMY written on both sides. But Ricky – Ricky had borrowed Paul's Portable Door, the secret weapon that'd make it possible for Judy to bring across her storm troopers by the hundred, not one by one over a long period as she'd been doing previously. If Ricky was . . . There was a kind of grisly logic to it. As far as Paul knew, the Door had somehow been lost or hidden until he'd stumbled across it three months or so back; maybe Uncle Ernie or someone like that had deliberately hidden it away – that's right, hidden it until the predestined saviour of mankind *(me, fuck it)* turned up to claim it. As soon as that happens, the traitor nips in and makes some excuse to get his paws on it, then vanishes. That would explain a lot of things: why Ricky hadn't been in the cell with Paul and Monika; why he'd been put in Ricky's department, apprenticed to him; why Ricky had always been so nice to him, bought him lunch on his first day and everything. *Ricky* was the traitor; and all that stuff about pretending to help Paul and save him, that night when Ricky had burst in through the window – that was just play-acting, intended to trick Paul into trusting him. *The bastard. Never should've trusted a man with wavy blond hair in the first place. They're all scum, those wavy blonds.*

Right. He'd see about that. If Ricky was the traitor, did that mean he still had the Door? Unlikely; Judy'd have taken possession of it for herself. No matter; he had the rest of Uncle Ernie's magic set, objects so powerful that they'd made Mr Tanner's mum turn pale. True, what Paul really wanted right now was some kind of very powerful but simple and easy-to-use weapon, and none of Ernie's bits and bobs really seemed to fit that description – well, maybe the Sea Scout badge, but he'd contrived to lose that right at the start. But he had the rest of the stuff; screwdriver, watch, chalks (*memo to self: must burn chalks. But* how?). As far as weapons went, he could pick up a tyre lever or a length of lead pipe along the way. Simplicity was the way to go where the fundamentals were concerned. He was, God help him, a hero, whether he liked it or not; he'd been born and trained to it, and in the opinion of JWW he'd passed his indentures and qualified. Fine. If they wanted a hero, they'd just got one, and the best possible sort: a thoroughly bad-tempered, pissed-off, grudge-laden hero. Their look-out.

Paul patted the jacket pocket containing the watch, the chalks and the screwdriver, ate a slightly dilapidated Polo mint for luck, and reached for the door handle. On the point of leaving the room he stopped, dithered, then pulled down the photo album he'd just been looking at. It fell open at the picture of the fat kid with the ice cream. He looked at it again, both with and without the wyvern stone. There had been something about it, but he couldn't quite figure out what.

It was a pretty bad picture – a bit dark, slightly blurred, the kid looked fatally constipated, with a strained expression and bulging eyes turned red by the glare of the flash; and the photographer, an adherent of the Boadicea school of composition, had cut him off at the ankles. Paul wondered who the brat was, and at once the wyvern stone provided him with handy subtitles: *Derek Carpenter, age ten, Richmond Park.* He ransacked his memories of endless dreary teatimes-with-visitors and dredged up an Uncle Derek who wasn't really an uncle at all, just some species of cousin. He considered the data and concluded that whatever the big deal was, he hadn't figured it out yet. The hell with it; he threw the album back on the shelf and went to war.

All very well saying that. But, as Paul emerged into the corridor, he was painfully aware that he had no idea what to do next. His only fragment of a plan of campaign was to find the Fey dormitory and wake up the dreamers; but that was like putting *Bring about world peace* on the top of his Things-to-do list fixed by a small magnet to the fridge door – fine in principle but a tad vague as far as the practical aspects were concerned.

All right: step one, burn the chalks. Even that was something of an ask, slap bang in the middle of the City of London, not exactly known for its plethora of unguarded open fires. Finally, with great reluctance, he decided that if anybody might know where a fire was, it'd be Mr Tanner's mum. He set his course for reception.

'Fire,' Mr Tanner's mum repeated, frowning. 'What d'you want a fire for?'

'To burn something,' Paul replied.

'No kidding.' Mr Tanner's mum narrowed her eyes. 'Well, there's a couple of whatsits, Bunsen burners in the lab. They might do the trick, depending on what you want to torch.'

Paul looked at her. 'There's a lab in the building?'

'They call it that,' replied Mr Tanner's mum. 'But really it's just a converted bathroom, up on the third floor. It's where Theo van Spee and a few of the others go to play about with chemicals when they're brewing the love philtre and stuff like that. They used to have one of those really big propane furnaces,' she remembered, 'so they could melt down Rings of Power without having to leave the office, but they had to throw it out. Fire regulations, or something.'

'The Bunsen burners sound like they'll do just fine,' Paul told her. 'Where on the third floor did you say it was?'

He found it eventually. It looked more like a kitchen than a laboratory: worktop along two walls, a third lined with what looked like MFI's most basic range of pine-effect melamine cupboards, a fridge and a stainless steel sink. But there was no cooker, and two Bunsens sat in the corner next to the sink, partly hidden behind a stack of perspex dishes with a dog-eared box of Swan Vestas perched on top. There was also a bolt on the inside of the door, which pleased him; privacy, he felt, was likely of the essence.

In the event, the chalks burned quite easily once Paul had fiddled with the collars to get the Bunsens up to maximum heat. He had a feeling that real chalk didn't flare up like that, suggesting that Uncle Ernie had modified them somehow to serve a more demanding role than writing on blackboards or keeping score in darts tournaments. Once the last one had resolved itself into smoke and residue, however, he was back where he'd been just a short while ago: planless, clueless and alone. For want of anything better to do, he perched on a lab stool and turned the empty chalk packet over in his hands. Go find Countess Judy's source. Easy-peasy.

Well, it had to be somewhere, didn't it? Unfortunately, the world is made up of billions of contiguous somewheres, and any single one of them could be anywhere at all. Indeed, given the tricky nature of the Fey, it could just as easily be in Montana or Burkina Faso as in England, which would make getting there as much of a challenge as finding it. Unless, of course, he had a Portable Door, or something very similar.

Yeah, right, Paul told himself. *In your dreams.*

In my—

When he was a kid, there used to be a poster, with a picture of some suntanned female sitting on a golden beach, and a caption: *In your dreams, you've been to Tunisia.* Weird thing to remember after all these years, but the point was a valid one. In a dream, you can go anywhere. Unfortunately, as a mode of transport, dreams share one regrettable common feature with Ryanair and South-West Trains: you have no control over where you're likely to end up, or what state you'll be in when you get there. Hitherto, Paul had always assumed that was because dreams are just mental indigestion, stray thoughts from the waking day glopping up into the unconscious mind like gas in a swamp. Now, of course, he knew better. If he had a dream about Blackpool, it was because some freeloading Fey wanted to go there. Trying to use dreams to get where he wanted to go was about as likely to work as disguising yourself as an airliner and sitting on a runway, hoping someone would come along and fly you to your chosen destination.

Unless—

Well, it was worth a try, given that he had no alternative whatsoever; and if it went wrong, the worst that could
happen – no, bad line of argument, the worst that could
happen would be dying in his sleep, harvested by Countess
Judy and her terrifying associates. Better to dwell on the
no-alternative-whatsoever aspect, with a healthy wodge of
semi-hysterical prayer to fall back on as a contingency plan.

Paul sat down in the corner of the room, head resting
against a cupboard door, and tried to picture her as she'd
been, that time he'd seen her. It was hard: her face slipped
through the meshes of his mind like whitebait in a cod-
fishing net, morphing into other faces, more immediate but
less helpful. Finally, once he'd got what he reckoned was
the best fix he was likely to get, he opened the cupboard
door next to him and looked inside for something suitable.
In the end he had to settle for a big, chunky, old-fashioned
brass microscope: rather heavier than he'd have liked, but
the only artefact he'd come across that looked capable of
doing the job. He took a sheet of plain white copier paper
from a pile by the sink and laid it on the worktop, with
one edge projecting slightly. Then he put the microscope
on the paper, and sat down on the floor directly underneath.

Here goes nothing, Paul said to himself, and tugged the
paper as hard as he could.

The paper slid out, jarring the microscope over; it toppled
and dropped off the worktop directly onto Paul's head. *Ouch*,
he remembered thinking just for a split second; and then
he was sprawled on the floor, bleeding freely from a long
but superficial scalp wound, fast asleep.

Once he knew he was asleep, he looked round frantically.
Hello? he called wordlessly. *Are you there?*

A very long and distressing pause; and then, quite

suddenly, there she was. As before, pale golden light glowed all around her, fuzzy and hazy as the fur on furry pink slippers. Where her short, flaxen hair ended and the pale glow began was hard to say, but the way it reflected off her golden skin was really quite— Paul pulled himself together. No time for any of that stuff now.

'You're strange,' said the Girl of His Dreams. 'Did you summon me here to watch you knock yourself out with obsolescent scientific equipment?'

'You're her, aren't you? My dream girl.'

'You say the sweetest things.'

'Yes, but you're *her*, aren't you? The one that came persecuting – came to talk to me a week or so back. You told me to buck my ideas up and get involved and stuff.'

She nodded. 'You were wearing red paisley pyjamas,' she said, with a very faint grin.

'You're her,' Paul said, with a sigh of relief. 'Right, please listen carefully, because we need to get this right—'

'We? Am I part of this? What are we doing, then? Will it be like that time when you had three glasses of red wine on an empty stomach, and you had this dream where we were on this tigerskin rug on the beach at Mustique—'

'No,' Paul said with a faint quaver in his voice (and he was thinking: *Some dreams I wish I could remember when I wake up*). 'Look, you're a Fey, right? A good Fey.'

She frowned. 'Depends on what you mean by good. If you mean it like in the phrase *a good Catholic*, then no, probably not.'

Paul shook his head; just as well it was only a dream, since his real head would've hurt like hell. 'There're two sides in this civil war thing, yes? Good Fey and Bad—'

'Ah.' She smiled. 'You mean *good* as a synonym for *on the losing side.* Yes,' she added before he could interrupt. 'I'm a Fey and I'm on our side. What of it?'

Paul breathed out. 'In that case,' he said, 'could you possibly give me a lift to somewhere?'

She frowned. 'Depends. Where?'

'Don't know.' Not the best answer. 'What I meant to say was, there's somewhere I need to go, but I don't know how to find it or how to get there. I'm not even sure it's possible to get in there if you're awake. Can you help me?'

Her frown turned itself inside out and became a smile. 'You're out of your tiny mind, you know that? Do you seriously want to go back to Countess Judy's castle?'

'Of course I don't *want* to,' Paul growled. 'But I think it may be the only option. I need to find out where she stores her Source – you know, the poor bastard who's dreaming her.'

'Find him, right. Then what?'

'Then,' Paul muttered, 'wake him up.'

The Girl of His Dreams let out a low whistle. 'What's come over you all of a sudden?' she asked curiously. 'All the time I've known you, you've been this timid little wimp. Now you're talking about storming the enemy stronghold and killing the queen. Have you been on one of those self-assertiveness weekends or something?'

Paul shook his head. 'It's her or me,' he said. 'She's going to kill me if I don't get her first. Look, if I get through this ghastly mess in one piece, I promise I'll go back to being a spineless piece of cheese, if that's what you want—'

'No, not at all. Besides, it probably didn't occur to you, but if you get the snuff, I die too. Helping you would probably be a good move for me at this point.'

'Fine,' Paul said, 'great. Can you do it? Get me there, I mean?'

'Oh, I can get you there,' she replied. 'That's easy. Keeping you alive for more than two seconds once we've got there is going to be the challenging part, particularly now you're so brave and resolute and all. There're no half measures with you, are there? Straight from not saying boo to geese to strangling lions with your bare hands.'

Paul looked her steadily in the eye. 'Please,' he said.

'Oh, all right. Just this once — it's entirely against my better judgement and it'll all end in tears, but why the hell not?' She raised her right arm in a graceful, dramatic sweep, then paused. 'Just one thing,' she said. 'You do realise, don't you, that when we're over there, your physical body'll still be here?'

Paul shrugged. 'I hadn't, actually,' he said. 'Will that make much of a difference?'

'Think about it,' she replied, not unkindly. 'For a start, supposing you find this Source. How are you planning on waking him up?'

'Oh,' Paul said.

'That's all? Oh?'

'All right: oh dear, that's not going to work, then, sorry to have bothered you. Is that any better?'

'There's no need to get all snotty with me,' she said. 'I'm not the one who never thinks things through. What you need,' she went on, ever so slightly patronising, 'is a dream telescope.'

'A what?' Paul was about to ask; but he was interrupted by a sharp blow to his groin. He yelled.

'Baby,' said the Girl of His Dreams mockingly. 'Well go on, look at it.'

The cause of his profound discomfort proved to be a long brass tube with bits of glass in each end. 'For looking at the stars,' she explained. 'When we get there, look for the Great Bear, third from the right. It usually works.'

Paul knew that he had that bewildered-half-to-death expression on his face, but he couldn't help it. 'Excuse me?' he said.

'Idiot,' she said. 'When you wish upon a star, your dreams come true, right? To a certain extent, anyway. And please be careful with that thing; it's old and fragile, and I had to sign for it when I checked it out of the stores. I take it you know how to find the Great Bear?'

'I think so.'

'He thinks so. Fine, just crane your neck back as far as it'll go and search for something that looks like L. S. Lowry's idea of a rotary cultivator.'

'Third from the right?'

'And straight on till morning. Sorry, forget I said that, it'll only confuse the issue. Ready?'

'I've had a better idea,' Paul said, as she raised her arm again. 'How'd it be if you drew me a map of how to get there, and I just—'

The light that surrounded her flared out and smothered him. At the same moment, he fell upwards, like a suddenly weightless Australian. The world exploded, then closed around his head like a plastic bag.

'—Got the bus or something.' Paul wobbled, waved his arms for balance, steadied himself. He was in total darkness, apparently alone. The telescope was still in his left hand.

Crane your neck back, she'd said, *as far as it'll go.* He did that, then slowly lifted the telescope to his eye. Through it, he could see a sprinkling of white dots, like dandruff on God's collar. To begin with they were just a random scattering but he concentrated until the shape of the Great Bear emerged from the jumble. He counted, three from the right. 'Wish,' he said, 'wish wish *wish* . . .'

Something hit Paul so hard in the small of the back that he fell over onto his knees. It was only when the lights abruptly snapped on that he realised it was his own body, catching him up and embracing him like a large, friendly dog.

The disturbing thing was, he recognised the place. He'd been there before, in dreams. Mostly it looked like a hospital ward, a huge one with lines of beds stretching away out of sight in all directions, each bed with a chart and a name tag clipped to the end rail, and someone asleep between the cold, crisp white sheets. But it put him in mind of other things, too: a morgue, a battery-chicken farm, and also the stockroom at the back of a shoe shop. There was something industrial about the sparse cleanliness, the silence, the order. Somebody used this place to store valuable stock-in-trade, and wasn't making any false economies when it came to upkeep.

At least he hadn't triggered any alarms, or any that he could hear; but what would the Fey need with electronics, anyhow? It was inevitable that they were monitoring Paul, and surely they'd be here any minute to whisk him off to the dungeons of Grendel's Aunt – the real ones this time, not the prettified imitation he'd found himself in before. Maybe if he was really lucky he might have thirty seconds in which to identify and find Judy di Castel'Bianco's dreamer and wake him up. He glanced up and down the rows. He'd never been much good at quantity surveying; his mental counter only went up to six, and anything over that was just *lots*. At a guess, though, there were somewhere between thirty thousand and a million billion of the poor bastards. Even if they had the names of the parasites they were playing host to printed neatly on their clipboards, thirty seconds wasn't really long enough, was it?

Idiot.

Yes, well. While he was here, he might as well do *something*. If he could wake just one of them up, that'd be a Fey colonist switched off at the mains for ever. Paul doubted whether it'd do the woken Source any good, but you can't have every damn thing in this imperfect world.

All right, then, one sleeper chosen at random. Out of all these. *Um.*

Most of them, Paul noted idly, were women; young women, mostly, which made sense, since presumably the main quality you'd be looking for in your Source would be durability. Women live longer than men, and the younger you catch them, the longer they're likely to last. If he'd been there doing scientific research, he might have speculated as to whether a male human could only dream a male Fey, or whether it didn't matter a damn. As it was, he resolved his decision-making problem by closing his eyes and pointing.

The specimen he discovered he'd chosen was a little thin wisp of a thing: dark, wiry hair, a pointed face, thin lips that moved as she breathed, just as Sophie's did. In fact, the resemblance was striking, except that Sophie, though as thin as a politician's excuse, wasn't that scrawny. Rather, she looked as Sophie might have done if she hadn't eaten for a week—

Christ, Paul thought. For quite a while, he couldn't move

at all, even though every heartbeat that rocked his body reminded him of the passing of that painfully finite resource, time. When he unfroze, he came close and peered down at the girl. Definitely; but so starved and drawn it made him ill to look at her. Then he noticed the IV drip plastered to her arm; just enough to keep her alive, presumably, but too weak to wake up. Thorough, the Fey, and quite methodical.

'Sophie.' His voice echoed disastrously, like a fart in a cathedral. 'Sophie, it's me. For God's sake wake up. Please. Now.'

A tiny little grunt, like the sound of a far-distant pig; then she stirred slightly and rolled over. She was lying on her left arm. She often did that, and then woke up with pins and needles and a really bad temper for the rest of the day. Sowing the seeds of carpal tunnel syndrome, too. After all, what'd be the point of rescuing her from this place, this fate that might even be genuinely worse than death, if she ended up with permanent cramp in her little finger?

'Sophie,' he repeated, trying to make his voice loud, but it wouldn't cooperate. Every inherent instinct was against it (*Paul, keep quiet; Paul, don't you dare make a sound or I'll take you straight home again*). 'Please,' he added, just in case she was ignoring him because he was being bossy and over-bearing. 'Fucking hell, Sophie, what've they done to you? Please wake up, they'll be here any minute, I haven't got time—'

And then it occurred to Paul to wonder: whose Source was she, anyway? Who was in her dreams right now, drawing off her life like beer from the wood? Not that it mattered, but . . .

'Mr Carpenter.' The voice made Paul spin round, almost

losing his balance as his feet lost traction on the hard, tiled floor. 'Please step away from the bed immediately.'

'You,' was all he could find to say, even though it was scarcely original, not to mention a disrespectful mode of address to use to a partner, to her face. 'You did this to her.'

Countess Judy nodded, her face grave and still. 'Ms Pettingell was assigned to my department,' she said. 'Also, she is, like yourself, the property of the firm. She's my personal assistant. And that,' she added severely, 'is none of your concern. Please step away from the bed.'

'She's dreaming you. She's your Source.'

'Correct.' Countess Judy took a step forward and, just for a moment, looked down at the sleeping girl. 'She looks so fragile, doesn't she? Waiflike, vulnerable, almost beautiful in a vague, pre-Raphaelite way. Pity she has such a vile temper.'

'There you go,' Paul said grimly. 'Sweet and sour Source.'

Perhaps he shouldn't have said that. 'If you don't step away this instant,' Judy growled, 'I shall have no alternative but to call security and have you restrained.'

'But why?' Stupid question. 'I mean, what did you need her for? You must've had a dreamer already, or how could you have been there before we joined?'

Countess Judy clicked her tongue, a suffering-fools-gladly sort of noise. 'My previous Source died,' she said, in a bored voice. 'She was a hundred and six, after all. Most fortunately, her last illness was diagnosed early, so I had enough time to find a replacement. Ms Pettingell should ensure me at least eighty more years before I have to go through that particular chore again. I will give you one last chance, Mr Carpenter. Otherwise—'

But Paul shook his head. 'You don't dare,' he said. 'If

you could touch me, you'd have done it already. But you can't – you're scared she'll wake up. That's right, isn't it?'

'Absurd,' Countess Judy replied, but her voice had risen a semitone or so. 'I am simply trying to spare you the consequences of your stupidity. You can't possibly understand the issues involved. And even if you did succeed in waking Ms Pettingell up, the consequences for you would be most regrettable.' She shook her head, as though in disappointment. 'I can see – it hasn't even crossed your mind that she wouldn't want to be woken up. For a human, the sheer joy of dreaming one of us is – well, quite beyond the power of language to describe. You would destroy her, Mr Carpenter, and yourself as well.'

'Balls,' Paul said. 'You're the one who's going to die when she wakes up.' Without breaking eye contact, he groped down at the bed until he connected with something: Sophie's nose, by the feel of it. He closed his fingers and squeezed hard, then let go a little. 'She breathes through her nose when she's asleep,' he said (and if there was no more than a fifty-fifty chance that he was right about that, since he hadn't actually noticed, he was betting Judy didn't know that). 'If I do this, she'll wake up.'

'Actually,' Judy said with a slight yawn, 'she'll suffocate. Is that what you want? Are you prepared to kill her in order to injure me?'

'Yes.' *Liar, liar, pants on fire*; but could she see that in his face or hear it in his voice? 'I'm a hero, remember? You had your traitor train me, remember? That's the sort of thing heroes do; and then they spend the rest of the series beating themselves up over it, but by then it's too late.'

'My traitor.' Judy smiled wryly. 'What a talent you have for melodrama, Mr Carpenter. What you obviously consider betrayal was merely his job, nothing more. After all, we all work for the same firm, don't we? In order to carry out my duties and bring in very substantial fee income, I do need to be alive. The rest of the partners authorised this, of course. I would never do anything without the knowledge and approval of my colleagues.'

'Like it matters,' Paul said.

'Mr Carpenter.' Her eyes were as cold as winter. 'I have refrained up till now from calling security because if I do they will take you, shred your mind and then kill you. Since you too are the firm's property, representing a not insignificant financial outlay, I would prefer to resolve this matter another way. However, I must insist that you do as you are told immediately. Otherwise, I will not be responsible for the consequences.'

'Piss off,' Paul tried to say, but it came out as 'Pppsf'. He shuffled closer to the bed, grabbed Sophie's shoulder and started shaking it as hard as he could. She flopped about, alarmingly easy to move; the drip feed came out of her arm, and that panicked him even more. But she didn't wake up.

'It's pointless,' Countess Judy said. 'She won't wake up, not without the right medication; and if you carry on like that, you'll do her an injury. I'm sorry,' she added, 'but I did warn you.'

Whether they came out of the shadows or whether they'd been there all the time Paul couldn't tell, but there were ever so many of them: silvery grey, like snow clouds, hard to see and harder to keep an eye on, as they merged into the grey walls. But their faces were hard and smooth and their eyes were cold, like those of deep-frozen children, and it seemed like a fair bet that they weren't crowding in on him to shake his hand or teach him card tricks. He dug his nails into Sophie's shoulder, begged her, 'Sophie, *please* wake up'; but her head lay flopped on the pillow, and the only sound she made was a very faint snore. The closest of the grey shadows was almost within arm's reach now; as he stretched out, the sleeve of his robe fell away from his hand, revealing a set of broad, bitten fingernails—

(*Odd*, Paul couldn't help thinking, in a small backwater of his mind that even then had nothing better to occupy its time with. *Bitten fingernails*. But why would a dream bite its nails?)

— Which closed, disconcertingly, around his ear lobe, and twisted it. Paul yowled with pain and shrank back, at which the grey shape wobbled, and suddenly appeared to break in two at the waist. The upper half toppled forward, let go of Paul's ear, and crashed to the ground, slipping out from under the robe in the process. 'Idiot,' it said. 'Clown,' it added, as the stilts it'd been standing on clattered to the floor.

'*Benny!*' shrieked Countess Judy, in sheer fury. 'What the hell do you think you're playing at?'

Chapter Fourteen

Benny? Benny *Shumway*?

Which explained the need for stilts, Benny being a dwarf. But what was he doing here, disguised as one of the henchmen of the Queen of the Fey? *We ransomed him, didn't we?* And why, not that it really mattered an awful lot, was Countess Judy calling him by his first name? Paul had never heard her use first names with anybody—

'Sorry,' Benny said, scrambling to his feet in such a way that he stood between Paul and the grey shapes. 'It's been fun, Judy. But I quit.'

The look of fury on Countess Judy's face was extraordinary; not just because of its ferocious intensity, but because it was there at all. Also, what did he mean, 'quit'? This was hardly the time to be concerned about whether he had a job to go back to at JWW.

'Bastard,' Judy spat. 'You pathetic, deceitful, *small* bastard.'

She gestured with her hands and the grey shapes all took a step forward, perfectly in time, like soldiers on parade. Benny growled like a dog, then pulled something out of his pocket and shoved it in the face of the closest of them, who rocked back and staggered as though he'd had an aerosol squirted in his eyes. The rest of them hesitated, and Benny swung whatever it was in a wide arc; they cowered out of the way, one or two of them tripping over their feet or the hems of their colleagues' robes. Judy was screeching something, either at them or at Benny. As his arm swung back the other way, Paul caught a glint of light off the mystery object in his hand, and recognised it. The Sea Scout badge, which he'd last seen nailed to the wall in the great hall in the top drawer of Melze's filing cabinet—

'Benny?' he said, but Benny was too busy with other concerns.

Which was great, in fact, because the grey shapes didn't like the Sea Scout badge one little bit. Judy could swear and scream at them till she was blue in the face; the badge was worse, and they were starting to give ground, edging back a few inches at a time. How long Benny would be able to keep swinging the badge around, however, was another matter; not indefinitely, in any event. Just to drive the self-evident point home, Benny tilted his head as far sideways as he could without taking his eyes off the enemy, and hissed, 'Piss off, Paul, for crying out loud.'

Good advice, profoundly shrewd reasoning; except that Paul couldn't leave without Sophie. In which case, he was going to have to take her with him, which in turn would involve picking her up and carrying her, and how exactly are you supposed to go about lifting a completely inert body? Firemen are trained to do it, and so presumably are ballet dancers and film stars; but if they'd covered it at school, it must've been on one of the days when he was off sick.

'Paul, you dipstick,' Benny yelled, flailing his arms like a short windmill. 'Get out of here, now.'

Fine. With a quick, jerky movement, like someone plunging his hand into very hot water, Paul grabbed the bedclothes and dragged them off; then he bent over Sophie, awkwardly slid one hand behind her back and the other into the crook of her knees, and tried to lift. Various components in his spine and shoulders shrieked abuse at him and for a moment it was touch and go whether he was going to fall over; but her weight shifted in his arms, he straightened his back and staggered backwards a step or two. He had her. Now, provided he didn't drop her and he could find his way out of this place—

'Oh, you're pathetic,' Judy snarled. 'Get out of my way.' She was elbowing past the grey figures, and from somewhere or other she'd produced a knife with a thin blade, sharply curved. 'Put that thing down, Benny,' she said, 'or so help me—'

One of the grey shapes suddenly squealed; Judy had inadvertently stuck it in the thigh with the tip of the knife. Paul couldn't quite see what was going on over the top of Sophie's head (he kept bumping his chin on it and biting his tongue, and her hair in his nose made him want to sneeze) but the slight accident must've given Benny an opportunity to make a strategic withdrawal; fast as a rat up a drainpipe, he ducked under the neighbouring bed, scuttled its width like a spider, and straightened up running. Three of the grey shapes fell over each other trying to follow him, and the elbow of one of them landed in Judy's solar plexus just as she was in mid-yell. Under other circumstances, it'd have been a sound to stop and relish.

'Well, are you coming or not?' Benny panted at him, grabbing Paul's elbow with his free hand. 'This way's the quickest, but mind you don't drop her, for fuck's sake. Now come *on*, will you?'

'Sorry,' Paul mumbled; by that time, Benny was yards away and making good ground, while the grey shadows were streaming towards him. *Bugger*, Paul thought. His arms felt like they were being wrenched messily out of their sockets: how the hell could he be expected to run, lumbered with all this weight? On the other hand, he was back in no-choice mode. He ran.

Benny stopped dead, balled his left fist and thumped it into the wall. Immediately a panel shot back, revealing the entrance to a tunnel or cave. 'Move, can't you?' he roared, as Paul shot past him into the opening. Then something scraped back into place, and all the lights went out.

'I've shot the bolt, that'll hold them for a bit.' He heard Benny's voice in the dark. 'But not for long, it's just a door, not a hardened-steel gate. Carry on straight ahead,' Benny added. 'I'll follow on with the shield. Just carry on up the passage, and mind where you're putting your feet. You mustn't drop her, understand?'

'I wasn't planning to drop—' Paul stumbled over something; his fingers lost their grip, he juggled, caught Sophie again just in time. 'Look, slow down, can't you?' he muttered. 'I'm having problems, all right?'

The click of Benny's tongue echoed off the roof and walls like a rifle shot. 'God, you're feeble,' he said. 'Look, this is no bloody good, give her to me.'

Yes, Paul thought; and then, *No*. 'Actually,' he said, with what little breath he had left, 'I think I won't do that. I mean, I can manage, it's okay.'

'No, it bloody well—' Something was crashing against the door behind them; maybe it drowned out Benny's next words, or maybe he decided not to finish his sentence. 'All right,' he said, 'but be careful. If she wakes up—'

'Yes?' Paul said. 'What'll happen if she wakes up?'

Benny didn't reply, and for what seemed like a very long

time Paul heard nothing except his own breathless wheezing and the pounding of his heart. Eventually, however, they came to a fork in the tunnel. He wouldn't have known it was there, but Benny warned him in plenty of time. By this point, Paul wasn't all that surprised to discover that Benny was so well informed about the geography of the place.

'Up the left-hand spur,' Benny told him. 'It's only about three hundred yards, and then we go right. It'll bring us out at the top of some stairs. You've got to let me carry her then, you won't be able to manage. Believe me.'

'Sure,' Paul said, 'I believe you.'

He had a lot to think about after that, quite apart from the practicalities of not falling over or passing out from sheer exhaustion. They were inappropriate thoughts for someone who'd just been rescued, but they wouldn't go away until a more convenient occasion; they dug their little heels in and growled at him when he tried to shoo them off.

Benny was absolutely right with his directions; when he abruptly called out 'Stop!' Paul did as he was told; a moment later, he could feel a faint draught coming up at him, as though from a stairwell. 'You know your way pretty well, don't you?' he said.

'Whatsisname, eidetic memory,' Benny grunted. 'Now, give her here.'

Paul hesitated; but even if he was right, there was no reason not to. 'Right,' he said; and a moment later the weight had gone from his poor abused arms and shoulders. 'You got her?'

'No problem,' Benny replied. 'Take care on the stairs, they're a bit slippery and there's no handrail or any of that mimsy health-and-safety stuff.'

'Fine,' Paul said. 'And how many stairs are there?'

'A hundred and seventy-three.'

You'd know that, of course, Paul thought. He counted them as he went down, more to give him something to do than because he needed the corroboration. 'Actually,' he said, as his feet found the level again, 'you were one out. Hundred and seventy-four.'

'Nobody's perfect. Now, a hundred and fifty yards straight ahead, then we follow on round to the left, and that should bring us out directly under a manhole cover.'

Paul kept quiet. Only sensible. After all, without Benny he'd be completely lost; indeed, if Benny hadn't shown up like that . . .

But.

Benny had to hand Sophie back to Paul while he climbed up the short ladder and pushed open the manhole cover. Light cascaded in like water flooding a submarine. Benny came down the ladder again, put Sophie over his shoulder as though she was a camera case or other small accessory, and shinned back up again. He even reached out a hand to help Paul up.

'Where are we?' Paul said, looking round. Behind him, he could see a tall, spiky, bare-topped mountain, set in a flat plateau of black shingle. Volcanic ash? Should've paid attention in geography, instead of doodling Klingon battle-cruisers on the back cover of his exercise book.

Benny said a name, but it didn't mean anything to Paul. 'I meant, what country?'

'Oh,' Benny replied. 'Iceland. Very remote, see. In the middle of fucking nowhere, nobody can hear you scream. Come on, it's a long walk to where I parked the helicopter.'

Benny was right about that; but he didn't seem concerned

about the possibility of pursuit, and if there'd been one, Benny wasn't the sort to turn a blind eye to it. That was comforting, at least.

'Benny,' Paul said, after about an hour.

'Hm?'

'I think I know why you don't want Sophie to wake up.'

Longish silence. All Paul could see was half the back of Benny's head, the rest of it obscured by Sophie's hair. 'Well,' Benny said, 'you aren't stupid. In fact, I'm surprised it took you so long to figure it out.'

'So,' Paul said. 'So you're the—?'

He couldn't say the word; but Benny laughed and said it for him. 'The traitor? Yup, that's me.'

'And you don't want Sophie waking up because that'd be the end of Countess Judy.'

Half the back of Benny's head nodded slightly. 'That's right.'

'Because you, um, you're in love with her.'

Benny's silence was thoughtful rather than anything else. 'Not sure about that any more,' he said. 'Oh, I was once. Very much so. Wouldn't have married her otherwise.'

'Married her?'

'Yup. She's my third – no, scratch that – fourth wife. I keep forgetting Tanya, because she only hung around for a week. That's right, Judy was number four, after Tanya but before Heidi. I think,' he added after a moment. 'Anyway, yes, we were married. She left me, of course, but not for anybody else, which is a consolation, I guess. Actually, it isn't, but who cares?'

Paul nodded, though of course Benny couldn't see. 'So you weren't captured by the Fey at all. You were, well, bait.'

'Yup.'

'For Ricky?'

'Do me a favour. For you.'

It was as though Benny had momentarily lapsed from English into an obsolete dialect of Portuguese. 'Me?' Paul repeated.

'Well, naturally. You're the one she needed to get shot of, after all.'

'*Me?* Why, for God's sake?'

Benny sighed. 'Because you were whatsername's boyfriend; you know, this one here. Name's on the tip of my tongue.'

'Sophie. But that can't be right, because she dumped me.'

'You reckon.'

'Yes,' Paul snapped, 'it was hardly a grey area. She wrote me this letter, and—' He faltered. 'She wrote me a letter,' he mumbled.

Benny's laugh came out as a thunderous snort. 'I don't think so,' he said. 'You might've got a letter, and it might have been in her handwriting, but I'm prepared to bet you my front teeth in a simple platinum setting that Judy wrote it, for reasons so obvious they're visible from orbit. All that stuff about a transfer to the Los Angeles office . . . You believed all that?'

'Well,' Paul said. 'Yes, actually.'

'Good God. Anyway, that's why Judy wanted you killed; but of course when she asked the rest of them for permission, you being partnership property and all, they said no, find someone cheaper. So she had to find some other way. First step, naturally, was getting you assigned to the heroism department, because she figured someone as monumentally feckless as you'd only last two minutes.' Benny sighed. 'But something went wrong there.'

'It did? I mean—'

'Yes,' Benny said slowly. 'At the time we thought it was dead handy, since Ricky had shoved off to try and use your Door thing to find this place; it meant you'd be put in with me, and I'd have no trouble at all arranging for you to meet with a nasty accident. But—' Benny shook his head, as though he still couldn't believe it. 'I couldn't,' he said. 'Dunno why; I mean, look at you, what's to like? But I just couldn't. So I had to go and do all the monster-fighting and vampire-staking, all on my own, enough work for two people full-time, while I had you swanning round the office filling in bloody stupid forms. I kept asking myself, why am I doing this? Apart from anything else, it was getting embarrassing every time I had to go and report to Judy; nope, not dead yet, still not dead, wasn't all that dead last time I looked, sorry, will try harder. I had to make out you were some kind of naturally gifted superhero, one look at you and the dragons and chimeras and enormous man-eating slugs just rolled over and died of fright.'

'Oh,' Paul said.

'You can bloody well say that again. Anyhow,' Benny went on, quickening his step a little, 'since that obviously wasn't working, she got a little bit anxious. That's why she had me plant the bomb in your office.'

Paul nearly choked. '*You.*'

'Me. Oh, come on,' Benny added scornfully. 'You very nearly caught me at it, remember? I practically had to throw you out the door, that night. Dunno whether I was trying to do it right or not,' he said thoughtfully. 'I mean, I made a lovely job of the arming mechanism and all that stuff – I'm a dwarf, after all, we're good with mechanical things. But I still reckon that if I was really trying to scrag you, I wouldn't have told the first goblin I met that you'd got a pound of raw liver stashed in your filing cabinet. Greedy little buggers, goblins,' he added with distaste. 'I told him, don't you go stealing it, mind, you'll get into all sorts of trouble. Would he listen? Would he hell as like.'

'I see,' Paul said; and even as he said it, he knew it was something of an understatement.

'Judy wasn't half pissed off about it,' Benny went on. 'The rest of them, they're not stupid, they knew perfectly well she must've had something to do with it, but of course they couldn't say anything; not with the amount of money she brings in for the firm every year. So she blamed me — even then I don't think she guessed I'd done it on purpose, just thought I was useless. She's always made that mistake, where I'm concerned. That's when she decided killing you wasn't the right approach; you just didn't seem to want to hold still and be killed. So she dreamed up — sorry, no pun intended — she *cooked* up the hostage-rescue scenario, sent me off to the basement and sent you to fetch me. Now that really ought to have worked; would've worked, too, if that bloody goblin hadn't stuck her oar in. See, I couldn't quite bring myself to kill you, but I had no trouble kidding myself that if you got locked up in the dungeons, that'd be all right. Sooner or later, Judy'd decide you weren't a threat any more and let you go; maybe I'd be able to persuade her, given time. Deep down, I realised that was all bull; if you ended up in the dungeons, you'd stay there till you rotted. But it wasn't the same as actually finishing you off, so that was all right. I was mad as hell when Rosie burst in and whisked you away. Anyhow,' he said, 'there's the helicopter, look. And in case you're wondering, no, I'm not going to chuck you in the ocean halfway across the Atlantic or anything like that. No point any more, I've blown it completely as far as Judy's concerned. No bad thing, either. Incredible pair of legs, but not a very nice personality.'

Paul hesitated. He could see the helicopter below them in a small hollow; he wasn't entirely sure that he wanted to get in it. 'We're taking Sophie, right?' he said.

Benny shrugged. 'Well, I was assuming you'd refuse to get in without her.'

'Quite right. So if you deliberately crash the helicopter into a mountain or something, Sophie'd be killed too. She'd die in her sleep.'

For a moment, Paul wondered if Benny had got the point. 'You know what,' he said, 'that hadn't occured to me. Smart. But don't worry about it, I'm not the self-sacrificing type. Besides,' he added, almost carelessly, 'my fiancée wouldn't like it.'

'Your—'

'Oh, didn't I mention that? I'm engaged. Again,' Benny added, rather superfluously. 'Come to think of it, that's probably why I decided to pack it all in with Judy and save you. She's quite fond of you, you see, in a motherly sort of way; it was one of the things we talked about, actually, when we were locked up together in the fake dungeon, waiting for Judy to come and let us out. Nice kid, soft-hearted; and of course, it's never exactly bad business to marry the boss's sister.'

Oink? Paul thought; then he understood. 'Monika?' he gasped. 'You're planning to marry my *car*?'

Benny tutted disapprovingly. 'She's not *your* car,' he said, 'she belongs to the firm. And anyway, you'll be better off getting the bus or the train – it saves money. Trust me on that,' he added, 'I'm the cashier, remember?'

'But—' Paul couldn't think of a polite way to put it. 'She's a *car*, dammit,' he said. 'Won't that, er, make difficulties?'

Benny shrugged. 'I like a challenge,' he said. 'There'll be some way to put her right again, you can bank on that. Till then at least, I'll know I've got a significant other I can trust implicitly. Like the telly ad used to say, why can't everything in life be as reliable as a Volkswagen?'

As if on cue, it started to snow. Benny pulled open the helicopter door (he had to stand on tiptoe to reach the handle) and swung Sophie in as though she was a bag of shopping. 'You can ride in the back with her,' he said, 'and for crying out loud, make sure she doesn't shift about, bang her head, anything like that.'

Paul looked at him. 'She's going to wake up sooner or later,' Paul said, 'I won't leave her like this.'

'We'll cross that bridge when we come to it,' Benny replied. 'Now, if you wouldn't mind getting in. Quite apart from the fact that every second we're here we're risking getting caught by Judy's people, it's perishing cold with the door wide open.' He sneezed like a cannon shot.

'All right,' Paul said, and he scrambled in. 'Where are we going?'

'Home,' Benny said, with a faint sigh. 'Lots of things I've got to do. What sort of a fist has that dozy little tart of Judy's been making with my job, by the way? If she's mucked up my filing system, I'll wring her insubstantial bloody neck.'

'Actually, she seemed to be handling it okay,' Paul replied mildly. 'What was the point of her, by the way?'

'Plan B,' Benny said. 'If you were in love with your child-hood sweetheart, you wouldn't worry too much about what had happened to your previous bird. I wasn't keen on the idea from the start, to be honest with you. I mean, she was just too perfect, too tailor-made, even a complete nitwit like you had to realise that. Presumably that's what happened?' he queried.

'Well, partly,' Paul told him. 'Also, the real one happened to phone me out of the blue; or rather, someone got into her dreams and made her want to. And—' Paul grinned, though Benny couldn't see; he was busy with the controls. 'She wasn't the girl of my dreams after all.'

'Close, but no cigar, as Bill Clinton would say?'

'Sort of.' Paul shrugged. 'Come to think of it,' he said, looking down at Sophie's still, pale face, 'the Girl of My Dreams isn't the girl of my dreams, either.'

'Not sure I follow,' Benny said. 'Not sure I can be fucked to try. Hold on tight, now; I'm a bloody good pilot, but the pedals on this thing are a long way down.' Paul sniffed. By the feel of it, he'd caught Benny's cold; the same one, presumably, that had been floating round the office for weeks. Or not, because Benny had been away long enough to have got over it, if it was the office special. Did the Fey get colds? Like it mattered.

Never having done much flying, Paul didn't realise quite how soporific the experience can be until it was nearly too late. He caught himself just as he was on the point of closing his eyes; bad business, that would be, when the Queen of the Fey was after him and he was in the same confined space as her at best ambivalent ex-husband. He dug his fingernails into his arm, blinked furiously, made a point of ignoring the flock of sheep that dogged his periph-eral vision as they formed up to spell out the words COUNT US! Sleep lapped at the backs of his eyelids like the sea against a wall, gradually eroding, continually probing for a way through. It had been a long time since he'd had any proper sleep, and his adrenalin reserves were more or less played out. Sooner or later—

Damn, Paul thought; *but I only closed my eyes for a split second, to rest them. I must wake up, right now. I really have to wake up now. I shall count to three, and then I'll wake up.* Snff. *Bloody cold.*

Zzzzz.

Paul was in Countess Judy's office, sitting across the desk from her. She was reading some big fat document, and he knew that he wasn't important enough to interrupt her till she'd finished. On the desk in front of him lay a strange collection of objects; a screwdriver, a pen, an old-fashioned wind-up watch that had seen better days, a Sea Scout badge and a bit of glass out of a busted flame-effect electric fire. There was also a photograph album, and since he was bored and Countess Judy didn't look like she even knew he was there, he decided to flip through it to pass the time. So he picked it up, but the pages were all hazy and fuzzy, as though he hadn't got his reading glasses on. But of course, how stupid. Paul took the lump of coloured glass and pressed it carefully into his eye socket. At once the fuzziness cleared, and the photographs were as sharp as could be.

The first one: taken out in the country somewhere on a bright, frosty day. Sophie was sitting on a gate, wearing a red bobble-hat and knitted mittens; Paul was standing beside her, holding her hand, looking at her rather than at the camera. They were both laughing, and the laughter had solidified into a little cloud of white vapour, the way your breath does in winter. He knew, of course, that the picture was false; there had never been such a day, they'd never had time for romantic country walks in cheerful primary-coloured knitwear, and he was prepared to bet cash money that Sophie had never owned a red bobble-hat in all her life. It was a pretty image, but a plain lie. He turned the page.

The second one: Paul recognised the setting as the landing beside the Rialto bridge in Venice, because he'd Portable-Doored there many times during solitary lunch hours, before he and Sophie got together. It was moonlight in the photo; she was sitting with him at a café table, with the steep span of the bridge behind them, a gondola slightly out of focus over his right shoulder. She was wearing some kind of evening thing (Paul's grasp of the technical vocabulary was vague at best) that made her bare shoulders look slim rather than bony, and seemed to drink up the moonlight and glow with it, and on her feet were high-heeled glass slippers. False, fake and phoney, just like the first one. *Tsk.*

The third one had no place in an album that might fall into the hands of children or persons of a nervous disposition. The background was lush green grass sprinkled with fat white daisies, and presumably it was meant to be warm midsummer weather, since neither of them exhibited so much as a single goosepimple. That hadn't happened, either. Paul would have remembered if it had.

The fourth one was even more bizarre. In the background, a golden-thatched country cottage, doorway an impenetrable entanglement of climbing roses in full bloom. Sitting in deckchairs on the lawn on either side of a small rosewood tea-table, a handsome, well-preserved elderly couple watched their grandchildren playing tennis on the full-sized court next to the pony paddock. Paul had to look twice before he figured out that the principals were supposed to be Sophie and himself.

Then Paul realised that Countess Judy was looking at him, and had been doing so for some time. He snapped the album shut and mumbled an apology, but she waved it aside.

'Would you like to keep it?' she said.

Paul shook his head. 'Thanks,' he replied, 'but it's not real. None of that stuff happened, or else it won't happen.' He sneezed. Fortunately, he had a dream handkerchief in his pocket. It even had his initials embroidered in one corner.

'That could be changed,' the Countess said; and a young woman stepped forward out of the shadows behind Judy's chair: Sophie, but with a blank, empty look on her face. 'I'm not saying you wouldn't notice the difference,' Judy said. 'You'd be very conscious of it. This,' she went on, flicking a thumb in the direction of the girl at her side, 'is the young woman in the photographs. She'll never criticise you, belittle you, make you feel stupid or awkward; she'll never cheat on you or get bored with you or make demands or stop you doing what you want to do with your life. She'll always be there for you, no whining or complaints or recrim-inations, no unfathomable mood swings; she won't expect you to be telepathic or tell you to do something and then yell at you because you did it; she'll appreciate you, admire you, love you till the day you die. She'll be the girl of your dreams, but her face and voice and mannerisms and every-thing you recognise the real thing by will be exactly the same.' Judy's voice was soft as water, soothing and gentle, the way a mother's voice should be but Paul's mother's never was. 'I'm sorry I tried to fob you off with that cheap, tacky Demelza Horrocks; I underestimated you, assumed you were shallow, insensitive, immature; I thought that so long as you had a girl who was prepared to love you, you'd be happy. I was very stupid. But now I can make it up to you. I can give you perfection.'

Paul frowned. 'No, thanks,' he said.

Judy laughed, and the fake Sophie vanished. 'Of course,' she said. 'It was worth a try, I suppose, but I knew you wouldn't settle for a walking, talking, living doll. Never mind.' She leaned forward slightly and folded her hands on the desk. 'Here's the deal, Mr Carpenter. Give me ten minutes to set my affairs in order; I've found a replacement source, so all I have to do is vacate Ms Pettingell and move across. I trust there are no hard feelings.'

Paul wiped his dripping nose and looked at her. 'I've won?'

She shrugged. 'It's no big deal,' she said. 'I've moved before, it'll mean a day or so to adjust but that's only a minor inconvenience, nothing more. Far more important to get matters settled before this ridiculous feud disrupts my schedule any further.'

'But you tried to kill me,' Paul pointed out.

'Yes, so I did.' Judy sighed. 'But you're too much trouble to kill, Mr Carpenter. Trying to dispose of you has wasted my time and my energy, and I'm getting behind on the things I ought to be doing. My fault; when I had you posted to the heroism department, I foolishly failed to notice that you are indeed a hero; and heroes can't just be snuffed out as easily as palace guards in a swashbuckler. It's far more convenient and cost-effective for me to give in and admit defeat. Take back your girl, Mr Carpenter, and may you both live happily ever after. As a residence, she isn't worth the effort.'

Now there was a bed, the hospital type with little wheels,

standing beside the desk; in it lay Sophie, the way she'd been in Judy's dormitory. As Paul watched, his eyes itching (but it was only the cold, he assured himself) she muttered something and turned restlessly in her sleep, the way she generally did just before she woke up. Very tentatively, he reached out and touched her, as if to check that she was real.

The shock was painful, like brushing against an electric fence. It was the same sensation he'd felt when the fake Melze had tried to hold his hand. 'No, thanks,' he repeated. 'I think I'll stick with the real real Sophie, if it's all the same to you.'

Quite unexpectedly, Countess Judy laughed, even clapped her hands. 'Well done, Mr Carpenter,' she said cheerfully. 'You know, just occasionally, now and then, I can see a little tiny bit of your great-uncle in you. I have to say,' she added, as the bed and the most recent fake Sophie vanished, 'that one would've fooled most people in the trade. So, I think we understand each other now, don't we?'

Oink, Paul thought. 'Do we?'

'I believe so.' Countess Judy leaned back in her chair and rested her chin on her fingertips. *Molto elegante*, like a middle-period Sophia Loren without that slightly bovine quality around the jawline. 'You're in possession right now, but dear Benny won't let you wake her up; more to the point, you may have her, but I have you, since you haven't got the stamina to stay awake.' As she said it, Paul felt steel clamps snap shut around his arms, pinning him to the chair. 'Sorry about that,' Judy said. 'A bit too James Bond for my taste and scarcely original, but I can't make the effort to be subtle right now.'

But Paul only shook his head. 'There's some reason why you can't kill me, isn't there?' he said. 'Otherwise you'd have done it already, as soon as I dozed off. And you can't lock me up in your stupid dungeon, either. And these gadgets—' He raised his arms, which passed through the clamps as though they weren't there, which of course they weren't. 'Seems to me that your effective magic's a bit of a contradiction in terms. Doesn't work on me any more, does it?'

Judy clapped her hands again, but this time slowly, and she wasn't smiling. 'Only certain very elementary procedures; the ones that don't hurt, mostly. We can try the ones that *do* hurt if you like, and see if they're still working.'

At once, Paul felt as though all his teeth were being drilled at the same time, without anaesthetic. 'Pain, you see,' Judy was saying, 'is effective magic in its purest form. There is no such thing as pain, it's always all in the mind, that's how it's supposed to be. A few drops of liquid or a whiff of gas puts it out of action completely. But without the drops or the gas, you can know as surely as anything that it's just electrical impulses in your nerves, and it'll still hurt enough to stop your heart or burst a blood vessel in your brain.' She shook her head. 'If ever I have the time, I'm going to write a book about beauty and pain. They're so alike in so many ways: neither of them really exist, but both of them are strong enough to override the strongest human mind and turn the wisest and bravest of us all into clowns. Someone who can command beauty *and* pain – well, they'd have all the bases covered, as we say where I come from. Don't you agree?'

There was only a tiny bit of Paul's mind still sticking up above the flood of pain, like Mount Ararat in the Bible. 'No,' he whispered. 'It's bullshit. And you can't kill me or put me in your bloody coal cellar, so fuck you.'

Whereupon the pain stopped, and Judy jerked back in

her chair as though she'd been slapped. 'How dare you talk to me like that?' she said; and Paul thought that if she had a heart, it wouldn't have been in it.

'What were you planning on doing?' he asked sweetly. 'Going to fire me?' He laughed. 'I think I'll wake up now, if you don't mind. And when I do, I'm going to wake up Sophie as well. And then you'll be finished. For ever. So if anybody's getting the sack—'

This time, the pain was in Paul's chest and left arm, presumably intended to simulate a heart attack. There was an awful lot of it, but it didn't actually hurt; it was a back projection of pain, as phoney as the polystyrene rocks in the old *Star Trek*. 'Don't bother,' he said. 'You're wasting time, and you haven't got a lot of it left. You know,' he added thoughtfully, 'apart from that little dragon thing – and I sat on it by accident, so it doesn't really count – you'll be the first living creature I've more or less intentionally killed. I won't feel good about it, but it could be a whole lot worse. Like, I could've trodden on an ant or something.'

'You idiot.' Anger and fear, and some contempt in there too. 'He can't always be in there to protect you, and if you kill me, my people will hunt you down and you'll die in your sleep, and then we'll see. We're always there, as soon as the light goes out, as soon as your eyelids start to itch. Just think about that, will you? You think you're tired now, you just wait, when you're dying of exhaustion because it's better than what'll happen if you shut your eyes just for a second. And when you do—'

'Oh, piss off,' Paul said wearily, and opened his eyes.

He was in the helicopter. He was awake, and in the real world, flying through a storm in total darkness over the icy-cold Atlantic Ocean, with a treacherous dwarf at the controls and the only girl he'd ever really love lying in a coma beside him. So that was all right. 'Benny?' he called out.

'What?'

'How much further?'

'Search me. I'm lost.'

Paul grinned. Lost, in a storm in total darkness over the ice-cold Atlantic Ocean. 'No worries,' he said cheerfully. 'Wake me up when we get there – I'm going to have forty winks.'

Which he proceeded to do; and dreamed about being back at school and being called up to recite a poem he hadn't learned in front of the whole class, with everybody sniggering at him. Just that: no girls, no dungeons, no grey shapes, no death threats, just humiliation, inadequacy and ordinary stuff like that. It felt like coming home again after the War.

When Paul woke up again, feeling cheerful and refreshed (bizarre enough in itself; usually when he woke up he felt like he'd just crawled out of a sporadically cleaned toilet), they were still flying, but it was bright daylight, and through the window he could see an endless blue-grey carpet with white frilly bits. 'Benny?'

'It's all right, I know where we are,' Benny called back. 'It's not where we're supposed to be, but what the hell. If nobody ever got lost, they'd never have discovered America.'

'I'm not bothered,' Paul sang back; then he sneezed. He still had the cold, apparently, but it wasn't interfering significantly with his general euphoria. 'It's not like I had much on for today, anyhow. No, I wanted to ask you: What're we going to do? About Judy, I mean.'

Silence. Then Benny sighed. 'I've been thinking about

that all night,' he said. 'And you're right, we can't leave your bit of stuff asleep for the rest of her life – we're going to have to wake her up. But first, we're going to try something. You still got that watch?'

Watch? Oh yes, watch. 'You know about that?'

''Course I do, you think I'm stupid or something? Anyway, the idea is, use the watch to make one second that'll last for ever, and then stick Judy in it. It'll be boring as hell for her and she won't like it, but it's got to be better than killing the bitch.'

Paul thought that over for a moment. 'You can do that?'

'No idea,' Benny replied. 'It's never been done before, and I wouldn't have a clue how to go about it. But Theo van Spee might, or Mr Wells senior, John Wellington; but God only knows where he's buggered off to. Someone'll know how to go about it. Agreed?'

Paul nodded. 'Whatever,' he said. 'So long as there's no risk to Sophie, you can do what you like.'

'You sound cheerful,' Benny growled. 'What's got into you?'

'A good night's sleep,' Paul replied. 'Does wonders for you. You should try it some time.'

'Very funny.' Benny didn't sound all that amused. 'I haven't been to sleep since nineteen – when was the year when Eddie the Eagle was in the Winter Olympics? Whenever that was.'

Paul laughed, assuming it was supposed to be a joke. In mid-snigger, he realised that it wasn't. 'But that's impossible,' he said. 'No human being can—'.

'Not a human being, am I? Thank God,' Benny added fervently. 'Our lot may be on the compact side, y-axis-wise, but we can teach you tall bastards a thing or two about staying awake. No, that year – early 1980s, wasn't it? –

that was the year Judy dumped me, and I got the distinct impression that the Land of Nod was off limits to me for the duration. I could be wrong, but it's not an area where trial and error seems the wise approach.'

'But Benny,' Paul said quietly. 'If I wake Sophie up, it'll be over, won't it? You can finally get some sleep. Wouldn't that be worth it?'

Benny thought for a moment. 'No,' he said. 'To continue the Olympic theme, another thing we dwarves can do pretty well for ever is carry a torch. We'll try it my way, or not at all. Got that?'

'Got it,' Paul said, and sprayed the back of Benny's chair with a fine dew of nasal residue. 'Don't blame me,' he added, reaching into his pocket and finding that the hanky had just been a dream. 'It's *your* rotten cold I've got.'

'Dwarves don't get colds,' Benny said airily. 'Now shut up while I try and land this thing.'

'Oh, right. What's the matter, turbulence or something?'

'No, I've never done it before.'

'Eek,' Paul said. 'I mean, you must've. You can't learn to fly without being taught how to land.'

'Who said I ever learned to fly?' Benny replied. 'Now, I wonder what this knob here does.'

It's not visible from the street, or from the air, come to that, unless you know what you're looking for; in fact, it's only there if you say the magic words in the right order and your security code is up to date. But there's a helicopter landing pad on the roof of 70 St Mary Axe, and Benny landed on it as gracefully as a mayfly settling on the petals of a rose. Which meant that either he'd been kidding or he was very, very lucky.

'It's all right,' he called out over his shoulder, as he cut the engine. 'It's safe, you can come out now.'

Paul uncurled slowly. 'You sure?'

'Chicken,' Benny replied, leaning across and opening the passenger door. 'Anyway, that was the easy part. Now we've got to get to our offices without Dennis Tanner seeing. Not supposed to leave the office without telling reception. He can get really snotty about it sometimes.'

Benny led the way across the roof to a trapdoor. He grabbed the iron ring and tugged, but it wouldn't move. 'Bolted,' he muttered in disgust.

Paul looked round. No other way off the roof that he could see. 'What're we going to do now?' he said.

'And you're the one who's supposed to be the trainee sorcerer,' Benny replied. 'Magic. Just watch.'

Benny walked back fifteen paces, took a run-up, jumped and landed with both feet together on the trapdoor. It collapsed under him, and he vanished. A split second later, Paul heard a dull thump.

'Are you okay?' he called down the hole.

'Fine,' replied a somewhat ragged voice from down below. 'Good magic, that – I learned it from some guys at a rugby club I used to belong to. Hold on, I'll get the ladder.'

Getting Sophie down was a grim business; Paul was terrified of dropping her, Benny was rather more concerned about waking her up, and in the end she slithered down the last few rungs on her back, until Benny was able to catch her. Fortunately, a gentle snore reassured both of them that no harm had been done.

'Problem is what to do with her till we've figured out how to do the swap-over,' Benny said, hoisting Sophie over his shoulder. 'Not your office, it's the first place Judy'd look.

Ditto mine. Strongroom's out, it's perishing cold down there and she might wake up. Ricky's room, maybe, but I don't trust him not to wake her. Which leaves the closed-file store or the women's toilet, and I'm not setting foot in there.'

'Why not?'

'Embarrassed,' Benny said shortly. 'Closed-file store, then. Good hiding place, nobody ever goes in there unless they're daft or crazy or suicidal or they want an old file really, really badly. We can dump her in the weapons locker. Reinforced steel door, and there's only two keys, mine and Ricky's.'

That sounded reassuring enough, though Paul had his doubts about whether any door could keep out Countess Judy and her followers. But he asked Benny if he'd mind taking off his Fey grey-shape robe and then folded it to make a pillow for Sophie ('Ah, how sweet,' Benny cooed, and mimed sticking a finger down his throat), and watched while the door was closed and locked. 'Right,' Paul said. 'Now give me the key, please.'

Benny looked at him for a moment, as though deciding what would be the most appropriate way to slaughter him. Then he handed the key over without another word.

'Now what?' Paul asked.

'I'll go and have a word with Theo van Spee, if he's in,' Benny replied. 'At least he may know where old Mr Wells has got to, even if he can't do anything himself. You,' he added thoughtfully. 'Dunno what to suggest, really. Piss off, keep out of sight and don't talk to any strange women. You could even,' he added, grinning, 'do some work. You know, the stuff they pay you for.'

'As opposed to getting killed and eaten,' Paul replied gloomily, 'which is what they bought me for. You know, there are times now and then when I wonder if wouldn't have been better off going to law school, like my mum wanted me to.'

Benny thought about that for a moment. 'Nah,' he said. 'Not a great deal in it, but at least this way you get to keep your self-respect,'

Do some work, Paul thought. *Well, why not?* If he could remember as far back as, what, the day before yesterday, Mr Tanner had dumped a thick wad of bauxite pictures on his desk and snarled something about *urgent*. It was all pretty remote, but if it came to a point where allies could help him, maybe Dennis Tanner would be more inclined to be on his side if he'd just pinpointed the biggest bauxite find of the last hundred years. Crazy enough to be plausible, he decided, and headed for his office.

In fact, it was remarkably soothing, scrying for mineral deposits in a reasonably comfortable chair, his feet up on the desk, nobody chasing him or smiling meltingly at him out of deep blue eyes or hustling him down subterranean passages a few steps ahead of a posse of poor men's Nazgul. If only there was some way he could get out of this ghastly mess with the Fey in one piece (and save Sophie, of course; that was the bit that mattered, wasn't it?) he'd quite happily take his triple vow of poverty, tedium and obedience and sit here prodding photographs with his fingertip until he was old enough to retire. None of it had been of his choosing, after all; and all that garbage about heredity and being the chosen one who'd drive the Fey out of the real world for ever was slipping away like – well, like a dream. Paul peered down at his wrists; he'd taken off his jacket, and most of the blood had gone on its sleeves. All he could see were two very thin reddish-pink scars, and a few black flakes of dried blood. Surely there'd be more to see than that if he'd actually succeeded and slashed his wrists badly enough to die.

Paul sneezed, and wiped his nose thoughtfully with the corner of his handkerchief. *Did I die? Really?* Unlikely. He ran over in his mind all the improbable things that had happened to him since Ricky Wurmtoter had come crashing in through his window. Wouldn't it make more sense if he himself had broken the window – it had a tendency to stick, maybe he slammed it too hard trying to close it, and the splintered glass had cut his hands. Then he'd passed out from the shock and the sight of blood, and everything since then had been hallucinations and dreams. Fine; except that if that was really what had happened, Sophie wouldn't be locked away in a steel safe full of rocket launchers on the floor below, and she'd really have left him and gone to California. That too was rather more likely than the alternative version, but there are times when you don't want to follow the odds too slavishly.

Melze, he thought, as a tingle crossed the palm of his hand, indicating the presence of bauxite beyond the dreams of avarice. He sneezed again. Had he really come within a gnat's whisker of falling in love with *that*? On balance, he'd rather get off with Mr Tanner's mum; she might have little round red staring eyes and teeth that you could open corned-beef tins with when the little key thing broke off, but at least she was real, once you got past the outer rind of super-imposed popsy. Memories, dreams, illusions, delusions: it occurred to him to wonder if there really was a stone-steel-and-concrete Dungeon of the Fey anywhere in the world. He was inclined to doubt it, because it wasn't necessary. Any human being, but particularly a human being like Paul

Carpenter, was capable of constructing a far more unbreakable prison for himself inside his own head.

'Hello.'

Paul froze, his finger between pictures. His nose was tickling again, but he fought back the impulse to sneeze. He didn't want to look up, for fear of what he'd see.

'So you came back here,' Countess Judy went on, crossing the floor until she stood over him, her shadow covering him like a gladiator's net. 'I couldn't believe you'd be that stupid, but I had to check.'

'You can't hurt me,' he said grimly. 'We've been into all this before. There's some reason I don't know why you can't touch me, so please go away.'

She laughed. 'That was there,' she said. 'This is here. And yes, I can't hex you or steal your soul while you sleep or stop your heart with a smile. But I don't need to. Hooray for basic technology, I always say.'

That made him change his mind and look up. Judy di Castel'Bianco was grinning, something he'd never seen her do before, and in her hand she had a big, broad-bladed knife. 'You wouldn't,' he said.

'Bet?'

Paul tried to get up; but the knife was ever so much more frightening even than the grey shapes or the dungeons of Grendel's Aunt. His knees gave way, and he flopped back into the chair.

'Your choice,' she said. 'Give me back the little Pettingell girl, or I'll cut your heart out, eat it and go ask Benny. He never could say no to me, poor little darling. Where is he, by the way? I looked in at his office, but he wasn't there.'

'I don't know,' Paul said. 'Look, you can't kill me, not really. You'll never get away with it.'

Countess Judy giggled. 'What, you think someone'll notice that you aren't around any more? Or notice and care? Anyhow, I've wasted enough time lately talking to you. I'm going to count to five. One.'

Paul closed his eyes. 'All right,' he said. 'She's in the—'

He got no further than that; because the door flew open, and there in the doorway was Ricky Wurmtoter, still wearing his rather tattered dinner jacket and holding a large steel crossbow.

'Not now, Ricky, I'm busy,' Judy said, not bothering to turn round. 'Two.'

'Pack it in, Judy,' Ricky said. 'I know about Benny, and he won't be helping you any more. Put that knife away before you do someone an injury.'

Still she didn't turn. 'Oh, right,' she said. 'And I suppose if I don't, you're going to shoot me. Like I'd even notice.'

'Oh no,' Ricky said, moving a step to the right, 'I know better than that – arrows just go right through you, wouldn't even smear your lip gloss. No; like I said, Benny's no longer an option for you, so Paul here's the only one who can tell you where the girl is. Which is why,' he went on, clicking some sort of catch on the bow, 'if you don't put that knife away and go back to your office right now, I'm going to shoot him.'

'What?' Paul said, and his voice sounded just like Judy's, probably because she'd said the same thing at precisely the same moment. 'No, please,' he added. 'I won't tell, promise.'

'It's okay,' Ricky told him. 'Don't worry about it. I know all about that stuff,' he added, with an exaggerated nod towards the photo albums on the shelf. 'Mr Dao told me about the nosebleed. When you get there, just ask for him, he'll see you right. Then, as soon as it's safe, I'll come down and fetch you myself, I promise.' Ricky was lifting the bow, squinting painstakingly down the arrow shaft for a sure aim, ever the craftsman. 'I know what I'm doing,' he said. 'There's nothing to be concerned about, trust me.'

'But there is,' Paul shouted. 'If you shoot me I'll die. Really.'

'Oh, don't be such a baby,' said Ricky scornfully. 'And keep still, can't you? These things are enough trouble without you wiggling about like a belly dancer.'

'No!' Paul squealed. 'You don't understand, it's not—'

But before he could finish what he was saying, Judy whirled round and lunged at Ricky with the knife. Quick as a cat, he sidestepped, swung the bow back on aim, and pressed the trigger.

'—There any more,' Paul said, as the arrow pierced his heart and killed him.

Chapter Fifteen

'You again,' said a voice from the heart of the mist; and then Paul opened his eyes onto darkness and knew exactly where he was. This time, though—

'When they paged me,' the voice was saying, 'I thought old Jacky Dao was joshing with me, because, well, their sense of humour's pretty basic around here. I thought, they're pulling my leg, I checked out the Arrivals board only the other day, and young Paul's not due down here again for donkey's years. But here you are,' Uncle Ernie went on, his voice tightening like a vice. 'In person, profoundly dead and unfashionably bloody early. What the hell do you think you're playing at, you stupid arse? Building up your Frequent Dier points?'

Paul looked up at him. 'I got shot,' he said, 'with an arrow,' he added, so that the full extent of the injustice shouldn't be lost on his great-uncle. 'Ricky Wurmtoter shot me, and now I'm dead.'

'Balls,' Uncle Ernie snapped. 'I've known young Ricky since he was strangling snakes in his pram. Not the sharpest rapier in the case, but a bloody good shot – he'd never have snuffed you by accident.'

'Wasn't an accident,' Paul mumbled.

'He shot you on purpose? Why? What did you do to provoke him?'

'Nothing,' Paul wailed. 'He thought he was saving me,

or the world, or something. He knew about the nosebleed, but not that I'd already died once and used it up.'

'Then why in God's name didn't you tell him?' Uncle Ernie exploded. 'Of all the—'

'I tried to,' Paul whimpered, 'but he wouldn't listen. He just kept saying, *It's all right, trust me,* and then he killed me.'

'You clown,' Uncle Ernie sighed. 'You do realise, for want of a little care and attention on your part the whole bloody project's fucked up. My life's work. The future of the human race. Screwed. All because you couldn't be bothered to pick up a phone or write a memo.' Tongueless, he could only synthesise a clicking noise out of vestigial memory and illusion. 'And it was going so well, too. You'd got the girl – I should've guessed it was that Benny Shumway, but at least he did the right thing when the time came, so maybe it was all for the best. If only you'd pulled your finger out and woken her up the moment you got out of the castle, everything'd have been just fine. But no, you can't do a perfectly straightforward little job without buggering it up. And I bet you forgot to burn the chalks.'

Paul was too upset and angry to speak, but he nodded. That seemed to calm Uncle Ernie down a little bit, though not much. He muttered something, and immediately they were standing in front of the bead curtain that served as a door for the safe-deposit vault. 'Stay there, don't move, don't touch anything,' Ernie growled, as he vanished through the curtain (he walked into it, but the beads didn't move). 'That's something,' he went on, as he came back holding the insubstantial outline of the chalks box. 'They're a bit crumbly, you got them far too hot, but they ought to work.' He paused, and scowled. 'You don't know what these are for, do you?'

Paul shook his head.

'Bloody hell,' Ernie said in disgust. 'First you were a waste of space, now you're a waste of interdimensional void. These chalks,' he said wearily, 'are for writing messages across the gap. You write something here, they can read it back home, where you just came from. Not,' he added savagely, 'that they're going to be a hell of a lot of use to us, because who are we going to write to? Not Benny Shumway, because we can't trust him; not Ricky Wurmtoter, because if I know Judy, he'll be arriving down here himself any minute, and besides, I'm not a hundred per cent sure he can read. You got any suggestions? Because I haven't.'

Not that Paul cared particularly. For the first time, he really and truly felt like he was dead; the affairs of the living seemed remote, distasteful and faintly ridiculous, like American politics. Soon, he knew, he'd have to make a tremendous effort to remember anything about his past life – and when you're dead, even the slightest effort is rather hard to justify. So what if the Fey overwhelmed humanity? Wouldn't make any difference down here, and probably it served them right, at that. Not his problem any more. In fact, he wasn't entirely sure he knew what Uncle Ernie was talking about—

'Fine,' Ernie snarled. 'Go ahead, give up. Dissipate and fade away, see if I care. I mean, what's it to you that now I can never go back, I'm stuck here just like you are. But so what? It's just twenty years of my life I've flushed down the toilet for nothing.'

'Go back?' Paul repeated foggily. 'Oh, right, yes, I forgot. You've got some blood of your own stashed away in your vault thing, haven't you? So that's all right.'

'No, it bloody isn't!' Ernie snapped. 'Because once the

Fey have taken over, the last thing I'll want to do is show my face Topside ever again. You should know by now, there's stuff they can do to you that makes being stranded down here seem like a beach party with cake and coloured balloons. I might as well chuck it away, or trade it with Jacky Dao for a virtual Snickers bar. Like it matters, anyhow,' he added sharply, 'compared with the inevitable extinction of the human species. Though I don't know why I'm worrying about it. I mean, it's not me the entire population of Earth's going to be pissed off with when they start arriving here by the billion.' From some hidden place in the air he produced a handful of ash and shook it out like a tablecloth; it became a sheet of white paper, on which he began to write. 'About the only one I can think of is Cas Suslowicz, and he's not even human, he's a frigging giant. Still, he owes me enough favours, he might just be inclined to help out. All he's got to do is collect a sleeping female and stick her head under the cold tap or something.' He stopped writing and looked up. 'Where exactly did you stash her?' he went on. 'I was able to follow you as far as the closed-file store, but it's shielded in there, I couldn't see.'

'I think Benny called it the weapons locker.'

'*Shit!*' Uncle Ernie winced as though he'd burnt himself, then hurled the chalk into the darkness. 'And let me guess: Ricky's got one key, you had the other. Oh, that does it, I give up. *Nothing* can get in there without the key, it's practically the securest place in the universe.' He crouched down on the illusion of a floor and curled up in a small, desperate heap. 'All that effort, all that work, all that aggravation I had to go through in order to get your revolting parents to fall in love, and what do I end up with? You. And you're *dead,*' he added viciously. 'Which means I'm stuck with you, for bloody ever. Oh, if it wasn't so totally miserable, I'd burst out laughing.'

It was at this point that Paul decided he'd had enough. He'd got past horror and despair some time ago; anger not long after that; detachment and not caring any more had been harder to shake off, but even they had worked loose and fallen away in the face of the monumental wave of irritation that was gradually building up inside him. It was time, he resolved, that he took the situation in hand, before it got too messy to bear. How he was going to do it he had no idea, but he knew he'd find a way, because—

Because?

Because, he realised in a blinding, contraflow-on-the-road-to-Damascus revelation, *I'm not what he says I am. I'm not stupid, I'm not useless, this isn't my fault, it's not fair and I'm not standing for it. So there.*

'Uncle,' Paul said.

Uncle Ernie looked at him as though he'd just found him stuck to the sole of his shoe. 'What?'

'I think I'd like to get out of here now.'

Uncle Ernie stared at him, then shook his head; *on top of all that, not drivel as well*, his expression seemed to say.

'No, really,' Paul said. 'If I go back, maybe I'll be in time to stop Judy finding where Sophie's hidden. I've got the key, and I'll do whatever it takes to wake her up, and that'll be that taken care of. Won't it?'

Ernie just laughed. 'Whatever you say, son,' he muttered wearily, 'whatever you say. Do whatever you like. I think I'll just carry on being dead for a bit, if it's all the same to you.'

'If you like,' Paul replied. 'Only, how can I find Mr Dao?'

Ernie didn't answer; he didn't have to. Mr Dao was standing in front of the bead curtain, bowing very slightly. 'Good evening,' he said. 'This is an unexpected pleasure.'

A small, tight grin crossed Paul's face. 'Actually,' he said, 'it's a bit of a mix-up. Someone killed me, thinking that I still had that blood from my nosebleed. Really, I shouldn't be here.'

Mr Dao sighed softly. 'Alas,' he said.

'Quite,' Paul said. 'But I was wondering. Maybe there's something we can do to, well, put it right.'

'I would be fascinated to hear your suggestions,' Mr Dao said politely. 'Although I have to say, I wouldn't recommend optimism at this time.'

Paul ignored that. 'Uncle Ernie's blood,' he said. 'The little bottle he's got in his box in there. I was wondering—' He paused to take a deep breath, then realised he couldn't. 'I was wondering if I could use it instead. Only,' he went on, as Mr Dao pursed his lips as though saying that of course you'd need a whole new gearbox, 'since Uncle and I are related – well, obviously we are – doesn't that mean that the same blood runs in our veins, or practically the same blood, or quite similar blood, anyhow? Carpenter blood, anyway. I mean, it works with marrow transplants,' he added hopefully, as the initial brilliance of the idea began to ebb rapidly, like a winter sunset. 'Only, I really do have to get back and save my girlfriend, you see. If it was just me, I wouldn't—'

'Hey!' Uncle Ernie had, apparently, snapped out of his cocoon of despondency. 'That's *my* blood you're talking about, you thieving little toad. That's my life—'

'Yes, Uncle,' Paul said pleasantly, 'but like you said just now, it's no good to you any more, is it? If Judy takes over, which she will if I don't get back there very soon indeed, you wouldn't be able to use it anyway, it'd just go to waste, and you'd be no better off. You do see that, don't you?'

'Yes, but—' Uncle Ernie was scowling, as if he was trying to crack an invisible walnut using his eyebrows alone. 'But if you take that, I'll be *dead*. Like, really dead.'

Mr Dao cleared his throat softly. 'I should point out, Ernest, that—'

'Shut it, you. No, Paul, listen, I need that blood, I can't stay here. I never meant to stay, you know, it was just something I had to do, for the sake of the mission. That's why I made sure I had a way out; otherwise I'd never ever have—'

Paul was looking at Ernie, calmly, with deep and refreshing contempt. 'No,' he said, 'I don't suppose you would. But things have changed, and you've got a choice: stay dead, or stay dead but help save a few lives in the process. Up to you,' he added. 'No pressure.'

Ernie looked at Paul, then back at the cold, solemn eyes of Mr Dao. 'You're bastards, both of you,' he said. 'He goes and screws everything up, and I'm the one who's got to die because of it. That's just so—'

Mr Dao coughed gently. 'Life was unfair, Ernest,' he said. 'Did you really expect death would be any different?'

'Oh, piss off,' Ernie replied. 'You can't make me do it, either of you. I'm not a hero. It's wrong. It'd be murder.'

The slightest of sighs passed Mr Dao's translucent lips. 'No,' he said, 'merely creative accounting. I should point out, for instance, that your account with the bank has been open for nearly one hundred terrestrial years, and in that time you would not appear to have paid any bank charges.'

'What? But that's—'

'In addition to which,' Mr Dao went on, 'there are administration fees, storage charges, facilitation and expedition
costs, plus interest and penalties. The Bank is entirely within
its rights to press for settlement of these outstanding items
at any time.' He raised his closed left hand, then opened
the fingers a little. Between them, Paul could see a small
glass bottle with a splash of something red at the bottom.
'Or,' he said, 'the Bank might see its way to waiving all
outstanding liabilities, in recognition of your outstanding
courage and self-sacrifice for the sake of your entire species.
As acting assistant deputy general manager, I do have that
discretion. But not,' he added briskly, 'if you keep whining
and swearing at me. Do you understand?'

The ensuing silence seemed to last for ever. 'Right,' Ernie
snapped suddenly. 'Fine, have it your way. It's all a complete
waste of time, though. It won't do any good. I mean, look
at him, my fucking useless great-nephew there. Save the
world, him? He couldn't even save bottle tops.'

Mr Dao turned away from him, and slowly reached out
his left hand towards Paul. When he received it, the glass
bottle felt burning hot – because of the minuscule amount
of heat left in the blood, he supposed. 'Thanks,' he said to
Mr Dao. 'That was—'

'Business,' Mr Dao interrupted. 'No human race would
mean no more dead, and no more living to send money and
valuables. The effect on the Bank's trade would be catastrophic. Purely business, you see.'

Paul nodded. 'Of course,' he said. 'Wish me luck.'

Mr Dao's face folded into a look of profound sadness. 'I
am sorry to be the one to tell you this, Mr Carpenter, but
there is no such thing as luck. There are coincidences, and
humans naturally seek to find some vestige of a pattern in

the random vicissitudes of events, since they cannot face the grim reality that nothing is preordained, there is no plan, no grand design, no—'

'Mr Dao,' Paul interrupted. 'Wish me luck.'

'Good luck, kiddo,' said Mr Dao. Then he reached over and flicked the stopper out of the little glass bottle.

It was getting so that the walk back from the Bank to the door leading to the cashier's office was practically routine; an alarming thought in itself. *If I do this a few more times,* Paul told himself, *I'll probably count as a commuter.* Interesting thought; with property prices in London the way they were, and all this open, empty space—

Paul didn't have to look for the door; he knew where it was in the same way that you can find your alarm clock in the pitch dark. It was shut, of course, but he'd got that point covered. If his calculations were accurate (bottom of the class in maths, first-year primary school to seventh-year secondary school inclusive), it was nearly time for the cashier to do the banking. He knew JWW well enough by now to know that come what might – murder, treachery, civil war, the obliteration of the entire human species – somebody would be along to pay in the takings and draw tomorrow's cheques, even if Dennis Tanner or Theo van Spee had to do it. He sat down by the door, shooed away a couple of his great-great-grandparents, drawn by the smell of Carpenter blood, and waited.

Time passes differently in the grounds of the Bank; a century can slip by in a minute, a second can seem like a thousand years. Even making allowances for that, Paul reckoned that he'd been waiting there rather a long time. The nasty thought occurred to him that whoever was doing the banking today might have done it early, in which case the door wouldn't open again for close on twenty-four hours, by which time the tiny dribble of blood would be all used up.

The chalks, he thought; *the chalks that Uncle Ernie made me burn, which can write messages across the Line.* He could go back and borrow them, and write a message on his side of the door – *HELP!!* or something equally succinct. But what if whoever was doing the banking came through while he was off chalk-scrounging? *Fine*, Paul decided; *I'll sit here till five-thirty, and then I'll know they've done the banking already, and then I can go back for the chalk.* Except that, after five-thirty, there'd be nobody left in the building but goblins, and he was by no means convinced that they'd be either willing or able to open the door.

"Scuse me.'

He didn't look round. 'Go away,' he said.

"Scuse me.'

'Piss off. I can't spare you any blood, I'm sorry. Goodbye.'

"Scuse me.'

Not now, Paul thought, *please not now*. He looked round. A small, wizened, elderly goblin was standing over him, so old and little and funny-looking that it wasn't in the least alarming, though you wouldn't want it standing next to the sauce bottle while you were eating a cooked breakfast.

'Yes?' Paul sighed. 'Can I help you?'

'Just thought I'd say hello,' the goblin replied. 'Never seen you before, see. Before my time, you were.'

'Well—' Paul said, shrugging vaguely. Then the dropping penny landed. 'Hold on,' he said. 'If you've come to see me and we can talk to each other and all – Does that mean we're *related*?'

The goblin didn't appear to have heard him. 'I always try and make a point of coming and saying hello, every time one of our lot checks in. Just to be friendly, you know. First time in a strange place, it's nice to have someone to meet you, I always think.'

'Excuse me,' Paul said warily, 'but are you a goblin?'

'That's right. Well, nice meeting you. I'd better be getting along now. Hope you settle in all right. Oh, and give my best to our Dennis when you see him.'

Before Paul could stop him, the goblin had vanished. Paul thought about the implications of what it had said just long enough to realise that he really didn't want to know, then turned his attention back to the problem of not staying dead. He'd just made up his mind to risk going back for the chalks when a thin knife blade of fire burst through the door frame. It was so long since he'd seen anything like it that it took him a moment to realise that it was light, the glow of the hundred-watt bulb in the cashier's room showing through as the door opened.

Paul bounded to his feet like a dog expecting a walk. 'Hello—' he started to say, then froze.

'Hello yourself,' replied Mr Tanner. 'Don't tell me, the door slammed and you got stuck.' He grinned, and then the grin slid sideways into a scowl. 'What are you doing in here, anyway?' he said. 'You should be in your office, scanning those photos for bauxite deposits. I thought I told you, I need them by tomorrow.'

'Sorry,' Paul said. 'I, um, got sidetracked. Well, actually,' he amended, 'I died. Ricky – Mr Wurmtoter, I mean. He shot me.'

Mr Tanner shrugged. 'Always was a clumsy prat. Hold on, though. You can't have died, you're alive.'

Paul smiled feebly. 'It's rather a long story, actually. So would it be all right if I just slipped past and got out of here while you go to the Bank? Then you won't have to rush, I won't outstay my time here, and I can tell you all about it when you get back, if you like.'

'Forget it,' Mr Tanner said. 'As long as those pictures are back on my desk with the bauxite clearly marked by ten tomorrow morning, I don't really give a damn. Go on, get out.'

Gratefully, Paul scuttled past him and back into the world. Then something tweaked his mind, like biting on a bad tooth, and he spun round. 'Mr Tanner,' he called out, 'could you wait a moment, please?'

'What?'

'It's just—' This was going to sound so ridiculous, Paul thought; *I'll never be able to look him in the face again. But—* 'It's just,' he said, 'are we related?'

For the first time since he'd met him, Mr Tanner seemed to be at a loss for words. 'Well,' he said, 'sort of. Very distantly. On my mother's side,' he added, as though that somehow made it less awful. 'How the hell did you find out?'

Paul looked away. 'I met this dead goblin, back in there, and he said he was, well, family. And that started me thinking, about a photo I saw in an old album. The guy in the photo, my Uncle Derek, though really he was just a cousin. And he didn't look much like a goblin, but he did have red eyes; and at the time I thought, that's just the flash, turns your eyes red. But I just remembered: the picture was taken outdoors.'

Mr Tanner scowled. 'Still don't see why you thought we were related,' he said.

'The person in the picture reminded me of someone,' Paul mumbled. 'I just figured out who.'

'Oh, I see. My mother?'

'No. More sort of you, actually.'

'Yes, well.' Mr Tanner was fidgeting with the handle of his briefcase. 'Just don't make a big deal out of it, all right? In fact, why don't you keep it to yourself and not tell anybody, ever, under any circumstances. Agreed?'

Paul nodded. 'Sorry to bring it up,' he said. 'But one last thing: is that the real reason why your mother keeps saving me from certain death and stuff?'

The expression on Mr Tanner's face would've curdled all the milk in Jersey. 'No,' he snapped, and walked swiftly away.

Paul managed to get as far as the chair behind the desk; Benny's old chair, with shorter legs than customary. He flopped into it, jarring his back somewhat, and felt the last dregs of energy seeping out of him. It had been rather a stressful couple of days, what with dying twice and then finding out that he'd been carefully bred, like a racehorse or a prize pig, and that part of his genetic heritage was shared with Mr Tanner and all those horrible red-eyed, beaked, clawed, inhuman *things* that took over the office as soon as the doors were locked. The last thought was, he realised, rather unworthy of him; one of the few people he reckoned he could trust further than a snail can move in a third of a second was Mr Tanner's mum, who was all goblin, goblin plus with added goblin. She was also, of course, a distant cousin. *Hellfire.* Now he had to go and wake up the girl he loved, and in doing so put a fellow sentient life form to death, coldly and methodically, because he had no choice unless he wanted the twilight of his species on his conscience for the rest of his short life. It was, Paul couldn't help thinking, all a bit much, particularly on an empty stomach. He tried to remember when he'd last eaten, or shaved, or had a bath, or changed his underwear. *Yuck*, he thought.

Still. No good sitting around when there was work to be done. (Which reminded him: after he'd rescued Sophie, killed Countess Judy and ensured that there would be a tomorrow for *Homo sapiens*, he'd have to find time to do those perishing bauxite pictures, or else face Mr Tanner's wrath first thing in the morning. A hero's work was never done, Paul reflected, and it was only the easy bits that got into the epic poems.)

Before Paul could reach the door handle, the door burst open and Ricky Wurmtoter came in. At least he had taken the time to change out of his shredded tux. (And do his hair, and shave, and trim his fingernails, and polish his shoes, and splash on about a quart of repulsive-smelling aftershave, and floss his teeth, and probably sign a couple of dozen eight-by-twelve photographs for his fan club's next prize draw.) He didn't have the crossbow any more, either.

'Hello,' Paul said. 'I was hoping to run into you.' Then, standing on tiptoe so that he could reach, he punched Ricky in the mouth as hard as he could.

Paul hadn't expected Ricky to fall over; in fact, he'd assumed that the punch would skid off, or he'd break his knuckles, or Ricky wouldn't even notice. But not a bit of it. Ricky staggered back a couple of paces, put his foot in the waste bin, lost his balance and went down in a manner that could only be described as arse over tip. It was, shameful to say, an incredibly satisfying feeling.

'Bloody hell,' Ricky mumbled, sitting up and rubbing his jaw. 'What's all that in aid of?'

Paul looked down at him. 'Oh, just getting in touch with my inner goblin,' he said. Then he added, 'YOU BASTARD, YOU BLOODY SHOT ME,' in a voice that he didn't recognise but which had to be his.

'But I kept telling you, it'd be all right. And obviously it is, or you wouldn't be stood there— No, please, put the chair down, don't hit me!'

Paul took a moment to relish the sight: Ricky Wurmtoter, master dragonslayer, champion vampire hunter, lieutenant colonel (retired) of the Riders of Rohan, huddled in a sprawl on the floor with both arms wrapped round his head. *I did that*, Paul thought, coddling his barked knuckles tenderly. *Nice punch, though I do say so myself.* 'It's all right,' he said pleasantly, 'I feel better now. I was just a bit uptight for a moment, that's all.'

Ricky looked at him through a grille of fingers. 'You sure?'

'I'm fine, really.'

'I think you've loosened a tooth.'

'Really?' And all these years, Paul had assumed that he couldn't punch a hole in a wet paper bag. 'I mean, sorry. I expect it'll be all right. You can use magic on it or something.'

Ricky muttered vaguely about magic not working on teeth, but he got up and looked at Paul warily. 'You sure you're over it, whatever it was?'

'Absolutely. I was just a bit narked about getting killed. Well, killed twice, actually; only the first time was suicide, I suppose, so—'

'You killed *yourself?*' Ricky had got over his fear, apparently. 'What in God's name made you do that?'

'Well, I thought a chat with my Uncle Ernie might be

in order, but he's dead. And I knew about the nosebleed blood, so—'

Ricky said something in German; it sounded like admiration for Paul's reckless courage, tempered by profound reservations about his mental health. 'And did it work?'

'No, not really. Well, I did get some good advice while I was down there, but the plain fact is that Uncle Ernie's a bit of a broken reed. Still, there we are. And I went to Countess Judy's place and rescued Sophie, so that's all right.'

'You rescued Sophie,' Ricky repeated.

Paul nodded. 'And then Benny Shumway rescued me. I know he was the traitor and all, but he seems to have got over that, now he's engaged to your sister—'

'He's *what*—?'

Oops. 'Forget I said that,' Paul said quickly. 'In fact, I may have misunderstood entirely, I wasn't really paying attention—'

'That evil little shit is messing around with—'

Paul frowned. 'Oh, don't be such a misery,' he said. (The words were out of his mouth before he realised that he was talking to a partner in the firm, management, the boss; but so what? Hardly likely to matter, since he'd just flattened the guy with a right cross.) 'Benny's all right. Like I said, he res—'

'That dirty, lecherous, sneaking, short bastard. I'll skin him alive and use his hide as a shammy leather. Him and *Monika*—'

'Look.' Paul couldn't help it. The reproving look and wagging finger were nothing to do with him, and he had no control over them. 'Benny's a good bloke. He risked his neck over and over again to keep Countess Judy from having me killed. And at least he cares enough about her to want to turn her back.'

'He's a *dwarf*, for crying out loud. Everybody knows they're only interested in one thing.'

Paul had heard that, yes, but he was under the impression that it was gold. *Oh well.* 'Benny's not like that,' he protested. 'He's sensitive, he's got feelings.'

'I hope he's got plenty of them in his bum, because I'm going to kick him from here to Burkina Faso.'

'He's got feelings,' Paul repeated sternly. 'And it's obvious that he doesn't just go by appearances. Do you think he'd be in love with your sister if he did? Her being a car, I mean? Obviously not. He knows that beauty isn't just paintwork-deep.'

'The hell with Benny Shumway,' Ricky snapped. 'I really don't want to think about that right now. Look, do you think we could get back to the job in hand, and I'll deal with him later.'

Paul shrugged. 'If you're horrible to him, I'll be very upset,' he said; and amazingly, Ricky stopped pulling faces and seemed to calm down a little. 'Fine,' he said. 'Now then, where've you hidden the girl?'

Paul was about to tell him, but hesitated. 'How can I be sure that you're really who you seem to be?' he said. 'For all I know, you could be a shapeshifter or something.'

'Don't be stupid,' Ricky said. 'I'm me – look. Now, where's Sophie?'

But Paul shook his head. 'I think it'd be a good idea if we went down to the main boardroom, where you've got that really clever trick table – you know, where you can see a person's true shape reflected in the polish. What do you reckon?'

'Waste of time,' Ricky said; and there was something in his tone of voice that made Paul wonder whether his right cross and new forceful personality were quite as impressive as he'd thought. And how come Ricky'd managed to get changed and tidied up so quickly? 'We need to get on,' Ricky continued, 'before Judy catches up with us.'

Paul nodded. 'True,' he said. 'Talking of which, how did you get away from her just now? When you shot me and I died, I mean.'

'Oh, Judy doesn't scare me,' Ricky said, with a slightly shrill laugh. 'I just turned and walked away. But—'

Paul let his right hand slip into his jacket pocket. He didn't have any sort of plan of action. If the man he was talking to really wasn't Ricky Wurmtoter, he was fairly sure that he was in deep trouble; and of course, he didn't have a weapon or anything useful like that, only a magic screwdriver and a magic time-freezing watch. But maybe the enemy, if that's who it was, didn't know that.

'What are you doing?' Ricky said.

'Never you mind,' Paul replied, grasping the screwdriver handle. 'But I'm giving you fair warning. Either turn back into who you really are and then get lost, or I'll have to do something about it.'

'You've got it all wrong. I'm Ricky Wurmtoter. Really.'

'Great. In that case, let's head on down to the boardroom. You can look at your reflection in the table top. You'll enjoy that.'

'You're starting to get on my nerves, Paul,' Ricky said, but Paul took no notice. 'It's you, isn't it?' he said, taking a step forward. 'Must be, because you know about what was said back there when I got shot, and you and Ricky were the only people in the room with me.'

For a moment, Ricky seemed to waver and flicker, like a faulty video; then he turned into Countess Judy. She didn't look the same as she had back in Paul's office, though: shorter, thinner, and was that a big red bruise on the side of her face?

'I underestimated you,' she said. 'Instead of being just a minor nuisance, you're a major nuisance. Congratulations on your promotion.'

Paul didn't move. 'First of all, I'd like to thank my agent,' he said. 'You don't frighten me any more, you know.'

'I don't?' Countess Judy looked puzzled. 'You sure? Because if I was in your shoes I'd be very scared.'

'And if I was in your shoes I'd be limping. You couldn't hurt me then, and you can't hurt me now.'

'Ah,' Judy said, and suddenly her face melted into a huge grin. 'But earlier, you had a cold. Now, it looks like you're cured. In which case,' she added, 'I'm gonna break your fucking neck.'

With that, she lunged forward, grabbing at him with her outstretched left hand. Paul weaved sideways; she didn't get hold of him but her nails ploughed his cheek, almost but not quite hard enough to draw blood. 'Tell me where that stupid girl is,' she snarled, 'and I'll let you go. Last offer, and then you're dead.'

'How do you mean, earlier I had a cold?'

'You know perfectly well—' She grabbed at him again, but he found that keeping out of her way wasn't so hard after all; he just had to watch her and move his feet. 'But he's gone, hasn't he? You're on your own now.'

'You mean Benny Shumway?'

'Don't play dumb with me,' she growled, just a trifle out of breath. 'I know everything that goes on around here, remember?'

'Ricky Wurmtoter, then.'

'Keep still.' Somehow, Paul didn't feel inclined to comply. Judy was trying to force him into a corner, but a neat little sideways shuffle solved that. 'If you don't tell me, guess I'll just have to tear the joint apart brick by brick. It'd take me about ten minutes.'

'Fine by me,' Paul replied, taking two steps back and one step left. 'Mr Tanner and Professor van Spee and Mr Suslowicz might get a bit uptight, mind.'

'Screw them.' Now she was definitely out of breath, and her face looked strange: out of focus, almost, as though she was being filmed through a smeared lens. 'Why do you care, anyhow? She dumped you, remember? Threw you out.'

'No, she didn't,' Paul said calmly. 'Would you like to stop and have a rest for a bit? You don't want to go over-doing it at your age.'

Judy shrieked and lunged at him; and when he side-stepped, her momentum carried her forward straight into the corner of the desk. She yowled as the sharp edge stabbed into her knee.

'You're getting weak,' Paul observed. 'Maybe she's starting to come round; you know, just dozing rather than the full REM stuff. I'm guessing that drip thing that was stuck in her arm was some kind of sedative, which is beginning to wear off. Am I warm?'

Suddenly, Judy stopped crouching and staggered back, until she was leaning against the filing cabinet. 'Is this what you want?' she said. 'Does it make you feel good, watching me die like this? Yes, you're absolutely right. That skinny little bitch is starting to wake up, and I haven't got enough strength to open a Coke can. Unless I can get to her in the next five minutes and put her deep under, I'm dead.' She was perfectly still now, like a statue or a painting; her eyes were huge and round, her hair floated like mist and her skin was soft and glowing. 'Do you think I'm so evil that I deserve to die, Paul Carpenter? Do I look like someone who's so dangerous that they've got to be put down like a savage animal? Look at me.'

'I'm looking,' Paul said. 'And, since you ask, yes.'

Judy's lips parted, making Paul catch his breath. 'I'm begging you,' she said. 'Please don't kill me. You can have anything you want, just ask and it's yours. When we make a promise, we have to keep it, if we break our word we die. Just say what you want, and I promise you'll have it. Three wishes? Three wishes granted to you by the Queen of the Fey herself. Isn't that the best offer you'll ever get?'

Suddenly and unbidden, Paul's mind filled with a bewildering profusion of images, a vast, bustling, jostling multimedia 4-D Argos catalogue of the synthesis of human desires and aspirations. It occurred to him that with three wishes from the greatest power on Earth, a good man could change the world, could wipe out hunger, war and disease, could do all the things that humans so desperately need and can't seem to do for themselves. Surely, beyond any question, that was what Sophie would want him to do. Indeed, if he turned away this miraculous opportunity, how could she possibly love him or bear to be anywhere near him? And if he really loved her, he'd make the sacrifice, because you can't truly love someone and not love the whole world. Paul understood this clearly, it made the best possible sense, it was amazing he'd been stupid enough not to realise it from the very start—

'Anything I want?'

She nodded eagerly. 'Anything.'

'And you'd promise? On your word?'

'On my life.'

'The three things I want most in the whole world?'

'Yes.'

'Right,' Paul said. 'One, I want Sophie to wake up. Two, I want you to piss off to your side of the line and never ever come back. Three I'm not sure about; I'm torn between world peace and a roast beef sandwich with extra horseradish.'

Countess Judy screamed, and before Paul could move her hands were around his neck, her nails digging into his skin just above the collar of his shirt. 'Tell me,' she rasped in his ear, 'where you've got her hidden, or I'm going to kill you. Do you understand?'

She was crushing his throat — he couldn't breathe. Any moment now, she'd damage him beyond repair, and he really didn't want to see the expression on Mr Dao's face, not a third time. Maybe if he hadn't been there he could've been brave and noble, hoping for Valhalla or the simple switching-off of all the lights. But he'd been there and seen what it was like, and he had no wish to go back.

'In the closed-file store,' he whispered. 'The weapons locker. I don't have the key.'

Judy let go, and as Paul collapsed to the ground, he knew that he'd made the right choice, because still being alive was too wonderful, and nothing is worth dying for. 'Who's got it, then?' Judy said, gasping for air like a fish out of water. 'Benny? Wurmtoter?'

'They've each got keys,' Paul muttered. 'But you haven't got time to find them. It takes twenty minutes minimum to find somebody in this place. And just suppose you did get to them in time, you'd have all this performance to go through, threats and pleading and casting spells and shit.

You've got, what, two minutes left? Less, probably, with all the energy you just used up.'

She tried to kick his head, but her knees gave way and she toppled over, crashing into the edge of the desk. The expression on her face was sheer disbelief; she'd never imagined, in her wildest dreams, that it'd end like this. Paul watched her form the intention to stand up, then realise that she didn't have the strength.

'It's too late, isn't it?' he said quietly. 'We'd never get there in time to put her back to sleep, not even if I carried you and ran. For what it's worth, I'm sorry. If there was another way, like Benny thought, and I'd known about it, I would have tried. But this was all I could think of, and I was taking a huge risk as it was.'

'Fuck you,' Judy whispered, and her eyes closed. She was falling asleep. She realised what was happening to her with a spasm of pure terror, because she knew better than anybody what can happen to people who die in their sleep, and just how much her people despised waste. But she couldn't help it; her eyes were shut, her breathing was gradually getting slow and even, her muscles were relaxing. *Sweet dreams,* Paul thought – but who was he kidding?

Then he sneezed.

Hell of a time to sneeze, when your mortal enemy is dying in agony right in front of you; disrespectful and inappropriate, and you can't help feeling very foolish. An apology was on its way past Paul's teeth when he realised that he hadn't just sneezed, he'd sneezed *something*.

Yuck.

A big something; big, and growing bigger every second, sprouting arms and legs and a head, and a distinctly old-fashioned slate-grey pinstripe suit, and Oxford brogues, and a tie and little round glasses, and a small Arthur Lowe moustache and a shiny bald head, and *I know who that is, it's old Mr Wells, the senior partner, and what in God's name is going on?*

Even Judy seemed to have noticed; her eyelids fluttered open weakly like poisoned butterflies, and she tried to say something. Mr Wells, meanwhile, was picking himself up off the ground, dabbing at his face with a large red spotted handkerchief (quite possibly the only one still extant outside a textiles museum), smoothing down the sparse fringe of hair that lingered on the slopes of his head like a village under the crater of an active volcano.

'*Gesundheit,*' Mr Wells muttered. Then he turned to Judy, nodded once and clicked his fingers.

He looked like the man behind the counter in the Post Office whose queue you really don't want to be in, because it's very long and glaciers whizz past it like speedboats; but when he clicked his fingers, the room filled with light, and Judy sat bolt upright, her eyes wide open. 'Stay,' Mr Wells commanded, as he reached into Paul's jacket pocket and took out Uncle Ernie's broken watch, which he set and then buckled round Judy's motionless wrist. Then from his own inside pocket he took out a very familiar object, a rolled-up sheet of plastic the size of a large place mat, that grew as he spread it against the wall until it had changed into a door. Not the scruffy cavity-hardboard door that Paul had to make do with when he used the thing, but a fine Georgian-style panelled door, with an ornate brass handle and finely carved mouldings. It swung open of its own accord as Mr Wells lifted his hand and Judy drifted slowly towards him, her feet not moving, an inch off the carpet. Her face was still and strangely grave, no longer beautiful or scary or anything much, and with a certain degree of shock Paul realised that it was her own face, what she actually looked like. The door opened wide and she carried on through it; and if she said anything before it closed behind her, then turned back into a sheet of plastic and fell off the wall onto the floor, Paul didn't hear.

'Mr Carpenter,' said old Mr Wells. 'This, I believe, belongs to you.'

He slid the Portable Door into the cardboard tube it lived in and held it out. 'Come along,' he said briskly, 'it won't bite. Or don't you want it any more?'

That, of course, was a very good question. 'I – I don't know,' Paul said. 'I mean, it's not really mine, I just found it in a drawer. Actually, I thought it belonged to someone else – you know, in the office.'

Mr Wells raised an eyebrow. 'But you kept it anyway,' he said. Paul hung his head. 'Fortuitously,' Mr Wells went on, 'it does in fact belong to you. It was your great-uncle's; he lent it to me many years ago, and I'm ashamed to say that I lost it.'

'Easily done,' Paul mumbled. 'I'm always losing things.'

'In a game of canasta,' Mr Wells added, 'with Mr Tanner's mother and some of her friends. I suspect the game wasn't entirely honest. At any rate, shortly afterwards I was forcibly transformed into a stapler, as you will recall, and could take no steps to reclaim it or return it to your uncle. That it somehow found its way into your keeping suggests that you were intended to have it, and I see no reason to interfere. Keep it, by all means; and next time, perhaps you should be careful to whom you lend it.' He shook his head. 'Dietrich Wurmtoter is a very capable young man, quite brilliant in his own way, but in other respects somewhat *in*capable. Had

I been at liberty at the time, I would have advised you not to let him have it. It's caused a great deal of trouble since it fell into the hands of the Fey.' A great deal of trouble; you could put it like that, Paul supposed. He nodded; then he took a deep breath. 'Mr Wells,' he said, as politely as he could, 'what were you doing up my nose?'

Mr Wells's face twitched; it was almost, but not quite, a smile. 'For the last few weeks,' he said, 'ever since this most regrettable crisis started, I have been – to use the modern expression – undercover. Given the delicacy of my position with regard to the complex web of conflicting loyalties in which I found myself, I thought it would be advisable if I put myself entirely out of reach of all the parties involved, while remaining close to the centre of events. Accordingly,' he said, 'I disguised myself as a cold.'

There's ambient weird – everyday weird, stuff you can get used to, like tables that reflect shapeshifters as they really are, rooms that move through ninety degrees each month, toilets that flush directly into the interdimensional void, cheques that have *Bank of the Dead* on them in very small writing just above the sort code, cars that turn out to be the boss's sister and goblins that turn out to be the boss's mother, dragons in cash machines and doors you can fold up and store in a toilet-roll tube; and then there's can't-have-heard-that-right weird, when two pages of *The Book of Life* have got stuck together, and the sugar you just spooned into your tea proves to be salt. 'Sorry?' Paul said. 'As a what?'

Mr Wells frowned a little. 'A cold,' he repeated. 'Rather a good idea, though I say so myself. You've probably noticed that a cold goes round an office; everybody catches it and passes it on to everybody else. A unique opportunity, in fact, to keep the protagonists in the affair under the keenest scrutiny; unseen, unnoticed, one's presence not even suspected because the disguise is so commonplace. Somewhat taxing, I will admit; there are over fifteen billion germs in the average head cold, Mr Carpenter, and being all of them at once requires effort and concentration. But worthwhile, I think, in the event.'

Paul nodded. No point in saying anything, really.

'Well.' Mr Wells was looking at his watch. 'By my calculations, Miss Pettingell should be due to wake up in approximately three minutes and seventeen seconds. We should just make it.'

Paul followed him out of the office, thinking, *Three minutes to the closed-file store, that's cutting it fine even if we run.* He needn't have worried. The corridors of 70 St Mary Axe clearly knew what was expected of them when the senior partner was in a hurry. They shortened. The number of stairs in each staircase diminished. Paul told himself to deal with it and be grateful, and threw the matter out of his mind.

'Excuse me,' he asked nevertheless, as they turned a corner where usually there was a fire door, 'but what's happened to the Countess di Castel'Bianco? Is she—?'

Mr Wells didn't pause or turn, but the back of his head waggled from side to side. 'Not at all. By intervening when I did – timing was critical, of course – I was able to save the fundamental essence of who she was: her memories, experience, knowledge, personality. It has been removed for ever from this world and can do no further harm, but it will survive. She has gone away to the enchanted Isle of Avalon, where her kind can enjoy a hybrid existence, real but outside our reality. There she will not fade or wither, she will walk for ever beside the silver waters, through the silvery mists;

and she will also be available to do a certain amount of work for us on a consultancy basis, which will be extremely helpful vis-à-vis looking after our long-established clients in the political and entertainment sectors. It's also worth noting that since she will not be technically dead, the remaining partners won't be obliged to pay out the value of her share of the business to her estate.'

'I see,' Paul said. 'So that's all right, then.'

'Indeed,' replied Mr Wells, who obviously wasn't noticing sarcasm today. 'A most satisfactory outcome for all involved, considering the desperate nature of the situation. Since the Countess remains technically alive, she cannot be succeeded as Monarch of the Fey, nor can she give orders, formulate policy or direct operations. Had she died, we would have faced a renewed threat in a matter of days. Now, I'm delighted to say, the threat from the dream-folk has been effectively countered. Thanks in no small measure,' he added, 'to you. And, of course, to your great-uncle's watch. I assume that that was what he had in mind when he arranged for it to come into your possession.'

Paul bit his lip. 'I guess so,' he said.

'In any case,' Mr Wells said, as the door of the closed-file store came in view, 'it was in the right place at the right time, whether by accident or design, and that's what matters. The firm will, of course, compensate you financially for the loss of your property.'

'Thanks, but no, thanks,' Paul said. 'It wouldn't feel right, somehow. Besides—'

'As you wish. Now, if you would be kind enough to give me the key.'

'Key?'

Mr Wells pushed open the door. Probably just Paul's

imagination, but he could have sworn that the folders and dog-eared manila envelopes all stood to attention on their shelves as he entered the room. 'The key to the weapons locker. Come along now, we don't have much time.'

'Oh, sorry.' Paul reached into his pocket. The key wasn't there. Instead, there was a hole.

'Come along,' Mr Wells snapped. 'The key.'

'Um,' Paul mumbled. 'I think I've lost it. There's a hole in my pocket, you see, and it must've dropped out some-where—'

'Oh.' Mr Wells's forehead crinkled in annoyance. 'No time to look for it, I fear. Never mind. If you'd be good enough to let me have your great-uncle's screwdriver.'

Paul handed it to him without a word; glad to be rid of it. A touch from its flat tip, and the screws fell out of the locker door's hinges. A moment later, the door itself clattered on the ground.

Sophie didn't appear to have moved at all; her head still rested on Benny's rolled-up gown and her eyes were still beneath their lids. She was also still deathly pale, and even her lips were white.

'She doesn't look right to me,' Paul said. 'Not like she's just about to wake up. What if something's gone wrong and she's – well, stuck like it?'

Mr Wells shook his head. 'She has just passed out of the shadow,' he replied. 'She has been far away. It will take her a little while to come back.'

'I still think she looks pretty bad.'

'Well, she was no oil painting to begin with.'

Then Sophie stirred; her eyelids twitched, and so did her mouth. Her head lolled a little way onto her shoulder, and she grunted. It was one of the loveliest sounds that Paul had ever heard, even if it did remind him a little of a warthog eating a turnip, because it was the noise she usually made, just before she woke up. 'Sophie?' he said. 'Sophie, can you hear me?'

She snorted softly, but her eyes and mouth were still and set once more; she was slipping back into the shadows, and all Paul could do was watch. Or was it? No, certainly not, he was being even thicker than usual. Of course; he'd known exactly what to do in this situation ever since his mum had read to him from *My First Fairy Tale Book* in his pram. Rather tentatively, and wishing Mr Wells wasn't standing next to him with his left eyebrow raised, he knelt down beside Sophie and, gently, tenderly, kissed her on the lips.

'Gerroff,' she mumbled, and hit him in the mouth.

At least it proved beyond any faint lingering vestige of a doubt that she was the real Sophie, not some forgery concocted by the Fey out of mist and shadow. The real Sophie, as Paul now remembered as he massaged his cut lip, didn't like being disturbed when she was just waking up. She tended to react with violent spasmodic (but usually very well aimed) movement. Mostly she tended to catch him in the eye rather than the mouth, but there weren't any hard and fast rules.

'Miss Pettingell.' Mr Wells's voice was deep and solemn, like Gandalf reading the shipping forecast. 'You must wake up now. The dream has ended. You will not remember any of it. It has been wiped from your mind. Open your eyes now, if you please.'

Sophie's eyes flicked open. She blinked a couple of times, then wriggled up onto her left elbow. 'Paul,' she said accusingly, 'what the fuck am I doing lying here surrounded by stupid swords and stuff?'

'It's—' He'd wanted to tell her it was a long story, but he'd run out of words. 'Tell you later,' he said. ''S all right, though. Tell you later,' he repeated.

'But isn't this the—?' She frowned. 'And what's *he* doing here? Look, just what exactly is going on here, because—'

'Miss Pettingell,' Mr Wells said. 'You are at the office, in the closed-file store. Several weeks have passed since you fell asleep, during which time you were a prisoner of the Fey. You are safe now, and everything is under control.' He peeked at his watch again. 'I suggest that you and Mr Carpenter go home now; and, under the circumstances –' a ghost of a smile flitted across his face '– I think you might as well have tomorrow morning off work. I shall, however, be grateful if you would both report to me in my office at two o'clock sharp.'

Paul breathed out, something he hadn't done for some little time. 'Right,' he said. 'Thanks, we'll be there. Um, Mr Wells, what about Mr Wurmtoter, and Mr Shumway? And we'll need a new receptionist, won't we, because that wasn't the real—'

'I shall deal with all of that,' Mr Wells said firmly. 'You two run along; it's well after half-past five, and the goblins will be about, so please be careful on your way out.'

Paul reached out his hand to help Sophie to her feet; she ignored him (she didn't hold with patronising gender-stereotypical conventions) and wobbled for a moment before her legs remembered how to cope with her weight. 'Is that right, Paul, what he just said?' she asked. 'I've been held hostage for *weeks*, and all we get is one lousy morning off? Didn't I always say, this firm is such a—'

Paul smiled feebly at Mr Wells, put his hand behind Sophie's shoulder and shoved her out through the door.

Chapter Sixteen

Paul and Sophie arrived together at the office next day, and immediately separated. Sophie didn't say where she was going; Paul headed for his office, where he sat down and started to work his way through the bauxite pictures, which were now severely overdue. As he ran his fingertip over the smooth surface of the photographs, he did his very best to keep his mind from wandering; but it was as hard to control as a large, bouncy dog that's been kept inside for a whole rainy week.

All the way home Sophie hadn't said a word. Hers was the sort of silence that well-meaning chatter sinks into and disappears without even a ripple, so he didn't try. Paul sat next to her on the bus, staring at the back of the seat in front of him, and tried to figure out a few things, trivial as well as crucial. He didn't get very far. He couldn't concentrate.

When they got home, he'd offered her a cup of coffee. She said, 'All right,' in a neutral sort of voice, so he'd fled into the kitchen and made the best possible cup of coffee that he could engineer, using all his skill, experience and flair. He took it through and put it on the table beside the chair she was sitting in. Sophie made no move to drink it.

That was Paul all gambited out, so he sat on the sofa with his hands folded in his lap. By rights he should be shattered – violence, precious little sleep, fear, outwitting the Queen of the Fey, near as made no odds killing her, dying, let's not forget that, and when was the last time he'd had anything to eat? He just felt numb, the way your mouth feels when you've had a tooth pulled but the effects of the jab haven't worn off yet – you know the pain is there, smothered under the anaesthetic, but it'll be along soon enough, and when it gets loose it'll be no fun at all. He could sleep now, actually close his eyes and stop fighting off the pack of ravening sheep that had been poised at the foot of the wall for as long as he could remember; but he didn't feel sleepy. Or anything much.

'Paul,' she said at last.

'Hello?'

Sophie wasn't looking at him. 'When old Mr Wells told me I wouldn't remember anything about the dreams, he was wrong.'

'Oh,' Paul said.

'I can remember it all,' she said, 'right from the start.'

'That's—' *Yes, Paul, what was that? Sum up in one appropriate word everything Sophie's gone through. Alternatively, shut up.*

'Everything,' she said. 'Being her – that *thing* – all that time. Being someone else, someone who wanted to kill you, and everybody, all the people in the world.'

Just a minuscule flicker of annoyance sparked across the back of Paul's mind; *right*, it said, *I think I've got that, but what the hell am I supposed to do about it?* 'That must've been – pretty bad,' Paul mumbled.

'Pretty bad,' Sophie repeated. 'Yes, you could say that. The whole fucking deal was pretty bad, actually. Like feeling great chunks of me, who I am, just leaking out and not being able to do anything about it. You see, she was sort of growing inside me all the time, getting stronger, I don't know; but every time she grew, a part of me got displaced; and it's not coming back, Paul. It's gone for ever. Memories, feelings, things I used to like or hate. Like, when I was a kid we used to go to the seaside, and I know that one of my happiest memories was scrabbling about in rock pools for those little snail things with the shiny shells. But I can't *remember* that, Paul; there's just a hole, like an empty folder with nothing inside it.'

'I see,' Paul said.

'While she was still there I didn't really notice,' Sophie went on, 'because all the gaps and holes were filled with her stuff, her memories and emotions and all the things she was. Now she's gone, there's just the empty folders. I don't know, maybe they'll fill up again as time goes by, but the stuff that I lost won't ever come back. It's all gone.'

Paul knew what she was going to say next. 'Drink your coffee,' he told her. 'It's going cold.'

'One of the things I lost,' Sophie went on, cold and precise, as though giving evidence, 'was us. I think she made a point of getting rid of it quite early on, because it was something I could hold on to, fight her with, even. But she just sort of flushed it out, and I could feel it drifting away, like a dream when you wake up. I know, in an abstract sort of a way, that I'd felt a certain way about you, before she came; but it's just a historical fact, like I know who Edward the Third was. I can't find those feelings again. They won't be coming back.'

'Right,' Paul said. 'I understand. That's it, then.'

Sophie nodded. 'Yes.'

'You don't think – if we tried really hard . . .'

'No.' She turned her head away so that he couldn't see her face. 'I'm sorry,' she said.

'Not your fault,' Paul said.

'I mean, you did save me,' Sophie said quietly. 'Sort of. You got me out of that place she took me to; and I know it was Mr Shumway who did all the fighting and had the plan and everything, but at least you tried, as best you could. So I probably owe you my life.'

'Don't worry about it,' Paul said. 'Any time.'

Sophie shook her head. 'No,' she said, 'it's important, because you came to rescue me because you thought we were still, well, *us*. It'd be wrong just to say, "Very sorry but it was all false pretences." I need to make it right, or else she's won.'

Paul closed his eyes. 'But there's nothing you can do, is there?'

'I suppose not,' Sophie said. 'It's over, I can't pretend or anything. I'm sorry, Paul. I did love you, and I thought, maybe now she's gone, maybe I'll fall in love with you all over again, from scratch. But now I look at you and I just feel guilty.'

Sophie had insisted that Paul had the bed; she'd had plenty of sleep lately, she reminded him, and now she felt like staying awake for a while, which she could do perfectly well on the sofa. So he lay on top of the undisturbed sheets, his hands behind his head, staring at the lighter darkness where the white-painted ceiling was, and begged sleep to come along and rescue him from the nightmare that he'd fallen into. At seven o'clock, he gave up and went into the kitchen. All the milk in the fridge had turned to runny cheese, and the one tomato that represented his entire stock of food had white hairs growing on it.

She came into the kitchen an hour later and made herself a drink. 'This isn't the usual coffee,' she said.

'That's right,' he said. 'Ricky Wurmtoter drank all the Nescafé and got me that horrible muck instead. He said it's better for keeping you awake.'

'Is it?'

'Yes,' Paul replied. 'But it tastes disgusting.'

Sophie nodded, and tipped it down the sink. 'What are you going to do this morning?' she said. 'We've got a half-day holiday, if you remember.'

Paul shrugged. 'I think I'll go in anyway,' he said. 'I was supposed to scry a whole lot of photos for Mr Tanner – you know, looking for minerals – and I never got round to it.'

Sophie nodded again. 'I'd better go in too,' she said. 'I don't feel like hanging around here on my own. And there's some stuff I need to find out about before we see Mr Wells.'

So here Paul was, at his desk, fingering two-dimensional slabs some bit of Africa. The bauxite seemed particularly elusive today – either that or he'd lost the knack of finding it, which would probably grieve Mr Tanner more than himself. Maybe you couldn't find bauxite if your heart was broken. Probably something like that.

Julie came in around mid-morning. 'You're not supposed to be here,' she said.

'Very true,' Paul replied. 'I keep thinking that, but here I am.'

She wasn't having any of that. 'Mr Wells gave you the morning off. Why aren't you at home, enjoying yourself?'

'Well, Mr Tanner told me that I had to have all these done this morning. So I thought I'd better come in and enjoy myself here. I've done this batch, but I've still got these to do. Tell him that I'm sorry, and I'll bring them up to him as soon as I've finished.'

'Can if you like, but he's not in today. Had to go to a

meeting in Bloemfontein, so he won't be back till tomorrow. So there's no rush,' Julie added. 'You could've stayed home this morning after all.'

Paul's smile was like the mathematical definition of a straight line, the shortest distance in two dimensions between the corners of his mouth. 'Life's little ironies, huh. Never mind.'

Julie shrugged. 'Please yourself,' she said. 'I only came down to tell you that it's Mr Suslowicz's birthday tomorrow, so that'll be a fiver.'

'Huh?'

'For the cake. We always get him a cake on his birthday.'

'A fiver each? That's a bloody big cake.'

'He's a giant. I can come back after lunch.'

Paul sighed and disbursed five pounds. He'd been intending to buy his dinner with it, but what the hell, he wasn't hungry. 'Do we each get a slice of the cake?'

'No.'

'Fair enough. Do you want to take on these pictures or not?'

Julie shook her head. 'I'll come back when you've finished, otherwise I'll have to make two trips.'

Paul struck bauxite on the last photograph but one, ringed the spot in blue marker and looked at his watch. Quarter to two; that gave him fifteen minutes before he was due to see Mr Wells. Under normal circumstances the thought of an interview with the senior partner would've puckered up his intestines like a tulip about to burst into bloom, but he wasn't bothered in the least. When you've died twice and lost the only girl you'll ever love twice and done everything you could to kill the Queen of the Fey, getting frowned at by the boss slips a notch or two down your list of things to be upset about.

The door opened, and Sophie came in; Paul knew it was her by the way the door started to open, which was as weird as a ferret in a blender, but that's love for you. 'Hello,' she said.

'Hello,' he replied.

Sophie sat down in what used to be her chair. 'We've got to go and see old Mr Wells in ten minutes.'

'That's right.'

She picked at her fingernails with a biro cap for fifteen seconds or so, then took a small glass bottle from her jacket pocket. 'I've been up in her office,' she said; no need to ask who *she* was, in this context. 'They've locked the door, but it's one of those combination locks, and I've got her memory of what the code was.'

Paul frowned. 'What did you want to go in there for?'

'For this.' She held up the bottle. 'I remembered she kept some for emergencies.'

'Ah, right. What is it?'

Sophie was looking at him. 'I've been thinking,' she said. 'I told you last night, everything I've ever felt for you's just gone for ever, so I can't love you any more. But there's this stuff.'

Then Paul knew exactly what it was. 'That's the love philtre,' he said.

Sophie nodded. 'It's not fair on you otherwise,' she said. 'I mean, it's not right that I don't love you any more. If I drink this stuff, I will. It'll be back how it was, more or less.'

Paul stared at her. Inside his mind was a huge, complex tangle of thoughts and feelings, ranging from joy and relief to anger and disgust, and there was no way of knowing which part of the tangle was which. 'You'd do that?' he said.

She shrugged. 'I don't care,' she said. 'It doesn't really matter what happens to me, and you'll be happy. And me too, I suppose. After all, being in love with someone who loves you back – that's the main thing, isn't it? That's what we're all supposed to want, more than anything in the world.'

The tangle unravelled itself in a blur, and the blur became a mental image of Melze, the fake Melze, the one who loved him with every fibre of her synthetic being, and whom he'd loved back, until he found out that she didn't really exist. What had become of her, Paul wondered; and realised that he couldn't care less. 'But it wouldn't be real,' he said. 'It'd be an illusion, like the stuff *she* used to do – effective magic.'

'So what?' Sophie shrugged, a slight, understated movement of her thin shoulders. 'It's better than nothing, isn't it? And anyhow, it'd be as near real as makes no odds, because I *did* love you, very much. It'd be different if I couldn't stand you before, but it's just, well, like rebuilding a damaged house or something. Well? Do you want me to or not? I'm not bothered one way or the other.'

'No,' Paul said.

'Suit yourself, then.' Sophie put the bottle down on the desk. 'I offered, so don't go around looking all tragic and sad. Obviously, you don't love me as much as all that.'

He looked at her. 'I'd have thought it was obvious that I do,' he said. 'Which is why using that stuff wouldn't be right.'

Sophie yawned. 'Whatever,' she said. 'If you're going to be all picky, then forget about it.' She reached out to take the bottle back, but left it where it was and folded her hands in her lap. 'Which of us is going to stay in the flat? I can move back to my parents', I suppose.'

'Up to you,' Paul replied. 'I don't think I want to stay there.'

'Once I've gone, you mean. Couldn't bear to be alone with the memories.'

'Don't say it like that.'

Sophie shook her head. 'You should try sharing your skull with the memories *I've* got,' she said. 'I think I'd be better off going home. Being on my own wouldn't be a good thing right now.'

Paul looked at the wall. 'If you're sure,' he said.

'It'd be better,' she replied. 'I'll get my stuff at the weekend. If you want, I'll pay my half of the rent till you can find someone to share with.'

He grinned bleakly. 'I'm not the sharing kind,' he said. 'I'll look for somewhere smaller. Anything larger than a shoebox gives me agoraphobia, in any case.'

'That's not true.'

'No, it isn't. Does it matter?'

'No.'

Sophie was still looking at him. 'Paul,' she said, 'what happened to her?'

Not a question he wanted to answer. 'How do you mean?'

'I remember her leaving me, but that's all. Is she——?'

Paul shrugged. 'I don't know, is the honest answer. Mr Wells did something to her, sent her through the Portable Door. Said something about the Isle of Avalon, if that's any help.'

Sophie frowned. 'That's in Somerset, isn't it? Where they have the big rock festival.'

'Is it? I don't think that's what he could have had in mind. I thought Avalon was where King Arthur went; and probably Elvis and Princess Di and JFK and Shergar and all that crowd.' He thought about that for a moment. 'She'll fit in well there,' he said. 'Her kind of people.'

'I suppose.' Her brow furrowed. 'What I mean is, she can't come back, can she? I couldn't stand it if I thought she could come back.'

Good question, Paul thought, and he remembered what Mr Wells had said, about Countess Judy continuing to do consultancy work. Saving the human race was one thing, but JWW was in business to make money, and that, apparently, had been something Countess Judy had been very good at. 'Absolutely no chance of that,' he said.

'But what about the stupid Door thing? If that's how she got there—'

'Yes,' Paul said, 'but I've got that, and nobody's going to get their hands on it except me, promise. Unless you want it. You can have it if you like.'

Sophie looked at him, and he didn't know how to begin to interpret her expression. 'No, thanks,' she said. 'You keep it, it'll be safe with you. After all, you're a hero, aren't you?'

Paul actually managed a laugh. 'You're right,' he said, 'with me, it's about as safe as the Stock Market. But I think I know somewhere where it *will* be safe, if I can face going there again. Come on,' he added, 'we'd better go and see Wells.'

'Essentially,' Mr Wells said, steepling his fingers on his desktop, 'everything you've been told is true. You were both of you bought from your respective families by this firm, which is why we can force you to continue working for us against your will. Furthermore, Mr Carpenter, you were indeed bred – if you'll pardon the expression – with the sole purpose of concluding Ernest Carpenter's work against the Fey and their proposed invasion of our side of the Line. Ernest Carpenter was for many years a partner in this firm.'

'What happened?' Paul asked. 'Did he retire or something?'

Mr Wells's face betrayed a tiny trace of embarrassment. 'He was made to leave,' he replied. 'The partnership felt that his ongoing enmity towards the Countess di Castel'Bianco was having an adverse effect on the firm's business. Accordingly, he was paid the value of his share, and he left. He then proceeded to devote the rest of his life, and his entire financial resources, to carrying on his fight against the Fey. When his money was all spent and his credibility in the trade was damaged beyond recovery, he took his own life – intending, as we know, to return once you had completed the job. It's a tragedy that his obsession should have cut short a quite brilliant career.'

'Just a moment,' Paul said. 'He saved the human race, didn't he?'

Mr Wells nodded slightly to concede the point. 'Arguably,' he said, as though Paul had won a trivial point on a technicality. 'To return to the matter in hand,' he went on. 'I've discussed the matter with my partners, and we've decided that since neither of you were what one might call free agents as regards your part in recent events, it would be inappropriate to take disciplinary action against either of you. We feel that, although your actions were directly responsible for the loss to the firm of a partner and a very considerable proportion of the firm's income, you were in effect acting under duress and therefore can't be blamed for what happened. In consequence, as far as the partnership is concerned, the matter is closed.'

Before Paul could say anything, Sophie was on her feet. 'This is a test, right?' she said.

Mr Wells looked at her. 'I beg your pardon?'

'A test,' she said, 'to see if I'm really me or something; because it can't be for real. You can't be saying, "You just went through the most incredibly horrible experience ever and saved the human race, but it's OK, we aren't going to fire you." Even *you*—'

'Miss Pettingell.' Mr Wells seemed offended. 'I fail to see what could possibly prompt such an outburst. Your actions have indeed damaged the firm and cost us a great deal of money. However, we accept that neither of you are to blame—'

Sophie called Mr Wells a part of the male anatomy. This didn't seem to help, but at least it shut him up for a moment. 'I can't believe it, even coming from one of you lot. My life's been totally ruined, Paul nearly *died*—'

'Actually, I *did* die,' Paul said mildly. 'Twice.'

'—And you seem to think I actually *want* this lousy job. Well, all I can say is, you must be even more of a stupid fat jerk than you look, which I wouldn't have thought was possible but apparently you managed it. You got that? I quit. I'm leaving. Goodbye.'

Sophie swirled round and marched to the door, which wasn't there any more.

'Miss Pettingell,' Mr Wells said slowly, with the air of someone wrestling back his temper with both hands and a cattle prod. 'When I mentioned the possibility of disciplinary action, it wasn't dismissal that I had in mind. The firm has lost quite enough money recently without forfeiting the substantial capital investment represented by our purchase of you. What I had in mind was rather more along these lines.'

Whereupon Sophie burst into flames.

How long Paul sat in his chair and stared at her, he could

never quite figure out. It seemed like a very long time indeed, but he also knew that he was on his feet and lunging at her before she started to scream, which was almost immediately. Mr Wells tried to stop him (he had remarkable reflexes for a man his age and size) but Paul slipped past him and grabbed at Sophie with both hands, trying to beat out the fire. He was vaguely aware of the pain, and of Mr Wells shouting; and then Paul's eyes went dark and all he could think about was the unbearable heat, which he couldn't get away from whatever he did. He could feel his skin shrinking and melting; and then nothing mattered apart from how much it hurt. He lost his balance and hit the ground, and he wondered what Mr Dao would say to him this time—

Paul, someone was saying, and he had a hazy recollection of having known someone with that name, a long time ago in a very bad place. He wondered why he was lying on his back with his eyes shut. He opened them.

'Paul,' said Benny Shumway's voice, which was odd, since Paul was looking at a car. *His* car, his maroon Volkswagen Polo, with the chip in the windscreen where the gravel had hit it, that time when he went to Gloucestershire.

'He's awake,' said the car; and Paul remembered that her name was Monika, and that she was Ricky Wurmtoter's sister. That reminded him.

'Sophie,' he yelled, and tried to get up, whereupon a large hand pressed down on his chest, squeezing all the air out of his lungs. This was, presumably, for his own good.

'She's fine.' Now Paul could see Benny's face, looming over him like a bearded rain cloud, and in the background the plain whitewashed walls of the cashier's office. He wondered for a moment what a car was doing in the smallest office in the building; then he thought, *Magic, what the hell.* 'So are you. It's all right, you're safe.'

'But—' Either he could share this bloke Paul's memories, or— 'But she was on fire. That bastard Wells—'

'Relax,' Benny growled. 'It was only trick fire. J.W. Wells patent non-oxydising flames – it burns but it doesn't consume. God not included, bush sold separately. Amaze your friends and hurt your enemies a lot.'

'Quiet,' the car said. 'Paul, the fire only *felt* like it was burning you, it doesn't actually do any damage. The same with Sophie. She's all right.'

'Oh,' Paul said. 'Oh, right. But why did he do that? I know she lost her rag a bit, but—'

Benny laughed. 'Sounds to me like you're under the impression that Jack Wells is a nice man; you know, a bit pompous and gruff but all right really, and always on hand at the end to rescue everybody and make everything all right. I have to tell you, that's not really how it is.'

Paul sat up, and this time Benny let him. 'I'd sort of gathered that,' he said. 'Did he really do that to Sophie, just to punish her for being *rude*?'

Benny shrugged. 'He's old-fashioned,' he said. 'Doesn't hold with attitude and bad language. Or with anything that doesn't make money for the firm. Losing money is pretty much guaranteed to piss him off on the quantum level.'

Paul shook his head, as if he could get rid of the weirdness just by shrugging it away. 'But Sophie was right,' he said. 'We rescued the whole bloody *world*—'

'Which is fine,' Benny said. 'Provided you do it in your own time, and it doesn't screw up the balance sheet. But don't expect any thanks, least of all from Jack Wells. He's not evil, like in Dark Lords and stuff, but he'd probably only save the human race if he was sure of getting a valuable prize once he'd collected the whole set. The point is—' Benny hesitated, then made a what-the-hell gesture with his hands. 'Let's face it,' he said, 'you're a hero, capital H and everything. True, you don't look it, but so what, Cas Suslowicz doesn't look like a giant, but you should watch him eat some time. Or not,' he added with a slight shudder. 'Fact is, you were a hero before you were even fucking born; your uncle Ernie saw to that, every gene in your body practically hand-picked. You've got hero instincts, including a heavily edited version of the self-preservation thing, and sad to say, but it's perfectly obvious, you've got hero brains. Don't get me wrong, I'm not saying that all heroes are as thick as school custard; but in certain respects, they're not smart. Couldn't be, or they couldn't do the job. Paul, my friend, you're all hero, and you've just got to face up to it and come to terms. And part of being one is, you can't see mankind in the crosswires or a damsel in distress without getting this overwhelming urge to leap in and help. Even when it's the dumb thing to do. Even when it's not wanted.' He sighed. 'But most people aren't like that, and particularly people in our line of work. Think about it, will you? Guys who can do magic: think of all the good they could do, the differences they could make. Just cast a spell, wave a wand, and you've got an end to hunger and injustice, you've got world peace, you've got a sea full of whales and everybody learning to get along with each other, and God only knows what. Or so you'd think, you being a hero and all. But we, people in the trade, our minds don't work like that. We think, *How do I use this special gift I've been given to make an obscene amount of money without getting noticed and locked up in a government research lab or a funny farm?* And you know what? It's good that we think that way, because nothing in history ever did more harm to the innocent and defenceless people of the world than well-intentioned people with power trying to make things better. That's why they threw Uncle Ernie out of the firm, Paul; he tried to breed a monster – magical powers, and a hero mentality. That's you.'

'Oh,' Paul said. 'Right. Well, thanks for telling me.'

'No charge. But now you can see why Jack Wells and the rest of them forked out a small fortune for you – and they got a bargain, at that, because you're the only specimen in captivity. Add to that the special bonus features, like the fact that you're part-goblin, which means you can find mineral resources just by looking at aerial photographs; you're a walking goldmine, no pun intended. Getting the two of you together—'

'Benny!' snapped the car. 'That's enough.'

'What do you mean, the two of us?' Paul said urgently, but Benny just shook his head. 'Not for me to say,' he said. 'But here's a clue: if you can figure out why Judy was so dead set on getting your Sophie for her replacement Source, you'll be in the right area. And that's your lot, on that topic. I've said too much already. Probably still a bit dizzy in the head, after Ricky bashed me and locked me in the strongroom while you two were dealing with Judy.' He sighed. 'Which was the right thing to do, I guess, because I would've tried to stop you. Oh, I'm over her now,' he added quickly, as the car revved ominously. 'Because she's gone, after all, and so her power's gone too, I'm out from under her spell, thanks to you. Both of you.'

'That's better,' the car said, a trifle grumpily. 'She was a very bad person, and you should be ashamed.'

Benny grinned. 'I am,' he said. 'Trust me.'

Paul thought it'd be a good idea to change the subject. 'So,' he said awkwardly, 'you two are, well, you know—'

Benny nodded. 'Talking of which,' he added, 'it's my sad duty to break it to you that you haven't got a company car any more. Dennis Tanner handed me the keys this morning.' Monika's engine purred involuntarily. 'Ricky was pretty uptight about the whole thing – told me that if he ever catches me giving my car a good polish and wax, he'll rip my lungs out with a garden fork. But he'll come round,' he added cheerfully. 'They always do. I mean, when you consider he was so desperate to get her off his hands that he was prepared to try and fix her up with *you*—'

Anything that Paul might have said was drowned out in the blare of Monika's horn, which carried on until Benny apologised and promised to be good in future. 'It's true, though,' he added. 'Obviously he thinks well of you; birds of a feather, I guess, because Ricky's all hero, from his toothpaste smile to his carbon-fibre-reinforced socks. I'd assumed you'd figured that out for yourself, actually. I mean, why else would a junior nobody like you get assigned a company car?'

Don't go there, Paul told himself, *it's never worth it*. 'Well,' he said, 'I suppose I'd better be getting along. Thanks for – well, thanks. I guess.'

But Benny shook his head. 'Small job I'd like you to help with,' he said. 'Just the usual, trip to the Bank, paying in and drawing tomorrow's cheques. Only, I thought you might want to come along.'

'What, me go back in there?' Paul shuddered, and in

doing so felt the edge of the cardboard tube that held the Door rub against his ribs. 'Actually,' he said, 'yes, why not? I'd like a quick word with Mr Dao, if there's time.'

'Good lad.' Benny nodded approvingly. 'Right, we'd better go.' He smiled, rather nauseatingly, at the car, which indicated back. 'See you later, honeypot,' he said. 'Thought we'd have a quiet evening in, just you, me, a gallon of transmission oil and a Haynes manual.'

If Monika had made a noise like that while he'd been driving her, Paul would've taken her straight to the garage. Now at least he knew what it signified, which was something. The disturbing thing was, his dad had had a Rover 2000 that made exactly the same noise when going up hills.

'You again,' said Mr Dao, but Paul knew him well enough by now to interpret the tiny discrepancy between the levels of the sides of his mouth as a smile.

Paul grinned weakly. 'Me again,' he said. 'But this time—'

Mr Dao raised his hand. 'Quite so. And Mr Shumway: what a pleasure it is to see you again.'

Benny grunted something that Paul didn't catch. 'Business as usual from now on,' he said. 'You heard about the doings Topside, I take it.'

'Indeed,' Mr Dao said. 'I would imagine it is all for the best. The Fey have never been regular clients of the Bank, for obvious reasons. Naturally, when an unfortunate situation arises, we tend to look kindly on those who favour us with their custom. Beyond that,' he added, 'we find it hard to motivate ourselves to take more than a passing interest. We are peaceful people down here, Mr Shumway. We prefer it that way. Excitement disturbs our tranquillity of mind, reminding us of what we once were and can no longer be.'

Benny shrugged. 'It's a point of view,' he said. 'Anyhow, we're pretty much back to normal on our side of the Line, so with any luck we won't be doing anything to upset you for a while.'

There was a slight but deep sadness in Mr Dao's smile. 'Nothing *upsets* us, Mr Shumway. We are incapable of feelings so intense. Now then,' he continued briskly, 'here are tomorrow's wire transfers, and statements for the deferred deposit accounts. I regret to have to tell you that a cheque drawn on the Commercial Bank of Isfahan was only partially burnt by the gentleman who's been looking after your duties during your absence—'

'Dennis Tanner,' Benny interrupted, scowling with exasperation. 'He's never got the knack of holding the very edge of the corner, so of course he burns his fingers and lets go. Still, he's management, so what can you do?'

Mr Dao nodded sympathetically. 'If you could see to it, I should be very greatly obliged. I have in fact processed the cheque so as not to cause embarrassment.'

'Thanks,' Benny said. 'Oh, and the kid's got something he wants you to keep safe for him. *Very* safe,' he added, 'as in you-know-where.'

Paul didn't know where, and he wasn't entirely sure he liked being called *the kid*, but he decided not to take the point. 'Just this,' he said, taking the cardboard tube out of his pocket. 'If it's all right, I'd like it so that nobody but me can get near it. Nobody,' he repeated, reproaching himself as he did so for unnecessary melodrama.

'Of course,' Mr Dao said. 'And in the circumstances, I think the Bank will be prepared to waive storage fees, given the nature of the item.' A rather frosty look passed across his face.

'We're very proud of the fact that over the last two thousand years, nobody has even tried to rob the bank, knowing that it would, of course, be impossible. However—'

'Actually, Jack, that's not quite true,' Benny put in. 'There was that Brooklyn gang about forty years back—'

Mr Dao nodded. 'Technically, I suppose. But since they could find no way of getting in here other than suicide, and had omitted to make arrangements for their passage back, I tend not to count that as an attempt, but more as a fitting punishment for stupidity. That incident aside, then, there hasn't been any trouble of that sort in our long and distinguished history. However, once I became aware of the existence of *that*,' he went on, glancing down with distaste at the cardboard tube in his hand, 'I must confess to certain misgivings. Whether it would be capable of breaching the Bank's security I have no way of knowing, since the experiment has never been tried. I would prefer to keep it that way, and accordingly I shall rest in peace more easily knowing that the only instrument in the world that might be able to break into our vault is safely inside it. I should warn you, however, that you will be able to retrieve it one time only; once it has been withdrawn from our keeping, the Bank's standared terms and conditions clearly state that should you wish to return it to store, a standard administration fee will be payable.'

'Oh,' Paul said, thinking: *Aggravating, but that's banks for you*. 'How much?'

'A life,' Mr Dao replied calmly. 'Either your own, or that of someone prepared to die willingly in your place. A similar fee will be incurred,' he added, with the merest shadow of a grin, 'on each subsequent removal. We are, after all, a business, not a charitable institution.' He held out his hand.

'Goodbye, Mr Carpenter,' he said. 'It's been disturbing knowing you.'

Benny didn't seem his usual chatty self on the way back to the office, which gave Paul a chance to agonise over whether he'd done the right thing in effectively getting rid of the Portable Door. *Probably just as well*, he decided; recent events had shown that the wretched thing wasn't safe to leave lying about, and hiding it or never letting it out of his sight was simply inviting abduction, torture, murder and other similar inconveniences. Being able to nip out to Copacabana for a lunchtime drink wasn't really worth it, all things considered; and besides, he had nobody to go with any more, so it really didn't make any odds.

When Paul returned to his office, he found Sophie sitting in her old chair. 'Hello,' he said.

She looked past him. 'Please don't,' she said. 'Just pretend I'm not here or something. I'm only here because I haven't got anywhere else to sit, and that bastard Tanner's sent me down a whole stack of these bloody things to do.'

Paul hadn't noticed the heap of Mortensen printouts on the desk in front of her. 'How are you feeling?' he asked.

'Oh, fine,' Sophie said. 'After you did your stupid heroics thing, Wells put us both out; I was okay straight away, but you'd lost consciousness. Then Mr Shumway turned up and took you away, and Wells said I'd better get back to work. So I came here, and found this lot waiting for me, with a note.'

Paul nodded. 'I don't think they're very nice people in this office,' he said.

'I think you're right. Shame we're stuck here for the rest of our lives, really.'

He sat down. He could only see the top of Sophie's head,

because of the pile of printouts. 'Here,' he said, 'I'll help you with them. Don't refuse,' he snapped quickly, 'just don't. All right?'

'Please yourself,' she said. 'If it makes you feel better, you carry on. Only I thought you had bauxite to scan for.'

'I'll work late,' Paul replied. 'The goblins won't bother me getting out, and I've got nothing in particular to go home for.'

'Don't start.'

'I'm not starting – it's true. Now, you take the top half and I'll do the rest.'

It seemed like old times, sifting meaningless paperwork together in sullen, embarrassed silence. Paul couldn't help remembering also the last time he'd had this job to do, when Countess Judy had used it as a trick to make him fall asleep and dream her invasion force over the Line. As far as he knew, they were still out there, albeit cut off from their chain of command and lines of supply; hundreds or maybe thousands of the Fey, masquerading as malignant children somewhere in the Greater London area. Cheerful thought; but not something he was allowed to worry about on the firm's time, apparently. *All right*, he told himself, *I won't worry about it, then. Screw it. Somebody else's problem.* He thrust the matter out of his mind, turned the full force of his attention on the printouts, and soon drifted into sleep.

'Hello,' said the monsters—

'Wait a minute,' Paul objected. 'I'm through with all this stuff now, aren't I? Countess Judy's gone, why can't I have my proper dreams back?'

The monsters giggled. 'We're the *good* Fey, silly,' said the younger specimen. 'Remember us? We dropped by to warn you, that night when She had the bomb planted in your metal-thing-for-keeping-old-letters-in. We just wanted to say thanks, that's all.'

'Yes, I remember you now,' Paul said, oddly touched in spite of everything. 'Well, it's nice to have somebody appreciate me, even if—' He hesitated. *Even if it's only hideous monsters* wouldn't be very gracious. 'Even if this crowd here don't seem to think much of it,' he said clumsily.

'Oh, we're very grateful,' said the elder monster. 'Mostly on account of I'm Queen now – well, acting queen, because She's still queen theoretically. Did I mention she's my big sister? You'd never think it to look at me.'

'Oh, I don't know,' Paul replied. 'Same eyes.'

That seemed to please the monster no end. 'That's very sweet of you to say so, though you're just being nice. Anyhow, all we wanted to say was, you won't be seeing us again. Any of us. From now on, your dreams are off limits to all the Fey, us and them.'

'Which means,' said the younger monster, 'I won't be able to come and visit you any more. But that's probably just as well, for your sake.'

'Sorry?' Paul said. 'Do I know you?'

'Silly,' the monster said, as her face and shape dissolved and re-formed. 'Now do you recognise me?' the Girl of His Dreams said, smiling nicely. 'It was fun, but it's time for you to move on, isn't it? You won't be needing me any more.'

'Won't I? But—'

She giggled. 'Don't worry about it,' she said. 'Can't say any more, not with the skinny girl here. After having Her camping out in her head all that time, I wouldn't be surprised if she can hear us. But it'll be all right eventually, one way or another. You'll see.'

Before Paul could say anything, they'd gone, and he sat up with a start. 'What?' he said.

'You were asleep,' Sophie said. 'You were muttering. I hate it when you do that, it's spooky.'

'It was— Sorry,' Paul said. 'It shouldn't happen again, anyway.'

'Good. Look, why don't you get on with your bauxite stuff and leave this to me? After all, I don't care how long it takes me, if I get it all done they'll just find me something else to do.'

Paul sighed. 'Fair enough,' he replied. 'Look, I know we can't be – I mean, I understand what you told me, and if that's how it's got to be, that's that, I suppose. But we've still got to work together and be in this rotten little room all the time, so can't we at least be friends? Otherwise it's really going to get to me, and I've got enough to put up with as it is.'

Sophie looked at him for a moment, then nodded. 'Well, not enemies, anyway,' she said. 'How about allies? Us against them.'

'All right,' Paul said. 'Two heads are better than one, and all that sort of thing. We stand a better chance of getting out of here in one piece if we team up. And then—' He looked away. 'Then we can go our separate ways and not bother each other any more. How's that?' As he said it, he thought of Mr Dao: *It's been disturbing knowing you.* And then he thought: *If I still had the Door, couldn't I just step back through time to before Judy started squatting in Sophie's head, and maybe we could figure out a way—* He frowned. If ideas like that were anything to go by, putting the Door where he couldn't get at it might well prove to be the best thing he'd ever done.

Sophie left at chucking-out time; Paul stayed behind to finish the last hundred or so pictures. Either there wasn't any bauxite in wherever the hell this was, or he'd lost the knack of finding it, temporarily or for ever. Like he cared; dutifully and methodically he traced each photograph with his fingertip, then added it to the *Done* pile. When the last one went face down, he stood up and reached for his coat.

'Waste of time,' said a voice behind him. 'I could've told our Dennis that, but he wouldn't listen to me.'

'For crying out loud,' Paul said, once he'd started breathing again. 'You nearly scared me to death.'

'Sorry,' Mr Tanner's mum lied. 'Only you were so deep in it all you didn't hear me come in. You look so sweet, prodding photos. Like our Dennis when he was learning to read.'

Paul realised that she hadn't bothered to transfigure herself into a beautiful girl this time; she was all red eyes and claws and teeth. For some reason, he felt vaguely proud that he hadn't noticed it straight away. 'Yes, well,' he said. 'I've just been forgiven for saving the world, and then set on fire. I can do without a bollocking from your son into the bargain.'

'He's not that bad, really,' said Mr Tanner's mum. 'Well, no, I tell a lie; he gets that from me, probably, because his dad's a real sweetie. But I didn't come here to talk about our Dennis.'

'Good,' Paul said. 'I'd hate to say anything to upset you.'

'You couldn't, trust me. No, what I wanted to ask is: I went to see the doc earlier today and he reckons the baby's due the middle of next week.' It took Paul a moment to remember that she was pregnant. Hard to tell, with goblins. 'Anyhow, Pip and I are having real trouble settling on a name. He wants to call him Christopher Vincent Horatio, after his dad, and I'd sort of set my heart on Azog Grishnakh Rupert, after my favourite uncle; and we talked about it and we were sort of thinking, since Pip and I would never have got together again but for you, if it'd be okay if we called him Paul.'

'Paul?'

She nodded. 'Paul Azog Christopher. It'd mean a lot to both of us.'

Paul blushed. 'Um,' he said, 'yes, right, by all means. I'm honoured,' he added, and to his surprise he was telling the truth. 'Thanks,' he said. 'Thanks a lot.'

Mr Tanner's mum smiled. When she wasn't being beautiful she had a nice smile, though you had to look quite hard to see it behind the tusks. 'Also,' she went on, 'it's this sort of big tradition with us goblins, it's very important who you ask to be the kid's godfather. Like, we had Theo van Spee for our Dennis, and Kali Grandma was my godmother, and my dad had the Dark Lord himself, rest his soul. We take it seriously, you see, it's got to be somebody you respect and admire who's still alive, not under sentence of death by excoriation, and unmarried. So we thought we'd ask you.'

Paul didn't know what to say. 'Seriously?'

'Yes, seriously, you clown. You don't have to do much; you've got to strangle a manticore with your bare hands at the ceremony, but Ricky reckons he knows where he can get us this really old, sick one with no teeth; and you're expected to buy Paul Azog Christopher his first scimitar, but our Snotnast knows a bloke who can get you one at trade, and anyway, that wouldn't be for a couple of years. Please say you will,' she added, 'it'd mean a lot to both of us.'

'All right,' Paul said. 'I mean, yes, I'd be delighted. It's really nice of you to ask, actually.'

She spoiled it a bit by slapping him on the back, jarring half the bones in his body, but he forgave her. 'Cheers,' she said. 'I'll tell Pip, he'll be chuffed to nuts.'

'Will he? Great,' Paul said. 'And really, it's the least I can do. I mean, you helped me a lot, rescuing me from High Wycombe and everything.'

'Ah, but I had an ulterior motive,' Mr Tanner's mum said, with a rather unnerving chuckle. 'And just because I'm asking you this doesn't mean I don't still fancy you. But it's all right,' she added quickly, 'I promise I'll behave at the service, you don't have to worry about that.'

'I'm sure you will,' Paul replied feebly. 'Let me know as soon as you've set the date, all right?'

"Course. Right,' she went on, 'it's time you weren't here. Young lad your age, you should be out enjoying yourself, not stuck in a mouldy office all night.'

'Yeah, right,' Paul mumbled, and he headed for the door. Then something occurred to him, and he paused. 'Is it true,' he said, 'that we're related? That – well, that I'm part-goblin?'

Her eyes opened a little, then she nodded. 'Who told you that?' she said.

'I sort of worked it out for myself,' Paul replied sheepishly. 'And then Mr Ta—'

'Call him Dennis,' she interrupted. 'After all, you're cousins.'

'He confirmed it,' Paul said. 'Cousins? What sort of cousins?'

She shrugged. 'Dunno. Lots of times removed; distant *enough*, if you see what I mean.' Paul looked away till she'd stopped leering. 'But yes, you're family all right. One of us.'

One of us. Amazingly, that sounded rather good. Goblins, for crying out loud; but yes, he liked the sound of it. 'Well,' he said, 'you can't be any worse than my human relatives, that's for sure.'

She sniggered. 'So I gather,' she said. 'I mean, we can get a bit boisterous sometimes and maybe we break stuff and sometimes when a party gets out of hand or whatever we have been known to eat people, just occasionally; but we don't go selling our kids, no matter what.'

Paul nodded. 'I'm surprised you're prepared to acknowledge me,' he said. 'Black sheep of the family, and all.'

'Not a bit of it,' she replied cheerfully. 'Take people as you find 'em, that's our way, or just occasionally with salt and vinegar. And anyhow, it's us that should be proud. I mean, it's the first time we've ever had a genuine hero in the family.'

'A what?'

'Hero. You.' Mr Tanner's mum shook her head. 'Honestly, you get this simple look on your face, and it's a wonder nobody's hollowed you out and used you as a canoe. Actually,' she said, 'one of these days when you're not busy, you ought to come down and meet the gang.'

'I—' Paul looked at her. 'I'd like that,' he said, and if he didn't mean it, maybe it was mostly because he was shy anyway. 'But not for dinner,' he added quickly. 'I mean, I'd hate you to go to any trouble.'

When she'd said goodnight – he was just fast enough to get out of the way of a cousinly kiss – and he'd heard the front-door lock turn behind him, he walked down the road as far as the bus stop. It was coming on to rain, and part-mage, part-goblin or not, there was bugger-all he could do about that except get wet. He'd been standing there for maybe three minutes, just long enough for all his clothes to get saturated, when a low, sleek red sports car drew up beside him and the passenger door opened.

'Hop in,' said Ricky Wurmtoter. 'I'll give you a lift home.'

'No, thanks, really,' Paul heard himself mumble. (*Why? It's pissing it down.*) 'It must be miles out of your way.'

'What way?' Ricky said. 'Don't worry about it. Jump in, before you drown standing up.'

All right, Paul thought, *might as well*. He didn't like getting wet, though whether he could get any wetter was a moot point, even if he jumped in the sea. He opened the door, moved an axe and a medium-sized can of SlayMore off the seat, and climbed in.

Ricky drove the way he'd have expected, so Paul spent most of the journey with his eyes shut and his fingernails dug into the web of the seat belt. 'It's all right,' he heard Ricky say eventually. 'We're here, you can come out now.'

'Wbbl,' Paul replied. 'I mean, are we? Good. Um, thanks for the lift.'

Ricky grinned. 'It wasn't that bad, was it?'

'No, it was fine,' Paul muttered. 'Any faster and we'd have arrived before we left, but—'

'You sound like my mother. What's the time? The clock in this thing doesn't work.'

Not surprised, Paul thought; *and if you don't know why, ask Einstein*. 'Five past seven,' he said.

'Fine. Come and have a drink. I know this nice little pub just round the corner.'

Paul hesitated for a moment; he wasn't really in the mood

for any of Ricky's dragon-hunting stories, but he could use a drink that he didn't have to pay for. 'All right,' he said. 'It's not the Three Tiles, is it? Because they have live jazz on Tuesdays, and—'

'Not the Three Tiles,' Ricky confirmed. 'Follow me.'

Ricky's idea of a nice little pub turned out to be a hidden door in the side of a disused warehouse, where you had to knock three times and ask for Chalky; whereupon bolts graunched and hinges creaked, and a tiny little man in a leather jacket with spiked studs on the cuffs let them through. It was at this point that Paul realised that he didn't know all that much about Mr Wurmtoter, and maybe he'd have been better off going home and having a cup of tea. But he followed Ricky down a long corridor and through another small door, and found himself in, for want of a better description—

'Here we are,' Ricky said. 'What'll you have?'

—A mead-hall, complete with high rafters, long tables and benches, rush-strewn floor, a long fireplace running the length of the room, and smoke you could carve. 'Not many in tonight,' Ricky commented, and that was probably just as well, since everyone in the place was shaggy-bearded, mail-clad and armed to the teeth, and as soon as Paul walked into the light they all turned and stared at him. Ricky was networking like a radio station and most of the people he nodded to nodded back, though some of them muttered and turned their backs. They sat down at the end of a bench, and a large red-headed woman slopped down a huge jug and two horns in front of them. 'What is this place?' Paul whispered.

'Valhalla,' Ricky replied.

'Oh,' Paul said. 'Sort of a theme pub, you mean?'

'No,' Ricky said. 'Drink up. The regulars tend to get a bit tense if they see someone not drinking.'

The whatever-it-was in the jug tasted rank, but slightly less alcoholic than ginger-beer shandy. 'I thought you had to be dead or something,' Paul said.

'That's right,' Ricky replied, wiping his mouth ostentatiously on his sleeve. 'At least, you've got to have died in battle, which of course you have. I can put you up for membership if you like.'

'Thanks,' Paul said, with all the sincerity of a cabinet minister. 'So, um, you must've—?'

Ricky nodded. 'Technically, anyway,' he said, 'breaking into the Underworld to steal the three-headed hound of Hell counts as dying, though they had to refer it to the membership committee. I think it's nice to have somewhere you can get away from the usual crowd.'

Paul drank some more of the whatever-it-was. The taste sort of grew on you, like verdigris on copper.

'Actually,' Ricky went on, 'I wanted to have a chat about a couple of things. Mostly, I guess, to say thanks. You were a great help; the business with Judy, and so on.'

'That's all right,' Paul mumbled, somewhat flustered. 'I'm just glad someone thinks I did the right thing.'

Ricky frowned. 'You haven't exactly made yourself popular at the office, I grant you,' he said. 'I can see that it must be a bit confusing for you, since you're still pretty new to the business.'

'I'm getting the idea,' Paul replied. 'Gradually. Benny Shumway explained a bit about it earlier today. It just takes some getting used to, really.'

'You could say that,' Ricky said, grinning. 'I've been in the trade – well, a good many years now, anyway, and I still don't know all the rules. You just have to do the best you can, and try and see it from their point of view wherever possible. Take Judy, for instance. Very good example, in fact. On the one hand, she's a total menace; on the other hand, she makes an obscene amount of money for the firm. Obviously, when it comes to the crunch, you have to take a view. From my standpoint, it's fairly clear-cut. If she has her way and the Fey wipe out the human race and take its place, in the long run it's going to have serious repercussions on my corner of the market. Humans need heroes; the Fey don't. They don't use money, hence no banks; no banks, no large accumulations of wealth, therefore no dragons; and dragons make up a good forty per cent of my workload. Sure, by reprofiling and maximising returns I could make up maybe half the shortfall in other areas, such as vampires and the Evil Overlord sector, but it still means a shortfall, and if I don't meet my target come the year-end partners' meeting, I'm going to have some explaining to do. So, basically, one of us had to go, her or me. It's a pity,' he added wistfully. 'She had a stunning client portfolio in entertainment and politics, and we're bound to lose a fair slice of that regardless of who we get to replace her. Still, it's a hard old world, and you can't make omelettes without killing the goose that lays the golden eggs, as we say in the trade.'

Just a moment, Paul wanted to say; *all that stuff, fighting the Fey, losing Sophie, dying, and it was all just office politics?* He wanted to say it rather a lot, but he knew instinctively that Ricky wouldn't understand what he was making such a fuss about. 'Oh well,' he said, and refilled his horn from the jug, which was still full to overflowing. Time to change the subject, before he said something he shouldn't. Ricky might have turned out to be no better than the rest of them, but an indebted bastard is rather more use than a resentful one, and offending his only ally on the letterhead probably wasn't a good idea. 'Funny thing happened earlier,' he said. 'Mr Tanner's mum asked me to be her baby's godfather.'

'Is that right?' Ricky turned and looked at him. 'Congratulations. That's quite an honour. It's well worth keeping in with that crowd, especially in our line of work.'

'Really?'

'Oh yes.' Ricky nodded gravely. 'Not much in the way of dragons, of course, but they do get a lot of pest trouble — cave trolls, gnomes, gremlins and so forth. Nice little filler jobs you can do when things are quiet. And from time to time they have wars, border disputes and so forth. A good goblin war can mean serious billable hours, especially if the other side's got in outside help too. Of course, Dennis has got the goblin sector pretty well in his pocket, being family and all, but it never hurts to have contacts of your own.'

'I see,' Paul sighed. A couple of tables down, two very large men had started bashing each other with axes. Their armour seemed to be standing up to the blows, and they were laughing. Probably the local equivalent of a friendly game of darts. 'It's good about Benny Shumway and Mo—' He stopped abruptly, unable to remember whether Ricky — the real Ricky, not Judy in disguise — knew about that yet. Fortunately, Ricky smiled.

'Yes, I think so,' he said. 'They'll be good for each other, I think, and if he can find some way of turning her back, that'll be a nice bonus. Though at times I get the impression she's happier as she is. She was a very difficult teenager. Being a car's been mostly a positive experience for her, I think.'

'Right,' Paul said vaguely, and stood up. 'Well, thanks for the drink. I think I'll go home now.'

Ricky nodded. 'I might stay on for a bit,' he said. 'Never hurts to be seen, you know. Oh, before you go, I've got something for you.'

Paul hesitated, and sat down again. 'Really?' he said, trying to sound enthusiastic.

'Here.' Ricky delved into his inside pocket and took out what appeared to be a small silver paperknife. He tapped it three times against the edge of the table, and it grew into a full-sized sword, complete with scabbard. 'If you're going to stay in the pest-control sector you'll need one of these,' he said, 'and to be honest, I never did get on with it, so you might as well have it.'

'Um,' Paul said. He took it reluctantly, as though it was liable to bite. 'Thanks.'

'Her name is Skofnung,' Ricky went on. 'Used to belong to King Hrolf Kraki. Go on, take a closer look. Rather a nice pattern, I think.'

Well, you have to be polite; so Paul gripped the scabbard with his left hand and pulled the blade out an inch or so. To his surprise, it wasn't bright and shiny; the edges were dark brown, with intricate patterns of silver specks and whorls, and the middle was a sort of sea blue. 'Damascus steel,' Ricky explained, or at least Paul guessed it was meant as an explanation. 'You never find two the same, which makes it easier, of course.'

All right, Paul thought, *I'll ask*. 'Makes what easier?'

Ricky narrowed his eyes. 'Finding her, of course,' he said; then, 'I forgot, you obviously don't know. It's a living sword, right?'

'Is it?' Somehow, Paul got the impression that the sword hadn't liked him saying that. 'I mean right, yes. Obviously.'

Ricky laughed. 'A living sword,' he said, 'is special because it has a life of its own – which is good, because it knows what it's doing when in use, so you don't have to. But it does mean you have to find its other half before it's much good for anything, and,' he added, grimacing slightly, 'I have to admit, I never did find her. And without the other half, of course, it's pretty much useless.'

Paul managed not to sigh, though he really didn't feel in the mood for any more of this sort of thing. 'Other half,' he said.

'That's right. A living sword has a human counterpart, and once you find – oh, excuse me,' Ricky said suddenly, and Paul noticed that a huge, ferocious-looking warrior type was standing by the door and waving. 'Bloke I need to see about something. Look, you hang on to the sword for now, and I'll explain another time. See you at the office tomorrow,' he added, and hurried across the room, leaving Paul sitting bemusedly with a large sword on the table in front of him.

Hesitantly, he picked it up; it was painfully heavy, and he couldn't imagine being able to do anything useful with it, except maybe weigh down an extremely large pile of paper. He considered just leaving it there, but Ricky might notice and be offended. Then he remembered; he picked it up and nudged the side of the table with it three times. At once it shrank – it was like holding a live fish – until it was paperknife-sized again. Paul looked at it. *Oh well*, he said to himself, *more junk. Screwdrivers and scout badges and bits of coloured glass, and now this. I'll have to get myself a garden shed to keep it all in*. Still, it was the thought that counted. Presumably.

He managed to find his way out of Valhalla without getting stabbed, walked slowly home and let himself into the flat. It was dark and very quiet, and empty. When he switched on the light, he saw empty spaces where things had been;

Sophie must have been there, picked up her stuff and gone. She'd hardly taken anything, but the gaps left seemed huge, unchartable, like the Atlantic before Columbus.

Well, Paul thought, *here I am.*

He found an old shoebox to keep the magic bits and pieces in, sellotaped the lid shut and stuck it on top of the wardrobe, where he wouldn't have to look at it. Then he brushed his teeth, hung up his suit, got into his pyjamas and went to bed.